Done Growed Up

Mary Morony

Westropp Press
ISBN: 0996328904
ISBN: 9780996328906

Dedication

To: Jim Samuels,
the smartest man in the world
with infinite gratitude for
teaching me how to train my mind.

Acknowledgments

Gratitude and blessings to
Lisa Tracy
for her brilliant editing
&
Denise Hood
for her excellent reading and suggestions

&

all my *chillins* for all of the lessons!

Chapter 1

They had seen a lot of Linda since the divorce. The first and the last times she and Sallee met happened within a space of eighteen months and a couple of hundred feet. Sallee would always remember that first time: Her dad picking Linda up outside of the hospital on a cold blowy Friday afternoon in early March, Linda running down the wide cement steps waving and smiling, and her father saying, "We should get some kites. March is the best time for flying kites. Gordy, get in the back so Linda can sit up front." Gordy started to turn around to climb over the seat when Linda opened the back door and jumped in with Helen and Sallee.

"It's fine, Joe," Linda said with a sunny smile that instantly melted Sallee's heart. It didn't hurt that she was wearing the coolest nurse's outfit Sallee had ever seen. The cap, what a cap -- starched with peaks and valleys like a mountain range and her nurse's pin! "I'd like to sit back here with the girls, if that's all right with you and Gordy?" Gordy looked dumbstruck while Joe's beam of assent lit up the car. Linda turned to Helen and Sallee. "I had heard that you were both such beautiful little girls, but I didn't realize that your Daddy wasn't exaggerating." She leaned in close in a conspiratorial way. "You know the way

Daddies do when they talk about their girls," she whispered and then winked. Linda–this remarkably exotic grownup sitting in the back seat next to Helen and Sallee–mesmerized them. She reached up and removed the bobby pins holding her nurse's cap, and a wisp of dark hair fell around her face. Seeing Helen's eager look, Linda placed it on the child's head, taking care to pin it to her soft blonde curls. Helen, never one to miss an opportunity for affection, plopped herself in Linda's lap and wrapped herself in Linda's willing arms.

The magic lasted longer than in a standard fairytale. They saw Linda every time they went to visit their father for months. Visiting Joe had always been an adventure, but with Linda everything was more–more zest, more laughs, more new things. The idea that a grownup would play dress-up was unheard of before Linda. And she had some of the most wonderful clothes for dress-up. Joe's house began to fill up with all matter of material for the purpose: a uniform that she didn't use anymore, complete with a hat, and all kinds of things she had left over from dance recitals. They learned songs and dance steps while dressed as princesses and queens, dripping with beads and glass jewels.

Linda possessed a vast storehouse of girl novels too, to go along with her encyclopedic knowledge of Nancy Drew. Sallee couldn't believe that she had read every single volume and could remember all of their plots as if she'd just read them. If Sallee happened to mention that she was reading a particular title, Linda was as conversant with the particulars as if it was lying open on her nightstand.

To say she loved Linda would be an understatement. Adored would be closer to the mark. If it had been possible, Sallee would have absorbed her into her being the way you breathe in the essence of a spring day–the sunshine, the birdsong and the fragrance of lilacs scenting the magical air, as if you could capture it forever in your lungs. Her clean smell, like sheets drying in that perfect spring air, had just the tiniest hint of flowers with a dash of earth. When Linda turned her gaze on Sallee, her eyes filled with curiosity and delight, as if what the girl had to say was going to change the world forever.

When absent, Linda consumed Sallee's conversations. Unfortunately, she had few people with whom she could converse. Helen was such a baby. When they were at their mom's house, talking about anything that went on at their father's tended to make Helen so nervous that Sallee had stopped bothering. Gordy was less than worthless, you were lucky if he even looked up from whatever he was doing and gave you a dirty look. Was it since the divorce, or since their old bloodhound Lance was killed or when he'd turned fourteen? She wasn't sure, but for sure he wasn't an ally any more.

Conversation with Ethel might have been passable if Sallee didn't have to worry about her mother walking in all of the time and if Ethel wasn't so fiercely loyal to "yo mama, Miz Ginny, doan you be talkin' like dat!"

So when Stuart asked Sallee on a hot August afternoon–it was almost exactly a year and a half since that magical day when Linda walked into their lives–when Stuart asked if she wanted to have a pedicure, Sallee could hardly contain her excitement. Time with her sophisticated big sister, whom she adored second only to Linda–and a pedicure–AND she could talk about Linda without worrying about who might be listening? Who could ask for anything more!

"Stuart, don't you just love that little car of hers?" Sallee quizzed, lying across the foot of her sister's everything pink bed, careful that her feet were not touching ANYTHING, watching as Stuart practiced blowing smoke rings. Stuart leaned up against her pillowed headboard, one leg casually crossed over the other propped-up knee as her newly painted toes nails dried. She nodded that she did, and then inspected her handiwork as she stretched her feet elegantly. Issues of *Seventeen* and *Vogue* lay around her like flower petals. The tissue she had wound between her toes had started to slip. She whisked it away with her cigarette-bedecked hand, a thin trail of smoke following before the tissue could mar the perfection of her new watermelon nails. "Do you like pink?" Sallee asked.

"Not particularly," Stuart responded. "Well, some things, like nail polish and lipstick, why?"

"I don't know," Sallee rolled her eyes around the room, "just wondered."

"Yeah, I know. Dad," she laughed, "he tries."

"He coulda gotten Linda to help. I'm pretty sure she wouldn't have…" Sallee dropped that train of thought, going back to where she had left off. "When I get a car I want a Renault just like Linda's. Re NALLT." Sallee rolled the new word off her tongue, bouncing her feet together in her excitement. Stuart shot her a cautionary look as if to say, *I'm not fixing them again.* Sallee immediately stopped and checked to see if she had done any damage to her very first pedicure.

"Before Linda." Stuart said. Sallee looked up quizzically. Stuart explained, "It was before Linda. He got some decorator to do this. All of it," she waved her arm to encompass the whole room, "as a surprise for me. It's better than all of those antiques at Mother's I suppose, but I'm not sure. It looks like a garden threw up in here." She looked around the room, at the dormer windows entombed in frilly little cape cod curtains that made a view from the windows impossible. The pink ribbon and flower-bedecked fabric matched the wallpaper that covered every inch of wall space including the ceiling. She rolled her eyes. "Too matchy-matchy girlie- girlie!" She gave a mock shudder. "So ME, too, don't you think? At least he didn't get bunk beds." She laughed. "There was a time that I would have died for bunk beds. Fortunately, he forgot about that aspect of my dream bedroom. But he sure did zero in on the pink and the flowers." They both laughed.

"And it's *RE NO,* by the way," she said, waving her elegant foot in a circle. "It's French. You don't pronounce the l or the t."

"Why do they bother to put them in, then?" Sallee wondered, then shrugged. "Lucky you, you didn't get those ballerina pictures like Helen and I did. What is it with those pictures? Almost every kid I know has the same ones? Aren't decorators supposed to make things look good? And poor Gordy, cowboy and Indian wallpaper! Yuck."

"Yeah, pretty awful. I think that was how he met The Rose. I think she is the reason for all this blah. She's a decorator." She rolled her eyes again and groaned, then changed the subject.

"How's Ethel doing? I'm sorta surprised that I miss seeing her as much as I do." Sallee and Helen and Gordy came to their father's on weekends, but Stuart had moved in full time after a particularly bad fight with her mother. "And hey, speaking of, um, *home*, do you know what's up with Mother? Hasn't she been acting odd, recently?"

"Ethel is great, still running the show at home. She doesn't stay as late as she used to when we were little. It's not like we can't put ourselves in bed or bathe ourselves." She laughed, "Besides, Mom knows that if Ethel left, the rest of us would follow, just like in that story about the goose. You know, where everybody gets stuck? Never mind. I guess Mom is acting a little strange." Sallee stopped for a minute, wondering about the question, then added, "I don't think she is drinking as much as she used to. Don't know. Don't care that much these days. She's such a pain." She shrugged and moved on to more important matters: "You know Linda told me she went to the University? Isn't that cool? I didn't know girls could go."

"Yeah, I know. Girls can go to nursing school. Does Ethel still bring sausage?" Stuart asked then added, "Almost nice, even, it's odd." Sallee looked up, trying to make sense of what her sister had just said. "*Mom* is almost nice," Stuart said impatiently.

"I guess," said Sallee, even though she wasn't at all sure. She waved a hand dismissively, "You could go, Stuart, and then you wouldn't have to leave home or at least go so far away and you wouldn't miss Ethel or her sausage."

"Slight problem. I don't want to be a nurse." A strand of pale hair fell across her face. With a toss of her head she flicked it away, then gingerly tapped her middle toe nail and gave her sister a nod. "They're dry. Besides, I want to go away to school. I can't wait." Her face lit up. "Only four more weeks and New York City, here I come."

"I thought you liked living with Daddy? Why would you want to leave, especially with Linda, around? She is so much fun. Don't 'cha think?"

"She's okay. You'll understand when you are older."

There was almost nothing anyone could say that made Sallee madder than "when you are older." If she hadn't been so interested in why Stuart was seemingly so apathetic about Linda she would have left the room in a fit of pique. "Don't you like Linda?" she dared to ask.

"Yeah, I told you; she's fine." Stuart snapped up a random magazine and started flipping through the pages, the ever-present cigarette swirling smoke with every flip of the page. Her long tan legs twitched and bounced. "Find something to do. I'm going to read," she said, lighting a new cigarette off the old one before stabbing it out in an ashtray that was fast moving beyond its capacity.

"You remind me so much of Mom when you act like that." Sallee said, falling back on her most reliable insult. It was handy, knowing that Stuart hated it when people told her how much she resembled their mother. But why? Sallee couldn't begin to fathom–if you had to look like your mother, wouldn't you be lucky that your mother was blonde-haired-blue-eyed-*Grace-Kelly* beautiful? Sallee certainly wished that she were as pretty as her mother. But no, she favored her daddy; leastwise that was what Ethel said. Ethel said that Mista' Joe was a good lookin' man, but Sallee pointed out to her that he was a man; she was a girl. It wasn't the same. Though blonde and blue-eyed like the rest of the family, she thought her nose looked more like a potato, and her hair resembled dishwater, dirty dishwater at that.

Had Sallee not been looking for it, she would have missed the almost imperceptible glare that was instantly replaced with a composed look, as if practiced. Stuart put the magazine up between them and shook it slightly, feigning indifference. Sallee slouched on the edge of the bed, baffled. Referencing Stuart's uncanny resemblance to their mother had never failed to get a response. Sallee knew that if she could get Stuart talking even if she were mad, she might be able to keep her going. She wanted to talk about Linda, and she wasn't going to be put off. Stuart made talking about people fun. She had a knack for capturing in a word, things at which Sallee could only hint. Besides, talking about Linda was the next best thing to being with her.

Years of prying information from people who weren't all that interested in giving it up had endowed Sallee with a certain skill set. She had begun to trust just how far she could push without getting yelled at, smacked or grounded. Since she didn't have to worry about the grounding part of the equation with Stuart, she seemed an easy target. However, Stuart was a thrower. She had in the past used just about anything within arm's length to throw. And she could give a bawling out with the best of them, a yell that could almost make you wish she had hit you. It was always best to be on your guard when poking at her. You just had to approach her the way you would approach a snake that you had accidentally happened upon--find a forked stick and go slow. *Hmmm. Look at what she's not saying. Then go back and look at what she did say.* "Sounds to me like you know something," she said.

"Would you GET?" Stuart didn't bother to peer around the magazine. That told Sallee a lot. If Stuart didn't want to look at her, Sallee knew she was on the right track. She had the stick; now she just needed to find the right spot.

"S o o..." she started, easing in slowly.

Stuart smacked the bed with the rolled-up magazine that only seconds before had been her whole world with such force that Sallee's head snapped back, and she bit her tongue. "Get the fuck out of my room!" Stuart shrieked.

Fuck was all she could hear spinning in her head; Sallee had never heard anyone use that word before. She sat slack-jawed in utter disbelief, staring as if Stuart had vanished before her, leaving only her watermelon-colored toenails. She finally croaked, "Stuart," as if the air had somehow lost every drop of moisture -- her tongue stuck on every syllable. When she had the presence of mind to focus her eyes, she saw that Stuart's shoulders were shaking. She was crying. "What?" Sallee implored. "What's the matter?"

"He's getting married!" Stuart blubbered.

"What? Who's getting married?"

"Daddy! He's marrying that – that – The ROSE!" She laid her head down on the bed and all but howled.

Fuck continued tumbling around in Sallee's head. She backed out of the room in a daze and almost jumped when the phone in the hall rang right behind her. She didn't even stop to think, just picked it up. "Hello?" she asked. Her father rounded the corner just as Sallee spoke. "Hey, Linda," she cooed into the phone. She twisted her fingers in the coils of the cord and placed a foot on one black square tile. She liked that her whole foot fit in the square. She walked around, stepping only on the black squares as far as the cord would allow. "I'm great. I just heard some news. Guess who's getting married? ... And guess who to?" She was so thrilled to be gossiping; she didn't even feel the growing tension. "No, silly, not me." Joe stood frozen in the doorway. "Daddy and Rosemary. Isn't that cool?" She thought she wanted Linda to tell her that it was, because she wasn't at all certain. She knew Stuart didn't' think so, but she felt like Linda would know for sure. She sensed the chill before she heard it. Realization dawned; Linda wasn't her friend, she was her father's.

Linda's sweet dancing voice had turned hard and stony. Her *R-E-A-L-L-Y* started off low and slow, hard-edged, but shot quickly up in volume and pitch as she wound her way through a series of double L's, finally ending in a shrill question mark. Sallee had never seen Linda angry, but she didn't have to witness the light dim in the velvet brown eyes or the recriminating look that she knew had replaced Linda's unfailing warmth. She put the phone in Joe's outstretched hand and willed herself outside. *Fuck.*

Chapter 2

The last time she saw Linda was after the ghastly recital. Sallee's overwrought mind simultaneously chided and praised her as she sat at the piano and the recital loomed only hours away: *No, not like that, you can do better, good, not fast enough, better, too fast. What a way to ruin a perfectly good summer weekend!*

If she played it as slowly as her teacher had insisted, the whole thing would be over in less than four minutes--three minute and forty seconds, to be exact. Sallee was pretty sure she could endure anything for three minutes and forty seconds. Besides, she had a new incentive, as her mind kept wandering back to what her mother had said at breakfast, so unlike her, so longed for, and yet so too late. "I know you can do it. Sallee, you are good at everything when you focus."

She dismissed her mother's words as she left the room trying to picture her fingering while she hummed the tune. At her bedroom door, she twirled around and headed back to the piano. *For the last time, this will be the last time*, she swore. She made so many mistakes, she had to resort to reading the music to find out where she was -- never easy at the best of times. Frustrated, she gave up and returned to her room, only to about-face again. On her way down the stairs, she bumped into Ethel.

"Honey, you is might near green as d' paint on de wall," she said. "Why doan you c'mon in de kitchen an' lemme fix you somethin' t' eat. It'll make you feel better." She looked at Sallee, shaking her head.

"I don't feel like eating. I'd throw up. My stomach is so full of butterflies."

"You gonna wear dem keys out. C'mon now, give it a rest," she chuckled. "I'm gonna heat up some of de soup we had fo' lunch an' make you a grilled cheese. You give it one mo' try, den it'll be ready fo' you. But only one try, you hear?"

Sallee nodded. It didn't make any sense to argue with Ethel. Food was Ethel's universal elixir, and no amount of logic could dissuade her otherwise. She went back to the piano and made her final attempt at getting the piece right. *It didn't make any sense*, she thought. *There were only, at the most, eight notes in any one of these measures. How could it be so hard?* She had played it perfectly a thousand times. Giving in to the frustration, she banged her fists down on the piano.

"C'mon now, Sallee." Ethel was standing just behind her. Startled, Sallee jumped. With a sigh, Ethel tucked her ever-present dishtowel under her arm and placed her hands on Sallee's shoulders. "Le's git you somethin' t' eat." She took Sallee by the hand and led her into the kitchen.

"Ethel, I can't do it." *I want Mom to be proud of me*, she thought. "It's no use. I can't remember any of it. My fingers won't work right. I can't go to the recital." Sallee whimpered as the dam that had been threatening to break all morning let loose. Dropping her head down on the kitchen table, she bawled. Ethel stood by, watching dispassionately with her hands on her hips.

"Cry. Might do you some good. When you finish wit all dat, here's yo' soup an' sandwich," she said, turned toward the sink and busied herself with the dishes.

When Sallee finally lifted her head, the grilled cheese didn't look half bad. Ethel had her head in the refrigerator looking for something in the vegetable drawer.

"G'wan eat some of dat soup. It'll do you a world a good." She insisted. It was as if she had eyes in the back of her head.

Sallee took a tentative spoonful of soup, blew on it, and brought it to her lips. then let the spoon drop back into the bowl and took a bite of the grilled cheese. With every chew, it grew bigger and soggier. No amount of chewing could render it into a form that she could swallow. With Ethel's back to her, she spat the wad that was threatening to expand beyond her mouth's ability to contain it out in a paper napkin and balled the whole mess up in her hand. "I gotta go get ready."

She assured herself she'd be fine - that she'd just gotten over-excited. After all, she knew the piece cold. She just needed to trust and not think so hard. None of her soothings quieted the flock of butterflies that had taken up residency in her gut, as they seemed to be expanding at an alarming rate. When she tossed the wadded napkin filled with the ballooned grilled cheese in the wastepaper basket, it thunked like a dropped melon. She started to gag as she remembered how that small bite seemed to take on a life of its own, almost choking her to death. She half-wished it had.

Helen, younger than Sallee by two years but who Ethel said *was born an old woman,* sat primly on her bed in their shared room, her light blond curls neatly brushed. Dressed and ready to go, Helen busied herself drawing pictures of horses, a pastime that occupied her every waking moment, looking as serene as a garden glade. "Aren't you nervous?" Sallee asked.

"Why would I be? I practiced, and I'm pretty sure I'll do all right. I am a little worried that Momma's not here yet. I hate being late and having to rush in at the last minute. Are you nervous?" she asked as if it was the most alien thought a person could think.

"Yeah." Sallee answered absently. Helen had given her a new avenue for hope. Maybe her mother was going to forget all about the recital or maybe she had a flat tire and wouldn't make it in time. As she yanked her long blond hair into a ponytail, she offered up this hope in the form of a prayer. The car pulled into the drive. "Darn," she groaned, as the butterflies redoubled their activity.

Their mother called from downstairs, "Come on, girls. It's time to go." Sallee hurriedly put on her dress and started downstairs with as much enthusiasm as if she had been going to the dentist. "For God's sake, Sallee, smile," Ginny directed as she headed out of the door. Feeling as if she had dreamt her mother's earlier praise, she followed with her music hanging limply in her hand.

"Where is that brother of yours?" Ginny demanded. *Why does she always make him mine when he isn't doing what she wants?* Sallee asked herself, then shrugged it off, since she had much bigger things to worry about.

"I don't know," she answered, trying to beat back her rising panic. "I don't even know how to play the piano. How am I supposed to know where he is?"

"Sallee, do you always have to be so dramatic? It's just a little piano recital. You've played that piece a dozen times. You'll do fine, just like I told you this morning," her mother assured her. "Just focus."

More like a million times, Sallee grumbled inwardly. "I guess," was all she could squeak out in response, at least assured that she hadn't dreamt the earlier praise from her mother. Her mouth was dry, and her tongue seemed to be swelling like the grilled cheese. In the car with no sign of Gordy, she suggested, "Let's wait for him just a little longer." Anything to delay the horror of walking into Miss Porter's parlor and sitting at the piano. She could already see the outcome. She was going to forget everything and probably throw up to boot.

Miss Porter would use the opportunity to make a point. Just like she did in Sallee's lessons where she would say things like: "See, Sallee, right there is an excellent example of why you never want to memorize your music. If you had been reading, you would have exactly known where you were, and you wouldn't have missed that phrase." She was always using one of Sallee's screw-ups to illustrate how it could have been better. She couldn't remember in all the classes she had taken from Miss Porter that the old bag had ever used anyone else as an example of what not to do. "Hear," Miss Porter would say, "how Helen stays on tempo. She doesn't race to the end like a horse running back to the barn."

Helen was just about to complain about being late when Gordy appeared from around the house. "Get in this car right now, young man," Ginny barked.

"I don't see why I need to go. It's just a dumb recital. If I have to, I am going under protest."

"Noted," was all that issued from Ginny.

He climbed into the back with Sallee. Sallee made a mental note, in the event that she survived the torture of the recital, to ask her brother what was up with this protest thing. *This going under protest foolishness,* she grumbled to herself. It wasn't the first time she had heard it or seen her mother's peculiar response to it.

Stuffed with her ten pupils and their relations, Miss Porter's dark, dreary parlor put them all at risk of incineration. The temperature had to be well over a hundred as more squeezed their way into the room. Sallee's eyes darted around, looking for a hiding place. She smelled her piano teacher's distinctively head-spinning scent of mothballs tinged with too much rose before Miss Porter came up from behind, placing her claw-like hands on each of Sallee's shoulders. "How is my star student today?" she asked. Sallee looked up and around in disbelief. *She couldn't possibly have been talking to me. Was she?* No. Helen was basking in the warm glow of Miss Porter's admiration while the old battle-axe held Sallee in her clutches as if she knew Sallee might bolt at the first opportunity.

Miss Porter had a singsong voice that raced high, then low, like a bad choir warming up. You would think that someone so interested in music would have more control over her voice. She started off pretty low, as she thanked all her students for coming -- *As if we had a choice*, Sallee thought. She wasn't the only one looking a little peaked. One boy was the color of boiled custard, and another looked like his necktie was choking him as he verged on a swoon. Miss Porter's voice shot up the scale as she remarked on the great turnout, and how absolutely delighted she was with her students' progress. Her unmodulated voice continued its erratic ups and downs as she added that some of her students were not as dedicated as others to practice, with a nervous little titter that sounded sinister to Sallee.

Sallee exchanged glances with her fellow non-compliers. "All in all," Miss Porter concluded, "I am happy to present my piano class of 1963." She ended on a shrill note that sent an involuntary flinch around the room. She clapped her hands, as a way of introducing her students.

It was worse than Sallee could have imagined. When Miss Porter croaked out Sallee's name, her hands started to shake so badly she was afraid to stand for fear the same would happen to her lower limbs. Never long on patience or kindness, at least as far as Sallee was concerned, Miss Porter made a joke. Finally, Sallee managed to take her seat at the piano. She had left her music on the floor. Miss Porter swept it up, placing it on the music rack in one fluid, albeit accusatory motion, enveloping Sallee in another cloud of her old rose aroma. She introduced the piece, saying, "Sallee will be playing, Beethoven's *Sonatina in G*." Sallee's heart was pounding so loudly she could hardly hear her teacher, even though Miss Porter had plopped herself down on the seat next to her.

She tried to take a breath and collect herself. Miss Porter hissed, "Put your thumbs on middle C." Sallee's hands shook so badly she was lucky to find the keyboard. She watched her spastic limbs as if they were possessed. Miss Porter grabbed Sallee's offending hands and plunked them down on the keys. It was no help. Frozen in terror, she almost lost consciousness. God knows she wished she had. Miss Porter, again, picked up Sallee's hands and formed the shape of the notes with her student's fingers banging them down on the keys, hoping, Sallee supposed, to jump-start them. Finally giving up, she announced, "That will be all. Sallee, you are excused." As Sallee, slunk in shame and mortification back to her seat, Helen pranced up and played *Fur Elise* flawlessly.

Gordy reached over and poked Sallee, offering his reassurance. She couldn't look at him. It took every ounce of control she had to endure the next fifteen or twenty minutes. As the last note played and the clapping ceased, before the refreshments were served in Miss Porter's dining room, Sallee sidled away. Without speaking to a single soul, without even a glance in any direction, she slipped out the back door and didn't stop running until she got home. Making her way into the kitchen, she took one look at Ethel and dissolved into a torrent of tears. Ethel pressed the child to her body and rocked gently while the girl wept.

It was three days after her humiliation at Miss Porter's that Sallee saw Linda. She was with Ginny in the drugstore across the street from the hospital. Sallee was sure that, had she been kidnapped and brought into the store blindfolded, she would be able to tell the police later exactly where she had been. The tinkling bell, coupled with the smell of grilled cheese, tuna salad, perfume and powders, with medicinal overtones, was unmistakably Chancellor's. There was no doubt in her mind, she would make an excellent crime victim, she decided, or a detective. *Maybe I should be a policeman when I grow up*, she thought.

Ginny had just finished an enlivened conversation with the piano teacher; at least it looked so from Sallee's vantage point behind the brush display. *Of all the people in town you'd most want to see on a Thursday afternoon, what were the odds of running into her here?* Sallee asked herself as she willed herself to become several sizes smaller. *Didn't she have any victims at home to torment?* Ginny was standing in the back, talking to the pharmacist. Sallee sipped her milkshake and lurked clandestinely, looking at the display cabinets and maintaining as much invisibility as possible while keeping a watchful eye out for her teacher. Spying Miss P. coming her way, she ducked behind a rack of shower caps, hot water bottles, and ice packs. She turned the spinning display just enough so that she could keep the old bag in her sight without being seen herself. She wanted to know exactly when Miss Porter exited the store. She stealthily moved toward the lunch counter to get a better view of the door, positioning herself behind the rack of comic books. Brenda Starr, Archie and Jughead leered out at her, and she immersed herself in the latest *Archie*. After the awful piano recital, she was not interested in running into her teacher under any circumstances.

Every time the bell on the door tinkled, Sallee looked up from her comic, hoping the old bag had left -- and then there she was, Linda, coming in. Their eyes met, and Linda looked like she was going to bolt, but then instead came over and gave Sallee a long hug. They both teared up. Linda asked how Sallee had been while trying to wipe away her tears as if she had something in her eye. As suddenly as she was there, she was gone, as if evaporating through the door just as Sallee's mother made her way down the aisle to where they had been standing. Sallee was dizzy trying to track so many fronts at once.

"Was that your father's little nurse friend?" Ginny asked as Sallee watched the door where Linda had disappeared. Sallee ignored her, pretending she hadn't heard, working to put Betty and Veronica back in the rack. Ginny shrugged, "Suit yourself." she said as they left the store. "Oh, did you see Miss Porter? She was asking about you."

Sallee's eyes darted up and down the street, then checked across University Avenue to see if Linda was on those same steps where she had first seen her. She hoped she was wrong, but she knew in her heart she'd never see her again. Even years later, Sallee never went by the hospital that she didn't look for Linda.

She stuffed the sadness that was whelming up. It took every ounce of will she possessed. For once she was grateful for her mother's habit of backbiting. Hearing Linda referred to as Daddy's "little nurse friend" made it easier to focus on her rage at her mother than the sadness of Linda's loss and her part in it.

Ginny's badgering lectures on her inappropriate behavior while in public had given way to snide comments about people she saw or services she did or didn't receive. Sallee didn't know when it happened. She just remembered that recently she didn't feel so much like a turtle, particularly when they first got back in the car. Her mother's criticism of others was far easier to ignore. She could agree or disagree as the situation dictated without listening. Though she couldn't be on total autopilot, because nothing made her mother madder than being pandered to, whatever the *fuck* that meant. That word again. She couldn't get it out of her head, and she was beginning to like it.

Ginny prattled on about Miss Porter until they had gotten to the car, lulling Sallee into thinking that the encounter with Linda might pass without any further comment. She was wrong. As Ginny was about to pull into traffic, she said with a sour giggle, "I bet that little girl was some kind of mad when she found out that her darling Joe was two-timing her with Rosemary."

"FUCK YOU," Sallee screamed. She jumped out the car and ran as fast as she could. At first, angry tears streamed down her cheeks. By the time her lungs picked up the burn, her tears had dried. When the stitch in her side became unbearable, she slowed her pace.

She was in a neighborhood she'd never seen before. In order not to be followed by her loathsome mother, she had taken turns as they came, not even interested in where they might lead, as long as it was away from her, and all the pain she was so adept at inflicting. Sallee was pretty sure her mother wouldn't have been able to keep up with her, with all the late afternoon traffic. Right then, she would have been happy to have never seen or thought of her mother again. She told herself she had long outgrown the need for her mother's approval, realizing that any attempts at pleasing her were in vain. But at just twelve hardly anything was long ago; it just felt like it, and she was fed up with her mother's judgments and was just ready to show how *much*.

As she looked around, she realized she had no idea where she was. There weren't any sidewalks, just dirt paths along the pitted, dusty road. The too-close-together wooden houses all shared a faded, gray-yellow lack of paint. A dog chained in a dirt yard barked monotonously as she passed, the only living thing that she could see. There were no cars parked along the road, nor was there any grass, except for an occasional overgrown clump or a patch of weeds that only looked like grass for their shared color. Most yards were washed-out patches of rutted soil broken by gnarled roots, with hard, worn paths leading to steps--some wooden, others rock or a broken piece of cinderblock.

Worn out from the exertion, she looked for a place to sit. Just ahead of her, a tree, with huge snakelike roots twisted around in and out of the ground, the perfect spot to sit and contemplate what the heck she was going to do now. She dropped down, thirsty, hot, sweaty, but strangely at peace, until she started thinking about how her mother must feel. Instead of the elation from this new sense of freedom that had so recently broken through, she began to feel as if she had betrayed *her*. She mulled over the absence of the anger that had sent her down this path, anger that had threatened to overwhelm her so completely just minutes before -- gone. Replaced with: How did *she* feel, *she*, her mother? It was as if her mother's feelings were more important than her own.

This utter betrayal by her brain infuriated her, all over again. No shred of empathy for herself, how did she feel--*guilty* of course, but of what? She couldn't say. Then she remembered just the other day when Stuart shrieked at her and for the first time she heard the word that had so much power, heard it out loud and directed at her. She couldn't stop thinking about how that felt, so empowering. It was as if something wild and wonderful broke loose inside.

Silly. It was just a bad word. Certainly, one that nice girls like Sallee shouldn't use, but still, just a little word. Her upbringing didn't include a primer in bad language, but here she was shouting it at her mother of all people, and feeling wonderfully elated and depressed at the same time. She must be going crazy. She picked up a handful of rocks and tossed them one after another into the road as she sat on the tree root, rolling her feelings around in her head, trying to make sense of them.

"What ya doin'?" The strange-looking kid was standing way too close.

Startled, Sallee jumped back, but she didn't even hesitate to snap with a sneer, "Where'd you come from? I didn't even hear you come up."

The kid indicated with its head a direction behind the tree. At first glance, Sallee couldn't tell if the apparition was a girl or a boy. Lank colorless hair hung in stringy hunks all around its head, as if it had been chopped, not cut. "What ya doin'?" it asked again, then added as if to itself, "Nice, like my mama say t' do," then broke out in a self-satisfied smile.

"I don't know. Sitting on this tree root, throwing rocks." Stating the obvious seemed the best approach. The kid could have been Sallee's age or way younger. It had a thick babyish body but was nearly as tall as Sallee. It certainly didn't act like it was twelve. Something wasn't exactly right, Sallee thought. Then; *Simple, maybe?* -- like Ethel's sister Hughberta who Sallee had only heard of. She wasn't sure.

"I never saw ya before. Kin I throw some too? Where ya come from?"

"If you want," she said, electing not to answer any questions that gave away information.

"Mama say I'm s'posed ta ask ya -- " the child stopped in mid-sentence, as if thinking, then slowly proceeded with exaggerated contortions of the mouth, "-- if ya want some water?"

Sallee looked all around trying to figure out where this kid's mother was, that she would even know Sallee existed, much less be able to read her mind. "Where's your mama?"

The kid again indicated with its head behind the tree. Sallee stood up and walked all the way around the tree. No mama, no house, no nothing. "Where?" She demanded. The kid took, her by the hand. Sallee noticed that the kid's hands looked like her baby brother Dennis's did--chubby and like there had been a rubber band around the wrist where it connected to the arm. She let this odd child lead her through an overgrown row of privet that at some point in the very distant past might have been a hedge. Sitting on a ramshackle porch attached to what looked like a pile of boards thrown in a heap, not ten feet from where Sallee stood, was a tall, angular-looking woman. She smiled at the kid as if it had just brought home a great prize. As Sallee turned and looked over her shoulder, she could plainly see where she had just been sitting. "Oh," was all she could think to say.

"Charlie," the dark haired lady chirruped. "I am so proud of you. You did what I asked exactly, and you were so brave. What's your friend's name?"

Charlie's doughy face broke out in a broad beam as she swung their interlaced hands back in forth in a wide arc, then looked up at Sallee with small brown eyes. "Wha's yer name?"

"Sallee," she offered, though reluctantly. As kind as this woman sounded, the whole thing had a dreamlike quality that she wasn't all that happy about.

"Mama, her name is Salwee. My name is Charwie."

"That's right, your name is Charlie. Why don't you ask Sallee if she'd like to come in and get some water? She looks hot," the woman said smiling at Charlie. Sallee noticed that the woman enunciated every word and spoke directly to her child, making sure of eye contact.

"Yer wanna water, Salwee?" Charlie asked, still swinging their arms back and forth, looking about to burst with pride.

"Sure, I'd love some," she said as Charlie continued to clutch her hand and swing it vigorously. "Would you like me to help you?" she asked hoping that it might stop the swinging.

"No, Charwie do it."

Charlie let Sallee's arm go in mid-swing and lumbered onto the porch and into the tumbledown house. Sallee smiled at the mother awkwardly. She smiled back easily, as if they had always known each other. She patted the step next to her. "Sit," she offered, half question, half imperative. "You look tired. And hot, too. But then it has been hot for the past few weeks," she added, as she picked up the paper plate lying next to her and began to fan herself. She offered it to Sallee, who shook her head, declining the proffered plate.

Sallee, usually eager to talk with anyone about anything, couldn't think of a topic of conversation. Finally she asked, "How old is Charlie?"

"She's ten. I have never seen you around here. Do you live nearby?" she asked.

"Oh," Sallee stumbled, grateful that she hadn't asked how old *he* was and surprised that she could have been so confused. She didn't think she had ever mistaken a girl for a boy or vice versa, ever. Well maybe a baby, but certainly not a kid. "I -- don't know," she stammered, flummoxed by mistaking Charlie for a boy. She certainly hadn't wanted to admit that she didn't know where she was, but here she had gone and done it. Besides, it seemed impossible to speak anything but the truth to the calm brown eyes that enveloped her with such open interest.

"Are you lost?" she asked, stopping her fanning and looking at Sallee, her eyes full of concern.

"Not exactly," Sallee said trying to come up with a plausible story as the truth tumbled out of her mouth unbidden and, from her perspective, wholly unwished-for. She soon heard herself telling the woman what she'd shouted at her mother as she jumped from her car. *Oh, nooo, what am I doing?* She put her hand on her forehead. *This woman is going to kill me*. She hadn't known her two seconds, and already she'd said *fuck* in her presence. *What is the matter with me?*

The woman moved toward her as Sallee cringed away. "Oh honey, you must feel just awful, poor dear." She put a long, slender arm around Sallee's shoulder and pulled her close. Charlie clambered out of the house with two mismatched jelly jars holding maybe a tablespoon of water apiece.

The woman turned, gently releasing Sallee. "Well done, Charlie."

"Charwie wanna hug Salwee too," she said as she dropped both glasses and wrapped Sallee's head in a vice-like grip. The jars proved stronger than the rotten floorboards and rolled under Charlie's feet. Charlie started to slip as she clung to Sallee's head, increasing the pressure until Sallee thought she was going to pass out.

The woman's voice rose sharply. "Charlie, stop right now. Stop it!" Her abruptness frightened Sallee. Charlie's grip lessened while Sallee sucked in much-needed oxygen. The girl's mother pulled her off Sallee tenderly as if nothing had happened. Charlie bawled, "Mama, I sawee, I din't mean t' break da glass."

"Honey, you didn't. See," she said, holding the two jars up for her daughter's inspection. "Why don't you try it again?" Happily, Charlie went back in the house with a jar clutched tightly in each fist. Several minutes later she arrived the glasses filled with enough water to quench a thirst.

"Mama, tell us a stowee," Charlie begged. "Tell the one 'bout da billwee goats grumps."

Charlie's mother said, "I have a better idea let's pretend that we are the three billy goats. Charlie, you can be the smallest one."

Charlie grinned. "I wanna be the billwee goat grump."

"Okay Mr. Billy Goat Grump, how are you today?" Her mother inquired.

"I'm grumpy," cackled Charlie, thinking her joke was hilarious. "Hi ho I ho," she sang, "Is yer bed jest right?"

Charlie's mother winked at Sallee, "Sallee can be the small billy goat, and I'll be the medium billy goat. Ok?"

"Ok, Salwee better get in bed den." Charlie insisted. It took Sallee a few minutes to figure out that Billy Goat Grump was a distillation of Goldilocks, The Three Billy Goats Gruff, Snow White and whatever else Charlie the director had in her mind. She willingly gave herself over to the game. "Say Fee, Fi, Foam, Foam, Salwee," Charlie insisted, "This is the bridge." Charlie pointed to a table, "Mama, you get under here." Laughing so hard at a combination of her frayed nerves and the nonsensical storyline, Sallee couldn't catch her breath. She decided she and Helen should play Billy Goats Grump sometime.

Charlie's mother steered Billy Goat Grump into a guessing game that Charlie insisted could only be played under the bridge. All three of them crawled under the table and laughed until they cried as Charlie would periodically crawl out from under the table and climb on top of it shouting "Hummy Dummy twidlin' pie. Eat the troll and make him die!" Then would break into a sinister, "mwhahah," which sent her mother and Sallee into convulsions of laughter.

Later they played a game of hop-scotch, though Charlie's mother only drew three squares in the dirt--the one a single and the two and three together. As she folded herself back up to standing, she announced to Sallee with a wink. "We don't need all those other numbers. The best hop-scotchers only use three." Charlie and Sallee both chimed their agreement. Sallee couldn't believe it when the Woolen Mill's five o'clock whistle blew. Charlie asked her if she would like to stay for dinner.

"Is it that late? I guess I should go home," Sallee said, completely forgetting why she was there in the first place. "Oh," she looked around wildly. She didn't want to leave. She didn't want to go home, even if she knew which way that was. But she knew she had to.

"Bless your heart, sweetie," the kind woman said. "Do you know your address?"

An indignant, "I'm twelve," almost slipped out, but, fortunately she was able to reel it back in before she offended anyone. "Yes, I live over near the University, behind the law school."

"Oh, I know. How about if Charlie and I walk you home? It isn't as far as you might think."

"It's okay, if you just point me in the right direction, I think I'll find my way," Sallee said, ashamed of being ashamed of them. She didn't want them to walk her home.

As if she could read the child's mind the woman said, "Okay, we'll walk you as far as the law school. You can find your way home from there, can't you? Charlie, I don't think tonight is the best night for Sallee to have dinner with us. Maybe another time?"

"But we's got baloney and mustard," she offered and then as if it were the most amazing thing in the world, "and bread, too."

Sallee waved goodbye to her new friends in front of the law school and slipped around back, down the hill and across the street. All the rest of the way home she wondered if anything had ever engendered as much joy for her as the thought of a baloney sandwich did for Charlie.

Chapter 3

Ginny stormed into the house, slammed the front door and marched into the kitchen. "Ethel," she snapped, "Where is Sallee? Have you seen her?"

"No'm, is jest me an' Helen. Gordy's off at George's," she said looking wide-eyed at Ginny. "Helen is up in her room las' I saw her," she added to Ginny's back as she stomped from the kitchen.

"Wait until I get my hands on that child. I will make her..." Ginny muttered. Ethel followed at a safe distance.

"Is everythin' all righ'?" Ethel ventured.

"No, everything is not all right," Ginny retorted. "Everything is decidedly not all right. I don't know what I am going to do with that child. She's now shouting profanity at me. In public no less!"

"Miz Ginny, you doan mean it?"

"Ethel, she sounded just like a little guttersnipe. She yelled the most disgusting thing you can imagine at me, then jumped out of the car, while it was moving, and ran away. I was sure she would be home by now. I can't even imagine where she heard such language." She stood at the bottom of the steps with her hands on her hips. "Sallee Mackey, you come down this instant. Do you hear me?" she shrieked up the stairs.

Ethel kept her distance. "Miz Ginny, I tell you, she ain't here."

Helen appeared at the top of the stairs.

"Honey, is Sallee up in y'all's room?" Ethel called up to her.

Helen shook her head, deep blue eyes staring at her mother. "What's wrong?"

"Where is Sallee?" her mother demanded.

"I don't know," Helen whimpered, then asked, "Did she do something wrong?"

"You bet your life she did. And she is going to be mighty sorry about it, too," Ginny growled.

Ethel, hoping to change the subject asked, "Miz Ginny, do you needs some help wit' de groceries?" *Lord, what has dat child gone an' done now?* "Helen, c'mon down here an' help ol' Ethel wit' de groceries," she said. The girl reluctantly came down the stairs, pressing close to the wall when she neared her mother.

"Hell's bells," Ginny moaned, "Ethel, I didn't go to the darn store. I was so upset by that child it slipped right out of my mind. I'll go now to Reid's Market and while I'm out I'll slip by Snow's Garden Center and get some mums. When Sallee gets back, you tell her to go straight to her room. No dinner, no television and no company!" She glared at Helen. "Do you hear me, miss?" Helen nodded that she did.

"You doan have t' go back out. I kin do 'til tomorrow," Ethel said as she wrapped her hands in her apron.

Just then Gordy banged open the front door. Thinking it was Sallee, Ginny turned on him, venom practically dripping from her lips. "Young lady, you get upstairs this… Oh for God's sake, Gordy, don't bang the door," she snarled, snatching up her purse and slamming out of the very same door.

Gordy looked to Ethel for an explanation. "Doan look at me, boy. I ain't gots no idea an' if I did I wonne' be tellin' you no way." She marched back into the kitchen, shaking her head, "Lord, if it ain't one thing…" then clucked under her breath about respect.

Helen said, "I heard Momma tell Ethel that Sallee yelled something bad. *Profane*, I think is what she said." Helen shrugged. "Then she ran away."

"What's profane?" Gordy asked.

"I don't know," Helen said, "But whatever it is, it's bad. She's mad."

"No kidding," Gordy allowed. "Jeez, what did Sallee do this time? I would have thought she'd be more careful, after all the trouble she got into when she left that piano recital. I don't think we'll ever hear the end of that."

"Doan y'all got better thangs t' do den standin' out chere talkin' foolishness?" Ethel glowered at both of them.

"Ethel, I didn't do anything wrong. Don't get mad at me. And ya don't know that Sallee did either. You know as well as we do that Mom lies if it suits her," Gordy said, his voice cracking slightly at that last remark. He hated it when that happened. It seemed that he couldn't control anything these days, even his own voice.

"Boy, doan be talkin' 'bout yo' momma like dat. How many time does I has te tell you? You s'posed te respect yo' momma, you hear me?"

"Yeah, yeah," he sighed and turned to go. "Believe me, Ethel, I would if I could." He climbed the stairs, wearier than an old man. Helen followed him to his room. She went over to his bookshelf and took out a dictionary. "Man, what is it with you girls? Always looking things up!" He rolled his eyes and fell across the bed.

"I want to know what she said to her, is all." Helen looked up at Gordy. "You better take your shoes off the bedspread or Ethel will be all over you, too."

"I don't give a shit," Gordy stated flatly. "I don't care."

Helen looked wide-eyed at him, thinking he better be glad Ethel wasn't around to hear him cuss, but decided to keep it to herself. "She didn't *say* profane. She said something that *was*."

"Was *what*?"

"Was ... '*obscene*'?" Helen reported dubiously, after reading for a while. "I guess."

"My point exactly. Why does anybody bother looking things up in a dictionary? I don't know any more than I did before. Do you?"

"Well, some," whimpered Helen. I know she didn't yell *profane* at Momma."

"That helps! Jeeez. *Girls*." He rolled over, turning his back to his sister.

"I don't have any place to be," Helen pleaded. "Momma said I had to leave Sallee alone. Can I --? Never mind."

"I don't want you or anybody else around," he snapped. "Get out."

She was out of the door before he finished. She ran down the stairs to her room, snatched up her drawing pad, took it to the kitchen and sat down at the table with Ethel. Neither said a word. By the time her mother returned, Helen had drawn an entire herd of horses. When the door slammed for the fourth time that afternoon, she flinched. She sat tensely waiting for what, she wasn't sure.

Ginny walked into the kitchen carrying a bag of groceries and a pot of rust color chrysanthemums. She placed them on the counter. "I love walking around Snow's. They have so many lovely flowers." She laughed, "I bet if I took you there this place would look like a jungle in no time. Back yet?" she asked, much calmer.

Ethel busied herself with the groceries. "Mighty pretty flowers, "She shook her head. "Ain't seed hide 'n' hair o' her. Do you think we should call someone?"

"No, I imagine, she'll be home soon. It's past five. She'll probably want to see you before you go."

Ethel looked up sharply to see if that was a barb directed at her. It didn't seem to be. "I got a 'ppointment, so I'm leavin' a li'l early dis evenin'. Remember?"

"Yes, I remember. You go ahead and go. I'll take care of things."

"Miz Ginny," Ethel said. She started to say, *Doan hurt her* but thought better of it. Ginny nodded goodbye and left the room.

Going home was worse than Sallee could have dreamt. She expected the household to be in a tizzy, everybody so distressed by her absence that her homecoming would blot out any of the earlier unpleasantness. Not so. She was surprised at how disappointed she was that her running away had so little impact. Her mother was sitting on the front porch reading the afternoon paper as she always did. Ginny hadn't yet seen Sallee. Sallee's mind was racing. *Was she sorry? Should she say so? Should she pretend like nothing happened and see what did?* Sneaking around to the kitchen door would be useless. Neither Helen nor Gordy was anywhere in sight. Ginny hardly looked up as Sallee started up the steps. Her grunt was her terse greeting. Then she indicated a chair. "Sit," was all she said.

Sallee sat and waited while her mother finished the paper. The idea of a loving mother and daughter on a dilapidated porch, free, easy and open with one another, stood in stark contrast to this scene of forced silence, definitely intended to shut down any hope for escape or forgiveness. *As if.* Sallee steeled herself for the coming onslaught. Then her mind went back to the fun she had had that afternoon, and she realized she was smiling. It was unsettling, but it gave her a flash of courage. This waiting was going to have to stop; so, better now - maybe on her own terms? Taking what she hoped was an unnoticeable deep breath, she lurched into an apology. "Mom, I'm sorry I said what I said to you this afternoon. I didn't mean it. I hope you'll forgive me."

Nothing from her mother. Sallee made a move to leave. Ginny shook the paper to get her daughter's attention, then glared over the top of it with a scowl toward the chair indicating that staying put was Sallee's only option. She couldn't tell how long she sat before her mother finally finished the paper. She folded it with excruciating exactness before placing it on the rattan table beside her, up under one of the enormous begonia leaves that took up most of the space, along with an ashtray.

She then with equal preciseness folded her hands in her lap and stared at her daughter. Sallee held her breath, feeling woozy and lightheaded. It seemed that her safest course of action was to wait. Her head began to spin. She couldn't focus her eyes and beads of sweat began to gather on her upper lip. She propped her elbow on the barrel-shaped chair she was sitting in and leaned her head heavily on her hand, trying for all she was worth to keep her eyes open. When Ginny finally started in on her, Sallee couldn't understand what her mother was saying as she slipped deeper and deeper into the chair, quite unable to hold herself up. It was as if she was talking on one of those phones made out of two oatmeal boxes and a piece of string. All she heard was noise. Her mother must have told her to go to her room. She woke much later in the night with a headache that felt as if someone had cinched a belt around her head at eye level and was squeezing it, intending for the top of her head to blow off. She moved. Sharp electric pains zinged up and down her back, causing every muscle to shriek in protest. She had to go to the bathroom but was afraid to move again so as not to start the spasms over.

"Helen," she croaked. She began to shiver, her teeth chattering. "Helen, help." Helen was dead to the world.

Sallee pushed the covers off, keeping her head as still as she could. The arctic blast that engulfed her almost made her give up, but then it felt good, too. She slid her legs over the side of the bed and felt for the floor. There wasn't one. She had slipped into the abyss. Was that Helen's head floating above her? Then silence, then her mother's voice. Voices wafted overhead, *Wa, Wa, Wa.* She felt a vague tugging, floating and then nothing.

When Sallee finally woke she was in a dull green-colored room, with a brigade of what looked like overgrown baby beds or cages for zoo animals lined up against the wall. The room was huge. She lay in one of those cages taking in the room, trying to make out where she was. A woman was sitting by her bedside. When their eyes met, the woman gave a little jump and chirped as if startled awake. Then as if she had forgotten to breathe, she sighed, "Oh thank *God*." Tears streamed down her cheeks. She looked tired, old and not at all like Sallee remembered. Her long blond hair was down, and much longer than Sallee thought it should be. She'd never thought of her as having hair -- just the bun, which never equated to hair in Sallee's mind. She was wearing a pair of pants, not jodhpurs. Sallee didn't know she even *owned* pants. And she was wearing what looked like one of Dad's old shirts, a sight decidedly more out of character than all the rest of it put together.

"Mom???"

"Oh sweetheart," Ginny whispered as she stood and gently let the bars down that separated them. "I can't tell you how marvelous it is to hear your voice." She leaned over and gave her daughter a kiss and a hug that lasted too long, though Sallee didn't want it to end. It made her feel almost dizzy again, but she gritted her teeth until her mother finally let go.

"Mom?" She still wasn't sure this apparition was her mother, though she truly wanted it to be. "What am I doing here? What happened?" Too weak to sit up, she gazed around the room, moving her head slowly side to side on her pillow. There didn't seem to be more than three other kids there, but it was hard to see through the bars. "Am I in jail?"

"No, silly, you've been very, very ill." Ginny sweetly smiled as she stroked her daughter's head. A cloud of concern swept over her face, "Does your head hurt?"

Sallee shook her head slowly. "But I am hungry." She noticed she had tubes going into her or out of her, she couldn't tell and was not crazy about the thought. When she moved, much to her horror, she peed.

Her mother must have read the alarm on her face. "What, what is it?" she asked, looking frightened. "Are you all right?"

"I just wet the bed," Sallee blubbered.

Ginny laughed that sweet, musical *tee-hee* that when Sallee was little made her think of how angels must laugh. "You have on a diaper. I'll call the nurse." She pulled up the bed rails, turned and pushed a button on the wall.

"A diaper!" Sallee cried out, wishing that she could vaporize that very moment and cease to exist. She prayed her heart would end this all by stopping -- now. "Please don't call the nurse," she pleaded. "Can't I just go to the bathroom and clean myself up?"

"Shhhh," Ginny ordered softly but firmly, with her finger to her lips. "I don't think you understand how sick you've been," She told Sallee she had just been moved there from intensive care that very morning, which meant she was getting better, but that didn't mean she was very strong. She needed to rest so that she could recover.

"There is no way I can rest in a diaper. So forget about recovering," Sallee moaned, ready to throw the towel in on life. Then, suddenly feeling like she had just run a fifty-yard dash -- too tired to fight -- she conceded. "Okay. Call the nurse." It was clear that as horrifying as wearing a diaper might be, wearing a wet one was a thousand times worse.

A few moments later a woman swept into the room in what Sallee immediately saw would make the perfect nurses' Halloween costume, until she remembered that she *was* a nurse. The nurse let the bars down again and somehow managed to soothe the girl's embarrassment and maintain her privacy at the same time, no easy trick. Discovering that she was also encased in a pair of rubber pants just like her baby brother Denny had only added to Sallee's humiliation and dread. She gritted her teeth again, but as the nurse disappeared from the room, Sallee thought of their old bloodhound Lance. She giggled. "Don't her shoes sound like when Lance's tongue would stick to the roof of his mouth?"

Ginny looked at her daughter quizzically, then laughed her magical laugh. "You, dear, have the most vivid imagination. Never would I have come up with that, but you know, they do!" She burst out laughing again, louder than Sallee ever remembered hearing.

She fell asleep and didn't see her mother again until . . . vague images of people coming and going floated dreamlike in her spotty awareness. A familiar drawl brought her back to semi-consciousness. Were those voices? Whose? The last time she woke, the light had hurt her eyes so much that she had lain with them shut, trying to identify who was in the room.

"I didn't realize that you were a designer. Does one have had to go to school for that?"

Is that Mom? It had to be, no one else could sound that disapproving while asking something so seemingly normal ... Who is she talking to?

She heard another voice answer, stiff and anxious. "There is a degree one could pursue in interior design, but it's not necessary in order to be a decorator."

Sallee scoured her brain trying to put a name with the voice. *Oh, God, That can't be The Rose, can it?* It was a ghastly thought -- her mother and The Rose in the same room together, and worse yet, in *her* room.

She debated venturing a peek until she heard her father speak. "Rosemary is quite good at it, too. She decorated my entire new house --" He swallowed the word *house* at the end of the sentence as if he'd thought better of it, but as usual far too late.

Good old Dad, always blurting things out before he thinks. I guess that's where I get it, Sallee groaned inwardly.

She heard her mother's too-polite voice dripping with derision, "How lovely for *both* of you." Sallee would rather have paraded around naked than risk opening an eye now. Lying there listening to the awkward silence of feet shuffling, throats clearing, and chairs legs scraping, she prayed that they would all leave and she could just fall back to sleep.

After that, she never woke without listening to who might be in her room before venturing to open her eyes. She made it a practice to feign sleep when she heard a visitor's approach, opening her eyes only when she was sure her parents were not both present.

She woke once to discover a well-worn book tied with a yellow ribbon lying on her pillow. She carefully untied the bow, opened the book and leafed gently through it sensing that it had been precious to someone. On the first page 'Linda Todd' had been neatly penned in a child's hand along with a star and an exclamation point. A note fell onto her bed.

Dear Sallee,

This book Half Magic was one of my very favorites when I was your age. In the book, four children find a coin that grants wishes but only half of a wish at a time. It is a little get well/goodbye present. I have a new job closer to my parents and will be leaving at the end of the week.

When I heard you were sick, I came by as soon as I could. Your rest is much more important than chatting with me. As hard as it was not to wake you, give you a hug and have a little cry together, I'm writing this to let you know how special you are to me. I'll always remember the fun we had.

You will be all better soon. I know, because I checked before I wrote this.

Please take good care of yourself.

Love,

Linda

Stuart came to see her in the hospital twice before she left for school. Her unusual sweetness slightly mitigated the shock of her newly dyed black hair. She brought comics and candy and sat on the bed though there were signs all over the place saying not to, and also something about leaving the bars up. She pulled the bars down crawled into bed with Sallee, then pulled the bars back up. The girls giggled, laughed, hugged and kissed. When Stuart got under the covers with her, Sallee was grateful beyond belief that she no longer wore diapers. She'd made her mother swear that she would never tell a soul, cross my heart and hope to die, *really*.

"I have missed you so much, you little squirt. Boy, you had us worried. It's bad enough having one dead sibling. Would have brought Ethel to drink." Stuart snickered.

Sallee cut her eyes up sharp as if to ask, "Is she?" -- praying that she wasn't.

"No, but I tell you one thing, you had better be strong and healthy when you get home because she'll bowl you over before you get out of the car. She's taken your room apart and cleaned every single square inch of it. I suspect with a toothbrush. She washed, ironed and starched your curtains so that they could stand on their own. Last I heard she was planning your favorite dinner for your homecoming. Liver, beets and cabbage, right? And for dessert mincemeat pie?"

"Aw, noooo," Sallee groaned. "She doesn't think those are my favorites, does she?"

Stuart giggled, "What do you think? Oh wait, I almost forgot." She stood up on the bed and climbed over the rails. "They're here somewhere," she said rooting through her things. "Hmm, oh yeah. Here!"

She tossed an aluminum foil wad into the bed then climbed back in. While they talked and laughed, they stuffed themselves on Ethel's marmalade tarts until there wasn't a single one left and the bed was covered with crumbs.

With a mouth full of tart Sallee asked, "Hey Stuart do you know why I am in here? What wrong with me?"

"I don't think I have enough time before I have to leave for school to tell you all of the things that are wrong with you." Stuart teased.

Sallee gave her a little sneer. "No, really do you know why I am in here?"

"What I heard," Stuart started then stopped and started again, "they didn't tell you?" Sallee shook her head. "They think you had meningitis from swimming this summer. A couple of kids got it. I can't…" Stuart stopped abruptly, as Joe and Rosemary walked in.

Joe laughed, "You look like two little monkeys in a cage." He came over and rubbed the top of Sallee's head while placing a new Nancy Drew book on her bedside table. "Can I get you something? Oh, I see you've had a few of Ethel's tarts." He brushed the crumbs from the bed. "You could have saved me one."

"Stuart, you shouldn't be in there. You could get sick," Rosemary fussed and fumed looking around, worried that someone might see Stuart breaking the rules, "That's why they don't want you on the bed. Stuart, you really ought to get out…" Stuart cut her off before she could go any further.

"Okay, for Christ's sake," She stood up and hopped over the rails again. "I gotta go. See ya, kid." With that, she was gone.

The second time she visited was the day before she left to go to New York. The almost-black hair had undergone a drastic change, to look more grown-up, harder with a razor sharp cut. "Sophisticated," she said. *Tougher -- and mean*, Sallee thought, but kept it to herself.

"This early? School doesn't start for another week, right?" Sallee asked. "I come home tomorrow. Can't you wait?"

"Kid, you haven't got any idea. Labor Day is this coming Monday, and my school starts the next day, so I have to get there and get settled. Besides, you aren't coming home tomorrow, I think I heard you were going to be here awhile. I can't stand it another minute. I love Dad more than I can say, but God, his taste in women. It seems that his perfect woman has to be a B-I-T-C-H. The Rose makes Mom look like she's standing still." Stuart whistled. "Phew, I'm talking full-time bitch. She'll wear you down like Chinese water torture. Not like Mom, who's just mean, The Rose just keeps at it, nag, nag, nag! How she was able to be nice long enough to reel him in is a mystery unless he likes it, and that makes me want to throw up."

"Linda wasn't a bitch," Sallee said forlornly.

"Yeah, I know. Makes ya wonder if Dad is all that wonderful. He sure treated Linda like shit. I think that is what I hated the most about the whole Linda thing. I had to entertain the possibility that my father wasn't Prince Charming. As Bets says, I had to grow up. My father is as big a bastard as any of them."

"...any of them who? Who's Bets?"

"Men. Just a friend I've known for ages."

"Oh."

Stuart didn't stay as long this time. Sallee was grateful that Joe and The Rose didn't come, nor her mother while

Stuart was there. Both the girls cried when it came time to say goodbye. Stuart promised she would write. Sallee didn't believe her, and she knew she was lying about Bets. Whoever Bets was, she was new and for some reason Stuart didn't want Sallee to know how new. Sallee was glad her sister had left. *Stuart sure was using a lot of bad words a lot more than usual these days. It's a good thing Ethel wasn't around to hear her, she'd probably wash her mouth out with soap*. The thought of her own little bout with cursing brought a shudder. Sallee lay in the hospital bed thinking about how strange it was that Stuart wasn't the only reason she was sad. She understood why Stuart was leaving. She thought she was even a little jealous that Stuart was leaving home. But she didn't want to go with her. Stuart was too much of a hater, and Sallee was getting tired of even listening to her. It was funny she didn't even mind that she had to stay here a bit longer. Now that she was feeling better, she realized that she was actually enjoying being here in the peace and quiet of the hospital.

Yes, her older sister was angry and odd, there was no doubt, but she was no Gordy. Stuart wasn't going to take her anger out on defenseless little birds, sitting under their feeders, with his BB gun snuffing out little lives because his life sucked. And when that didn't give him the peace Sallee guessed he was looking for. He'd put Helen in a box and shot at her!

What was Helen thinking? Helen was the biggest mystery of all -- her very nature a conflict, a pleaser and a worrier, she had to have been awfully upset when she'd let Gordy put her in a box. What kind of sense did that make?

A big unhappy mess pretty much summed up the family. Except for Ethel, it was like nobody loved anybody. They made Sallee sad, so she guessed she loved them. They were like planets floating around the sun, lonely and solitary in their own pathetic little orbits. Staying in the hospital was vacation compared to that, if only Ethel would visit.

Sallee received one letter from Stuart about a week after her big sister left. She couldn't remember if she had ever gotten a letter before, except maybe a birthday card from her grandmother that clearly hadn't made much of an impression. This letter, though, was something else entirely, addressed as it was to: Miss Sallee Mackey, University of Virginia Hospital, Pediatrics, in Charlottesville, Virginia. Right away she recognized that it was from Stuart even before she saw her sister's fat round letters printed neatly across the envelope front. She had coveted the powder-blue stationery ever since her mother had given it to Stuart for her birthday last summer, in anticipation of her leaving for college. Not only powder-blue *real* stationery, it was engraved with Stuart's name and her soon-to-be school address. Before Stuart got the stationery, Sallee had never considered college as a place that she would like to go, but now with the possibility of her very own stationery, she couldn't wait. After much consideration she decided she would like the same style as Stuart's, but pink with darker pink engraving.

She opened the envelope with care. Without a letter opener she had to tear a tiny bit off so that she could wedge her finger in to pull gently along the crease. It hurt her that the tear wasn't straight along the crease as it was when her mother opened her mail. There were jagged tears on both sides of the envelope. That she was here alone in her room when the letter came only heightened her excitement. Two pages slipped out of the ragged-edged envelope. Sallee eagerly gathered them up and started to read.

Dear Sallee,

College isn't anything like I expected. We have a schedule just like high school except we pick the classes ourselves. I counted on that being the case. What I didn't count on was that they take attendance, and if you miss too many classes, you are put on a thing called academic probation. God, it's like going to boarding school. I am so beyond that. Not what I had in mind at all. I'm not sure I'm going to stay. You keep that to yourself. Since I have told no one else, I'll know where they heard if Mother and Daddy get wind of it.

My friend Bet disappeared almost as soon as we got here. I never see her. I thought we were going to be roommates. Instead, I have this dumb blonde idiot of a girl who can't think beyond how to match her purse and her shoes. She reminds me of Mother. Just my luck to go all the way to New York and end living with someone just like my mother.

I hope you are feeling better and are going to be leaving the hospital soon. Hey, has Daddy married The Rose yet? I'd be the last to know since he knows how much I hate her.

I miss you. Say hello to Ethel for me.

Love,

Stuart

P.S. Tell Gordy and Helen I say hi.

After reading the letter three times, she very carefully folded it in half and stuck it in the front of *The Mystery at Lilac Inn*.

Voices wafted in from the hall. Ginny's soft drawl was easily recognizable. Sallee couldn't make out the other, a male voice. She strained to overhear the garbled conversation. They were talking about her. It must be the doctor, she reasoned. He said, "She is a lucky girl. I can tell you. I was very concerned when she first came in. It was thanks to your quick actions that we were able save her. Bacterial meningitis is a serious and life-threatening disease that can cause all kinds of complications afterward. Sallee appears to have come through whole and healthy, I am very glad to say."

"I thought that she had polio, which only shows how terrified I was. She had been vaccinated just like everybody else. Polio was such a scourge for so long, every mother's nightmare." Ginny mused. "When I called Dr. Nelson and described Sallee's symptoms, he told me to wrap her up and wait for the rescue squad, and then he hung up without even saying goodbye. He called that new rescue squad himself. I was impressed with how professional they were."

"Yes, we are very pleased with them. It is something this community has needed for a long time. If she continues to improve as she has been, she should be able to go home by Friday."

"Oh, that is wonderful," her mother gushed. "It's safe, right? She's not contagious, is she?"

"Absolutely not," We wouldn't let her go home if she were. The important thing is that she gets plenty of bed rest. Sallee will fully recover from this."

Oh no, she was leaving the hospital! She had gotten that much from eaves dropping -- she was getting well. The thought surprised her at first until she realized that since she had been sick, people had acted better around her. They seem to put themselves out a little more. If she didn't count the two times her family ran into each other, her stay at the hospital had been peaceful, almost fun. Sort of like that afternoon she spent with Charlie and her mother. She longed for that sort of life, as she drifted off to sleep.

Do I have to be sick my whole life just so things can be a little better? she wondered. At the moment, it seemed like a small price to pay. She sure hated all of the fighting she remembered from before. *What would it take for the whole family to actually get along?*

Chapter 4

"Gol-lly, Sallee, I can't believe it, I actually missed you! Wow, you're really skinny. It seems like a year since you went to the hospital. Do you hurt? Did it hurt? What was it like? Man-o-man, nothin' happened here. I mean not one thing."

Gordy plunged on without even pausing for breath. "Well, Ethels stayed with us after you went to the hospital until school started. That was fun. Too bad we didn't have school when you were first sick. We could have missed it."

He stopped and looked at her hard. "Your eyes got so much bigger! You look kinda gray. And boy, that day you went to the hospital was crazy. Mom called the rescue squad after you fainted. You had a temperature of a hundred 'n' five. No, wait, I don't think you did. I think you die if you have a fever higher than one hundred and four. Anyway, the doctor said to call the rescue squad. You might have been one of their first cases, you know? The truck that took you away was brand new. I wonder what people did before rescue squads?

"I woke up when I heard the siren comin' up the driveway. I had to stay here with Helen while Mom went to get Ethel. An' now Mom's got Ethel a phone cuz of emergencies like this. She went straight to the hospital after goin' to Ethel's. Early brought Ethel over.

"Your lips are all chapped." He peered in close like he was looking into an anthill, careful not to get bitten, while not wanting to miss anything.

Taking a breath, he continued rapid-fire, "Mom stayed at the hospital with you the whole time, only comin' home to change clothes and sometimes to eat somethin'. It was nice not havin' her around and havin' Ethel stay. I got to stay up 'til eleven every night. Helen and I went home with Ethel an' Early to help him with his chores. He'd bring us back after we finished. He said one day I could milk Janice. You know, milkin' is hard. Ya gotta squeeze just right. If you don't the cow'll kick you, and no milk comes out. Didja know you can aim that stuff?

"They wouldn't let me come see you. They said no kids allowed. Dad is talkin' about getting married, I guess that is something. Stuart said he just up and said one day, Rosemary and I are thinking about getting married. Now she is around all of the time. She is a real bitch. Stuart cried for three whole days, I think. She was talking about coming back to live with Mom until she made this new friend."

He stopped to think. "So huh, Stuart has this new friend. I think her name is uh, I don't know, but let me tell you she is one odd ball." Gordy didn't stop talking as he wound his index fingers in circles on either side of his head and crossed his eyes. "After she met what's her name she was all gung-ho to go to New York. She wears black all of the time and is weird, really *weird*. Oh did you see she dyed her hair black? BLECHHH!"

"Who?" Sallee was just able to get in. "Oh, yeah."

"Stuart! Who else?" he snapped. "It's who I've been talking about. Haven't you been listening?"

"Uh--" was all Sallee able to say before he continued his barrage.

"Ethel doesn't think much of her and you bet Mom doesn't. That's her name, Bet. What a dumb name. Who's named Bet? She lived in New York before her family moved here. You oughta hear the way she talks. You'd think she could say New York right. She says Noo Yawk, looks just like a fish when she talks. She says Noo Yawk is da coolest place in the woyld and that Stuayt and she are goin' t' have soooo much fun when they get t' Hunter. She says they can go t' da *pahk*. Hunter is *neah da pahk*. It's on *Pahk* Avenue. " She does *this* all of the time too." He wiggled both his uplifted hands as air quotes, and then he shrugged his shoulders around his ears as he rolled his eyes to show his complete disdain.

"Me, I'm glad she's goin'. She is such a bitch most of the time, just like Mom. And the rest of the time she is cryin' or actin' like she was some, huh, movie star or somethin'. You'd think she was the only one that had shit to deal with. Jeeze."

"You have shit to deal with?" Sallee asked.

"Duh, whattya think it's been, a picnic? ee, Sallee did somethin' happen to your brain in that hospital? Did they take it out? Remember, Lance got poisoned? My DOG got POISONED, right? And then that old bastard Dabney tried to kill me and get me arrested, Ethel and Mom drank all of the time, the divorce. Then Dad goes out and finds some other bitch out of the blue. I don't know why he didn't like

Linda," he stopped and wondered, then continued, "Yeah, I'd call that shit. Wouldn't you?"

"I guess," she said, "you forgot Denny." Sallee's eyes closed. "I got a … I'm really tired. I'm supposed to sleep, rest." She rolled over facing the wall.

"Right, want anything?" he asked as he got up to leave. Sallee couldn't tell if he waited for an answer. None came.

The time Sallee had spent in the hospital had been so peaceful, or at least the parts she could remember, except when her father and Rosemary were there. She had forgotten all of the drama, all of the anger that she and her siblings had been steeped in for so long. She certainly wasn't glad to get it dumped right back on her, either. Gordy may have been filling her in, but he seemed to bring up more questions than she liked.

Time had a way of compressing since she'd been sick. She couldn't tell if she had just fallen asleep when Ethel bustled into her room with a tray filled to the brim. "Here ya go, sweet pea. I brung you some good homemade vegetubl' soup. You hungry?" Ethel put the tray down on Helen's bed, then turned to Sallee. She placed her big warm hand on Sallee's forehead. "You a speck warm, darlin'. You feelin' all righ'? Gordy didn't wear you out, now, did he?"

Sallee shook her head. "I'm okay, just tired. It's funny cuz I didn't do anything but ride in a wheelchair down from my room to the car, then take a little ride in the car home. I guess I fell asleep, cuz I don't remember anything 'til Gordy came. When was that?"

"That was 'round noon. It's suppertime now. I thought I'd set wit' you a spell 'til yo' momma git home. Honey, I did miss you so." Ethel, always the old hen, was clucking over Sallee, plumping pillows and straightening bedclothes. "Here lemme help you set up so you eat somethin'. You gotta gets yo' strength back." She had managed in one fluid motion, before Sallee was able to protest that she could do it, to get her sitting up and her pillows propped up behind her. As she tucked the sheets in so tight that Sallee wondered if the circulation in her legs would be cut off, Ethel asked, "Do you wants me to feed you?" Ethel eased her bulk into the chair by the bed, picked up the bowl, scooped up a spoonful, blew on it, then held it up to Sallee's dry lips. "Lord, honey, you is dry as a August creek bed. Dis here soup will do you a world of good. C'mon now, it ain't too hot. Jes' a little, there you go. Now ain't that some kinda good." Ethel beamed down on Sallee.

"I missed you too, Ethel. Why didn't ya come see me in the hospital?"

"Darlin,' I did. Most times you was sleep. At first dey won' let no one 'cept yo' parents in t' see you. I couldn' git away no how, wha' wit' Gordy an' Helen. When you could see folk, de vistin' hours was hard on Early tryin' to get de chores done 'n' all an' me t' de hospital. We gave it a good try two- three time. Yo' momma took me oncet, but you was sleepin'." She held up another spoonful of soup. Sallee willingly let Ethel feed her, though she had been managing to feed herself for at least the last week or two.

"Ethel, it feels so good to be home." She whimpered. "It seems like I've been gone for ages." She took another spoonful of soup. It was good, Ethel was right about that.

"I made you some tea. Or a cok' cola?"

"Coke, please."

Ethel handed Sallee a straw and held the glass of coke up for her to sip. "I 'spect you do feel like you been gone a good while. Truth is you was. Lord knows. It sho weren't the same without my Sallee."

Helen stuck her head into the room. "Can I come in?" she asked.

Ethel said, "You finished yo' supper already?" She handed Sallee a tiny piece of buttered bread. "Try this, but doan choke on it."

Sallee laughed," Ethel I didn't lose my teeth. I can still chew. I might need a bigger piece. This piece is too small to chew."

Ethel chuckled, "I 'spect dat is right hard t' chew, ain't it?" She tore off a larger piece, buttered it and handed it to Sallee. "Want mo' soup?" Sallee shook her head.

Helen crawled up on her bed, looked over at her sister and flashed a big smile. "It sure is good to have you home. It was so lonely without you. Hey, I've gotten good at drawing horses. Lemme show you." Helen jumped down to root around in her desk drawer pulling out her drawing pad and colored pencils. "Look. I like this one a lot." She held up a headshot of a dappled gray horse with a dark mane and huge expressive eyes. Its neck was curved around looking backward.

"Wow, Helen that is good. Look, Ethel, look how good Helen is getting. You are a real artist. I'm so impressed."

Sallee exclaimed. Helen beamed and crawled back up on the bed with her sketchpad.

"Thanks, Sallee, I'm going to try drawing people next." The little girl beamed. "Are you gonna drink the tea?" Sallee shook her head, again. "Can I have some, then?"

Ethel poured Helen some tea, stirring in a lot of milk and a large spoon of sugar, before holding the cup and saucer out for Helen to take. "Now be careful. Doan wanna be spillin' it. Two hands, now." Helen took the saucer in one hand while holding the cup steady with the other and placed it expertly down on the bedside table like she was an old hand at drinking tea. "You getting' t' be a such a big girl. Afore too long y'all ain't gonna be needin' ol' Ethel." Ethel picked up Helen's drawing, looked it over for a long time, then looked up, nodded her head and smiled at Helen.

Helen stated the obvious in her matter-of-fact way. "That time will never ever come, Ethel. We will always need you, right, Sallee?" Sallee nodded an emphatic yes.

Ginny blustered into the girls' bedroom. "Oh, what a day. Sallee, honey, I am so sorry! I had no intention of being gone for almost all of your first day home." She turned to Ethel, "Thanks so much for staying, making dinner, and taking such good care of Sallee. She actually looks better. Probably has much to do with your soup. I am sorry I missed that too."

"No'm you didn't. I know you likes it so, I left it on the stove so's you kin have it fo' supper. You jest needs t' turn it on fo' a minute t' warm up. Glad t' be here t' help my girl Sallee." She patted Sallee's leg and gave her a big wink. "All my babies. And, you too, Miz Ginny."

Ginny, as far as Sallee and Helen were concerned, did the most remarkable thing they had ever seen: She bent over and gave Ethel a big hug. "Ethel, honestly, I don't know what I would do without you. Thank you." She had tears in her eyes.

Helen and Sallee exchanged amazed glances.

"Helen, you are going to have to sleep with me until Sallee's feeling stronger. So get your pajamas and whatever else you're going to need. It's getting time for bed." Helen started to protest and then decided against it, gathered up her things, and followed Ethel out of the room. "Ethel go ahead and give Early a call. I'll take care of getting Helen ready for bed."

"Miz Ginny -- " Ethel turned back into the room -- "I hafta to say I weren't all that 'cited 'bout gittin' a phone, but now we's got one, I swear, Lawsy, I doan know how we got along so long wit'out it." She chuckled, waved good-bye to Sallee, and hustled Helen across the hall to her mother's room.

Sallee drifted off to sleep. Later Helen crept back into their room. "Sallee, are you awake?" she whispered. "Sallee," she shook her sister gently. "Wake up."

"Helen?" Sallee tried to will herself conscious. "Is something wrong?" She grasped for words, struggling up onto one elbow.

"No, I'm okay. I just wanted to talk to you. I wanted to tell you how it's been since you got sick. Ever since she came back from staying with you in the hospital, she's been like this. Never so far as hugging Ethel, but she doesn't drink, and she's nice. I mean *nice.* She thanks you when you do things, she doesn't yell anymore. It's like she's the way Ethel always said she was. It's like Ethel knew."

"Ethel knew what?" Sallee was trying hard to follow what Helen was saying, but it wasn't making any sense. She finally gave up and fell back on her pillow, exhausted

"Ethel always said that Momma was sweet. Remember?" Helen whispered. "Try not to make any noise. I'm not supposed to be in here. I sure don't want to get caught and have her decide to go back to her old ways."

Sallee whispered, her head still on the pillow, too heavy to hold up, "She's different? Wow, you know the whole time I was in the hospital I prayed that I could have a mother like Charlie's. Wow, do you think?"

"Think what? Who's Charlie?" Helen peered toward the door in the darkness, then whispered, "I think you better go back to sleep. We can talk about this tomorrow. 'Night."

"Gordy didn't say," Sallee sat up, then flopped back again, "Gordy didn't say that Mom changed. He sounded like everything was just like it always was or worse."

"Shhh! Gordy is so mad about I don't know what, he wouldn't see it if it hit him over the head." Helen spoke in an exaggerated stage whisper now. "I'll tell you tomorrow. I've got to go." She hurried from the room, carefully closing the door after her.

After Helen left, Sallee tried to stay awake long enough to think about what she had heard. She woke later when her mother came in to check on her. "Mom, I'm sorry for getting sick and causing so much trouble."

"Sallee, you…I…no trouble…Oh God, Sallee, I love you." Ginny took her daughter in her arms and held tight. "I love you so much. I'm the one that is sorry for all of the hateful things I've said and done to you and Helen. I think I still stand a chance with you two. I am afraid Stuart and Gordy might never forgive me." Sallee could feel her mother's tears. "I do love you. I hope you know that." Sallee's head nodded up and down on her mother's chest. She wondered how long she had waited for this moment and how long ago she had given up hope that it would ever happen. Her last thought before falling back to sleep in her mother's arms was having a relationship with Ginny just like Charlie and her mother.

Helen brought Sallee her breakfast the next morning. "Ethel said she'd be up after she got breakfast cleaned up. Look, she made you fried apples and sausage, hers."

"I don't think I can eat it." Sallee felt a little sick just from the smell of the food. "Will you, so she doesn't get her feelings hurt? If you don't feel like it, at least make it look like I tried to." Helen took a bite from the sausage, and stirred the apples a bit. "Are you thirsty? She handed Sallee a glass of fresh orange juice.

"I can't, Helen. Can you pour it out and get me a little bit of water?"

Helen jumped up to leave and bumped into her mother, who had just come into the room. "How are you feeling?"

"Not so good," Helen offered. She can't eat this -- " she indicated the tray -- "or drink this --" holding up the glass of orange juice. "I was going to throw it out and get her some water."

"Oh, why? Here, I'll drink it." Ginny said reaching for the glass.

"I don't want to hurt Ethel's feelings," Sallee said, "She went to so much trouble. I just can't eat it." Sallee was worried that it might make her mother mad, but she didn't have the energy to make up a story and didn't want to.

"I'll take care of it." Ginny said as she sat on Helen's bed and picked up the fork, then began to eat the sausage and half of the apples. "I don't think I can eat the toast," she smiled at her daughters as she patted her belly. "Let's just let this be our little secret, okay?"

Sallee stole a quizzical look at Helen. Helen pursed her lips and shrugged. Ginny gathered up the tray, humming. "Can I get you anything? How about a little ginger ale and really, really dry toast?"

"Ginger ale, please."

Her mother nodded. "I've got an appointment, and I'll be gone for most of the morning, but I'll be back before lunch. Helen can you bring the ginger ale?"

"Sure." Helen waited until Ginny had gone, then whispered, "See I told you. She's so nice. I think I am afraid to trust it. I'll be right back." She was back within minutes. "What do you think?"

Ethel stuck her head in the door. Helen jumped up. "Bet' not see them shoes on the spread again." She gave Helen a stern look, then smiled in Sallee's direction. "How you feelin'? Did my heart good to see yo' appetite comin' back. Knew you wouldn' say no t' apples an' sausage."

Sallee gave Ethel a weak smile, "Not so much though, okay? Helen and Mom had to help me eat it all. The orange juice made my stomach hurt."

"Ethel! Are you upstairs?" Ginny called from the hall.

"Yes'm, I'm here." Ethel stepped out to the top of the stairs.

After she'd left the room Sallee faded in and out for a minute before saying, "I have been having some weird dreams. I think this is one of them." She reached over and touched Helen. "You seem real enough, but you can't tell with dreams." The front door slammed. She could hear angry voices and threatening shouts. Sallee flinched, "I knew it was a dream. Too good to be true."

"That's Gordy. He does it all of the time, especially when Momma asks him to cut the lawn or do some other chore. He has some doctor he sees a couple of times a week. I don't know why. I don't think he's sick. He sure is a pain in the neck." She lay down on her bedspread, propped her feet up and continued. "I hate being around him. He's kind of scary."

"Scary? Gordy?"

"Yeah, Gordy. You know that time he put me in the box and shot BB's at it?" She put one leg over the other and began to swing it back and forth. The more she talked, the faster her leg swung. "He told me if I didn't get in the box, he'd shoot me. I started to walk away, and he did too. Right in the butt, it hurt. He said if I cried or told anyone he'd get me back." Her leg was pumping. "He meant it. I could tell. I try to stay away from him. It's not too hard. He's almost never here." Her leg slowed its swing, then picked up as fast as before "You know I told, too. I'm scared he's going to get me back."

"Gordy?" Sallee tried to wrap her head around what Helen was saying. "Gordy wouldn't hurt you. He makes a lot of noise, but he wouldn't hurt you. He probably said it cuz he heard it on television."

Ginny appeared with Ethel close behind her. She stopped in the doorway. "That was your father on the phone," she said. "He's coming over to see Sallee. He's bringing Rosemary." There was a flash of the old Ginny on her face as she cast her eyes to the sky. She looked at Sallee, then laughed, curling up her nose and making a face.

Sallee laughed, knitted her brows, and looked at Helen as if to ask, *Dream?*

Helen sat bolt upright on her bed not even trying to hide her incredulity. "Daddy's coming here? With The Rose? You're *kidding*, right?"

"No," Ginny giggled. "Is that what you call her? The Rose? Huh?" She laughed out loud. "I don't think that is what you should be calling your soon to be stepmother." She had to stop and gasp, she was laughing so hard. "But I have to tell you, I love it."

Ethel was looking around like a cat in a room full of snarling dogs. "Don't worry, Ethel." Ginny struggled to compose herself. "I told them you were off this afternoon, and if they wanted to come, they'd have to sit until I got back, because I had errands to run." Ginny chuckled. "It was very convenient that he called when he did."

Joe ran his hand through his sandy-colored hair, looking as perplexed as Helen had when he and Rosemary came into the room. "Hi sweetie, how're ya feeling?" He came over and gave Sallee a kiss on the forehead. Rosemary hung around the door looking every which way, clearly not liking much of what she saw.

She waved hello, "I thought the rooms would have been bigger." Helen, who had followed them in, flopped on her bed and rolled her eyes at Sallee.

"I'm okay," Sallee said, stifling a giggle of her own. "The doctor says I can start getting up for a little bit starting tomorrow." Joe pulled a Nancy Drew book out from his jacket. "Oh, wow, another new one. *Mystery at Lilac Inn*," She read the title and looked at the publishing date. "Wow, brand new! Thank you, Daddy. I've read all of the old ones a hundred times!"

"A hundred?" He laughed, "Are you sure?"

Rosemary ventured farther into the room, gingerly taking a seat on the end of Helen's bed. "You look like you are feeling better. I guess being home makes a big difference, huh?" She reached out to pat Sallee's leg. Sallee moved it before she had a chance. "I know how that is," Rosemary added, looking at Joe like she wanted him to do something.

"Where's Gordy?" Joe asked with an askance glance.

Helen volunteered that he was supposed to be out mowing the lawn. Everyone stopped to listen. Helen stated the obvious, "Doesn't sound like he is, so I don't know. He doesn't spend much time around here these days."

While Joe and the girls played games and read all afternoon, The Rose spent the time leafing through magazines, turning the pages with more effort and noise than necessary and sighing. Sallee struggled to stay awake, finally saying just before they were ready to leave, "I've got to take a nap. I'm so sleepy." She sank into her pillow, murmuring, "I love you Daddy," before falling fast asleep.

School had already started for everyone else. As much as Sallee thought she would like being home while they were in school, she was fast running out of things to do in bed. She had read *Half Magic* the book Linda had left so many times that she could almost recite it. Linda's note threatened to split in half from the many times Sallee had unfolded, read it, and refolded it. With every read she hoped for a little something more. Devouring *The Secret of Red Gate Farm,* which Joe had brought her in the hospital, and the newest Nancy Drew book, twice partially distracted her from the boredom. After a reread of her entire collection she moaned. "Ethel, I'm bored," as Ethel was making Helen's bed.

"Dat's a good sign. You be outta de bed in no time, den." Ethel looked across at Sallee, giving her a big smile while she tugged the bedspread to make it tight like only she could.

While Ethel dusted, she hummed. Sallee pulled out her mother's locket from its hiding place in her special box along side Linda's note, sequestered in the drawer of her bedside table. She opened it and peered at the face of the boy inside. His name was Cy. She remembered that much about him, probably because that was almost all she'd ever heard, besides that he worked as her grandparents' stable boy. She knew there was more to the story and found herself emboldened enough to ask. "Hey, Ethel, do you think Mom would tell me about Cy now?" *Now that she was so different, so nice,* she elected not to add.

Ethel's head whipped around like she had seen a snake. "What wou'd make you ask a question like dat?" She noticed the locket in Sallee's hand. "Where'd you git dat?"

"Mom's dresser a long time ago," Sallee said deciding to tell the truth. "Mom told me once that her father gave her a locket and that she had put Cy's picture in it. She said she got in trouble for it. I was just thinking about it, is all. I just wondered."

Ethel shrugged. "I doan know, honey. Dat was a long time an' a heap o' hurtin' ago. It might be best t' leave it alone."

Thinking about Cy reminded Sallee of the crush she once had on Ethel's grandson Lil' Early. "Where is Lil'Early? Why doesn't he ever come with you anymore?"

"He live in Washington wit' his momma's folks. His Daddy, Junior, you remember Early's son? He got hisself in some trouble. Dey took Lil' Early away from him." She pressed her lips hard together and shook her head. Sallee noticed with gratitude that the four knots that Ethel routinely tied her dark hair in, on either side of head, were neat and tight. The days of using those little buns as barometers of Ethel's sobriety were long gone. "Durn fool got caught up in one a dem *set-ins* dey had in Al'bama or Mis'sippi. Doan remember which. He ain't from neither one, why he think he gotta go down dere on a bus wit' a lot o' other fools an' set is more'n I kin say."

"Why couldn't Lil' Early live with you, then?" Sallee sat up in bed, interested in something for the first time in a long while.

"Junior didn' cotton t' our politics, he say. Didn' want no son a'his growin' up steppin' an' fetchin' fo' no white folk. He say so much foolishness." She sniffed, "He was never quite right in de head after de war."

"What happened to him in the war. Did Early go to the war? Did Daddy?"

"Early didn'. You know yo' Daddy went t' war. I heard 'em tell you stories my ownself."

"Oh yeah, I forgot. Why didn't Early go?"

"Early was too long in de tooth t' be goin' t' war, but he kep' hisself busy in de war effort at home. Got an extra job at night workin' in de uniform factory, cuttin' cloth.

"Long in the tooth?" Sallee asked. Ethel pulled up a chair next to Sallee's bed and sat down. The chair protested with a groan.

"Old." Ethel said. "Glad of it too. Doan know what I woulda done if I had Early t' worry 'bout too. 'Tween Junior an' Mista' Joe goin' off an' not knowin' if dey was comin' back. It's what started me takin' a nip now an' again," Ethel admitted, looking to Sallee a little sheepishly. "Think that was when it started comin' a habit, like dey say." She paused.

"I mighta started drinkin' because I was worried 'bout Mista' Joe an' Junior, but I kep' it up 'cause I was bored like you is now. Doan you go an' start drinkin', now, you hear?" Ethel chuckled, shaking her head. "I'm here t' tell you, it doan do you no good." Sallee laughed too.

"Bein' bored didn' last too long. Might' near de time Junior landed, in a place somewhere in England, he got shot in de head. It almost never happened dat Early an' me was both at de house at de same time, but we was dat day de news come. Sweat broke out all over Early when de boy handed him de telegram." She shifted in the chair. "He couldn't hold his hands still t' open de envelope. 'You open it,' he say t' me. Dat ol' yellow paper flapped like a flag 'tween Early's shaking hand an' de breeze."

She drew a long breath. "I s'rprised myself, calm as I was. I smiled at him like t' say, It gone be all right. My insides was all squirmy, but dat was fo' Early, not Junior. I couldn' stand seein' my man in pain like he was. Whatever happened,'tween me an' Junior, was long ago an' mos' fo'got ..."

"What happened between you and Junior?" Sallee asked, suddenly alert.

"Never you mind." Ethel cleared her throat, clearly flustered. "Das 'nother story. Ya wanna hear de one I'm tellin'?" Sallee nodded, yes, making a note to ask later about what happened between Junior and Ethel.

She put her hands in her lap and continued, "Folks I ain't seen in years, followed dat delivery boy t' our house--like a mournin' parade. It was somethin' t' get a telegram back den an' not a good somethin' neither. Dose times, dey almost always carried news you didn't wanna hear. As we stood on de porch lookin' out int' de dirt yard, people just kep' on filin' in. Before I could get de envelope open, dey was fifteen folks easy, standin' lookin' at us wit' dere sad eyes. I go to hand Early de telegram an' ever' last one of us holdin' our breath. 'Tell me what it say,' he say, backin' away f'm me.

"I couldn' make out all of it, but I was might' sure it didn't say nothin' 'bout Junior bein' dead. Las' thing I wanted was t' cause Early any mo' hurt. I look up, hopin' t' see someone I know dat could read better'n me. Just about dat time my sister Roberta, you remember Roberta, doan 'cha? Use t' set fo' you."

"I remember." Sallee shook her head with more vigor than was actually necessary, "Boy, do I! Drove like a crazy person. Go on."

Ethel chuckled. "Anyhow, 'Berta step up on de porch an' look over my shoulder. 'Tween us two, we's able t' make out most of what it say. He ain't dead. I look up f'm dat telegram t' see my husband bitin' his lip, tryin' hard not t' cry out dere, front of all our neighbors an' friends. T' effort like t' kill 'em. Finally, he jes' sat on de stoop, put his face in his hands an' cried like a baby. His shoulders all hunched up, dey jes' shook as he sat dere sobbin'."

"Poor Early. That must have been awful for him," Sallee said, then quickly added, "and you too. Then what happened?"

"Course I knew he loved his son, but I didn't know how much 'til Junior ended up in one o' dem veteran hospitals in Was'ington. Early went t' see him most every week. No easy trip, wit no car."

"He didn't have his truck? How come?"

"During de war mos' people didn' have much. Even if you did have a car you couldn' put no gas in it, rationed like it was."

"Oh." Sallee thought about asking about *what rationed like it was* meant, but decided she'd rather have Ethel tell her story.

Ethel went on. "De trains weren' reliable. He'd go up Sat'day evenin's after work an' would spen' Sunday mornin's wit' Junior. If he lucky an' de trains was runnin' he'd get home real late Sunday night. Sometime, he'd have t' go direct t' work. Colored folk couldn' buy food on de train. Dey had t' tote dey own. When Early couldn' get off work in time t' pick up what I had cook fo' him, he'd go widout. Since he was workin' two jobs, he wouldn' be home fo' days at a time, meant he didn' eat. I went wit' him a few times, but we couldn' leave de animals, so most times I stayed home." Ethel looked up at Sallee like she was startled. "I got work t' do. I can' be sittin' here talkin' t' you all de live long day." She pulled her great bulk out of the chair and smoothed the covers on Sallee's bed. "Good dat you bored. Means you feelin' better."

Sallee stayed out of bed a little longer every day. Within a week, she was back to her usual schedule and almost ready to try going to school. She followed Ethel around all day asking questions, just like when she was younger. "Ethel, what happened between you and Junior?" Sallee asked one afternoon as Ethel was ironing in the kitchen.

Ethel thought for a minute like she was deciding if and what she was going to say. Then she shrugged and started in. "Junior'd been livin' wit' us fo' a spell, just afore he enlist in de army. He was closer t' my age dan Early were. He an' I use t'go out sometimes. We'd ask Early. He say, 'Go'n wit' yo' young selves, I's got thangs t' do here.' We'd go out an' dance an' drink just like Early an' I used t' do. I'd fo'got how much fun we had.

Three nights afore Junior was t' leave we was out dancin' like we was ol' Sain' Vitus hisself. Junior had more dan he shoulda t' drink. Truth is, we bot' did." Ethel stopped ironing, and looked out the window for a long time, her thoughts traveling back twenty years and more.

What'm I doin' here? Ain't gon' tell this young'un how he took me over int' a corner so dark, an' kissed me hard. How he breathed all whiskey breath, "I love ya, Ethel, I truly do."

Even if I did say, 'Git on outta here,' an' tried t' pull away, but, Lord knows, I liked dat kiss all d' same. 'Y'ain't got no idea what yer sayin.' Can't tell her that neither. Ethel stared out over the ironing, looking into the dark dance hall.

"I do, I know 'xactly what I'm sayin'. I want you t' be here waitin' for me when I gits back. I wants you an' me t' go away after de war, together. Daddy too old fo' you."

Ethel picked up the iron and shook her head. *Kissed me again an' much as I didn't want him t', I did. We didn' go home dat night. I can't say none o' dis t' Sallee.*

She shook her head again and went back to her ironing. "Sallee, I have no notion why I'm tellin' you dat story 'cept you asked. 'T'weren' nothin'."

She worked steadily now but silently, lost in thought, her head down. Sallee opened one of Ginny's magazines that was lying on the kitchen table, looking idly at ads.

Early done already lef' for work when I slipped in de house t' get ready t' go t' work. Junior come up behind me an' wrap his arms 'round me an' whisper all close in my ear, "Why don't we just stays here today? I'm leavin' day after tomorrow. I'll help wid the chores, den we kin take de day off, easy like.' An' I will regret dat all my days.

She shook her head as if clearing a cobweb and put the iron down on its heel to fold a shirt, still ignoring Sallee.

"Junior, What we is doin' is wrong. Early loves me. He been good t' me an dis ain't no way t' be treatin 'im. When he gits home tonight dis an' yestiddy didn't happen an' it ain't gonna happen again. You bet' be understandin' me cuz I ain't gonna be sayin' it a second time. Y'all go'n off t' dat war an if it makes you feel good den go head an' think o' us like dis, but I wants you t' know it ain't happnin' 'gain.'

Ethel snapped back to the kitchen, looking older to Sallee, older and worn out.

"Were you so sorry when he left?" Sallee asked. "To go to war, I mean."

"Lord, child, I felt bad about dat day fo'a good long time. I think it was one of dem thangs I was trying t' get outta my head when I drank so."

Sally had made up her mind she was going to say it today no matter what. She had practiced her argument over and over and decided she'd run it by Ethel. "Whaddya think? Do you think she'll let me give up piano? I hate it, and I really hate that old bag that teaches it too."

"Young as you is, you doan know nothin' 'bout hatin'. I 'spect you doan like it cuz it ain't easy. Dat's de bad part o' havin' most things come easy t' you. Jest doan have de stick-t'-it-ness when a thang is hard. I doan think I'd let you stop if I had a say in it."

"Could you please not say that to Mom when she comes home?" Sallee implored.

"I'll keep my thoughts t' myself, miss, but you bes' be in dere practicin' like you momma told you 'til she say ot'erwise. G'wan now.

"Ethel, come on. What's the point if I'm going' to quit anyway?"

"You ain't quit yet. G'wan."

Sallee groaned, acting put upon. "Don't ask me to help you out," she muttered not entirely to herself.

Ethel looked up from what she was doing, "Whadda you say?"

"Nothing," Sallee said as she dragged herself off of the chair, making a big show of the hardship Ethel was foisting on her.

"I gotta go practice my piano."

"You is a mess, girl." Ethel chuckled as she watched the child leave the room.

She hadn't been practicing more than a minute or two when Ginny arrived home. "Mom, I've got to talk to you," Sallee cried, jumping up from the piano to run greet her mother at the door. "It's important." A little insecure now that she knew Ethel wasn't on board with her plan, she thought she had a better chance of getting what she wanted if she struck now before Ethel got a chance to add her two cents. Sure, Sallee heard Ethel say she wouldn't say anything, but you just couldn't tell what might happen.

Ginny came into the sitting room and perched herself on the sofa. "Yes?"

Here was her big chance. She took a deep breath and started, "I've been thinking about this for a long time. You know how good Helen is when it comes to the piano? Well, pretty much anything?"

"Yes, I do. She is very good at a lot of things. She takes pride in what she does." Ginny responded. "So she takes her practicing very seriously." She raised an eyebrow at Sallee, "I suspect you would be good, too, if you practiced."

This was not going at all the way she had planned it. "Well that's the thing. I hate playing the piano. That's why I don't practice. Mom, I mean, I *hate* playing the piano." She could kick herself. She wasn't using any of her well thought-out logic. How it was such a shame for Helen to have to share the piano since she loved it so much. How they always did everything together, and it would be so much better for Helen if she didn't always have to follow in her older sister's footsteps. She should be allowed to strike out on her and not be in Sallee's shadow all the time.

"Have you something else you would prefer to do? A life-long skill that you would like to learn?" Ginny asked.

Not half bad after all, she thought. "Yes! I want to learn how to ride horses like you do." She had never thought of this as even an option. What a win it would be to be able to give up piano and get to take riding lessons instead. "I would love to learn how to ride and go to horse shows." Sallee's energy was bubbling over. "Really, really love it."

"You know, to be good at it, you'd have to practice, just like piano," her mother cautioned. "Even if you ride your whole life, it's not the same as being able to play a musical instrument."

"I know, but shucks, ask Miss Porter, you have to be musical to be able to play well, and I'm not all that musical. Have you heard me sing? I can't carry a tune. But I would practice every day to get better at riding, cuz I'd like it," Sallee insisted.

"How do you know you'd like it? You've only been on a pony a few times."

"Just being led around on a pony is a million times more fun than playing the piano." Sallee had begun to warm to her subject. "Riding, and steering, and jumping and going to horse shows, and hunting and having your own horse. Wow, how great would all that be!"

"It's hard work, is what it is," Ginny said. "Your muscles will ache. You could get hurt. I don't know if you are up to it. You might quit when it got too hard."

A brilliant idea struck Sallee, "I know, to prove that I'm not a quitter, I'll keep playing the piano until summer vacation, if I can take riding lessons." Chuffed as she was with her plan she even threw in for good measure, "And I'll even practice."

"I don't know how you'll have the time to do both," Ginny pointed out. "They both take a lot of time. How about this for an idea: You keep taking your piano lessons until next spring. If you have practiced like you said you would and if you still don't like piano, you can take riding lessons. Does that work?"

"Yes!" Sallee exclaimed. She jumped up and kissed her mother, then sat down at the piano and actually applied herself to her practice of the first page of Bach's *Sheep May Safely Graze*.

Chapter 5

Life was beginning to normalize for the family now that Sallee was back in school, if only half a day. Gordy still remained withdrawn and antagonistic. Ginny hoped her news might lighten his gloom. Since Joe left, Gordy had lost his spark, she thought. *Being a boy in this family had to be difficult,* Ginny mused, *especially without a father. He'd grown so tall this last year – really shot up – almost as tall as Joe now. Poor kid, this should help,* she thought as she announced at breakfast, "I have such exciting news. We're moving!"

She rushed on, so excited, she was almost dancing. "The house is on the market, as of yesterday. People will be coming through to look at it, as a matter of fact today, even." She was feeling like a kid that had just laid eyes on Santa for the first time. "I've been looking for months for a house that would suit us. I think I've found it. I thought I would take you all to see it today after school. What do you think?"

"No way," Gordy shrieked. "You did not!" He rose to his full height and charged toward his mother like he was going to hit her. Helen, Sallee, and Ethel stared slack-jawed, rooted to their spots.

"Gordy --" Ethel mustered the presence of mind to speak before he cut her off.

"Shut up, you fat cow," he shouted at her, his voice cracking -- as it had begun to do regularly, adding to his fury -- and then turned on his mother. "God damn you! How dare you sell our house without even bothering to ask us how we felt about it! It's my house too. You can move to hell for all I care; I'm not going with you."

Ethel made a move to grab Gordy by the arm, "You'd bet not..."

Spit flew as he screamed at her. "Ethel, don't tell me what to do. No right, you have no right. Besides, I don't give a shit what you think," he snarled, "so shut UP!" He pushed past his mother, knocking her up against the doorjamb, and stormed out of the front door. The door slammed so hard that a picture crashed off the wall, covering the hall with shards of frame and glass. They could hear the change the newspaper boy had left as it bounced with the shattered glass on the hardwood floor.

"Glory be, Miss Ginny, you all rig't?" Ethel demanded as she reached for the broom. "I bet be gettin' dat up afore somebody get hurt." She patted Ginny's arm. Ginny stood stock still, stunned beyond speech.

Sallee and Helen wanted to go to their mother, comfort her if they could, and possibly get a little comforting of their own, but hesitated because they thought she might lash out at them. They stayed seated at the table staring at one another in dumb silence. Helen started to cry quietly.

Ginny moved trance-like to her side and held her, cooing softly to her daughter, "It's all right. Everything is going to be all right. I promise." Sallee, as much as she wanted to believe this motherly concern and affection was an honest show of Ginny's true feelings, was wary. Her mother had a long history of being less than honest with her children. When she thought about what had incited this tantrum of Gordy's, she wasn't altogether sure she didn't agree with him. *How did she get off just deciding to sell their house, anyway? Didn't they get a say in where they live?* she wondered. *Maybe Mom would really have to ask a judge. Since the divorce, that seemed to be the supreme authority about parents and children, as far as she knew.* Sallee was not at all sure how she felt about this latest development, not at all.

Ethel lumbered back into the kitchen mumbling to herself. "Got me so riled up, I plumb fergot de dustpan. Miz Ginny, I'm afraid dat pitchur is beyond fixin'. Frame's all busted up."

"It's all right. If you just get the glass up, so no one steps in it, I'll see what can be done about it later" Ginny had regained her composure. "Come on, girls, we need to get to school. Are you okay, Sallee?"

Sallee nodded. Ginny held Helen's chin up to get a good look at her and kissed her lightly on the nose. "Let's not let this spoil our day. Okay?"

Sallee and Helen grabbed their things, hustling by Ethel and the mess she was fast rounding up, in an attempt to get outside, alone, so they could discuss what had just happened. Sallee asked, "Was that real? Helen, am I dead? Is this all a dream? She didn't yell. She didn't scream. She didn't cry. But wait, how does she get to sell our house?"

"Beats me," Helen said. "Whatever I thought I knew, I don't anymore." The two girls walked slowly to the car, lost in their thoughts.

Mrs. Dabney, out hanging up laundry, stopped and waved, shouting across the yard, "Why, Sallee, it is so good to see ya up an' around. Heard ya had a rough time of it. Glad you're feelin' better." She threw a sheet over the line, "Feelin' up to some blueberry little men? I'll bring some by, leave 'em with Ethel when I get through hangin' up these sheets. Okay?"

"Thank you, that would be nice," Sallee answered hesitantly. Then in an aside to Helen, "I sure would like to see the look on Ethel's face when she opens the door and finds Mrs. Dabney standing on the other side." She laughed despite the strange feelings swirling around inside her.

Ginny strode down the walk, waved at Mrs. Dabney and said, "Good morning Mabel. That's very kind of you. I think Sallee would love to have some blueberry little men." Even Mrs. Dabney looked up startled.

Sallee couldn't stand it another minute she had to say it. "Are you my mother?" she asked when Ginny had shut the car door.

Ginny laughed, "Yes, I am your mother. I guess I am pretty unrecognizable." Both girls grimaced, nodding their heads vigorously up and down. "The Ginny you know is the one I don't recognize. I don't have time to tell you all about it now, but I promise when we get back from looking at what I hope will be our new house, I will tell you."

"Yeah, about that," Sallee heard herself say in a tone that she knew she would never have used with Linda. She softened it a bit, "Don't we get a say in whether our house is sold or not?"

"No, you don't. That's my job. You do get to have some input into where we move from here, but just input. You don't get to decide," Ginny said as evenly as if she were saying, "Pass the jam, please."

"Aren't you mad at Gordy?" Helen asked as Ginny started the car and backed out of her parking spot.

"Helen, sweetie," Both girls stole a quick glance. "*Sweetie?*" Sallee shrugged up her shoulders, screwed up her face and eyebrows while mouthing *sweetie* to Helen. "I am sorry you all had to deal with Gordy's rage. I know how frightened you both were. I was, too."

"I bet he is going to get in trouble." Sallee observed.

"Gordy is already in trouble, Sallee. He is getting help, but he needs a lot of love and understanding right now. So if you don't mind, I would appreciate it if you didn't say anything to him about this morning. I know that might be hard."

"I'd say!" Sallee exclaimed. "Gordy and I talk all the time about everything, well, we used to, before I got sick." She thought about what she had just said and realized that Gordy and she hadn't had a good conversation for a very long time. Probably not since she had planned to run away. When was that, two years ago? The more she thought, the more she realized Gordy wasn't talking to anyone and that he had gotten real mean.

"I know you two have always been very close. And I believe you when you say you talk about everything, but Gordy doesn't, and hasn't for a very long time. That is a big part of the problem. Gordy holds all of his anger inside. What we saw this morning doesn't even come close to the rage he is feeling. And with good reason, I might add." She pulled the car up to the front of their school. "We will talk about this later, too. I promise. Bye, I love you." She waved and drove off, leaving Helen and Sallee standing on the curb in awed silence.

As Ginny pulled away from the school, she was calculating how long it would take her to get to Dr. Anderson's office. She had to catch him before his first appointment. She congratulated herself for having arranged Gordy's appointments so that they were the doctor's first in the morning. If she didn't get there before his appointment began, she wouldn't be able to talk to the doctor without having to sacrifice a big chunk of her day sitting by a phone. She didn't mind making the sacrifices, but today there were so many to make. To streamline her day, she had stacked one appointment on top of another. She knew it was going to be close getting to the doctor's office before nine but decided that she would prefer to talk to the doctor in person, so she took the risk. She hoped to see Gordy, too.

It looked as if she'd made it to the office before Dr. Anderson – his parking space was empty. Realizing that she hadn't taken a full breath since Gordy blew up, she used the time while she waited to try to relax and breathe. *Gordy was, even in his present state, pretty level headed*, she thought, *so there isn't anything to worry about. He knows he has an appointment with Dr. Anderson. He's probably already sitting in the waiting room.* For a minute she debated going in and sitting with him, then thought better of it. *I don't want to upset him further and have him leave in another fit of rage*, she reasoned.

When she saw Dr. Anderson drive up, she climbed out of her car and waited as he did the same. "Hello, Mrs. Mackey," he said. "How are you today? What a perfectly beautiful morning. Gordy waiting inside?"

"Good morning. It is." she agreed trying to smile and finding her lip quivering. "I hope he is." The doctor gave her a *give-me-more-information* look. She blurted out, "I didn't think it through. I was so excited about the news, I didn't think. I told the children this morning at breakfast that we were moving, that I was going to sell the house." The doctor nodded for her to go ahead as he held the door.

"Let me get my office opened up. As you say, he may be here, so we will continue in just a minute. Would you mind sitting in the waiting room until I come get you?" He turned to unlock his office door. "Oh, Mrs. Mackey, if Gordy is there, don't talk about it." She nodded and headed to the waiting room feeling both anxious and hopeful that Gordy might be there. He wasn't. By the time Dr. Anderson appeared in the doorway, she was having a hard time keeping herself composed.

"I see that Gordy is not here," the doctor stated. "Was he?" She bit her lip, holding back tears and shook her head. "He may still show up," he offered. "Why don't you come into my office." He ushered Ginny back to his office. "I sit there. Feel free to sit anywhere, else," he said in what Ginny thought was becoming an annoyingly dispassionate tone.

You didn't have to point that out. It's pretty obvious, with your pen, your glasses, your pad, she wanted to scream. Fighting for a little self-control, she looked around the room slowly, deciding on the sofa. She had just placed her purse on the floor beside her when she was overcome with a feeling of bone-melting dread. She couldn't hold her tears back. "He was so angry," she managed to get out in a rush of tears. "I just didn't think. I had no idea that he would feel so... I thought considering all of the bad memories they would be happy..." She let her words trail off.

Dr. Anderson handed her a box of tissues and waited while she pulled herself together. "When you are ready, tell me what happened this morning. Don't rush. Only when you are ready. Take your time."

Grateful for some compassion, Ginny allowed herself to give way to another wave of sobs. After gaining some control, she took a few deep breaths, wiped her nose and started the account of the morning's breakfast. With just two minor interruptions for clarification, she was able to get through the story in its entirety and without another tearful outburst.

Dr. Anderson shared his thoughts on the progress of Gordy's therapy. They talked about how important the house was to Gordy, and what it represented.

"I was sure he would be here. I wasn't even worried. He's usually so sensible," she said, looking at the doctor for agreement, or maybe it was approval.

"Mrs. Mackey, these are not usual times for Gordy. He has had a lot of trauma in his young life." Ginny sank back into the sofa feeling as if she had just been punched in the stomach. "I understand that you feel responsible for that trauma, but let me remind you, you didn't kill your baby or the dog. You didn't, did you?" He seemed to be asking for a response.

"No I didn't kill..." she hesitated, deciding whether to say "the baby" or his name. She finally said, "Dennis, nor did I kill Lance." She felt a little irritated at his insistence that she deny this guilt out loud, but instantly noticed that she felt a bit better. "Maybe not, but I am responsible for getting a divorce, being mean. I did leave them to fend for themselves as I tried to drink myself into oblivion." She sniffled, surprised at her candor.

"That may be the case," he agreed, "but I suggest that you might have had very good reasons for your behavior. You know, Gordy didn't suffer those traumas in a vacuum. The family has been rent asunder; that has effects on all of the members, and everyone reacts differently to these major life events. Gordy is at a very vulnerable age."

Ginny shuddered. "I feel so responsible."

"My point is: it does Gordy no good for you to feel as if you are responsible for how his life has affected him. It is clear to me that you love your children. You are making efforts to put your life on track. Mrs. Mackey, you are not helping Gordy by blaming yourself." Ginny began to cry. "I am so sorry, but our time is up. We are encroaching on my next patient's time."

He scribbled a number on his pad and ripped the page off, handing it to her. "Please, I want you to call me at this number. Call me, when Gordy comes home. If you don't hear from him by dinner time, I suggest you call the police."

Hearing *the police* sent a shock wave through Ginny's body. She had to stop to steady herself. She looked at the doctor, fighting back panic, "Do you think he...?" She didn't know what to ask.

He said, "Just better to get right on it. He's a minor. They will want to know sooner than later. Goodbye, please stay in touch."

Ten minutes later, Ginny slid into a seat in the circle as quietly as she could and tried to hush her breathing. She needed to be here. Even if she was almost twenty minutes late, this was not a meeting to miss. After a man finished, the leader turned to Ginny. "Did you want to say something?"

She nodded yes then said, "I'm Ginny. I am an alcoholic."

"Hi, Ginny," twenty people responded.

"Like a lot of you know, I have been having some problems with my son recently, most of it due to my drinking." She thought she was going to be able to handle this without crying, but stuffing down sobs proved too much. The group waited while Ginny attempted to regain her composure, though she waved them to continue without her. Finally managing a bit of control over her emotions, she told the group about the morning's events. "Even though I know," she choked back a sob, "I know it doesn't help, I feel so responsible." She placed her thumb and forefinger at the top of her eyes sockets on either side of her nose and pinched hard to keep herself from crying anymore.

A tall, thin woman sitting nearby spoke up. "Ginny, I remember one of the first days you came here. It might have even been the first. You said, 'The day of my father's accident, I put on what felt like a coat called Dutiful. I've been wearing it ever since.' Do you remember what else you said after that meeting?"

Ginny shook her head, trying to catch her breath. "No, I don't remember."

"I'll never forget it," the woman went on, "You said, 'I feel like all of these years later, I have just now taken that coat off, and it feels fantastic. I feel so free.'"

Ginny started weeping, again. "Yes," she was just able to get out.

The woman finished: "Don't put that coat on again. It doesn't fit now."

When the meeting ended the woman came up and wrapped her arms around Ginny, holding the back of her head with one hand. She said, "It's going to be all right. I'll call later to check on you. I am going to walk home, and I'll keep my eyes peeled for Gordy. I don't need to pick Charlie up until later, so I can take the long way home, and I'll ask along the way."

Ginny looked at her and then at the clock. "Oh God, I've got to go. Thank you, Rebecca. I don't know what I would have done without you these last months." She blew a kiss over her shoulder and tore out of the room.

The day had been so many things unexpected, all exhausting. When he stormed from the house earlier, he had no idea where he was going. All he wanted to do was get away as far as possible and as fast. In a blind rage, he ran with no destination until he was out of breath. He was surprised to find that he was halfway to Ethel's house when he finally did stop, and also less than a half-mile from his dad's shopping center. It seemed like a good place to walk around without having to come up with more of a plan or until a plan came to him. In the Western Auto store, the shiny red Schwinn boy's bicycle called out to him. Having taken hold of the handlebars, he was just about to swing his leg over the crossbar when a salesman came up to him. "Hey kid, nice bike huh? Say, aren't you supposed to be in school?"

"Yeah, I'm waiting for my mother," Gordy lied easily, "I thought I'd just check this out to see if it fit." He backed away from the bike. "She's at the A&P. I gotta go. Said I wouldn't be long." Turning to leave he said, "Sorry," over his shoulder as he headed out of the door feeling like a criminal.

As she raced to her next meeting, she decided that it might not have been the best idea to chock her morning quite so full of meetings. She had to knock on her own therapist's door, she was so late. "Janet, I'm sorry I'm late," she said before she launched into the events of the morning, starting to cry again in spite of herself.

Janet said, "You don't give yourself enough credit. You have been through hell and back. Of course, you are emotional. I agree with Dr. Anderson. I think you should call the police, but now – as soon as you leave here. You don't have any more appointments, do you?"

"Right after this, I have to pick up Sallee. She only goes half days until she's stronger."

"Can someone else pick her up? Janet asked.

"I suppose Joe could. But by the time I get to a phone, I might as well do it myself."

"Here," Janet offered, indicating her desk. "Use my phone. Call Joe. Tell him what's going on and ask him to pick Sallee up and then meet you at the police station. They, more than likely, will want to talk with both of you."

"And bring Sallee?" Ginny looked wide-eyed.

"No, Joe can take Sallee home first. Ethel's there, right? If any feelings come up that you need to address after you talk to Joe, we can talk through them." She gave Ginny an encouraging nod.

As Ginny got up to go to the phone, Janet stood and headed toward the door. "Where are you going?" Ginny asked, shocked.

"I was going to give you some privacy," Janet said. "I'll just be right out here."

"No," Ginny said, "Please stay. I want you to hear if I do it right."

"Ginny, there is no right and wrong in this, just be yourself. If you want me to stay, I will." She moved to the sofa as she offered her chair to Ginny.

Ginny dialed the number and waited for what seemed forever before Joe came on the phone. As she was explaining the situation, she started to cry again. When she hung up and moved back to the sofa, she said with a shaky laugh, "I can't seem to stop these water works. I don't know what's the matter with me."

"Ginny, you have had a lifetime of unwept tears and enough grief for six people. It's a good thing, a wonderful thing. Let them out." Janet handed Ginny a box of tissues and waited for her to collect herself before she asked, "What's the plan?"

"I must look a sight," Ginny muttered running her hands over her hair, tucking in loose strands and then straightening her skirt.

"You look beautiful," Janet assured her.

"Joe is going to pick up Sallee and take her home to Ethel. Ethel won't like that, I can tell you. Ever since the divorce hearing, Ethel has been squirrelly about being around Joe. I don't know this, but I think he asked her to testify against me. Bless her heart, I imagine that was a terrible time for her."

"Well," Janet said, "you know that is Ethel's problem, right?"

"Yes." Ginny sighed, crumpling a tissue. "Joe is going to meet me at the police station in forty-five minutes. I think I have enough time to get a quick bite to eat and just sit for a minute. You know, Janet, I'm not sure it is such a good idea to stack these appointments on top of each other like this. Can I change my appointment next week to another time and even another day?'"

Janet cocked an eyebrow. "You think?" They looked at each other, and Ginny burst out laughing. "Done," said Janet.

Leaving the shopping center unnoticed, Gordy moved on to Ethel's house, where he knew he wouldn't be bothered. Nobody would be there until Early got home around four. The cows were out in the field, no more interested in him than were the pigs. He sat under a tree, throwing bark peelings from sticks as hard as he could in the direction of home while he thought about what the hell he was going to do now.

He heard gravel crunching on the road. Slipping quickly behind the tree and out of sight, he felt the bottom drop out of his stomach as the police car slowly rounded the bend. *What do they want?* he wondered. The men in the car appeared to be looking for something. As one drove, the other gazed from side to side intently. The car stopped in front of Ethel's house. Both men got out. One knocked at the door while the other walked from one side of the house to the other, checking under shrubs and finally circling the entire house. *At least they don't have their guns drawn*, Gordy told himself as he circled the tree to stay out of their line of sight. *Mom probably called the cops on me. It would be just like her*. He kept perfectly still, listening.

To his horror, he heard the two start to head his way. His hiding place was directly between the house and the shed that Ethel and Early called the barn. The tree wasn't big enough to completely conceal him if either man looked in his direction, which they couldn't help but do as they approached the barn. Gordy started to panic, willing his brain to come up with a plan, without success.

Just then there was a gravelly sound from the road. Both men stopped, turned, and waited, as Early's rusted Easter egg-green pickup pulled into view, rumbling and smoking. He stopped next to the police car and cut the engine, which backfired, shuddered and finally ground to a halt as Early got out and headed toward the men. Gordy's stomach flip-flopped as he realized it was going to be impossible to stay out of sight when the three men converged. If someone had to see him, it would be best if it were Early.

What he didn't realize was that Early had already spied him and was working to distract the policemen.

"Mornin'," he said gently tipping his hat, "Is dey sompin' I kin do fo' y'all?"

"Who are you?" the younger of the two policemen snapped.

"I'm Early Thompson. Dis here's my place." He gestured to the house and surroundings. "I lives here wit' my wife, Ethel. You fella's lookin' fo' som'pin'?"

"Yeah, there's a kid missing' you ain't seen him, have ya?" the young officer asked. "He's 14. About so tall," he added, holding his hand up to his own eye level. "Named --" he looked down at his notes -- "Um, Gordon, goes by Gordy -- Mackey. Got dark blond hair, crew-cut, blue eyes. Seen'um?"

"No, sir I ain't seed Gordy fo' mig't near a week or maybe two," Early lied. "Kin I get's y'all some water? Mighty warm fo' October." He was turning toward the house, hoping the two men would follow.

"You know him?" The older cop asked.

"Yes, sir'ah. Been knowin' him since he was knee high t' a jackrabbit, I 'spect. My wife works fo' his momma. Been knowin' her since way befo' Gordy was even a glint in his daddy's eye," He chuckled. "C'mon over t' de house. Lemme git y'all some water." He started toward the house. He looked around to see that they weren't following so he stopped and asked, "Why y'all lookin' fo' Gordy? Ain't in any trouble, is he?"

"He ran away. Chief said to keep an eye out if we had time, gave us a list of possible places he might be hiding. We were driving by and thought we'd check this place off our list." The older of the two officers was still gazing around the property sharply.

"Lord, Lord," Early shook his head. "Why you 'spect he gone an' done such a thang as dat?"

"Kids today," the young policeman complained. "Spoiled, probably wasn't getting something he wanted and thought he'd scare his mother into getting it for him when got home. He'd sure get more than he bargained for if he were mine, I'll tell you."

The older officer nodded. "Come on, he's not here." The two got in their cruiser without another word and drove away. Gordy let go a huge sigh of relief as the police car disappeared unhurriedly up the road.

As he was following the movements of the police, Early slunk around the other side of the tree. Standing within feet of Gordy when the police cruiser finally drove out of view he roared, "Boy, what y'all mean by scarin' de life outta yo' momma an' Ethel?" Gordy jumped a good foot in the air.

"Early, you scared me to death," he gasped.

"Ya ain't de onliest one scared. Ethel an' Miz Ginny is 'side dey selves. All cuz o' ya takin' off like nobody cared one wit 'bout what happens t' ya." He shook his head. "I'm here t' tell ya, Gordy Mackey, I'm mighty disappointed in ya. I 'spected better from ya. Why ya go do such a thang?"

Fighting back tears, Gordy looked to run. Early grabbed him, wrapping his arms around the boy. Gordy struggled for a second then dissolved into tears. Early turned him around and hugged him while the boy wept. "It gon' be all right, boy." Early whispered as he gently rocked and patted him. "Dey ain't nothin' a good cry an' set down won' fix."

After Gordy's tears had stopped, Early said, C'mon, now, les g'wan in an' gets us sompin' t' drink. Mighty thirsty work dis here." He chuckled as they headed into the house. "Set on down dere. Want some lemonade?" He pulled out a pitcher from the icebox.

Gordy nodded. "Do you have anything to eat? I'm starved," he said.

"Git on up an' git de peanut butter over dere," Early indicated, waving a half-full glass of lemonade toward a cabinet. "Knife's in de drawer dere," another indication with the now full glass. "I think Ethel done made a new loaf o' bread dis mornin'." He looked over near the window. "Yeah, over by de winda."

Gordy gathered up all of the fixings and proceeded to cut the bread with a table knife. Early handed him a better one, saying, "Son, you can't cut bread wit dat knife. Don't y'all...?" He stopped himself. "I doan 'spect so. Ethel won' let nobody do fo' dey selves if'n she be round t' do it. I doan know what I's thinkin'." He chuckled as he took the sandwich Gordy offered.

"Is there any jam?" he asked.

Early got up slowly, walked over to the refrigerator and rooted around for a big jar of homemade strawberry jam. He handed it over, then put a hand on his hip. "What, I doan git none?" He winked and handed his sandwich back to Gordy.

The loaf of bread was all but gone when they finished eating. "I 'spect if the peanut butter held out we'd a finished dat loaf. Sure hope Ethel didn't have a plan fo' it," Early laughed. "She'll have our hides. Now, le's go. We's got chores t' do an' I gotta te git yo' home."

Gordy tensed up. "Early I don't want to go. I hate it there. Can't I live with you and Ethel?"

"Ya know good as me dey is no way. 'Sides what ya hate 'bout living at ya house, anyway? You got a fine family who loves ya, cares 'bout ya. Ya live in a mighty nice house an' gots about as much as a body could want, doancha'?" Gordy looked as if he were about to cry. Early added hastily, "Now doancha be tunin' up again. Le's go do de chores, an' we kin talk 'bout all dis here hatin'." He cuffed Gordy gently on the side of his head as he started to make his way out of the kitchen. "Y'all comin'?"

Early handed Gordy a hoe, "Ya can hoe this row while I picks de beans." He didn't stop for even a second for acknowledgment from Gordy.

Surprised that he hadn't even asked for his help, Gordy whined, "I don't know how to hoe."

Early took the tool back and patiently demonstrated, with soft scritch, scritch, scritches in the dirt. "Doan git too close t' de plant, jest want t' work up de soil round it. See where dem weeds is sproutin' up." He indicated the green tendrils around his broccoli stalks with the tip of the hoe. "Ya doan have t' put a lot of back int' it." He chuckled, "No point wearing yo'self out, now is dey? Gentle like." Handing the hoe back to Gordy, he said, "Now, tell me 'bout all dat hate, dat seems t' be givin' you such a fit. Hatin' be a pow'ful thang to haul around."

Gordy grabbed hold of the hoe as he'd seen Early do and began hacking at the weeds as if he were carving out a trail through the Amazon.

"Whoa, boy, easy like. Dey ain't goin' t'gitcha. Slow an' steady like dat dere tortoise." Back at it with less vigor, Gordy looked up at Early, who nodded his approval. "Sompin' sure got ya all riled up. Wanna tell me, what is?"

"I hate her!" Gordy spit out. The hoeing became choppier. "She's a liar and a drunk. The only person she cares about is herself." By now the hoe blazed though the dirt. Early patted the air in front of him with an up and down motion slowly and took a few deep breaths. Gordy attempted to follow his lead as sweat stung his eyes. "I don't like this. Can I do something else?"

"Ya keep on wid it a while. Good t' git de hang o' a thang 'fore ya put it down. Ya gittin' there. 'Member slow an' steady." Early nodded that Gordy should keep talking as he bent down and unhurriedly stripped beans off the plants faster than Gordy thought possible. "Careful 'bout gittin' too close," Early reminded him, "Ethel is right partial t' her broccoli."

Gordy's hacking lessened, and though he wrestled with himself to slow down further, he never approached Early's sedate, even pace. They spent several minutes in quiet, Early lost in his thoughts, Gordy fighting his urge to bushwhack. Finally breaking the silence, Gordy indignantly sniffed. "Did you know she is selling our house?"

Early responded with a noncommittal grunt.

"Where does she get off selling my house?" The hoe hit a stone and sparked. Gordy slashed at the stone, wiped his brow then applied even more force to the rock, which clanked but didn't give.

Early straightened up, stretched his back and watched as Gordy banged away at it as he pulled a hankie out of his back pocket, peeled his glasses off and carefully whipped them. By now the boy had worked up a quite a sweat. "I's jest won-derin' if it wouldn' be easier on ya if ya jest bent over an' picked up dat dere rock an' tossed it aside?" he said. Older by decades and a head shorter than Gordy, Early – the boy noted – was still cool and calm without a drop of sweat on his brow. He wrapped his glasses back over his ears, bent back over, and continued picking beans.

Gordy whaled away at the rock, his dirt-streaked face pouring sweat. "It looks like you have the easier job," he observed. "Can we switch?"

"G'wan over an' git yerself some water. I'll finish pickin' dis here row an' ya kin do de nex'."

By the time Gordy had come back from the well, Early had finished picking his row and had hoed half way through the broccoli. "I thought you said to go slow. Look, you did twice what I did, in just a few minutes."

"Hum," was all Early said as he steadily scritched the earth around the broccoli. Gordy stood and watched. "Git on wid it," Early said, looking up at the boy evenly. He had finished hoeing the row and started picking at the other end. Denched in sweat, Gordy had a scant handful of beans picked when Early, still cool and dry, met him with only a quarter of the row left to do between. "Didja know if ya puts fertilizer on weeds dey grows big an' strong?" he said.

"Why would anyone put fertilizer on weeds?" the boy asked, trying to make sense of what Early had just said. His eyes and nose squinched up in perplexity as he wiped his brow with a muddy hand.

"I can't rightly say." Early replied, as he straightened up, bent backward a bit with both hands on his hips to stretch out his back, then looked at Gordy, "C'mon'?" he asked as headed toward the barn. Beans in the bag bumped along by his side. "I 'spect dat'll be d' last of them beans dis year."

"*Ew*," Ginny curled her lip as she helped Ethel unpack the groceries "What was I thinking? How on earth did I think I could…? Oh God, that man can make me so mad." Ginny snarled like her old self. She picked up a can of tomatoes and almost heaved it through the window. "Ethel, I can't believe he let that floozy bring Sallee home! Thank God he didn't tell me until after we had talked with the police. I might have killed him right there. Ugh, That would have been a fine kettle of fish." She started to laugh a little, "But it would have served him right, the idiot."

"I doan rightly know Miz Ginny 'bout all dat. What dey say 'bout Gordy?" She reached out and took the tomatoes from her employer and put them up in the cupboard. "Best be gettin' dese out yo' way." She chuckled as she folded the grocery bags and wedged them behind the hot water pipes. "Ain't goin' t' do, havin' you in de jail house, now, is it?

"No, but it might be worth it!" Ginny giggled and then taking on a more serious tone continued, "The policeman said --." She took a card out of her purse and read it. "Officer Timothy Hendricks said that they would alert all of the cruisers, I presume that means the police in cars, to be on the lookout for Gordy -- and the patrol officers, too. We had to give them a detailed description of what Gordy looked like. He did have on that red T-shirt that he likes so much, didn't he?" Ethel shrugged. "Well, I told them he did, anyway. We had to tell them we were divorced. They said Joe should check around his house, the basement and attic. He might have gone over there. Oh, that reminds me, I have to go check out in the garage. He might be there. They also asked if there were any fallout shelters in the neighborhood. Do you know of any?"

"Already did, Miz Ginny, basement, attic, too. No sign. I don't know nothin' 'bout no fallout shelters."

"He did," Sallee volunteered, "have on the red T-shirt. I don't think he would have gone to Daddy's. He doesn't like Rosemary. George said his neighbors built a fallout shelter, the ones behind his house. I guess he could be there. The Martins, I think is their name, but I'm not sure."

"Where did you come from?" Ginny asked clearly startled "I thought you were sleeping." She went over and reflexively felt Sallee's head for a fever.

"I've been here since you complained about the floozy bringing me home. Is Rosemary a floozy?" she asked. She wanted to ask what one *was* but instead decided to ask, "Are the police worried about Gordy being gone?" Her mother nodded, twisted up her mouth and shrugged one shoulder indicating *not so much*.

Sallee continued, "She was okay, Rosemary. We didn't talk that much. She waited for me in front of school. She said that you and Daddy were off somewhere and that she was going to bring me home to help you out. It was okay." Sallee slumped down in one of the kitchen chairs, leaned over the table and laid her chin on her crossed arms. "You wouldn't kill Daddy, would you?" she asked, surprised at her own boldness.

"Nooo, you know I wouldn't. You do *know* I wouldn't, don't you?" Ginny mewled.

"I guess." Sallee shrugged. She was sorry to have seen her mother angry after almost coming to believe in the new, improved version of Ginny.

"Sallee, I was joking with Ethel. Just like you do with Helen and Gordy when you say 'I'm going to kill you.' You don't mean it. It's just like that." Her voice trailed off. As much as she wanted Sallee to understand, she just didn't have the energy to pursue it anymore. "I'm sorry you heard that." When the phone rang, she hurried from the room to answer it.

As they set off toward the barn, Early began calling the cows. "Sook, sook sookie, c'mon girls, sook, sook. Git on up here." He sing-songed as they walked along.

"Why do they come for you? They didn't even look up at me when I called to them." Gordy grumbled, put out by the rejection. "Do you have to yell *sook*? You don't always, do you? I don't remember the last time I was here that you did.

I thought you just called Janice and Mattie, and they came right along."

"Whoa there, one question atta time, boy. I'm old an' slow," Early chortled. "Dey come when I call'em. Doan much matter what I call, jest dat I be doin' de callin'. Dey doan know ya. Ol' Lance would'na come if'n I gave 'em a shout – now, would'e?"

"No, I don't guess he woulda." Gordy bounced off that old twinge of pain and hurried around it, "But they're cows. Cows don't know the difference, do they?" He screwed his face up quizzically as he looked at Early and realized that he was taller by a lot. "I don't think cows are as smart as dogs. Are they?"

"I tell ya one thang. Dumbest animal in de world knows where dey food comes from. Cows ain't dumb neither," Early said, sounding a bit indignant.

"What does *sook* mean?"

"Ya do ask some kinda questions. Doan mean nothin' jest I use it enough dat dey know it means food t' dem. Git on over dere an' opens up dat gate, would ya?

"Early," Gordy debated about going on, then plunged ahead, "I called Ethel a fat cow this morning. I'm sorry. I didn't mean to. I was just so mad. She got in my way and was telling me I shouldn't talk to my mother like I was. It just slipped out." He tried to make himself look at Early but was too afraid of the anger he might see and the shame he felt. As he stole a look, he noticed tears running down Early's cheeks and that he appeared to be shaking. "Honest. I didn't mean it. I love Ethel." Gordy implored. "Please don't be mad at me."

At that Early let loose and laughed hard and long. When he finally was able to speak, he said, "I bet dat put a look on her face," then laughed some more.

"You're not mad?" Gordy asked, unable to believe what he was hearing.

"Did ya call *me* a fat cow?" Early asked when he was able to speak as he wiped away tears. He threw a bucket of slop in the pig trough and turned to Gordy. "Son, it ain't none o' my bid'ness what ya say t' Ethel. She a big girl an' kin take good care o' herself. I 'spect she had sompin' t' say 'bout all dat. If she ain't yet, ya best be believin' she will." He chuckled some more.

"I left before she said anything," Gordy said.

"Good move," Early replied. "Le's git dese here cows milked."

Still chuckling, he squatted over a short stool beside a cow and began to wipe her udders. "Here, you try." He handed Gordy the rag. Gordy poked at the cow's swollen teats, jumping every time her tail swung. "Quit yo' jumpin'. She won' be able to let dat milk down, ya git her so riled up. What's de matter? Ya done dis here afore."

"I forgot how." Gordy took a deep breath to calm his nerves and tried again. He leaned up against Early, gently wiping Janice's udders while breathing in the earthy barnyard smells and allowed the calm to wash over him. "I love the way cows smell."

Early planted his forehead into Janice's flank, chuckled again, grasped a teat in each hand and expertly guided white streams of warm milk into the stainless bucket between his knees. "Wanna try?" he asked.

"Sure," Gordy gave a delighted yelp.

"Pull dat stool up over on de other side an' do what I do."

Gordy pulled and tugged, squeezed and pumped and produced not a drop. "It's hard. You make it look so easy."

"Ya been doin' it as long as I has, ya'd make it look easy too. Here, lemme show ya." Early covered Gordy's hand with his own and began to milk. "Kin ya feel dat? You needs t' relax. Easy like, squeeeeeeeze as ya pull down. Dere, did ya feel dat? Ya got it." Gordy beamed as a thin stream of milk pinged against the side of the bucket.

"Oh Lord," Ethel said, "I fo'got all about de message. If it ain't one thing, Miz Ginny, it sho' is another."

As if she needed another thing to think about, much less worry about, the Dean of Students' office had called for Ginny. Ethel took the message and was very careful to take down the number, asking the secretary if she would repeat it so that she was sure she got it right. Ethel met Ginny as she was just though the kitchen door with the news. From Stuart's school, Ethel repeated twice, in case Ginny hadn't made the connection. She said, "all the way from New York," as if she couldn't conceive of telephoning long distance.

Ginny smiled, despite this new concern today. "Did she say anything other than to call them? What it was about?"

"No'm, jest as soon as you got in you was t' call, da's all dey say. I'm sorry as I can be I fo'got."

Ginny sighed. “Thanks.” she headed toward the phone in the back hall. Ethel followed, wiping her already dry hands on her apron. She stood a short distance away but definitely in earshot. Ginny wanted to dismiss her but realized that she was concerned too, and let her stay.

The dean came right on the phone when her secretary announced Ginny’s call. “Hello, Mrs. Mackey. Thank you so much for calling back so promptly. I don’t want to alarm you. Your daughter Stuart has not been attending classes. She has been on academic probation for the past week, as you know. I presume you got the parents’ copy of the notification.”

“I have received no such letter. What is the address you have listed? As I think you are aware, Stuart’s father and I are divorced. Oh, no, that notice would have been sent to him. Might I please give you my address so that you include me in your correspondence in the future? Do you know where Stuart is? You don’t!”

Ethel gasped.

Ginny continued, “Do you mean to tell me that my eighteen-year-old daughter is somewhere in New York City, and you have no idea? Oh, you don’t even know if she is in the city. Wonderful. I presume you checked with her friends and roommate. I understand. How long have you been aware that she is not in school? I see. And you have called the police? I will have to talk with her father. We will be in touch I assure you. Please keep us posted. Thank you.”

Ginny turned to Ethel after hanging up. “I don’t know anything other than what you heard.”

While Ginny was on the phone trying to get Joe, Helen opened the front door, leaving two men and a woman standing on the porch behind her. Seeing her mother on the phone, she went to the kitchen to tell Ethel. "I don't know what to do. There are these people at the door," she said.

"Lord o' mercy," Ethel mumbled and scurried down the hall. "C'mon in," she invited them, purely for form, for the man and his group were halfway into the living room when she arrived. "Miz Ginny be right here. She on the phone. Would you like some tea?"

"No, we are here to see the house," the taller of the two men said as he went to take off his hat, then thinking better of it handed Ethel a card instead. "We'll just look around. Kitchen in there?" He pointed to the way Ethel had come.

Ethel nodded, and was about to say, "Through the pantry," when he brushed by her and led his group into the kitchen, giving Ginny a casual wave. Like rats from the proverbial sinking ship, Helen and Sallee scurried from the kitchen, looking wild-eyed and frantic. Ginny quickly ended her conversation and made her way in to greet the real estate agent. Just as the group was heading back down the hall toward the stairs, there was a knock at the kitchen door. Again the man waved Ginny and Ethel aside as he passed them, directing the couple up the stairs. He fell back, came over to speak to Ginny, and finally removed his hat. He reached out a limp hand and nodded a greeting. "Didn't your agent tell you, we prefer if you aren't here during showings?"

"Ethel, will you see who is at the kitchen door?" Ginny mustered control before she turned her steely blue eyes on the agent. "I don't suppose your mother taught you any manners, sir. Please feel free to show your clients around and then leave as soon as possible. Good day." She turned on her heels and headed back toward the kitchen, followed close behind by Helen and Sallee.

Mrs. Dabney brayed. "Ethel, I brought these for Sallee. I almost forgot I told 'er I'd bring 'em. You tell her for me I hope she gets better real soon. I am so sorry to hear that she hasn't been feelin' so good."

Ginny held back just inside the pantry out of eyeshot from the kitchen or the front hall, hoping to escape, but not knowing where to go. Her nerves were frayed to the point that she wanted a drink more than air. "Oh God, help me," she groaned.

She heard Ethel's deep, melodious drawl, but was unable to make out what she was saying, although Mrs. Dabney's every word seemed to reverberate in her head. She stood gripping the doorjamb, fantasizing about downing massive amounts of bourbon, no ice, no water, hell, no glass, just booze. Helen came up and took her hand and gently led her down the hall to the living room. "They've already been in here," Helen said in her flat, unadorned way. Ginny sank into a chair, saying a little prayer of thanksgiving for her youngest. Too distraught to speak, she managed to give Helen a wan smile. Her hands shook in her lap. Sallee followed them into the room and dove onto the sofa, doing her best to disappear.

Ginny was unable to draw a decent breath until she heard the odious agent close the front door, droning as he went about the advantages of a such a prime neighborhood. Helen left, then came back back into the room and quietly announced, "Mrs. Dabney left. Can I get you something?" Ginny shook her head.

Sallee groaned, "Is that what selling your house is like? Sheesh, do we have to?" At which point Ginny burst into tears. Helen shot Sallee an accusatory scowl. "I'm sorry. I didn't mean to make you cry. I just thought it was awful. Those people snooping around, um, our house, ew! I didn't say it was your fault." Ginny fled from the room. Sallee defended herself from Helen's reproving stare. "Don't look at me. I didn't do anything." Helen shrugged and followed Ginny out of the room, leaving Sallee on the sofa feeling older than time.

She lay on the sofa listening to her stomach gurgle and wondering where Gordy might be. *He was pretty self-reliant and stubborn, too. He might just hole up in a fallout shelter if they had a television set,* she mused, *and make us suffer*. As mixed up as he clearly was...a thought interjected itself. *Whoa, he told Ethel to shut up. ...And then, called her, an old cow, man! He had better stay gone.*

She tried to imagine how he could come home without being *in trouble* for the rest of his life. As she thought about it, it occurred to her that Ethel had never spanked anyone of them. She threatened, oh, yes, she threatened, and she did apply a switch to the back of her legs on a few occasions, but only a few and without any real heat. It was funny how much she – and, she presumed, her siblings -- feared crossing Ethel. Until now, she had always thought it was because she would have suffered some horrible physical pain at Ethel's hand. As she dug around in these thoughts, she discovered that what she feared more than anything else was losing Ethel's love. She cringed into a fetal ball. She would rather endure the shame of a perpetual piano recital than consider losing Ethel's love. For even these few moments considering life without Ethel, because that is how it would be -- without her love, there would be no relationship with Ethel -- left her shaken, anxious, and bereft.

As paralyzing as the prospect was, she forced herself to delve deeper. What would make Ethel withdraw her love? *It would have to be something we did*, she reasoned. She explored all of the heinous things she could imagine. She could not conjure a single one that would change how Ethel felt about her. She examined every story Ethel ever told for clues. It certainly wasn't like Ethel loved everybody. After all, she was human. *I must know someone Ethel once liked that she doesn't anymore*, Sallee deduced in her best Sherlock-Holmes-Nancy-Drew mindset. Her mind made list after list of people; dismissing Hambone because Ethel only wanted something from him; she didn't love him. Cary and Ben who worked at the beach house, nope; her sister Alberta, no, she didn't' expect Alberta to be anybody but Alberta, so there was no disappointment there. Hmm, she knew there was somebody, and disappointment was a big clue, or maybe it was expectation.

I know, it's Junior, she practically shouted out loud. Ethel was disappointed in Junior. She didn't love him like she once did. Did she expect him to be something else? She wondered about that half-baked story Ethel told a few weeks ago. She knew there was more to that story than Ethel was letting on. He disappointed her, but how? She mentally ran through Ethel's story. Junior didn't respect Ethel. He didn't approve of the way she was. That was it.

Was that possible not to respect Ethel? *Nah,* she found herself emphatically shaking her head. Was it possible to disappoint Ethel so much that she wouldn't love me? She dismissed the thought entirely. *It wouldn't happen.*

But Gordy's words could have made Ethel think he didn't respect her? They could have hurt her so much that she would stop loving him? It wasn't possible. She had watched Ethel as she scoured upstairs and down, out in the yard, and the garage, acts of love, Sallee knew that. She also knew that had Ethel found Gordy she would have embraced him, not hit him.

She followed her thoughts back three years to just after her parents divorced, back when both Ethel and her mother were drinking so much. She remembered her despair so great that she even planned to run away. Now Gordy was in that same dark place. It hurt her heart. He was always the stronger one, the one that could see the sense in things. How was it that he was so adrift and so angry when she wasn't? Where would he go? She tried to put herself in his mind. The effort made her head ache, so she gave up and continued to follow her drifting thoughts.

Her mother, *did she change or was it an act?* Sallee hoped that it wasn't an act. As much as she wanted to trust this change, her mind kept taking her back to all of the little things her mother had done, or would have done if this change were not real, like selling the house, calling Rosemary a floozy and wanting to kill her dad. *Did she want to kill Daddy?* she wondered.

Change, she didn't like it any more than anyone else, she realized as she twisted the experiences of the day around in her mind. That surprised her, too. She had always thought she liked change: that things were different, that you couldn't count on a thing being a certain way. But here she was with a changed mother and she was very unsure. Could she trust this new improved version of her mother? Isn't this what she had always hoped for, a loving, kind, gentle mother? A mother more like Linda. She couldn't want her mother to stay mean and drunk because she knew how to handle that kind of mom– could she? *Maybe*, she thought, *I don't want her to change because I don't know what that looks or feels like; I might get hurt all over again in some new way, some way I can't even think of?*

She wondered about that day at Charlie's, just before she got sick. Would she have a life like Charlie's if Ginny had changed as much as Helen said? Maybe it had only been fun at Charlie's because she was there. Maybe Charlie's mother was just pretending that life was fun because they had a guest. It sure didn't seem fun to live in that house that looked as if it would blow away in a big wind. How fun could it be, to be that poor? Ethel's house wasn't so hot, either, but Ethel seemed happy.

Did happiness have anything to do with money? Sallee thought about all of the people she knew. Most had more than Ethel; most had more than Charlie and her mother. None seemed to Sallee to be as excited about anything as Charlie was about a baloney and mustard sandwich. *Maybe they were starving, Charlie and her mother. If you don't get to eat regularly, baloney probably sounds pretty good.* But Charlie approached everything that happened that day with the same enthusiasm. *Maybe you have to be simple to be happy.* She laughed at the irony of that thought because there was nothing simple about happy, not at least from where she lay.

Helen entered the room with a purposeful walk full of conviction. This was a newly adopted attitude, Sallee noted. "Mom's in the kitchen talking to Ethel about having a drink. Uh, I hope, uh, she, oh, Sallee don't let her," she pleaded.

"What am I supposed to do? If Ethel can't talk her out of it, I'm pretty sure I won't be able to. I didn't think this was going to last anyway." Sallee heard herself sounding more like Stuart than she liked.

"You don't know," Helen whimpered. "You didn't see her when you were in the hospital. She was different. I bet you didn't know she stopped drinking in January. That's," she stopped and counted on her fingers, "ten months ago. Did you know that? She wants to change. I know she does. I heard her talk to a friend of hers-- someone she met at AA."

"Arrogant Ass?" Sallee asked. "What are you talking about?" Confusion knitted her brows together.

"I am not!" Helen cried looking crestfallen, "why would you say that?"

"Aunt Lisbeth called Dad *AA* all the time." It means *arrogant ass*. Cousin Jilly told me." Sallee explained. "I'm not calling you one. I just don't get what that has to do with what you are saying."

"Alcoholics Anonymous, dummy." Helen, feeling a bit vindicated, took advantage of her superior knowledge in this particular area.

"Nuh-uh," Sallee protested. "Mom? She was drinking before I got sick. I remember."

"Yuh-uh, since this past winter sometime. I told you she's been going to AA meetings. And no, she wasn't drinking. She had stopped, like I just told you, ten months ago!" Helen asserted vehemently, "Sometimes you miss the most obvious things. How did you not know?" She looked at her older sister in astonishment.

"I don't know. I stopped caring about what she had to say and avoided her, so I guess I just missed it." Sallee shrugged.

"Anyway, Mom said she would do anything in the world to keep you alive and bring you home. She said she would never drink another drop of alcohol, ever, no matter what, if you came home well. So you need to go in there and remind her," Helen urged, "stop her."

"Sure," I'll just say, "Mom, remember that promise you made to some lady I don't even know? Well, here I am, don't break it. Yeah, that'll work." Sallee sat up indignant that all of a sudden the mighty burden of her mother's sobriety rested on her inadequate shoulders.

"I can't keep her from taking a drink. Helen, do you know what was the matter with me? I think I asked, but nobody ever said."

Helen shook her head. "Nobody ever said that I heard except that you were gravely ill. Is that like near the grave?"

"I guess, definitely serious!" Sallee shrugged, "Gosh, that's scary. I'm glad I lived."

"Me too," her sister agreed.

"Maybe I should remind her, in case God decides to make me sick again because she broke her promise." Sallee said getting up slowly as she tried to convince herself that what she had just said was a good idea.

Before entering the kitchen, she stood just outside listening. Ethel was humming softly to herself. Helen stood just behind Sallee. "Go on," she urged.

"Okay, give me a minute, this is not as easy as you seem to think," Sallee hissed. After a minute, "Ethel," she called. "Are you in the kitchen?"

"Yeah, I'm here. You need somethin', sugar?" Ethel called back as she slipped around the counter and looked Sallee in the eye. "What you doing standin' there hollerin' at me?" She went back to the sink, picking up her knife and the broccoli she was preparing for dinner.

"Where's Mom?" Sallee asked.

"She had to go out for a bit. She say to tell y'all she hoped to be back in time to take you to see the new house. C'mon in here an' set down, you too, Helen," Ethel directed.

Sitting at the table with her head cradled in her arm, Sallee asked, "Did she have a drink?" Helen leaned forward in her chair, intent on hearing everything Ethel might have to say on the matter.

Ethel whittled at the broccoli tossing it into the pot when it approximated the size she wanted. "What you talking 'bout? Did who have a drink?" Ethel gave Sallee a quizzical look. "Yo' momma? Lord, girl, she stopped her drinkin' las' winter."

"Well, she could start up again. Helen said she heard Mom talkin' to you 'bout wantin' a drink. I don't want her to drink cuz I'm afraid God might make me sick again if she breaks her promise to him." Sallee looked up at Ethel with big watery eyes.

She put her paring knife down, picked up the edge of her apron to wipe her hands, then made her way over to Sallee. "Darlin', God ain't goin' make you sick no matter what yo' momma do." Her face broke out in a warm smile as she tried not to laugh while rubbing Sallee's back. "You doan need t' be worryin' 'bout dat." Ethel bent down, giving the child a peck on the top of her head, "All you gots t' do is take good care o' yo'self an' get stronger. You gonna be jest fine. So stop yo' worryin'. It ain't good fo' you." She patted her gently. "Lemme fix you a little warm Ovaltine. That would be good now, wouldn' it? You want some, too, Helen?"

"Ethel do you know what was wrong with me?" Sallee asked, a bit relieved by what she had heard.

"Once, I think yo' momma thought it was de polio 'til she remembered you done had de vaccination. I think, dey decided it was de meningitis. Didn' nobody tell you?"

"Polio," Sallee's eyes popped open wide. "Am I gonna be a cripple?"

"No, you ain't got nothin' wrong wit' you now. You jest need t' get you strength back is all. You be fine. Child, you worry too much."

She chuckled as she poured milk in a pan. "Helen, could you get me some mugs outta de cupboard, please?"

Lumbering over to the stove, she turned the burner, then dug into in a drawer, looking for a spoon.

Since she was unable to get Joe on the phone, Ginny drove over to his office, furious. *How dare he not tell her that Stuart was on academic probation! How dare he let that floozy bring Sallee home. How dare he draw breath.*

As she pulled into the parking lot, she was reminded how much she resented his fancy office at his beloved shopping center, a monstrous blight on the landscape as far as she was concerned. She stomped past Judy, the secretary, and into his office, slamming the door after her. Joe, on the phone, looked up in shock. He hastily ended his conversation and hung up.

Ginny was gearing up for a full-on attack when she caught site of the pictures on the wall. Dozens of photographs depicting the progress of the shopping center's construction arranged artistically matted and framed in colors designed to complement the painted wall hue, s*o decorated,* she thought with a pang of jealousy.

Just as she was about to let him have it with both barrels, he asked with a quavering voice, "News about Gordy?" Reading her expression, Joe looked stricken. "Oh, God, tell me, Ginny, what is it?" He came over and took her by her elbows imploring her "Tell me, what? What happened?"

"Stuart is missing," she squeaked out, fighting with all her might to keep from crying. Her anger began to melt away as he held her arms. She wanted to lean into him. She wanted his embrace, but resisted by clinging to her very last shreds of anger. "Why didn't you tell me? Why didn't you tell me she was on academic probation?" She started to beat on his chest.

"What?" If possible, he looked more stricken. "What do you mean she is missing? Academic probation? What are you talking about?" He asked and denied simultaneously as he pulled her close to him. Out of habit, she pushed away.

She recounted her recent call from the dean. "For God's sake, what else can go wrong?" she demanded then slumped up against him for a minute before regaining her composure.

Joe was beside himself. He sat down to make a call, realized he didn't know to whom, then jumped up and took Ginny by the hands, looking desperate. "What now?"

"I guess one of us is going to have to go to New York. I think I should stay here, since Gordy might come home. Can anything else go wrong?"

"Jeeze, don't say that! Plenty of things can." He went to the door and shouted to his secretary to get him a ticket on the next flight to New York.

She was on the phone in a very engaged conversation. "Hold on a minute, I'll put him on." She turned to Joe. "For you." She transferred the call to his line. "It's Stuart."

Ginny dove for the ringing phone. "Stuart," she cried out, "Oh thank God, you're safe. Where are you?"

"Mother? Is that you? What are you doing at Daddy's office?"

"Where *are* you?" Ginny asked. Joe reached over the desk and put the phone in speaker mode.

"Stuart, what's going on?" he shouted to make sure he was heard. "Your mother and I got a call – your mother got a call," he corrected himself, "from the dean of students saying you were on academic probation and that you were missing. What is going on, young lady?"

Ginny put her forefinger to her lips shushing Joe. "You don't need to shout. You can hear him, can't you, Stuart?"

It was hard to tell if Stuart just ignored Ginny or was too intent on delivering her message. She forged ahead. "Oh Daddy, it's why I'm calling. My roommate is an idiot. She told the dean's office that she hadn't seen me in over a week. She doesn't like me very much and thought it would be funny."

"Stuart, are you telling me the truth? I am having a hard time believing this." Joe said while Ginny rolled her eyes. "Sounds a little cooked up to me." Joe smiled at Ginny's eye roll.

"Honest, Daddy. I am so sorry." While they talked, Ginny rocked her head over and back and mouthed, *She is lying.*

"Maybe so, but I'm coming up as soon as I can get a flight," Joe informed her, in his best not-interested-in-any-flack way.

"Don't!" Stuart was practically shouting. Then in a more controlled voice, she continued, "I'm fine. There is no need for you to go to the expense."

"I'll worry about my expenses, thank you. I plan to see the dean with you. I want to find out about this academic probation and why neither your mother nor I got a notice. I will be there as soon as … hold on a minute." He went to the door, where Judy handed him a list of flight times. "Tonight at 6:10, gets in at 7:30," he read aloud. "Stuart I'll meet you up at your dorm a little after 8:30. I expect you to be there waiting. Do you hear me?" His voice had risen to a shout again.

Stuart answered with an exasperated "Yes," and a click was all they heard.

"You know she is lying through her teeth," Ginny said. "Thank you for going up there. I don't know what she's up to, but my guess is it isn't good. I wish she would talk to me. I think you did a good job, by the way. I knew it was better for you to handle it since she hates me so much."

"I don't think she hates you. I think she is confused, angry and scared. She tries to be a real tough guy, but she isn't. None of this has been easy on her."

"My drinking certainly didn't help," Ginny admitted, "I'm sorry for that. Hell, I'm sorry for lots of things." She said as she gazed out of the large window that overlooked the shopping center. *It's not all that bad looking from here,* she thought.

"It's not your fault," he added hastily.

"I know. I forget it sometimes, but mostly, I know it. I don't suppose you have heard anything more about Gordy have you?" she asked turning back toward him. "I'm guessing not, considering how you reacted when I first came in." He shook his head.

She picked up her purse and headed for the door. "When's the big day?" she asked as she reached for the knob.

"What? What big day?" He answered looking puzzled.

"The children said that you and Rosemary were getting married." She said it just a little too testily.

"Oh, for God's sake! That's more of Stuart's lies. She was mad when I told her that Linda and I were just friends. You know who I mean?" Ginny nodded. "On her own, she decided that it was because of Rosemary. She's very manipulative."

"Who? Rosemary or Stuart?" –she just couldn't help herself– "I know," Ginny agreed. "Do I know!"

"My guess is, she set Sallee up, poor kid -- she was devastated. Linda called minutes after Stuart told Sallee I was getting married to Rosemary. You can imagine how that went over. Linda had more plans for the relationship than I."

"Hmmm," Ginny smirked, "Don't cha just hate that? But, I don't see how Stuart used Sallee?"

Joe opted to ignore Ginny's dig. "You know how Sallee is. She loves being in the know. The way I figure, Stuart told her, knowing that Linda was going to be calling."

"I completely agree that Stuart can be manipulative. I don't see how she could have known your little friend –" she couldn't help taking another shot – "was going to be calling or that Sallee would answer the phone."

"Because I told Stuart earlier that I was expecting a call from Linda we were going to make plans for the day," he explained, "and as luck would have it, Sallee was primed and the next person she talked to just happened to be Linda." He started to laugh.

"You are a heartless rake, Joseph Mackey," she laughed. "I think you are stretching more than a bit with your notion that Stuart set the whole thing up."

"You had to have been there," he insisted, laughing.

Ginny giggled. "Just as happy as can be that I wasn't."

Joe looked over at his former wife, his blue eyes sparkling, "It was priceless. The phone rang. It's Linda. Sallee picked it up seconds before I got there. I have to stand there and listen as I see what is about to happen, and there is nothing I can do about it. I mean it was like a Noel

Coward play, the hapless hero stands by as he is handed his life on a…"

Raising an eyebrow, Ginny says, "Hapless, yes. Hero?" She shook her head.

He shrugged and continued his story, "Just after Sallee delivered her lines she handed me the phone, walked outside and shouted "*Fuck*" at the top of her lungs. I swear it was all I could do not to bust out laughing. Timing is everything. That kid's got it." They both laughed.

"She's been doing a fair amount of that recently," Ginny said, remembering the incident before Sallee got sick.

"More Stuart," Joe added.

"You let that woman pick Sallee up from school today!" Her voice rose with her remembered indignation.

"Ginny, she's a decent woman. She was here when you called. Before you called, I had just told her I had a meeting I couldn't get out of, so she asked if she could help. She is a friend, that's all."

"Hmm, friend, humph, if you and The Rose," Ginny smirked, "weren't getting married, why on earth would you bring her by to see Sallee the day she came home from the hospital? And for that matter to the hospital, twice?"

Joe's secretary stuck her head in the door, "You had better hurry up, or you'll miss your flight."

Joe grabbed his coat, without thinking kissed Ginny on the cheek and ran out of the door. "I'll call you later." As he rushed by her desk, he said to his secretary, "Call what is the name of that store? Uh, could you look it…"

"Paul Stuart." Ginny called behind him. "The store is Paul Stuart. It's on Madison. Ask for Phil."

Joe's head whipped back toward Ginny, "Impressive! Thanks," he said, then to his secretary, "Tell him to get together some clothes. He'll know. Send them to the Carlyle. A suit and shoes too. Bye."

Ginny smiled and waved, "You don't live with someone for seventeen years and not know something about them."

Gordy, dirt-streaked and weary, strode through the big front door, daring anyone to speak, hoping that this aggressive demeanor would protect him from any more confrontations. Despite the promise he made to Early, he wasn't quite sure he was all that willing to make amends, at least not right now. To his surprise, the house was quiet. He expected a fracas equal to this morning's –had steeled himself for one, in fact. He was ill prepared for the business-as-usual quiet that surrounded him. He debated whether he should seek Ethel out. He was mad this morning, sure, but he didn't mean to call her a fat cow, just like he said. He didn't want to hurt Ethel. Ethel was the only person he knew that loved him except maybe Early. They, he could count on. With one hand on the banister, he paused as he weighed his options; he could go into the kitchen, apologize to Ethel and feel better, like he told Early he would. She always made him feel better, but then he'd have to listen to her lecture him about how he should treat his mother. Or he could go upstairs to his room sad, but alone and with no lecture. Suddenly weary to the bone, he started up the stairs. Voices drifted from Sallee and Helen's room. He crept by as quietly as possible, taking great care not to step on any squeaking floor boards – grateful he had spent an entire afternoon last summer investigating which board squeaked and which didn't and that the door to the girls' room was only partially open. When he finally made it up to his room, he threw himself onto his bed and cried. The last thing he heard was Ethel calling up to the girls, "I'm goin' now. Tell yo' momma dinner's in de oven. Bye, now. Oh, an' doan forget t' call me if'n you hear anything 'bout Gordy."

Gordy had almost fallen asleep when Ethel huffed into his room under a full head of steam. Not waiting to catch her breath, she grabbed him up in her arms, practically knocking the air out of him. She all but suffocated him as she held him up against her large heaving breasts. "Darlin,' you scared me good dis time," She gasped for air. "Please, baby, doan ever do dat again."

Gordy listened to Ethel's racing heart and tried to catch his breath while she held on tight. A muffled, "I'm sorry I told you to shut up," emanated from between her breasts. "Ethel, I love you."

"I know you do, darlin'. Early tol' me, he say you s'pposed t' come talk t' me. Why didn't you?"

"I was too tired to get yelled at anymore," Gordy said as he struggled out of Ethel's embrace.

"Why you think I gonna be yellin'? I know how unhappy you is. I want t' do my level best t' make de sun come back int' my precious boy's eyes. Ain't gonna be no yellin'. From you neither, you hear?" She lifted his tear-streaked face up to hers by his chin and looked him in the eyes, "Hear?"

"I'll try," he promised. "But she makes me so mad. She..."

Ethel raised her hand up flat in front of his face to indicate stop. "No mo'. Yo momma's doin' her bes' t' change. She needs yo' help. I knows you don't think so, but yo momma loves you every bit as much as I do and mo'." She seemed to stop and think about the implications of what she said, then allowed as that it might be true, but for good measure added with a chuckle, "Not dat I knows how anybody could love you mo' dan I do." Then she took in the dirt. "You is a mess, boy. Bes' be gettin' int' de shower afore you turn dis here bed int' a sty." She laughed. "Did you leave any dirt in de garden?" It was only a matter of time before she was bound to ask, "Have you had anythin' t' eat? I made some marmalade tarts t'day?"

Gordy's face lit up. "Man-o'-man, thanks Ethel. Early and I had some peanut butter and jelly sandwiches. That sure was good bread you made, and jam, too."

"Oh, Lord wid de two o' y'all loose on it I 'spect I gonna have t' make some mo'." She chuckled and rubbed the boy's back. "I thought I would die gettin' up dem last steps. Sure do wish you done done what Early told you. It a saved me a heap o' steps." She laughed.

Sallee and Helen stood in the door. "What y'all lookin' at? Say hello t' Gordy an' git on down stairs." Ethel tried to sound gruff, but everybody knew she was just trying to hide how shaken she had been by Gordy's disappearance. Patting Gordy on the knee, she stiffly stood to leave. "You comin'?" Gordy shook his head. "It be easier on you if you did. I promise dey ain't gonna be no yellin' You be downstairs when yo' momma gits home you'll see how much she loves you."

Ethel leaned over and gave him another big hug. "I'm so glad you's home safe an' sound. You sleep tight, you hear, an' remember, no yellin'!" Gordy smiled as she let go.

"Okay, I promise, no yelling. Can we have French toast tomorrow?"

"We'll see bout dat in de mornin'."

Before she set foot on the top step, Gordy ran out and said. "Ethel, I didn't mean all those hateful things I said. I hope you know that."

"I know, darlin,' doan you worry none 'bout dat. 'Night."

Gordy watched Early's truck pull out of the drive, and then watched his mother turn in just afterward. As he thought about it, what Early had said that afternoon made a lot of sense. He did have lots of people that loved him; he was sure of that. He didn't doubt Ethel. His mother, he was pretty certain did love him. How she did it was the problem. The idea of no yelling was great, but how did he go about achieving that? Every single thing his mother said to him was like fingernails on a chalkboard.

Dr. Anderson was no help. He just made out like there was something wrong with *me*, Gordy thought. Reasons to be mad, hell he had a ton of them. Being mad with reasons isn't crazy. It's when you make reasons up--that's crazy.

As he lay there, he wondered about Sallee and Helen -- excepting that episode with that old bastard next door, they pretty much had the same shit happen to them. *Why weren't they mad like he was? Stuart sure was. She might even be madder. Was it cuz he and Stuart were older, or maybe it just really wasn't all that important? Of course. it was important. His little sisters might just be too young to know better.*

But like Early said, he lived in a mighty fine house, but then the bitch has gone and sold it. He felt himself get angry. Rather than feed the anger like he usually did he tried thinking about milking Janice. He thought about how good it felt to finally get some milk to come out. The anger disappeared a little. Thinking again about his mother selling the house didn't make him quite so mad. He switched his focus to making sandwiches with Early, and again what little anger had disappeared. He actually tried to get mad about the house to see if he could. Nothing. *Hmmm, that's interesting,* he thought.

With absolutely nothing to lose, Gordy decided he'd pull out the mother of all things that made him mad, Mr. Dabney killing his beloved bloodhound, Lance. Closing his eyes, he lay there on his bed and purposely brought back the memories of Lance writhing in agony on the back porch. Feeling his heart beating faster and his muscles tense up, he remembered how he and Sallee watched mesmerized by the horror of the scene until they were shooed away by his father. He remembered how he felt like his blood had turned to fire. He remembered how he hurt all over and how hard it was to hold in the tears, how hard he had to bite down on his lip to keep from bawling like a baby.

Hot tears pricked at his eyes, rather than stuff them he let them come. Feeling all of these memories wasn't as terrifying as he had always thought it would be, so he decided to go deeper. Remembering how mortifying it was when the police hauled him out of the Dabney's basement he tightened his jaw and brought up some more rage. Maybe now he had enough stuff he was pissed off about to see if it would work again, to see if he could make the mad go away. With closed eyes, he allowed the memory of his afternoon with Early wash over him. Walking to the house with Early's arm over his shoulder, felt so good, so safe. Safe was what he missed feeling. The realization that what had been missing for so long was feeling safe felt fantastic. Gordy broke into a big smile for the first time in a very long time.

Ginny appeared in the door and hesitated. "Can I come in?" she asked with a nervous little smile. "I am so glad that you are home safe and sound."

Laughing, he said, "That's what Ethel said." Then he added more softly, "Me too."

Ginny came over and hugged hard. At least one of her lost lambs was back in the fold. "I have missed you so much, so so much." She sniffed, holding him tight.

Chapter 6

The question of Cy had been gnawing at Sallee for years. Now she reasoned that if her mother had truly changed, she would tell his story. There was no question there was a story. That night as they were all watching television before bed she ran to her room and pulled out the locket. She brought it to her mother in the den and asked, "Will you tell me his story now, please?"

Ginny sighed, fighting back the impulse to refuse the request. She sighed again, and took the locket in her hand, looking down at it soberly. "Get ready for bed, first, and then come back here." She hardly had the words out of her mouth before she was sitting alone in the room. She marveled at how good it felt to sit by herself alone with her thoughts, if for only a moment. Minutes later all three children were gathered around waiting expectantly.

"Cy was two years older than I and the most beautiful man I ever saw," she began.

"I thought he was your boyfriend, not a man," Helen said indignantly. Ginny almost asked Helen how she even knew of Cy until she remembered that Sallee would have shared all of her thoughts on the matter with both siblings.

"That was just an expression. I can't say he was the most beautiful boy because Gordy is. How about I say, he was the next most beautiful boy I ever saw, better?"

Helen nodded her approval while Gordy beamed his.

"His eyes reminded me of water, light gray with the tiniest hint of green flecks. My whole life, since his death..."

"He's dead?" Helen gasped. "but he was a *boy!*"

Gordy poked her. "Would you let her tell the story?Then he pinched his lips tightly together while nodding quickly several times at his mother to continue.

"Since he died, I've always looked, but I have never seen eyes like his on anybody. Great big honey-colored curls framed his face. Everything about that face was perfect except that it was the face of a colored boy."

All three children gasped.

"There was no way you could tell, except that his speech was not as educated as mine, but then he wasn't as educated either. Don't get me started as to how unfair that is." Her voice rose, then softened, "His singing voice was divine. He'd break into a spiritual without even thinking, like Ethel does."

"Oh," Sallee meant to say to herself, but it came out louder as an oft nagging question finally made sense, "now I see. That's why you don't like it when Ethel sings her hymns." She looked to her Mother for confirmation.

Ginny bit her lip and nodded then continued. "I never met his mother. She was Bertha's sister. You know Ethel's mother, Bertha?" They all nodded their heads, *of course*, while urging her to go on with the story. "I think, but I'm not sure, she died when he was a baby. People said that she was a beautiful octaroon -- not *woman,* but *octaroon*.

"What's that, *octo-roon*?" Sallee interrupted.

"It means that three of her four grandparents were white. "Another gasp from the children.

"How can that make him colored, then?" Gordy demanded.

Ginny continued, "Well, his father, Wilson, was colored, and so was Bertha, so I don't know. I have never been able to understand it. There was always something strange to me about all of it. Wilson was darker than his son, but only just. He wasn't even as dark as Ethel. And you know Gordy has more color than Ethel does when he's been in the sun all summer. It is such a strange thing to me making someone an inferior because of the color of their skin.

"Anyway, this is going to get complicated so you'll have to pay attention. Black Sam, I'm sure you heard about him. He worked for Daddy. He and Daddy were the same age. They were like brothers, which was odd, but understandable at the same time. Sam's mother was Daddy's nurse, wet nurse."

Helen asked, "What's a wet nurse? Sallee and Gordy tucked their heads abashed, hoping that their mother would ignore the question, both having a cursory grasp of the service provided.

Ginny considered for a minute how to explain or even if she was up to the embarrassment of the explanation if she could explain. Finally, she just dove in. "You know when a baby calf drinks its mother's milk?" They all nodded yes. "Well, before there were baby bottles, human mothers fed their babies the same way." All three children looked horror struck. Sallee squirmed. Gordy prayed that his mother would just go on with her story and that Helen wouldn't ask any more questions. "Some women would hire a woman who had a baby to feed their baby too. Those women were called a wet nurse." Sallee was quite sure she could have gone her whole life not having to hear this explanation.

To everyone's great relief, Ginny continued without further explanation, "Isn't that strange that people hate you because of the color of your skin, but, you can suckle their babies?" Her audience shuddered. "It makes no sense. Anyway, Black Sam was always called Black Sam even though he was about the same color as Ethel, light skinned. Sometimes I could remember as a youngster mistaking Sam for Daddy. One day laughing at my mistake, I told Daddy. It was the only time he ever struck me, and right across the face, too. My mother was furious. I cried for days. He bought a pony to make amends." Eyes rolled.

"I have never said this to a single person before, but I think my grandfather was Sam's father too!" Another gasp.

"Does that mean we are colored?" Helen looked around, shocked as she asked.

"Nooo, jeeze!" Gordy couldn't contain his exasperation. This was the most interesting story he had ever heard. "Think about it, dummy!" Ginny raised an eyebrow by way of reprimand. "Sorry," he apologized hastily. "She's saying her white grandfather had sex with Sam's black mother and made Sam." Ginny raised two eyebrows in shocked amusement.

"Not to put too fine a point on it," she laughed. "Remember, Sam was Cy's grandfather. Sam's son, Wilson, was Cy's father and also very light skinned. So I'm thinking that Cy had a lot of white grandparents or maybe great grandparents himself. At least two, if not more."

Sallee cut in, "Cy and you would have been related then. You would have been – cousins!"

"Gross, Mom, you were in love with your cousin?" Gordy made a gagging gesture. "Ick!"

"Would you shut up?" Sallee demanded.

"Stop, everybody," Ginny ordered. "Stop being so mean to each other."

All three children exchanged glances as the thought came to each of them unbidden, *look who's talking* and each felt guilty for thinking it.

"We don't have to continue this story," Ginny said briskly. The children straightened up and moved closer to each other, doing their best to demonstrate demure behavior.

"I don't know if Cy and I were related. I never, until recently, even had the courage to think it, much less examine what I believed about it. I must have suspected all along. One thing I do know, Cy looked as white as you and me."

"How did he die?" Helen wanted to know.

"That is another one of the many mysteries of my childhood. There certainly were a lot of them. Lots of questions with few answers."

Sallee rolled her eyes. *I know how that goes,* she thought.

"Daddy, Sam, and Cy were all coming home. I don't know where they had been or why all three of them were together. It certainly wasn't a usual thing, and as far as I know, no one ever said why. I think Daddy was driving, but it could have been Cy. Now that I think about it, it probably was Cy. Daddy liked to put on airs, so he was most likely in the back, but again I don't know."

She stopped for a minute, thinking about the implications of what she had just shared. The words that Cy was at fault for her father's death had never coalesced in that order before, and they chilled her for an instant -- almost as if someone had walked over her grave, as Ethel would have put it.

She finally continued. "There was a terrible wreck on our drive --" She stopped again, wondering, H*ow would the car have gotten from the road to around the tree like that?* "Hmmm," she said out loud, "I don't know."

"Don't know what?" Gordy asked.

"Oh, another mystery. I was wondering how the car could have gotten wrapped around the tree like it did. Unless they were going very fast and skidded off the road, and if so, why? Or they were run off the road, and if so, who caused it, and why didn't *they* stop to help? I guess I'll never know." she mused.

"I'm going to stop right here for tonight. That was a lot of stuff, and thoughts I have never thought out loud, and lots of old painful feelings to deal with on top of a very long day." The end of the story was met with a chorus of groans. "I'll tell you more, I promise, just not tonight. I am exhausted. Digging around in unanswered questions from your childhood is very hard work." All three children understood that all too well.

"Is that why you would never talk about things in your childhood?" Sallee asked. "Because you were afraid?"

"So many painful things happened one right on top of another," her mother said, putting a hand gently on Sallee's shoulder. "I felt like it was safer to stuff the feelings and the memories away, so I didn't have to look at them or feel them." She straightened up.

"I was wrong. It made me mean, small-minded and miserable. And I think it's bedtime." She looked around at the three children. "Sorry we didn't get to look at the house today, but so many other wonderful things happened instead." She smiled at Gordy and he smiled back. She prayed the luck would hold out for Stuart too.

Joe was shocked when he saw Stuart, barely able to stand, on the sidewalk outside of her dorm. She looked like she hadn't eaten in weeks. "Oh God, What have you done to yourself? You haven't been at school at all, have you? Have you taken something? Are you drunk?" He sniffed but couldn't detect any smell of alcohol. "A drug?"

"Noooo," she said with slurred indignation.

"I suggest you climb off that high horse of yours. We're going to your room and get your things. You are staying with me tonight, and tomorrow you are withdrawing from school and coming home."

"No need. There's nothing up there." He could tell she had to concentrate to speak without slurring and she was weaving as if she were about to pass out. He also noticed that she was sweaty, though the night was cool.

"Did somebody give you something? What?" He grabbed her by the arm and swung her around to get a good hard look at her. "Jesus, look at you. What did you take? How much?" He hailed a cab and barked, "Closest hospital?"

"Presbyterian? Or Bellevue?" the cabbie asked.

"Presbyterian, I guess." He had a vague memory of a doctor, his father's doctor being there.

He bundled Stuart in the cab and prayed she hadn't overdosed. *How had she even managed to meet him?* he wondered. She was pasty white and clammy cold. Not good. He looked at her nails -- blue. "Shit," he said out loud and then to the cabbie as horrible old memories flooded in on him. "Hurry, I think she's overdosed." He quickly pushed up her sleeves to see if there were any track marks and breathed a sigh when he didn't see any. "Stuart," he shook her. She was no longer responsive, "Hurry for God's sake, hurry!" he shouted to the driver.

When they got to the emergency entrance, Joe hardly waited for the cab to stop before he threw a twenty at the driver, gathered Stuart up in his arms and plowed through the door into the hospital.

Someone with a gurney arrived out of nowhere, and hardly waiting for an explanation he placed Stuarts' limp body on the gurney and disappeared through double doors, leaving Joe winded and frightened. A woman soon appeared with a clipboard and raft of questions, most of which Joe was unable to answer. As the woman plied him with unrelenting questions, he attempted to ask some of his own. By the time their interview was over Joe was spent. Like a beaten puppy, he curled himself up in the waiting room where he had been directed to sit and waited for news.

Joe spent an insufferable two hours in the overheated grimy waiting room cheek by jowl with some of New York's ripest citizenry. He was sure he had told the cab-bie Presbyterian. How had he ended up at Bellevue? His mind ping-ponged from calling Ginny and telling her what was going on to waiting until he knew something. That she would be worried if she didn't hear from him was a foregone conclusion. Besides, he wanted to know if there was any word of Gordy. He got up, heading toward the empty -- at least for the moment -- phone booth, then talked himself out of it, hoping to have something definitive to say before he called. Then he looked at his watch and realized he'd have to make the call. It was nearly ten. Ginny knew the time he and Stuart were scheduled to meet--just after eight. She would be frantic. Just as he turned back to make the call, a young doctor, who didn't look much older than Stuart, came up to him.

"Mr. Mackey? Dr. Hampson." He held out his hand,. "We have your daughter stabilized." While he talked, he indicated that Joe should sit.

Joe turned toward his former seat and saw that it had already filled. "I'm fine standing," he said. "What about Stuart?"

"Sir, I am sorry to have to tell you this." Dr. Hampson spoke rapidly and sounded as if he were reading from a medical textbook, or at least a prepared script, and without meeting Joe's distraught gaze. "Your daughter is suffering from a heroin overdose. We have done a series of test and have administered a narcotic antagonist. I am admitting her for observation while awaiting results of our tests. She will be in the hospital for at least 24 hours." Hampson sped on, not pausing for breath. "She does not appear to be a long-term drug user, at least not intravenously. Depending on what we find, the test results will determine our next move."

He paused, then concluded, relaxing just a little. "My initial recommendation is to seek a drug rehabilitation program for her so that when discharged she can be immediately readmitted into a rehabilitation facility."

Joe looked around. He wrestled with his pride and shame, trying to grasp all of what this young doctor was saying. No one seemed to be paying the slightest attention, even though it felt as if the doctor had broadcast the saga of Stuart's fall from grace to the entire God-awful waiting room. Hoping the doctor would follow suit, he spoke just above a whisper. "She had *a heroin* overdose?" The doctor nodded.

"What did you say you gave her? He asked, still sotto voce.

"We gave her an oral narcotic antagonist," the doctor repeated.

"And that is what exactly?" Joe wanted to add, *You pompous ass*, but bit his tongue. The doctor's pedantic attitude was irritating him beyond reason.

"An antagonist, in this case, attaches to the opioid receptors, blocking them without activating them. A narcotic antagonist, as the name implies counteracts the narcotic, particularly in regards to the depression of respiration." The doctor adjusted his glasses and looked at his clipboard; he was in his reading-from-the-script mode again, and it was all Joe could do not to grab him by the lapels on his lap coat and shake him into some semblance of humanity. He resisted the urge and asked where he might find information on drug rehabilitation programs, but couldn't help adding, with just a slight edge in his voice, "Do you think it is necessary? Isn't this a little premature?"

"If she were my daughter --" the doctor started to say, and Joe thought, S*hit, if you were my father, I'd have been shooting up*. "-- it is what I would do. Street drug use at her age is perniciously seductive. Taking immediate and definite action might be the only way you can stop the addiction." The man's word stunned him. *Addiction? My little girl a dope fiend?*

"She is sleeping and will be for the rest of the night. I suggest you get a good night's sleep and tackle this in the morning." Dr. Hampson was glancing down at his clipboard again, segueing to his next task. He looked up and spoke earnestly, meeting Joe's eyes. "I am very sorry. I am sure this is a terrible blow." He smiled tentatively. "The good news is that all indications are she had not been using for long. I'll leave orders for a nurse to get you the information on local drug rehabilitation programs in the morning. They will be at the nurses'station." He paused, and getting no answer, cleared his throat and held out his hand to Joe, waiting a moment for a response. When none came, he turned and left.

Joe decided he needed some fortification before calling Ginny. As he stood outside of the hospital waiting to hail a cab he debated walking to the Carlyle. It couldn't be more than twenty blocks, he thought, but was too tired to do the math. It surprised him that, considering the events of the last few hours, he was still excited about staying at the hotel. He congratulated himself that he had had the presence of mind to get his secretary to book a room before he left Charlottesville. When a cab finally pulled up, he jumped in, glad he didn't have to walk after all, and gave the driver his destination.

This hotel was as close to home as it got for Joe Mackey. Pulling up to the black and gold portico and pushing though those revolving doors was a homecoming. His parents had had a small apartment here for years. *How long had it been?* He wondered. Some dark thoughts threatened to push their way into his consciousness. He pushed back

He strode through the revolving door and up to the front desk, feeling better than he had since before seeing Stuart. The night manager spoke as if they knew each other. Joe wracked his brain, but couldn't put a name with the face "Here's your key, Mr. Mackey. It's good to have you back, sir. Any luggage?"

"It's nice to be back. No, I had to leave in a hurry -- would you please have a toilet kit sent to my room?" Joe replied. "And may I have a phone brought to my table. I'll be in the Bemelmans."

There was a lot to be said for home, he thought -- a thought he hadn't allowed himself to think since he left Ginny and the children four years earlier. He decided then and there he was going to do whatever it took to put his family back together. Stuart was first up on the agenda.

By the time he got seated at a table, it was well past eleven. He debated about calling and then decided he had better. Ginny answered the call on the second ring. "Hello?"

"Hi, it's me. Any word on Gordy?"

"Yes, he is home and remarkably well, too. He spent the afternoon with Early, of all things." She laughed, but he could tell she was anxious for news of Stuart.

"Thank God. Early?" Joe let out a long slow breath possibly for the first time since climbing into the cab with Stuart almost four hours ago. "I wish I could give you as good news. Stuart is in the hospital. It's okay, she's going to be okay, a drug overdose, but she is going to be all right." He rushed to get in as much information as possible, knowing her propensity to worry before getting all of the facts.

"The doctor, who hopefully has more healing skills than bedside manner, thinks she needs to be admitted to a drug rehabilitation program as soon as she is discharged from Bellevue.".

"She's in Bellevue?" she asked in a mechanical I-need-to-ask-something kind of way. He thought it was odd that she would ask, since she knew nothing about hospitals in the city.

"The cabbie made the call. I wasn't thinking all that clearly at that point. Are you all right?" he asked.

"What's all that noise? Where are you?

"I'm at the Carlyle. I'm in the bar. I thought I'd get something to eat, since I haven't eaten since breakfast. Remember I was at the police station with you at lunchtime?" Mentioning the drink that he had just ordered and was looking forward to far more than he wanted Ginny to know seemed like unnecessary information. He asked again, "Are you all right?"

"Well, I'm not in a bar. I suppose I am as well as can be expected, considering the day I have had and this news." she answered testily. "Drug overdose" finally coming to grips with the important part of the message – "what do you mean, drug overdose? What happened? Where? Why did it take you so long to call?"

"She was a mess when I showed up." he said to her, nodding to the waiter that he'd like another, "Looked terrible, thin, and drawn, hardly able to stand. Then we were at the hospital for hours before I knew anything. The doctor doesn't think she's been using for long."

"*Using?* Using what?" Ginny asked.

"Heroin."

Ginny gasped. "Oh, Joe!"

Chapter 7

Sallee couldn't wait to get Ethel alone the next morning. She got up early and dressed so she could be there as soon as Ethel came in. Wanting to waste no time, she slid down the banister and raced into the kitchen. Ethel was already preparing breakfast. "Did you know Mom was in love with Cy?" Sallee demanded breathlessly. "Did you know that?" And then, as it just occurred to her, she said, "Like with Junior?"

"Whattya talkin' bout?" Ethel demanded. "How you know anythang 'bout dat?" Ethel held the egg she was about to crack over the rim of the bowl as if she had been turned to stone, not a muscle flinched. *Lord child, I need my head examined to be sayin' anythang t' you.*

"You told me," Sallee said, "then Mom told all of us last night. Do you think Mom's granddaddy was Black Sam's daddy?"

"Girl, what you talkin' 'bout?" Ethel's eyes nearly popped out of her head.

"Mom said she thought so, whatta you think?" Sallee pushed.

"I don't know nothin' 'bout none a dat." The egg down on the counter now, she turned to Sallee, "I ain't got no idea, atall."

"Ethel," Sallee put her bead right on her, "You can stop trying to protect her. Tell me what you know."

"Git on outta here, girl, 'fore I tan yer hide. You ain't too big, ya know." She picked up the egg and gave it a good whack on the bowl.

Sallee laughed at her, "So you do know something! Ha, I thought so. Don't you worry. I'll tell Mom. She'll get it outta ya." Sallee skipped out of the kitchen in search of her mother, leaving Ethel sputtering like an overfull teakettle while she prepared to beat the tar out of the eggs.

Sallee found Ginny already in the dining room reading the paper. "Mom, do you always get up this early? Ethel knows something about Black Sam."

"What? What are you talking about?" Ginny snapped, irritated by the abrupt interruption and not being to able follow what the child was saying.

"You said last night that you thought your granddaddy was Black Sam's daddy. Remember?"

"Yes," Ginny answered with an exasperated sigh. "I remember." *I don't know what I was thinking telling you, but I do remember,* she said to herself. "What, Sallee, have you done?"

"I asked Ethel," Sallee answered, pleased as she could be with herself. "She said she didn't know nothin', but I know she does. I can always tell when she's lyin'."

Ginny groaned, "Oh, Sallee. Could you please..."

"What? You want to know, don'tcha?"

"I don't know." Ginny poured out in a long, exasperated sigh. "I just don't know." She put her head down in her hand and then looked up at Sallee, "Will you go upstairs and tell everybody they had better hurry up, or we are going to be late for school." Trying her best to stay even-tempered, she added, "And Sallee, would you do me a favor? Leave what we talked about last night alone for a while. It's private, you know? I don't think you'd want people talking about your private feelings, would you?"

"Nooo … I wouldn't," Sallee agreed.

Upstairs Sallee said to Helen, "Ya know, I don't get grownups. Didn't you think Mom wanted to know if Black Sam was her daddy's brother?"

"No, she said that she thought maybe her granddaddy was Black Sam's father." Helen corrected as Gordy came in and flopped on the bed.

"Same difference," Sallee said, rolling her eyes impatiently. "Gordy, Ethel knows something about Black Sam. I'm sure of it."

"So what?" Gordy snapped. "You should leave it alone. If you run around asking questions all the time, she won't tell us anything. Just leave it."

"Am I the only one that wants to get to the bottom of this mystery?" Shaking her head, Sallee looked at her two siblings as if they had fallen from the sky. "I don't get you guys! Mom says to get downstairs, or we'll be late. Hey, Ethel's fixing French toast." Gordy was gone before she could finish the sentence.

While they were eating breakfast, Sallee asked Ethel one more time what she knew.

"I know I heard yo' momma tell you t' leave it," Ethel growled.

"She didn't mean us. She meant not to go telling other people. I'm not gonna do that. Whattya think..."

Ethel cut her off. "She mean leave it, *period*," she stated, with all her weight on the period, "I doan wanna hear another word 'bout it, you hear me?"

A natural early riser, Joe tried to force himself to sleep in. As he tossed and turned, he debated calling Ginny, then decided he was better off armed with more information. Besides, it was awfully early for her. Finally giving up all pretense of getting more sleep, he got up, ordered breakfast, then pulled out his address book. He perused the small leather book, trying to remember the name of his father's doctor. It was here somewhere, he was nearly certain, but thumbing through the book did little to jog his memory. Breakfast arrived. After showering and shaving, he had little to do but summon the name. When he needed to remember something that didn't just come to him, he'd apply a strategy that almost always worked: divert his attention to fill in the time until the memory came. He picked up the Wall Street Journal, and like magic, it floated up to just below his consciousness: *Stein* something? Stiel, Siebel, Steinburg? Burg, Burg ... Berke! Berke, that was it. *Jacob, I think*. Noting the time, he sat on the side of the bed, thumbing through the yellow pages. *Physicians, psychiatrists, hmm, he should be here somewh…, there. Jacob Berke, 96th & Park, great and not far at all.* He dialed the listed number.

On the third ring a refined accented voice answered. "Hello, Dr. Berke?" Joe said. "I am Lee Mackey's son Joe. I am not sure you …Oh, you do? Great. I'm surprised you answered the… I see! My luck then. Would you have time to see me today or talk now? My daughter was admitted to the hospital last night for a heroin overdose. I remember what great things my father used to say about you. I need some guidance. This problem is beyond me." He ran his fingers through his hair, noticing that it seemed thinner.

Joe answered all of the doctor's rapid-fire questions just as rapidly, "Bellevue, of all things. Stuart Mackey, last night through the emergency room. His name was Hangsum, something like that, I wrote it down. It's uhh mm. I didn't catch his first name … That would be fantastic. You have rounds this morning, but .. oh, good. I thought I remembered that you worked at Presbyterian, but you have contacts at Bellevue? Oh, I see. Of course. The psychiatric unit. Of course."

Joe heard himself heave a large but involuntary sigh of relief. He forged on. "After you see her can we make an appointment to meet? At six your office, I look forward to it. Thank you."

With virtually the whole day now ahead of him, he mentally flipped through his file of New York connections. *That was it. Yes.* Since he was here, he might as well try to make an appointment with his parents' attorney. He'd been putting it off since the letter a few weeks back. Last thing he'd expected after all these years: an inheritance, of all things, and from his father, no less. The notification -- *inheritance, sole heir, constraints, earliest convenience, etc., etc., etc.* – it was amazing how much it had actually irritated him. The lawyer's name he wouldn't forget: Leland Templeton Pettit, III. *Bound to be an ass of the broad A variety – Leland the Third – doubtless a good ol' member of Dad's cocktail club …* Joe groaned, thinking about meeting the fat SOB face to face. A little snot-nosed brat grown large, no doubt, and how many of them had he endured back at Horace Mann, New York's most exclusive enclave for the prep school crowd? "*… Acting under the strict awders of your fawther's will not to infawm you of the situation until ten yewrs after your sawviving pawrent's death.*" In his mind, Joe evoked what would be Pettit's well-rehearsed New York patrician accent and by way of amusement, added, "*Do come dowwwn to the yawwwcht club for a cawwwcktail, why dohhn't you?*"

He found L. T. Pettit, Esq. via information and called the great man's office and left a message with his secretary that he would like to meet at Mr. Pettit's earliest convenience, today if possible. "Tell him I will only be in town for the next two days. You can leave a message for me at the Carlyle. Thank you."

As he hung up, there was a knock at the door. Joe opened it to a bellman laden with two stuffed garment bags and several shopping bags as well. "Good morning Mr. Mackey," the short uniformed man chirruped as he strode to the closet with the garment bags. "And where would you like these, sir?" He held up the shopping bags, somehow managing a slight bow at the same time.

"On the sofa would be fine," Joe said as he slipped him a tip. "Thank you."

Stuart, he was sure, would be as excited as he when he told her about the good luck he had reconnecting to Dr. Berke. He wondered about telling her how he knew the doctor. But it wasn't his story to tell. *I'll ask Dr. Berke tonight*, he thought. *How does one go about telling a child about her grandfather's drug problems? Dr. Berke would be older, maybe even late seventies by now,* he thought. *He was good, though, and in a profession where age didn't make a difference.* An unbidden thought surfaced. *It was odd that he answered the phone, and that he could see me so soon.* "Trust," Joe, remembered reading recently, "was important," he reminded himself. While going through the clothes and putting away the things he wanted to keep, he dismissed his worries.

Changing into a sampling from his new wardrobe, Joe took stock of himself in the mirror. *Phil does know what he is doing,* he conceded. *This suit fits like it was made for me.* He fingered the light gray cashmere. *Nice. I'm not going to look at the price, just let Pops pay for it.* He chuckled as he closed the hinge on the last cufflink and gave himself a final once-over. "Not too shabby there, pal," he said out loud as he tugged both shirt sleeves into place. "Not too shabby at all. " He gave a quick check in the mirror to confirm that his hair was not thinner. Reassured, he strode out of the room.

In the lobby as he passed by the desk, he remembered to ask the clerk to send someone up to gather the remaining clothes and send them back. "Thank you," he said and whistled his way through the revolving doors. It felt good to be in the city. Funny, he'd missed the ease of it all. Who'd have thought? He couldn't imagine how complicated that simple clothes transaction would be at home. And since it was a glorious fall day, and he was feeling great, he decided to walk to the hospital.

When he arrived at Stuart's room, he was relieved to see her awake, although that awful dyed hair, now growing out, had kind of a skunk-like effect that gave him pause for a second. While she was not exactly the picture of health, she looked decidedly better than the night before. She hardly waited for him to kiss her before she began to negotiate for her escape." I am starved," she said with an obviously affected breeziness. "I know this great place for breakfast. Wanna go?"

"You narrowly missed dying from a heroin overdose, and you are talking about breakfast? Stuart, it is time for a *serious* talk," he announced in a tone dripping with condescension. "How long have you been using heroin?" He heard himself use the expression and quaked, missing his patronizing tone entirely. *This bad dream was not happening. His daughter a drug user, an addict, Heroin no less!*

"I don't *use* heroin," she stated emphatically. "*Use*" dripped with contempt.

"The doctor and test results beg to differ, young lady," he retorted. "I would very much appreciate your telling me the truth. I saw you last night. I brought you here. You probably don't remember that little fact, do you?" He was snapping now, his volume stair-stepping upward with every belittling point. "You displayed all the signs of a heroin overdose, let's get that straight."

"How would *you* know what a heroin overdose looks like?" she countered.

Her attitude riled him further, "Stuart, you are not getting out of this. I expect answers." To drive home the point that he was the one in power, he let fly the threat, "The doctor has recommended that you be admitted to a drug treatment facility. If you want to have any input as to where that might be," his condescension rising to dizzying heights, "I strongly suggest that you stop this game you are playing right now."

"*Drug rehab*! Are you *crazy*?" Stuart was screaming, as she swung her legs over the edge of the bed, looking for her shoes. "I had one little incident, and you are making me out to be a fucking drug addict!"

"Stuart, that's enough." Joe was up on his feet. It took the last of his self-control not to smack her. "I will not hear you talk like that again."

"Well, you'd better get the fuck out of here, then!" she shrieked.

Stunned, Joe stood stock still in the middle of his daughter's hospital room, struggling for control. Clearly he had none over her, and losing what little he had left over his own temper wasn't going to help the situation. *God, how did I let this happen? How did I go so wrong so fast?* Like a bad flashback, his father's brutish and bullying insolence had come up out of nowhere. He shuddered as he thought of how many times he had been on the receiving end of the haughty diatribe and how much he had hated the man for it. *Oh, Stuart, honey, I am so sorry. I swore if I ever had children, I would never treat them like this.*

"Calm down," he said, mostly for his own benefit as he started his backpedaling. "Look, I didn't handle that the best. So let's start over? Okay? Is that all right with you?" He hesitated with each question, inching his way back into his daughter's good graces. "I am sorry for being such a jerk." He started to move toward the bed. Reading her body language, he stopped. *Hell,* he thought, *like it or not, you're going to hear how this felt.* "You've got to know that this whole thing scared the hell out of me," he began, trying for calm but firm. "First, learning you'd left school, and then finding you like I did last night. The last thing I want to do is lose you. You do know that?" She nodded, but reluctantly, eyes planted on the floor.

He took a breath and went on, "I'm sorry I reacted so badly."

"Me too," she grumbled, still not making eye contact. "But..."

Joe put his hand up to stop her. Having bungled the situation about as badly as possible, he decided he'd leave Stuart to the professionals, at least for the short run. "Listen, I have a lot of things to take care of while I'm here in the city. So why don't you hang tight here? See the doctors and hear what they have to say. I'll be back around four. Then we can talk about what the options are. Does that suit you?"

"No! There is no reason for me to stay in this --," She looked around the room with contempt.

"Okay, could you work with me just a little here?" He was having a hard time maintaining his calm. Pressing his lips hard together, he continued, "The doctor that saw you last night in Emergency said that you would be here for two days." That wasn't exactly what the little prick had said, but he felt justified pushing the time a little. "I have no more control over that than you do." He hoped she would just believe this mild prevarication, it was all for the good. Tilting his head slightly to the right and down, he looked out from under his brow and gave her a tentative smile. When she didn't respond in kind, he grimaced and forged ahead. "Like it or not, you are here until a doctor signs an order to let you out. Heroin possession, you may or may not know, is against the law." She was about to protest that she didn't possess any heroin when he cut her off lightly with, "My suspicion is that having heroin in your system constitutes possession. And I think they could have you arrested if you don't comply with their wishes."

He smiled weakly, "I don't want you to become a jailbird. So could you please stay here? See the doctors? Pretend that you were well brought up?" He grinned. She stuck out her tongue. "While I see to it that I can spring ya from the joint." He ended in a lousy James Cagney imitation.

Stuart lay back on the pillow and groaned. "Well, I'm glad, at least, I don't have to spend the day listening to that. Get out of here."

———

For most of the next morning, Ginny avoided being alone with Ethel for fear she would ask her about that day, about Cy, Black Sam, and her father -- and then she'd know. As much as she wanted to know, something nagged at her, making her feel she would uncover a dreadful secret that might change her life forever. She busied herself in the study with some paperwork, but distracting thoughts kept crossing her mind. So when Ethel came into the study, Ginny decided that this was the time for questions that needed answers.

"Ethel, do you remember the day that Cy was killed?" Ethel nodded and stopped, waiting for the next question. "Do you know what happened? Do you know how it was that the car was wrapped around that tree like it was?

"No'm, I don't." Ginny was strangely disappointed now that she had summoned the courage to ask. "I was wit' you dat day, 'member? But I know who prob'ly do," she said. "I 'spect Momma know right smart 'bout dat day, but she ain't never tol'. I 'spect Mr. Dabney know somethin' 'bout it, too."

"Oh God, no, not him," Ginny groaned. "Maybe that's why I never wanted to ask. Eww. I feel sick. Do you think he had something to do with it?"

"I doan know de answer t' dat. What I do know is he live right next doo'."

"Do you think Bertha would talk to me about it?"

"I 'spect she would. 'Nough time done past," Ethel replied.

"Could I see her today?"

"Prob'ly. I could call down an' ask Johnson t' bring'er by," Ethel offered.

"No, but I would appreciate it if you would ask if I might come see her. It doesn't have to be today." Ginny felt a twinge of excitement as she thought about actually laying to rest questions that she had kept at bay for most of her life. "I would so much rather speak with Bertha than that dreadful man next door." She shivered just thinking about Dabney.

"Miz Dabney say he ain't well. Dat dey doan 'spect him t' live out de year. He got de cancer. So you bes' be makin' up yo' mind 'bout talkin' t' him. He an' Mama de onliest ones I know as would know 'bout dat day. Miz Pansy's long dead an' Wilson, too, po' soul. He never did git over losin' his daddy an' Cy on de ver' same day." She stood in the door looking far away and then added, "Roberta wasn' round dat day, but she make it her bid'ness t' know whatever folks gots t' say 'bout a thang. You might want me t' call her an' ask what she know?"

"I would love to talk to Roberta. Where does she work? Maybe I could go by."

"She work fo' yo' friend Miz Chambers. Be doin' fo' her fo' de last few years."

"Oh," Ginny said, sounding crestfallen, "Maybe she could come by here then. I'm not sure Betty would appreciate me coming to talk with Roberta while she is at work. She's funny that way."

"I'll ask Roberta t' stop by after she git off work." Ethel said as she thought, *I didn' think Miz Ginny would be goin' by Miz Chambers. I wonder what dey fell out 'bout?*

"Is there any way I could see Roberta at her house or if she would prefer here when the children aren't around? You know how Sallee can..."

Ethel chuckled. "She is one right smart detective, dat one. Doan give 'er even a corner o' a page t' get hold o' or she'd be readin' 'tween every line on it in no time. Dat girl's a mess. Hmmph" She chuckled again. "I'll ask if Roe can come by in de mornin' when de chil'ren is at school."

"Thank you so much. That would be perfect," Ginny said. For the rest of the afternoon, she vacillated between confronting Dabney and complete revulsion at the thought.

Shaken by the force of Stuart's fury and his own in response, Joe decided that he wouldn't bring up Dr. Berke. *The old guy can probably do a better job without my poisoning the well anyway,* he thought. After checking at the nurses' station that Stuart would not be able to leave without discharge papers from her doctor, he felt confident that he was safe to follow up on his appointments.

Ducking into a phone booth, he called the hotel. Good, he had an appointment with Pettit – Mr. L. T. Pettit, no less -- at 2 o'clock. Inside the phone booth, he checked his watch, did the math and decided that he had time to see the dean of students. He would have to grab a quick lunch along the way. He rummaged through his pocket for a dime, put it in the slot, and dialed information. Minutes later, he had an appointment to talk to the dean at noon.

Now he was cooking. He loved life when all the balls fell into all their appropriate slots. Efficiency was what it was all about. There was no doubt in Joe's mind that heaven ran like a well-oiled machine. As if it were waiting just for him, a cab pulled up as he stepped from the curb. Giving the college's address, he sat back and relaxed against the seat.

Orderly as his day was becoming, the episode with Stuart still unsettled him. He understood her rage. He chuckled as he thought about it. There was a girl who could stand up for herself. At her age, he had chosen to leave and never look back. There were too many of those fracases from his childhood to have a happy ending. God, he hated his father. He had forgotten how much. Homecomings are fraught with bitter and sweet, he decided. *I guess it's my time for the bitter, but I would so much prefer to have it in my drinks.*

Stuart's lack of attendance and the fact that she hadn't lived in her dorm room for the last month made the meeting superfluous. Suspension trumped withdrawal. However, the dean assured Joe that if Stuart wished to return, arrangements could be made. The whole meeting was over in less than forty-five minutes, leaving Joe with the nagging question of where Stuart had been living for the last six weeks. The dean was quite unable to answer that question.

He decided to pay a visit to Stuart's roommate. She might know something even if they hadn't hit it off. Balls were continuing to drop just so for Joe: Miriam was just leaving her room when he rounded the corner. As he had huffed his way up the four flights of stair to his daughter's former dorm room, he'd rolled name upon name around in his head, hoping to dislodge the roommate's. Seeing her did the trick. "Hi Miriam, I'm Stuart's father, Joe Mackey."

"I know who you are," she said, none too politely. "I remember you when we moved in. I guess I should say, when *I* moved in, since *she* never did." She finished with a sneer.

Joe chose to let the insolence go for the time being. "I'm glad to have caught up with you. Do you have a minute?"

She looked at him skeptically and then at her watch, "I'm on my way to class."

"Would you mind if I came along?"

"To class?" She looked as if something odiferous had died right there in the hall.

"No, I just want to walk along. I've got a few questions," Joe said, and since the girl had started toward the steps, he fell in step with her. "Do you have any idea where Stuart has been living?"

"Not here," she said defensively. "She met some guy. The first week, I think, of school. She would have moved out," she laughed, "except, like I said, she never moved in."

"I sure did lug a lot of stuff up these steps for her not to have moved in." He laughed, trying to appear casual to hide his dread. *Some guy?*

"Yeah, it's still here," Miriam informed him. "You need to take it. It's her clothes and stuff."

"She didn't take her clothes?" He was pretty sure Miriam could hear his panic, but he continued his charade, nonetheless. "Oh no, I've got to haul that stuff back down all of these stairs."

"The guy said he went to Columbia, but I don't think so. He was creepy in a dirty druggie sort of way," she volunteered while Joe's stomach turned.

He gave up all pretense of a casual conversation and drilled her. "Do you know his name? Where he lived? How I can get in touch with him? Where did she meet him?"

At the bottom of the stairs, she opened the door. As she looked back at him, she said, "All I know is that you have to get her stuff out of the room or I'm going to give it all away." The door swung shut as Joe stood there trying to think what his next move was.

"Wait, Miriam, wait!" he yelled as she disappeared through the outer door. He ran outside, looking around feverishly, and just caught sight of her before she vanished around a building. Calling, he wove his way through a throng of students, trying to catch up to her.

It was pretty clear she wasn't going to get rid of him, apparently, since he all but collided with her as he rounded the corner. "Look, the only thing I know is he said he was a student at Columbia. I think she called him Tad. He was gross and smelled bad. He looked like one of those beatniks –" she said the word with enormous disdain – "always spouting off poetry, political mumbo jumbo, and lots of dissension. I think he was a drug addict. He sure looked like one. Even had tattoos." She shuddered. "When are you taking her stuff?"

"You can have the stuff. What you don't want, sell, or give it away. Thanks for your help. If you think of anything else, please let me know. It's important." He handed her his card. "Call collect, and if I'm not there, leave a message with my secretary," he said as he made a mental note to call Judy and tell her to accept any collect call from someone named Miriam.

She took the card, and as if it just dawned on her to ask, said, "Is she okay?"

"No, she's not. Please call me if you think of anything, anything at all." He turned and walked away. As he made his way to the street, he wondered, *Why it was so important? Why did he need to know where she had been? She was safe now. Whoever the creep he was, he was out of the picture now.*

Bertha broke into a big smile. Her warm copper face had a few more wrinkles, and glasses now perched on her patrician nose. Otherwise, she looked as she always had. She greeted Ginny warmly. "Been a long time, ain't it? " she asked as she took Ginny's delicate hand in her large work-worn ones.

"I don't think I have seen you since Denny's funeral," Ginny replied, and was surprised at how easy it was to say."That was well over three years ago."

"Dat all?" Bertha said, "Lord, it seem like a lifetime ago." A cloud had come over her face when Ginny mentioned the baby's name, but it passed when she saw it didn't cause Ginny any pain.

"It does seem almost a lifetime," Ginny agreed. "But time looks as if it has stood still for you, Bertha! What is your secret?" Ginny laughed, and then she abruptly changed the subject. "Did Ethel tell you why I've come?"

"Yes 'um, she did." She indicated to a rocking chair, " Won't yo' set a spell. I hates t' tell yo' dat if I did know sompin,' I's forgotten. I put a lifetime int' fergittin' dat day." Ginny pulled up a stool and sat down.

"Oh, I don't want you to talk about it if it will upset you," Ginny assured the older woman.

Bertha waved her hand. "It doan bother me none now. Kin I get yo' sompin' t' drink?" Ginny shook her head no, and Bertha sat back in the rocker, looking relieved. "My feets been botherin' lately," she said, and then continued, "De onliest thing I knows fo' sure 'bout dat day was dat rascal C.L. Dabney had some kinda part t' play in it. I do remember someone, coulda been C.L., come in an' say Mista' Gus was drunk an' raisin' cane downtown somewheres. He say somebody best be goin' fo' him 'fore he gets hisself arrested. Sam was in de kitchen an' he say him an' Cy would go fetch him. He say not t' worry yo' momma, Miz Bess, wid it. He took Cy t' drive. Das all I know."

"Remember how the car was wrapped around that tree? And off the road so far?" Questions were flooding Ginny's mind. "Did anyone ask how the car got that far off the road, later? Was there an investigation? Did the police look into it at all?"

Bertha shook her head. "I doan remember. I is sorry as I can be dat I doan know no mo' ... but --. I doan think Cy was driving on de way back," she added, as if the thought had just come to her. "Dat C.L. would know. He be de one dat found 'em an' went fo' Wilson."

Ginny groaned. There was no way around it. She would have to talk to him, and if what Ethel said was true, sooner than later. "Back then the po'leece didn' do 'vestigatin' like nowadays," Bertha finished. I doan 'spect dey did nothin' mo'n ask a few questions, if dey even did dat."

Chapter 8

An extremely attractive older man glided into Stuart's room, indicated the foot of the bed for permission, then sat demurely on the indicated spot and gazed at her with piercing blue eyes. He took her hands in his perfectly manicured ones. "I cannot tell you how delighted I am to finally come face to face with the diaphanous creature that caused her usually taciturn grandfather, once upon a time, to wax positively lyrical. Although you are older, you are every bit as beautiful as he said those many years ago."

Stuart's hand shot to her hair, "Excuse me, I think you have the wrong room. I don't have a grandfather," she informed this apparition of sartorial elegance perched on the edge of her bed as she self-consciously let her hand fall into her lap. "I wish I had one and I wish he would say those things about me." The words coming out of her mouth shocked her as her heart opened like a lotus to this exotic man sitting beside her.

"Darling child, your wish it is my delight to grant. You not only had one, but you had an exceptional one at that. You are Stuart Mackey, are you not?" Stuart nodded that she was.

"Your Grandfather Lee Mackey told me on no less than ten occasions the exact color of your eyes down to the tiny gray rings around the pupils." He leaned in closer to inspect, "He may have even given me the exact dimensions of those rings. Let me take a look." He drew back gracefully. "He was a scientist, you know, with a tendency toward exactitude that defied description. In short, your grandfather was besotted by you."

She was rapidly finding herself besotted by this strange man. Had he suggested that she follow him to the ends of the earth, even at this early stage in their relationship, she might have considered it. "How did you know my grandfather?"

"I had the great privilege of being his physician for many years. A kinder gentler man did not exist. He was truly a gentleman. And one I miss to this very day. Please allow me to introduce myself. I am Jacob Berke. I have been a doctor of psychiatry for the past forty years. Your grandfather was one of my very first patients."

"You were my grandfather's shrink? Wow. Do you work here?" Stuart didn't remember ever meeting her grandfather. Grandfathers, in general, or at least in her mind did not have shrinks. That hers had was something unusual indeed.

"Ah, I am based elsewhere, but I have had – mmm -- connections here for many years." Not pausing to explain Bellevue's reputation among psychiatrists or his role as the occasional rescuer of wealthy clients' children, he gently placed his hands on either side of Stuart's neck just under her jaw, tilting her head gently. "And I would very much like to work with you. How do you feel about that?"

"Sure, I guess. It's sorta far out to think my grandfather had a shrink. And then to think we would have the same shrink." She laughed. "Yeah, okay, cool. My grandfather had a shrink, far out. Wait, why? Why did my grandfather need a shrink? That is weird, man."

Dr. Berke said, "Yeah, like really far out, man." They both laughed. "Your grandfather was addicted to heroin. I helped him get beyond his addiction."

"Wait, *what?!* My dad's father was a heroin addict? Ohhh." She wagged her head and sighed, "Just like Dad to overreact. Damn him," she swore, "I'm not addicted to heroin. I tried it once, big deal. Obviously too much, is all. I don't need a shrink. I'm not an addict."

"Obviously," The doctor said as he allowed the ambiguity hang between them before continuing. "I don't believe for a minute that you are an addict." Stuart broke out in a self-satisfied smile.

"See, Dad is such worry wart." She said. "He's always worries that I might get hurt or in trouble."

"You don't ever give him anything to worry about either. Do you?" Jacob laughed. His eyes traveled around the room, making his point.

"Well, I guess. I did get kicked out of school and did take some heroin, so yeah, I guess so," she allowed.

"Well, if you are satisfied with the way your life is going, you don't need my help." He looked over his half-moon glasses at her. "My suspicion is that someone who even *tries* a highly addictive substances isn't completely thrilled with the trajectory of her life." Smiling as he gazed at her two-toned hair, he tilted his head quizzically toward Stuart, who looked away. Then he continued. "I could be wrong. It's been known to happen. As far as your father is concerned, he knows first hand the pain and suffering of loving an addict. He watched his father struggle in the clutches of a severe heroin addiction for most of his early life. He had to go out on the street and buy drugs for him because his father was too sick to do it himself. He, no doubt would want to spare himself and you that anguish. I'm not so sure you can fault him too much for that."

"Okay," she sighed with a dramatic groan and eye-roll, If you are going to have be my doctor, you can get me out of here, right?" As entranced as she was with this new possibility, the hospital was definitely cramping her style. "My dad says I can't leave without my doctor's permission. If I tried, I could be arrested. Could you work that out for me?" Drawing on his earlier compliment about her irises, she turned them to their fullest effect, giving him a soft doe-eyed look in hopes of sealing the deal.

"I might have to work out a few things first. I assure you I will do my utmost to navigate the labyrinth of law and misappropriated emotion on your behest" – he gave a slight bow, with a hand flourish – "to deliver you to your father as soon as humanly possible." The mention of her father didn't sit well, speaking volumes to highly attuned older eyes. He gave her a benign smile, adding, "Let me caution you, we are dealing with New York State laws, where time and the tide waits for no man -- or miss, as the case may be. Let me away to do thy bidding, fair maiden. I shall return later this evening with news, and we shall talk at more length, yes?"

"Yes," she said shocked at how excited she was at the prospect.

He stood, bowed again with that flourish, and took his leave.

Nothing about home had ever suggested new, efficient and shiny rather old and complicated, but charming. This didn't look anything close to what they expected, not that they knew what they had expected. For as long as Sallee, Gordy, and Helen could remember, home had only looked one way: a big front facade, green-black shutters, warm butter color, a maid's room and bathroom far enough apart that you had to pity anyone in need of the facilities in the middle of the night; three stories, formal rooms with furniture to match, and Ethel's dated kitchen with the table smack dab in the middle.

As they sat in the car with Ginny holding her breath waiting for their reaction, there was a stunned silence. Finally, Helen broke the spell. "That's it?"

Helen's casual comment landed on Ginny like a kick to the stomach. "You don't like it?" she asked, far too fast. Her defensiveness was lost on none of them.

Ethel always quick to help Ginny out, offered up, "It sho' is a pretty spot. You know, it ain't too far away from my place, as de crow flies. I doan 'spect it's a half mile."

At this opportunity to ingratiate, Ginny jumped in, "I could ride to your place from here?"

"You mean on a horse?" Ethel asked. "It won' take you five minute. We's jest on de other side o' dat far hill."

"Wait, you have a horse?" Sallee asked.

"I'm going to get one if we move here. There's a little barn over there." She pointed to a small barn near the woods' edge. "See? There are three paddocks and two big fields, so there is plenty of room to keep a few horses and even some cows. The woods are part of the property. They are about twenty-five acres, and there is a pond, pretty good size too, over there." She pointed in the opposite direction.

"You mean this is a farm?" Gordy asked his eyes widening by the second as he took in all of the sites his mother pointed out. "It would be *our* farm?" He let out a low whoop.

"Yes, it would be our farm. It's not too far out of town. It has beautiful mountain views." She looked at her watch, "Where is that agent?" she muttered. " I want you all to see the house." She continued her sales pitch, "It is very different from where we live now." She turned to Ethel, "And you are going to love that there are only two stories. Most of the bedrooms are even on the first floor."

Helen grunted, "Hmmm, it looks pretty small for all of us."

When the agent arrived, the children poured out of the car and ran ahead, eager to get inside for a look around. Gordy pressed both hands to the glass and peered between them. "It's brand new! Is it? Wow, we would be the first ones ever to live here?" He was already mentally moving in. Ginny couldn't help smiling.

Sallee wandered around the side, only to return instantly at a gallop shrieking, "There's a swimming pool, there's a *swimming pool*!" All three children disappeared around the corner.

Ethel chuckled. "I think you sold 'em."

Ginny tried hard not to do a happy dance right there on the threshold. The agent opened the door, and Ginny ushered Ethel inside. "Look at this kitchen. Isn't it beautiful?"

Ethel turned around slowly, taking in her surroundings. The kitchen was tremendous, with shiny new appliances and sparkling counters. One entire wall was sliding glass doors, with a view of the pool. The open floor plan made surrounding rooms at least partially visible. "Miz Ginny, dis is beautiful, but yo' ain't gonna be needin' me no more, if yo' buy it." Ginny shot her a puzzled look. "Won't be nothin' fo' me t' do an' dis here house ain't set up fo' no maid. You doan want me in yo' bidness all de livelong day. Won' be no place fo' me t' be, 'cept --"

The children arrived just in time to hear the last of what Ethel had to say. Gordy piped up immediately, "I don't care how cool this farm is, even with a swimming pool, if Ethel doesn't come I'm not coming either." Sallee and Helen nodded their agreement.

Ginny fought back her initial urge to cry, "Hold on everybody. Let's not..." She looked around desperately trying to come up with a logical counter to Ethel's very real and legitimate concerns.

The real estate agent, quick to realize whom she needed to sell on the house, jumped in. "The house is deceptively large." She started a tour designed to counter Ethel's concerns while not in the least acknowledging them, heading through the dining room and into the adjoining living room.

She paused to point out a room that had not been in Ethel's view. "This den or library makes a wonderful sitting room. It is so cozy, with the fireplace and the built-in cabinets." Further down the hall she pointed out a large guest room with a bath and then the master bedroom. "It is so quiet back here," she purred, "large enough to have a very nice sitting area next to the fireplace." And then as if it never occurred to her before, she pointed out an alcove "Look, what a wonderful spot for a desk!"

"Wow," Gordy couldn't help himself exclaim. He more than anyone wanted Ethel to find a reason to be here.

Sallee and Helen remained staunchly impassive as they waited for Ethel to weigh in. Ginny bit her lip, praying that the real estate agent would find a way to earn her commission. When she swept open the door to the bathroom, everyone on the tour was impressed. Ethel said, "I take back what I say. Dis here baffroom alone would be a full-time job t' keep up wit'." Everyone breathed a collective sigh of relief.

Gordy asked, "Where are our rooms?" Ginny and the agent looked at each other and smiled.

"Here, let me show you," she said pleased to have averted a crisis that would have lost a sale. The tour headed down the short, wide-open flight of stairs into a large family room that also looked out at the pool. Three bedrooms opened off the family room. .

"There is no room for Stuart." Helen declared.

"Sure there is," countered Sallee, "we'd still share a room, wouldn't we?"

"I don't think so," Helen stated in her flat voice.

Sallee, surprised and more than a little hurt, could only say, "Oh."

"There's a guest room upstairs that could be Stuart's," Ginny quickly pointed out.

The chatter in the back seat was everything Ginny had hoped it would be. She was glad that she hadn't postponed showing them house because of Stuart's news. Even Ethel seemed pleased.

When Joe showed up at Stuart's room at 4:30, fresh from the meeting with his father's lawyer, he had a lot more to manage emotionally than he was used to or liked. Mr. Pettit's voice never once sounded patrician, but instead flat and nasal. It clearly emanated from a badly set nose that Joe suspected had been broken by accident, since the man did not look like he could survive a brawl. Although his suit was a nice cut, the effect was lost on his dumpy body, and his over-eagerness was more the proverbial beaver than the shark Joe anticipated. The appointment proved to be surprising in many ways, but – he was now reluctantly admitting – enriching on even more counts.

Of course he'd known his father was well off, but never, in his wildest dreams, as well off as Mr. Pettit intimated. In the course of their conversation, Joe had gone from a reasonably prosperous land developer to a multi-millionaire several times over. And now? It wasn't that he wanted to keep this news from Stuart, he just didn't think this was the time to tell her that he had just inherited a fortune. Or maybe he did want to keep the news quiet. The only thing he knew for certain was, he didn't know.

He'd laughed when Pettit gave him a copy of the assets inventory list of his father's trust. "Is this a joke?"

I assure you, Mr. Mackey, this is decidedly not a joke."

"Tell me again, why wasn't I told of the existence of this trust earlier?" Joe asked.

"I made every attempt. I sent you a letter in September on your birthday, as a matter of fact, and another a week later and..." He laughed a little, with a shrug, "...it seems that you didn't feel the need to respond until now."

"I wasn't interested in the old man's money." Joe replied lamely, recalling how the news -- all those years ago, at the time of his father's death -- that the will was "sealed," had struck him: As a final gesture of the bad relations between them. He sighed. "I still don't know if I am."

Pettit failed in an attempt not to look shocked, "Well, as I told you in the letter --" he corrected himself -- " *letters* -- your father was adamant that you know nothing of any inheritance until ten years after your last surviving parent's death and that you also had to have reached the age of majority, defined in his will as forty-six. Those events just happened to happen concurrently. A man needed to make his own way in the world, in your father's mind, so an inheritance was a double-edged sword. It had the capability of making a man settle for less than his fullest potential. Such a fate your father did not wish to inflict upon you." He paused, "I don't suppose he considered the possibility that the relatively minor holdings he had when he died would grow so exponentially and that his attempt to protect you from inherited wealth created a vast amount of the very thing. Ironic, wouldn't you say?" He rubbed his hands nervously, determined to make his point. "Some irony, eh?"

"Just like him, he couldn't get it right." Joe shook his head slowly, still grappling with it all.

Pettit recovered his official professional voice. "He made some brilliant choices in assets, as you can see here." He pointed to the inventory list. "DuPont, IBM, Coca-Cola and Ford Motor Company, Bell and General Motors. All are blue chip, all have had extraordinary earnings and growth since this trust was created at your father's death. It's amazing he'd have picked what he did, in some cases ... Oh, and Dow Chemical, sir -- you are a very rich man."

"You must feel like that guy, was it Mark or Mike Anthony, knocks on doors with checks?" Joe replied, shaking his head again and laughing. "You know, on that TV show -- what was it called?"

"*The Millionaire*," Petttit was back in beaver mode. "Yes! Yes, I have to admit it is exactly how I feel. I have never been presented with these exact circumstances. It is very exciting, I must say." He stopped for a second as if to say something, then thought better of it. Finally he continued, "I'm sure you will need some time to process all of this information. I can continue to act as fiduciary until you have come up with a plan as to how you want to proceed. And of course, do not hesitate to get in touch for any reason. I will leave the funds where they are for the time being, but as I think I told you, the trust dissolves now that the two stipulations have been met. The holdings are yours outright. My recommendation, if you choose to hear --" He stopped, waiting for a sign from

Joe. None came, so he stood up and held out his hand to shake Joe's.

"What is your recommendation?" Joe asked. "Roll it over into another trust?"

"It was, that's exactly that I wanted to suggest, and I would be happy to do that for you." Joe waved his hand indicating in his mind, *go ahead, do it.* Pettit asked, "Are you indicating that you want me to set up another trust? You know we'll need to get together and iron out the details."

"Write it up and send me a copy. I'll get back to you. I've got too much on my plate right now to worry about this. Just make it typical revocable boilerplate," Joe said. "That works for right now. Yes?"

Pettit couldn't help feeling dismissed, "Yes." This certainly is not how he would have reacted if someone told him he was an instant multi-millionaire. *People are strange,* he thought, *and this one is stranger still.*

For Joe, the whole thing was far too complicated to comprehend right now. His father and money had long been sore subjects, and more so when combined. Besides, all of this took the focus off of helping Stuart deal with whatever it was that drove her to practically kill herself with heroin. He still could not believe that his first-born had been near death due to *that drug.* Of all of the drugs she could have taken, it had to be heroin—the very same drug that his father had battled for the majority of his life. He just couldn't get away from the old man. *It is his city,* he thought. *No wonder I left.*

Already this ridiculous inheritance and his father's fears had brought up all his sense of inadequacy, feelings he was all too familiar with, especially in regard to Pops. All of this money and what could it do to help his daughter? Sure it could provide the best doctors, and treatments, but could it mend her hurting soul? Could it make the pain of her childhood go away? What could it mitigate? How was it going to make him more powerful than the forces that put Stuart here in this hospital bed?

Stuart was looking far more like her former herself than she had when he last laid eyes on her that morning. That strained look had disappeared. Her eyes even had a vestige of their old sparkle. Had a mirror been present and Joe happened to look at it, he might have seen the strained look on his own visage.

"How are you doing?" he asked, kissing her before he flopped into the bedside chair. "Feeling better, I hope."

"Ready to leave," she said, adding, "You don't look so hot. Actually you do, nice suit, but you look a little," she struggled to put a word to the look she saw on her father's face, "crazed," and flinched after she settled on her choice.

"Crazed fits." He laughed without mirth. "It's been a hell of a 24 hours. Wouldn't you say?"

"Yes," Stuart admitted, quick to change the subject:" What was Mother doing at your office?" Then she grimaced as she remembered why, and again wished she had made a better choice in topic.

"She came to talk about you. The Dean of Student's called her, remember?" Joe wished that Stuart would shut up. It was hard enough not to rip into her for getting into this mess. To have to maintain his calm and not take the bait she kept throwing to him was close to impossible. *Was she goading him? God, he was exhausted.*

"I had the strangest visitor today," she offered up in hopes of finding a conversation where they could both relax, at least a little.

"Do tell," Joe rubbed his temples and tried to stay present. "Visitor?"

He panicked momentarily. *Did that bastard, Tad, Brad, whatever the hell his name is, show up here?*

Stuart was so engrossed in trying to remember how Dr. Berke started off their conversation that she didn't notice the angry look on her father's face. "This guy, he said he was my grandfather's shrink." Joe instantly relaxed. "He was so good looking. Oh my, gosh, you should have seen how he was dressed. So debonair, so worldly, dreamy in an older man sort of way."

"Dreamy?" Joe sat up.

"Yeah, dreamy. He's going to get me out of her. He's my doctor. Isn't that far out? My shrink was my grandfather's psychiatrist. Nothing like keeping it in the family," she laughed.

"Nothing," he agreed. "When's all of this happening?" He was suddenly wearier than he could remember ever being before.

"He's going to get back to me later. He said it was a labyrinth of law and emotion. He called me a fair maiden, and it wasn't at all icky. Dreamy."

"Not icky, dreamy. Got it." Joe sank back in the chair. *God bless you,* Dr. Berke, he thought.

"Joe, so good to see you again, You don't mind that I call you Joe, do you?" Joe indicated that he didn't. "It has been such a very long time. You were about Stuart's age when we last met." Dr. Berke crossed his book-lined office in three easy strides holding out his hand to Joe. "It is such a great pleasure."

Taking the doctor's hand, he shook it in a vague, distracted way, as he was quite surprised by the man's youthful appearance. "It is good to see you, too Dr. Berke. I couldn't have been more than about nineteen when we last met," he said as he took in his surroundings. Dr. Berke's small office, more like a homey little library, was warm and comforting, with a brown leather sofa and an equally comfortable-looking chair. Joe had expected something expansive, cool – sophistication, perhaps with chrome, rosewood and black furniture, and metal blinds covering large windows.

He noticed a number of unusual books that appeared to be very old, many of them apparently Chinese or maybe Japanese. Small Oriental artifacts lay scattered on the few tables in the room and were tucked in among the books and scrolls. A magnificently carved Chinese warrior stood at least 18 inches tall ruled the windowsill. "Do you speak Chinese?" Joe asked.

"Mandarin, passably," he said, "My father and I left Germany in the teens before the first war – what we now call the First World War -- and went to China. He saw what was coming and wanted to get me out before I was conscripted. He chose China because of opium. He reasoned that since opium came from the Orient, the Orient might hold the key to healing the addiction. I spent most of my late childhood there. It was an extraordinary privilege to be one of a handful of occidentals in China at the time. We came to the United States in the early thirties.

"I remember clearly meeting your father. I was thirty-six. Lee was my very first patient. You know how exacting he was?" He lifted one eyebrow. "When you and I met, he pointed out that nineteen years separated the three of us. That wasn't how he put it. He had some formula -- a mathematical equation of some sort – never my strong suit. I remember thinking how frightening that in a mere nineteen years I would be as old as your father, who at the time seemed to me to be almost elderly. You must have had similar feelings in regard to me at the time."

Joe laughed, "In fact meeting you, just now, I was surprised. I had remembered you being quite advanced in age. Funny about time and our perceptions of it?" He instantly felt at ease. Stuart's assessment of the man was right; he was very urbane, *was that the word she used? Although he is, I'd say he is more elegant – and very much at ease.* Joe mused.

"Please, please won't you sit?" With a small sweep of his arm and a deferential bow, the doctor indicated to the seats in the room "And, please call me Jacob. Your daughter Stuart is charming. We talked for some time today. I was quite taken with her. She is very bright."

Joe sat on one end of the sofa. To his surprise, Dr. Berke sat on the other end, turning slightly toward him, as he crossed one leg over the other and casually laid his arm along the back.

"I wouldn't say nearly overdosing on heroin is indicative of being either charming or bright, but I am glad you think so," Joe acquiesced as he sat on the edge of his seat. "It horrifies me that Stuart inherited my father's weakness for heroin. One dope fiend in the family is enough for a lifetime." He sighed, feeling more like nineteen years *older* than the good doctor.

"I couldn't agree with you more. One dope fiend, to use your term, is enough for any family. My own father struggled with an addiction to the drug. Hence China." Joe nodded knowingly. "He worked with Heinrich Dreser, the head of the pharmacological laboratory at The Bayer Company in Elberfeld, Germany. Besides aspirin, the company gave the world heroin. Funny, did you know that heroin got its name for being considered a *heroic* drug at the time? It was created to alleviate the terrible suffering of tuberculin and pulmonary patients. Its highly addictive nature was initially unknown."

The doctor continued. "Both of our fathers suffered mightily from that ignorance. Your father had contracted tuberculosis while in the Army during the war. I don't know if you knew that." Joe shook his head indicating that he had not. "The heroin he was given to ease his physical suffering created his addiction. My father acquired his in the process of testing the drug for market."

"Where I disagree with you is in your assertion in regard to Stuart inheriting your father's weakness for the drug. The problem, we now know, with heroin is that it is a highly addictive substance. We all share the weakness you speak of."

"Okay if you want to split hairs," Joe started before the doctor interrupted.

"Not splitting hairs -- let me explain," he said with a languid wave of his hand, as he continued, "We are run by our minds. We don't have to be, but most of us have no concept of the power of our minds. If we do not control our minds, our minds control us. One way they do that is by setting us up to emulate our role models. And for most of us that would be our parents." He paused.

"Just by way of illustration, if you wouldn't mind, give me a short description of your father and then of your mother--your role models."

Joe grimaced. He sat back in the sofa and described his father as a know-it-all bully, who had to have things his way, or he pitched a fit and, as Jacob well knew, was an addict. His mother, he said, "meant well. She tried to be a good parent, but couldn't stand up for herself and left the job of child rearing to my father."

"Excellent," Jacob said leaning forward with his elbows on his knees and hands clasped in front of him. "When I spoke with Stuart, she briefly described your reaction to her present circumstances. Would you care to give me your perspective of that interchange?" he said, giving Joe an easy smile. "Only if you want. I think you will find it most illustrative."

"Sure," Joe said. "After I got over the fright -" he fidgeted and leaned back, crossing his ankle over his knee, then put his foot back down on the floor and sat up straight. The pattern was all too clear. "I was furious. I attacked, bullied and found myself acting exactly like my father. I then tried cajoling and decided that I would leave the heavy lifting to you. Interesting in light of what you just said. Does that mean I am destined to be like my parents?"

"That is an excellent question. Our minds operate best, most efficiently, with clearly defined goals. The human mind is a goal-seeking organism." He settled back into the sofa this time propping his feet up on the coffee table. "The default setting or lack of a specified goal leaves the mind to follow what has been instilled or has been learned in the past from our role models. For example, from what you have said, you vacillate between bullying and passivity. Neither works particularly well, but well enough. That's what gets us in trouble. What we have learned works well enough." He paused for a moment.

"My studies of the mind have shown me that if you set a specific goal and stay on track with that goal, you have immensely more power and control over your life -- which by the way, includes addictions." He finished with a nod in Joe's direction.

"I gather this is not considered conventional thought in your field," Joe said.

"No, but they will catch up eventually." Jacob laughed placing his hands behind his head. "I have a highly successful practice, but then I choose my patients carefully. My approach is not for everyone, although it would work for anyone open enough to try it. The problem is that it goes against -- to use your phrase -- *conventional thought*. Although I argue that is a misnomer. It is, in fact, *incorrect group thought,* not real thought at all." He laughed again. "Nobody likes to hear that."

Joe smiled, "I can see you wouldn't be for everyone." He leaned forward. "My question for you: would Stuart benefit from working with you? I see the logic in what you have presented. It makes perfect sense. What I am asking is, would your approach work with Stuart? She's so young."

Pleased with Joe's question, the doctor said, "Absolutely. She instantly understood when I explained to her how the mind works. She was very quick to see how she had been operating under her parents' modeling. Not blaming, but seeing how -- in the absence of a clearly stated goal -- the default setting kicks in, the setting that creates such chaos when emulating your role models. I strongly believe that Stuart would profit tremendously from our collaboration and very rapidly, too." He stopped to wait for Joe to speak. When he didn't, Berke continued, sitting up again, "I would like to make a suggestion if that is amenable to you?"

"I am all ears." Joe laughed, feeling freer about Stuart than he had since long before this heroin incident. He sat back into the buttery leather cushion and casually crossed his ankle over his knee.

"I would like to include her in the conversation. She and I will speak again tonight, and then I would like to suggest that we meet in her room tomorrow. There we can come up with a plan that we can all live with. It would be wonderful if her mother could be there, but I understand that circumstance will not permit. I do hope, however, to speak with her at length before we get too deeply into implementing our plan. Stuart is eighteen and therefore legally an adult, but I feel we can move ahead so much faster if we are all on board."

Joe hesitated for the first time since their conversation began. "I can't speak for Ginny."

"I'm delighted to hear that you know that" Berke laughed, "You'd be surprised how many men are under the mistaken impression that they can speak for their wives."

"You know she is my former wife?" Joe asked.

"Yes," Berke said, "I know. I think this collaboration could benefit your entire family."

"Where do I sign?" Joe laughed.

Chapter 9

Things rarely go the way they are expected to, that was for sure. Often they go better, Ginny reminded herself as she sank back in the chair opposite her real estate agent. Lord knows she'd been unspeakably relieved to hear from Joe that Stuart was much better. Not so with the purchase of the new house. She'd made an offer contingent on the sale of the present house, which according to Sharon, her agent, was standard procedure.

"What am I supposed to do now?" she whined in desperation. "I can't pay the listing price. Already this is a huge stretch for me. If our house doesn't sell I'll … I don't know what." She bit her lip to fight back tears.

"Don't worry," Sharon assured her. "I've been in this business a long time. We'll figure something out. Let's see, how many showings have you had? Hmm," she muttered -- more to herself than to Ginny -- then said, "I'll be right back," and left the room, while Ginny unsuccessfully tried to beat back a rising panic.

"If I have gotten the kids all excited about this house, and we can't buy it, I don't know what I'll do," she said out loud. "Oh God, I hate this! What if someone else buys it?" She felt weak in the knees at the thought. "I should never have taken them to see it." As she talked to herself, she paced around the office, trying to take deep breaths and calm herself down. The clock behind Sharon's desk set off a fresh wave of angst.

"Ohhh -- the AA meeting, hells bells!" She wrote Sharon a hasty note, asking her to call later in the afternoon, and raced out.

Rebecca caught up with Ginny as they were leaving the meeting, "Any time for coffee? Charlie's in school 'til 2 o'clock today. How I live for these days." Ginny couldn't hide her surprise – this, from the so comfortable and competent Rebecca? "Oh, I just mean I can get so much done. It feels so good to accomplish so many things. That's all."

"I can't today. I'm trying to buy a house, and it's not going well. I have to get home in case my agent calls. You wouldn't want to come home with me, would you?" Ginny immediately regretted asking. Even though she liked Rebecca very much, there was something about her that put Ginny off.

"Sure, that would be fun. Thank you. I don't have a car, so you wouldn't mind giving me a lift, would you?"

True to her upbringing, Ginny had recovered seamlessly. Rebecca clearly hadn't noticed a thing. "I'd be delighted. Here we are," she said, standing at the car.

As they pulled out into the street, Rebecca asked, "You don't live far, do you?"

"No, actually – I'm a little embarrassed I could easily have walked, but…lazy, I guess," Ginny confessed.

"Don't be silly! I'd drive everywhere if I had a car," Rebecca said.

"You mean you don't have one at all?" Ginny realized that she sounded far too surprised to be polite. "I mean – I wasn't thinking, it's just..."

"I know, everybody has a car nowadays. I get it all of the time. Not a problem -- I just don't need one. Honestly, everywhere I need to be is within walking distance."

"Do you know how to drive?" Ginny inquired and then flinched for having asked.

"Absolutely, I just can't afford a car. I have a very limited income. It definitely doesn't include owning a car. That's all. Since I don't need one, it works out just fine."

"I didn't mean to pry," Ginny apologized.

"You didn't," Rebecca said and then exclaimed, Oh, what a pretty, pretty street. I've never seen it before." Ginny turned into her driveway as Rebecca gasped, "Oh my God, what a beautiful house! Yours?"

Ginny felt more uncomfortable by the minute. She tried to dismiss it: Rebecca was not judging her in any way; she wasn't the least bit envious. But she cringed when she opened the front door to find Ethel coming down the stairs.

"Afternoon, Miz Ginny," Ethel said. With a nod of her head and downcast eyes, she said to Rebecca, "Howd'y' do?"

Ginny found herself in the most unusual position of trying to decide how or if to introduce Ethel -- something she was just discovering she had never thought of before. Before she had the chance, Rebecca stuck out her hand and said, "How do you do? I am Rebecca Levine."

Ethel reluctantly took Rebecca's hand, gave it a very small, quick shake – eyes still downcast -- and beat a hasty retreat to the kitchen without saying who she was. At the door, she turned and asked, "Can I bring you sompin'?"

"No, Ethel you go ahead and do what you were doing. We are fine." Then, before Ethel disappeared completely, she collected herself. "Wait -- Rebecca, do you want some coffee? On second thought, Ethel, would you make a pot of coffee? I'll be in to get it when it's ready."

"Yes'm." Ethel whisked through the kitchen door, wondering why Ginny didn't want her to serve it. She shrugged and set to making the coffee.

"I'm sorry about that," Ginny said to Rebecca, "that was Ethel. She has worked for me since I got married. I don't understand why I feel so awkward about it just now. I do apologize."

"I understand," Rebecca said. "I'm from up north. Down here people tend to feel judged by us Yankees," she laughed. "I think it is wonderful that you have Ethel and that you have been able to offer her employment all these years. How wonderful for both of you."

"I suppose," Ginny allowed, but she wasn't sure at all. *Offered her employment, what the hell did that mean?*

"Ginny, this house is magnificent." Rebecca eagerly took in the room, seemingly all of it at once. "This silk damask is the perfect shade of gold for the room, with the bold green on the walls; I would never have thought to use it like that. Stunning! You have such a great eye for detail. Your furniture, mostly American?" she continued. "It would make any house beautiful. I confess it makes me a little homesick. My mother collected antiques, but European, and since she lived in the city, she hadn't room for nearly so many. I can't even imagine what kind of house you are thinking of buying that would come close to replacing this one."

Suddenly remembering that Ginny was recently divorced, she stopped short. "Oh God, I'm sorry, now it's my turn to apologize. Please forgive me, I --"

"We are a sorry lot, aren't we?" Ginny laughed. "I loved this house, but it has too many memories. It's time to move on. The new house is brand new, and it's on a bit of land. I can have a horse and some cows. I grew up on a farm, so in a way I'm getting back to the good part of my roots. I am very excited. I think it's a wonderful place for the children. So how about that coffee?" She got up, "I just hope it will work out."

"I find that things almost always do," Rebecca assured her as she continued to peruse the room.

The phone rang just after Ginny had poured the coffee into two kitchen mugs. Ethel stood by watching, *Doan dat beat all*, she thought. What in the world would have prompted Ginny to use kitchen mugs? She started for the kitchen door. "You want me t' get dat phone?"

"No, I'll get it," Ginny said as she put the mugs down and raced out into the hall to answer the phone.

Ethel rooted around for some napkins, unsure of which to use, since she had never dealt with this particular dilemma, the proper service of coffee in a mug. She opted for some linen cocktail napkins and took the two mugs into the living room. "Can I git you a cookie o' a slice a' cake?" she offered.

"No, I am fine, thanks," Rebecca replied.

A few minutes later, Ginny came into the room, visibly shaken. "Oh, Rebecca, It doesn't seem like I am going to be able to buy the farm after all. I am heartsick." For the second time that day she bit her lip to try to stem the tears.

"I am so sorry," Rebecca said as she got up to give Ginny a hug. "I can't image how disappointed you must be."

"Ohhhh -- how am I going to tell the children?" Ginny croaked, doing her best not to sob while breaking free of Rebecca's embrace.

"Honestly, it will work out. Whatever you need, will come. It always does," Rebecca said with complete conviction.

"I'm glad you are sure," Ginny said sniffing as she delicately blew her nose. "Oh, my, look at the time. Don't you have to pick Charlie up?"

"No, I have to be home. She's getting dropped off." Rebecca stood up, slightly panicked, looking at the clock on the mantel. "Oh, dear -- can I impose upon you to take me?" She gathered up her purse. "She absolutely can't be home alone."

Glad to have something to take her mind off her disappointment, Ginny followed as Rebecca hastened out of the room.

After dropping Rebecca off, Ginny slowly pulled away from the dilapidated house, examining the shock she felt when they pulled up. Her feelings of guilt, judgment, and recrimination almost overwhelmed her. *What was the matter with her?* she wondered, *what kind snob was she?* No amount of self-analysis eased her niggling feelings. Rebecca just didn't add up.

The next day in her agent's office, Ginny learned the rest of the story. Sharon was clearly frustrated by the unexpected turn of events. "It seems that Rosemary Taylor was the builder's former wife," she said, with a who-could-have-foreseen-this wave of her hands. "You didn't know that, did you?"

"Absolutely, I did not!" Ginny snapped. "Damn it."

"Well, according to what I heard, she left him for Joe."

Ginny groaned. "So, I guess that's it, huh? Hell's bells, what are the chances of that happening?"

"Small town," Sharon said with a shake of her head, immediately moving on. "I've got two other properties to show you that you might like. Do you have time?"

"I don't know. I don't think so. I don't think I have the energy. What I want to do is have a drink," Ginny sighed.

"Oh, okay," Sharon brightened up, " let's do it! We can drown our sorrows."

"It's tempting, but I don't think so." Ginny got up to leave and then turned. "You know, there is no way Rosemary left her husband for Joe if she's already divorced. They didn't start seeing each other until sometime this past summer. I wonder what the real story is?"

"Beats me," her agent shrugged, clearly disappointed at Ginny's lack of enthusiasm.

"Damn, double damn," Ginny muttered to herself as she drove home. "It seemed so perfect. Too perfect." She sighed deeply.

As she pulled up the drive, she thought about Rebecca and the awkwardness of having coffee with her, that house of hers, her meeting Ethel – the whole thing, in fact. She certainly did have more than enough to talk about for at least a couple of therapy sessions with Janet, so many disquieting feelings. Rebecca couldn't be lovelier, but her life didn't make any sense, and for some reason it put Ginny on edge. "As if mine did," Ginny sniffed.

She had put off telling the children as long as she could, hoping that some miracle would occur, and the house would be hers. At dinner, she took a deep breath and plunged into it. "I've got some bad news," she started off. All eyes were immediately on her. "You know that house we saw, the farm? The man won't sell it to us."

"Why not?" Gordy demanded.

"I don't know, it's complicated." Ginny sighed. "It is silly. I guess it just wasn't meant to be."

"Why not?" Gordy demanded again, more disappointed than he would have believed. "Did somebody else buy it?"

"No," his mother demurred, "I can't explain it, I really don't even know. I understand how disappointed you are, though. It seemed so perfect for us."

They ate in silence until Sallee asked, "Are we going to stay here, then?"

Ginny hadn't thought that far. "What do you all want to do? I'm so disappointed I've sort of lost interest in the whole idea of making a fresh start."

Helen cut a sharp look at Sallee. Sallee grimaced and shrugged. "You aren't going to start drinking again, are you?"

"Oh honey, I am so sorry that you have that to worry about. No, I made a promise when you were sick that if you got better I would never touch another drink." Ginny gave them a thin smile. "It is a promise I intend to keep."

"I hope so," said Sallee, "I don't want to get sick again if you don't. I didn't think I would like the idea of moving, but after seeing that house, I haven't been able to think about anything else. So maybe you should keep looking. Do you think it could happen?"

"I don't understand. Can what happen?" Ginny asked, pleased that Sallee wanted to keep looking.

"Can God make me sick if you start drinking again?"

Gordy glared at Sallee, "You aren't that dumb, are you?" he snapped. "Of course you aren't going to get sick if she starts drinking." His words dripped with contempt. "Sometimes I can't believe the stupid questions you ask."

Ginny grimaced. "Gordy, don't. Sallee has every right to be concerned. I don't have the most stellar record for reliability. When you get God involved, it gets tricky without some faith, and we are in mighty short supply of that, I am afraid." *Again, my fault*, she thought.

"Ethel says God won't make me sick," Sallee added. "Ethel has enough faith for all of us. I just thought I would ask Mom what she thought, is all."

"I have to say the one thing, the most important thing I have learned in all the therapy and AA meetings I've attended, is that questions need answers. Stuffing your feelings to avoid asking the question creates bigger problems. So if you have a question, ask." Ginny inwardly groaned, knowing that she had just unleashed Sallee. That child asked more questions than the rest by times ten, easily.

Gordy looked up, surprise all over his face, "You go to a therapist? Anderson?"

"Yes, I see a therapist once a week, just like you do," Ginny responded, "but not Dr. Anderson."

"Did," Gordy quickly corrected.

"We'll see," Ginny said.

Helen, ever practical, brought the focus back to the issue of the house. "I want to move because I want my own room."

Surprised and a little hurt, Sallee was happy nonetheless, to hear that Helen was on board with moving. She suggested, "Why don't we make a list of all of the things we want in our new house? It could be fun. It might make finding it easier if we knew what we are looking for."

"That is a brilliant idea, Sallee," Ginny said as she leaped up to get a pad and pencil. Gordy gave her thumbs up with a nod of approval.

"I want a farm, and a swimming pool," he announced before Ginny had time to sit back down. "And a dog! A big one."

Chapter 10

Despite the revulsion she felt for the filth of her clothes, Stuart dressed in what she had worn the night she was admitted. She stood with her arms stretched stiffly by her side so that as little of the fabric could touch her body as possible, wondering if the hospital gown might be more acceptable but dismissing the thought. It couldn't take him much longer to get there. Gazing down at her attire she had to laugh. "I sure did go out of my way to piss people off, didn't I?" she said out loud. When Joe showed up with several shopping bags of clothes, she broke out into a big smile. "Hey Daddy," She kissed him, refraining from a hug until she was changed. "I see you got my message. I was worried that you might not have, so I went ahead and put this gross stuff on because that hospital gown was just too awful. I'll be right back." Armed with the bags her father had just placed on the bed, she slipped into the bathroom, shutting the door behind her.

"What do you think?" She asked as came out into the room and spun around toward him, dressed in a pleated plaid skirt, a form-fitting black belted sweater, simple black flats and a scarf around her head. "The hair could use a little work," she laughed. She had slicked it back and used the scarf as a headband to mitigate the look of skunk a bit.

"Much nicer than the grungy things you had on," he grumbled. "Very nice, actually."

"Kinda grumpy aren't you? I thought you would like these clothes. They are more in keeping with what I used to wear. Just a little more sophisticated than pigtails and bobby socks." She laughed. "Did you enjoy talking with Dr. J. last night?"

"Dr. J.?" Joe didn't bother to hide his contempt. "Is that what you call him? Seems a little fresh to me, miss."

She smiled, "I guess you two didn't get around to deciding on a goal for you, huh?"

"No we didn't, and I'm not sure that you should either. I thought about the malarkey he is peddling. I think the guy is a quack, a nut case. I got sucked in at first, but when I had time to think about it, I don't even think he's a real doctor. He went to medical school in China, for God's sake. I decided that the best course of action would be for you to see a conventional psychiatrist. As far as I remember, your grandfather never got his addiction under control."

"China, wow, that's cool. Wow! Strange about your dad!" Stuart exclaimed, sitting on her bed demurely with her hands clasped in front of her. "I would still like to work with Dr. Berke. You did put us together, after all. I think he can make a big difference. He already has. Just one talk with him, I feel so much better about life. What he says makes so much sense." She looked at her father as if seeing him for the first time in a long while. "It doesn't make sense to you?

Maybe you should try setting a goal for your mind and see what happens." Stuart suggested evenly.

Jacob Berke suddenly appeared in the doorway, clearing his throat. "Ahem, I hope I'm not interrupting," he said.

Joe stood up defensively. "Morning," he replied with a grudging nod at the doctor, then started right in before Stuart could set the stage. "Last night I had time to think of what we talked about. I don't believe you are the wisest choice for Stuart. You are too unconventional, and Ginny would never go along with it." He caught himself pacing, sat down, then stood up, leaned against the wall and crossed his arms over his chest.

A nurse came to the door and handed Jacob an envelope. "This is for Mr. Mackey," she said and melted away.

"Hey Dr. J., did you go to medical school in China?" Stuart asked.

"I studied Chinese medicine while I was in China, However, I earned a medical degree in the States along with a PhD in psychology," he said as if he were commenting on the weather.

He carried the envelope over to Joe, who continued, "As I was saying, I think she is too young, certainly, for having any input into where we go from here. I don't know what I was thinking when I called you, since you didn't help my father with his addiction." He was furious with himself for inadvertently letting Stuart know about her grandfather. Actually, he was surprised that Berke hadn't told her. *I guess he wasn't going to crow about one of his failures,* he concluded. *Or did he tell her?* He thought back to what she had just said as he held the brown envelope.

The doctor acknowledged that he had heard Joe with a nod in his direction and a smile. He turned to Stuart and said, "Good day to you, Stuart. You look lovely this morning. I heard what your father had to say. What do you think?"

"Don't even start with your mumbo jumbo." Joe snapped, as he unsuccessfully fiddled with the envelope clasp.

Dr. Berke and Stuart smiled at each other. Stuart started again. "Dad, yesterday after you and Dr. J. talked, he and I talked a second time about goal setting. He told me that kids lots of times get what he says much faster than adults. I'm guessing kids have less time invested in being right." She laughed and leaned back on the bed, propping herself up on her elbows. "Anyway, he said that you might be bouncing off your default 'Dad' model when we talk this morning. He told me not to worry, because he knew you understood the merits of his teaching. You are just concerned for my safety, because you love me deeply."

Joe fought to control the sudden rage that threatened to boil over and engulf them all. *How dare that son-of-a- bitch turn my daughter against me like this?* The struggle not to lash out was overwhelming. Before Stuart had finished all he wanted to do was sit down. Dr. Berke meanwhile just stood casually watching, which only added to Joe's fury. He managed a tightly even tone.

"It is obvious I have been out-maneuvered here, which I find completely unprofessional and outrageous, and my opinion seems to be..." his voice trailed off. He sat down heavily, feeling old and beaten. How had he done this to himself, and how was he going to explain it all to Ginny? He was confronted with a specter of himself at Stuart's age, and of the family he knew then. He propped his elbows on his knees, his head in his hands, looking as defeated as he felt. Pamphlets fell out of the now opened envelope on to the floor in front of him.

No one said a thing for a while. Stuart looked up at Dr. Berke, who smiled back at her as he leaned against the wall, his arms crossed lightly in front of him. Finally she broke the silence. "You know what's funny, Daddy?" He looked up, "I have the same kind of role models as you do, so I know how it is to go from angry bully to defeated wimp." She laughed. "You're the wimp, by the way. Mother is the bully except when you are the bully and she wimps out by getting drunk. Really doesn't make any difference, same dynamic. Don't you think?"

Joe felt like his head was going to explode.

"Watch out," Stuart announced, "he's going to blow."

"Ha ha," Joe started with a sneer. But just as his rancor was about to reach a crescendo, he felt himself detach, giving way to defeat. "Okay," he said, "you've made your point. Stop." Stuart got off the bed and went over to her father. It was too awkward to hug him so she put her hand lightly on his shoulder, trying to make eye contact.

"You are the only one that can stop it, Dad, don't you see? It's what Dr. Berke says. You are the one that has to teach your mind a different way. A way to operate in the world that puts you in control, not your mind! It's outdated. Our minds, they're outdated, they don't give us a good model to work from." She spoke calmly but confidently. Joe looked over at Dr. Berke, who nodded, admiring Stuart's grasp of what he had so recently explained. Stuart was leaning over her father, still trying to look him in the eye. "Daddy, I love you. I promise I'm trying to help all of us."

The doctor shrugged at Joe, with a wry smile. "Sounds like she knows what she's talking about. Might be worth a try. I have found that the younger they are they easier this concept is to grasp. But many people have this sort of response. Clarity begets capability, creating confidence which in turn generates more clarity and on it goes to more and more success."

"Do you think it would help if I told you what my goal is, Dad?"

He shrugged, still looking down at the floor. "Maybe."

"Autonomy," she said proudly as she straightened up, returning to the bed, where she plopped down, stretching her feet out to admire her new shoes. "I had never even heard of the word until Dr. J. and I talked last night. I told him what I wanted in my life. He said that what I wanted was called autonomy. So here is my plan: Before I make a decision I'm first going to ask myself does this move me closer to being autonomous." She looked over at her father, giving him a big happy smile. "If it doesn't I'll make another decision. If I get stuck and don't know how to go, I'm going to ask myself how someone else might do it -- not necessarily you or Mom or Ethel," she added, "since you guys have been running the show for so long. The odd thing is all three of you have played the same roles, just changing up who was being passive and who was being the bully. That's strange, isn't it?"

"Slow down, there Dr. Frankenstein," Joe said. "Why don't we let the doctor have a say in what's going on?" Joe had to admit he liked the change he saw in Stuart. He couldn't remember her looking this happy since – when? Before the divorce, before ... so much, he thought. Since – maybe since she was a little girl. It seemed a little too much and certainly way too fast to be believable.

"She's doing a fine job." Berke said.

"Here is what I want to do," Stuart said with an assertive nod. "I want to go with you to talk to the Dean today. I want to ask if I can re-enroll under academic probation. I want to show myself and all of you that I can not only take care of myself, I can clean up my messes. What do you think?"

"What about that jerk Tad, Brad whatever the hell his name is?" Joe growled. "Is he going to be on the scene? Because I am telling you right now that if he is, I'm not having any of it." He made a move to stand up.

"Would you please stop being such a bully? Brad is not going to be a problem. I used him." Joe sat down, again. "I couldn't deal with being pissed off." He flinched at her language. "And angry all of the time, so I took a -- passive-aggressive?" -- she looked up at Berke for confirmation that she had used the term correctly -- "a passive-aggressive approach to that anger. I wouldn't do it now because I know what I want and more importantly I know how to get there. I want to be a successful, autonomous woman. Brad and drugs won't get me there. Hard work will."

"That's what you say now," Joe replied skeptically. "I don't know if I can trust this miracle cure you seemed to be experiencing. Seems a little too good to be true to me. A little too *Oral Roberts.*." The other two looked at him, confused. "A faith healer," Joe barked, then caught himself. *She was right, at that. The pattern of bullying ... his own family ...* He continued more calmly, "Besides, you don't know if the school will take you back."

"You're right I don't, but I sure won't know if I don't try. I want to continue to see Dr. J. regularly. I don't think I'm *cured,* but I do feel like the fear, and a lot of just not *knowing* has been replaced with some clarity. My hope is that you and Mom can help me keep my eyes on my goal. Dad, what I learned yesterday is the coolest. It is so simple and makes life exciting, not scary. Honestly, you of all people must understand."

He had to admit, that she sounded great. If only he could believe what she was saying and what he was seeing. Glancing down at the pile of papers on the floor he almost laughed out loud as he reached down and bundled the pamphlets for private psychiatric facilities back into the envelope, acutely aware of the irony. On his way out of the door, he tossed them into the trash. Seeing the Silver Hill pamphlet on top of the others cinched the deal for him. How many times had his father gone there? How many times had he come back and fallen into his old habit? He couldn't put Stuart through that hell. There had to be a better way. Maybe this was it.

"How'd I do?" Stuart asked Jacob Berke after Joe left the room.

"You did great." He reached over and patted her shoulder, "When you are talking with someone, it is good to remember that you need to speak their language. You did a good job of that when you said that you have to deal with rage and its counter, passivity." He smiled, clearly chuffed with his protégé. "Be careful not to bully. When a person is rebelling, they almost always pick the wrong target. In this case, your father picked what I teach and me. He tried to undermine it just like I suggested he might. I think your plan is a good one.

"Be patient and kind with your father. He'll get it because you will be modeling it for him. Assuredly he will be watching you like a hawk. And even if he doesn't, you have gotten it, and that makes all of the difference in your life."

"But I want him to get over being sad. And I want my mother to get it."

"All double negative goals, my dear, which leaves you right where you are. Double negative goals momentarily stop your mind. Minds like being busy, so rather than stopping, the mind falls back immediately to whatever the default is." He raised his eyebrows. "Make sense?"

"Yep," she said.

How could you recast those into single positive goals?"

Stuart twisted a lock of hair that had fallen loose and looked at him blankly, "I don't know what you mean."

Jacob smiled, "What would you have if your father got over being sad and your mother got it?"

"I'd get a happy father." She smiled.

"That's exactly it! I want a happy father, is a single positive goal— a clear statement of what you want. Remember: clear, capable, confident. He sat down in the chair opposite her and leaned toward her. "When you are clear you become more capable. The more capable you are, the more confident you become. Look at how you demonstrated that this morning." He beamed at her. "You are doing a great job."

"I don't see how saying I want my mother to get it is a double negative?" Stuart said, tilting her head and wrinkling her nose.

"There is an implied double negative in wanting your mother to get it. What you are really saying is: I want my mother to stop being how she is." He stopped and cocked his head. "With me?" Stuart nodded, so he continued. "The way to turn that desire into a single positive goal is to ask yourself, what would I get if she did *get it?*"He sat back in the chair crossed his long legs and steepled his fingers, awaiting Stuart's answer.

"A loving mother?" She ventured.

"Exactly," he said with a flourish of hands. "I want a loving mother, is a single positive goal! Think of it this way." He stood, crossed over to the window and perched on the sill. "Let's say you want to get a new dog and you have decided on the breed. Before you know it, you are seeing that kind of dog everywhere. Are there just more of those dogs being born all of a sudden?"

"No, you are just noticing them now, that's all," Stuart said.

"Correct!" the doctor said emphasizing the point with his index finger in the air. "In essence you told your mind to look for that breed of dog. So it does."

"So how exactly does this way of thinking help with addiction? My mother is an alcoholic."

"Why don't you tell me?" he said. "I'll fill in if you get bogged down."

"An impressive presentation," the Dean congratulated Stuart. *It wasn't all that bad considering some of the pleas she had heard.* "You have a very compelling argument." She had to admit the kid had done her homework and was putting on a good show. But she had been in education far too long to be taken in by this little show of contrition. *Might as well bring the hammer down on it now, get it over with.* "I am willing to reinstate you," she droned, "provided that you are on academic probation for the entirety of the semester. If you don't maintain a 2.5 GPA, I will have no recourse but to suspend you permanently." She held her breath, waiting for Stuart to start whining about how punitive her terms were. She had seen legions of girls just like Stuart, immature, spoiled and undisciplined, too young to be away from home, much less in the city by themselves. Pregnant, strung out on drugs, all manner of dysfunction showed up at her desk, some with their parents, most without, begging for reinstatement, promising great changes of heart and a newfound dedication to their studies. She had heard it all. If you were too lenient, things rarely changed. It was just plain more efficient to hold a tough line up front, easier on everyone. She puffed up just a bit to steady herself for what she anticipated would be the blow back. There was always blow back. None came.

Stuart gave a little excited jump clapped her hands and exclaimed, "Thank you. I have to run if I'm not going to be late for English." She turned, gave her father a kiss, and disappeared out of the door, leaving her two surprised elders staring at each other.

"I didn't see that coming," the Dean chuckled, "and here I'd thought I'd seen it all."

They exchanged parting comments, and in no time Joe found himself on the street, wondering what he was going to do. Should he just go home? Or wait for Stuart? The latter seemed fraught with more frustration. They hadn't made a plan, not that he figured into her plans, not unless he went along with this so-called doctor. He wanted to kick himself for getting the man involved. But then, he had to admit that three days ago in that taxi, this was a scenario he would not have been able to imagine. It was amazing. Why was he pushing so hard against what would appear to be a wonderful outcome no matter what led up to it?

And then there was his inheritance. He had to laugh at himself -- how many people would change places with him in instant, out of the blue a multi-millionaire? Maybe he ought to go see Berke himself. He had felt good when they talked. Where did all of this anger and distrust come from? Maybe Berke was right: just another inheritance, "Thanks Pop," he saluted the sky. If he didn't go see Berke, he ought to go see someone. He was beginning to think he was cracking up.

Chapter 11

It wasn't until two days after Ginny had seen Bertha that Roberta was able to come by. In the meantime, Ginny had plenty of time to fret over the questions that had begun to plague her, but when Roberta finally did arrive, she was no help. She did all she could to deploy her vast knowledge of community gossip, but came up short.

Of Ethel's three sisters this one had always amused Ginny. She was the epitome of contradiction, possessing two speeds -- very fast and extraordinarily slow. When thinking fast she spoke excruciatingly slowly and vice versa. "Miz Ginny," Roberta now said at the rate paint dries, "C.L. be de onliest one alive datta know somepin'. It wasn' a thang folks took t' spectulatin' on cuz o' Wilson – kin, yo' know, n' all." She shook her long thin face rapidly back and forth for emphasis and Ginny couldn't help but think of Mr. Ed. "Least ways round me, no one say nothin'. I sorry as I kin be I wasn' no help."

"I'm sorry to have you come over for that," Ginny apologized.

"Ain't no problem," Roberta drawled, "good t' see yo' an' ain't seen Ethel in I doan know how long."

"Thanks so much for your help," Ginny said, rising from her seat at the kitchen table where they'd gathered. "I'll leave you two to catch up. It was good to see you too." Knowing that she would have to see Dabney if she wanted any answers, she figured now was as good a time as any. She grabbed her jacket, marched with purpose out of the front door and down the drive, straight to the Dabney's kitchen door, where she knocked before she could talk herself out of it.

Mabel Dabney could have fainted from the shock when she opened the door to find Ginny Mackey standing on her kitchen stoop. "Is there something wrong?" she blurted out before Ginny had a chance to speak.

"No, everything is fine. Hello, Mabel." She nodded at the large woman, and then stole a look at her watch. "How are you? I was wondering if I might speak with your husband -- that is, if he is up to it?" Ginny hoped her wavering voice wouldn't give her nervousness away. "It's not too late, I hope," she added, then bit her lip. *Oh God, did that sound like she thought he might be dead?* "In the day, I mean," she added lamely. The last thing she wanted was to come off as nervous in front of that dreadful man. "By the way, that was so sweet of you to bring those muffins by for Sallee. Thank you."

"It was nothing, but my pleasure. I hope she's doing better. She is a sweet little thing, actually, all your children..." she stopped abruptly, remembering the incident where Gordy was arrested for breaking into their house. She wasn't ever sure what had happened, it just didn't seem like something he'd have done. But that was what her husband said and she knew better than to cross him. "Come on in," she opened the door wide. "I'll have to see if he's awake." Her voice dropped to a whisper. "Ya know he has cancer. They don't expect him to see Christmas."

"I am so sorry," Ginny lied, while thinking, *Serves the old bastard right,* and then felt terrible for having thought such an uncharitable thought and having used such language even if it was only in her head. She hoped Sallee was wrong about God, that He was not a bookkeeper constantly recording earthly actions in credit and debit columns. If Sallee was right, she was in for some pretty big trouble. "If he isn't well, I don't want to bother him." she hastily added.

"No, no, no trouble at all. Let me just slip in to the sitting room and see if he's awake." She returned momentarily and said, "He'd be happy to see ya. Can I get ya some tea, coffee?

"No thanks, I don't want to put you to any trouble. Thank you, though," Ginny said, fervently hoping not have to stay long enough for anyone to make tea. The stench of goaty unwashed male, potent acrid medicines and death assaulted her as she move through to the dimly lit sick room. She was unable to hide her shock when she saw him. Practically skeletal, his once beady eyes looked not only enormous, but also full of fear. She actually felt sorry for him. "I am sorry that you are not well," she said, and meant it.

"To what do I owe the honor of this little visit?" he croaked, his voice thin and dry, his tongue sticking as he spoke. There was a hint of his former churlish ways, but just a hint.

"Is it all right if I sit?" she asked. He nodded and she pulled up a chair by the sofa and sat down next to him. She decided that the best approach was just to get it over with. "I've come to ask you if you know anything about the wreck that killed my father."

"And yer boyfriend too, if I remember correctly." He struggled to sit up to take a drink. Ginny held the glass and steadied the straw, hoping that her hands weren't giving her away. She had no idea that he knew about Cy and was completely unnerved by this startling revelation.

"Yes," she said. It was clearly difficult for the man to talk. She wished now that she had not come. "Do you remember anything about that day?" she continued despite her misgivings.

"There hasn't been a day since that I haven't thought about it," he said. "Yer old man killed those people, ya know. They were niggers, so I guess it didn't amount to too much of a loss, but still, the old man wasn't half bad. That grandson, though, he deserved everything he got."

Visibly upset, Ginny made a move to leave. "Don't go," Dabney practically pleaded.

"I can't sit here and listen to your vitriol," Ginny said. "I would think in your condition you might actually consider the worth of a human life. I am sorry to see you don't. It is certainly your loss."

"Wait, don't go, please. I'm just mad. I *loved* you," he blurted out, shocking them both with his words. "It took every ounce of control I had not to kill that boy when I found out that you two were…" he trailed off, overcome with emotion and a convenient coughing fit. "I didn't kill him. Your father did. I bet he had insisted that he was going to drive home. You know he could be stubborn. I don't know if you knew that. When he drank he was a royal son of a bitch. He picked fights, beat on your mother."

"Do you expect me to believe these lies?" Ginny moved to leave.

"Ginny, I don't expect anything. Believe it or don't. Do you think as hard as it is for me to talk that I would waste my breath telling you a bunch of lies?" He spit and coughed and had to rest awhile before he could continue. "I'm telling you the God's honest truth. Your father was a black-hearted bastard when he drank. He was like that Jekyll and Hyde. I got paid fairly regularly to sit with him and keep him away from your mother. He broke a bone or two of mine back in the day."

"If that was the case, why didn't I know about it?" Ginny demanded. "There had to be enough people around that knew. Somebody would have said something. My brothers would have said."

"And how would they have known?" Dabney asked. "Where were they? In school and summer camp, not at home. Your mother was a smart old bitch."

Ginny flinched at his words. More coughing. She noticed that the tissues were bloody

"But the help would have known," she insisted.

"They were paid well to forget, let me tell you. Nobody wanted to rock that gravy train. Besides, Sam would have fired their sorry asses, if anybody breathed a word. Like

Bertha -- she had all those daughters. Sam told her if one of them ever breathed a word of what went on at the big house, she wouldn't work again. Bertha made sure those girls knew nothing." He was taken over by another coughing fit. Thrashing like a drowning man, he caught Ginny's arm with his claw-like hand. Ginny fought the revulsion she felt. It was all so horrible. But she had to push on, she had come too far now. "What happened? How did the car get so far from the road?"

"I saw them coming. I was walking back from making a delivery. I worked at Maupin's store."

"I know," Ginny said, "go on." He looked up at her eagerly. "Please just tell the story,"

"I had no idea that you even knew I existed." He looked at her with tears rimming his weak eyes. She nodded for him to continue. "I had been hanging around the house hoping to catch a glimpse of you. I went to that house every chance I got. Four or five deliveries a day I if could."

Ginny scowled. "Please go on." She wanted to choke the man.

"I heard the car coming before I saw them round that bend, you know?" Ginny nodded that she did, willing Dabney to continue. "Old man Stuart, he was at the wheel. I could hear Sam yelling for him to slow down. When he caught sight of me he went right for me. He stamped on the gas and came at me. The only reason I am here today dying is because that boy of yours grabbed the wheel and pulled. It sent the car into a skid and round the tree."

"If that's true, why do you hate colored people so much? He saved your life."

"Because you loved him and he was a nigger. That made me less than a nigger in your eyes."

Ginny involuntarily closed her eyes at the harshness of it, her fists clenching at her sides. Then she met his gaze. "How did you know?"

"I saw you two together a good deal more than once. Didn't take a genius to see what was going on," he said.

"I can't even pretend to understand. Thank you for telling me this story. I am shocked, but I do believe you, although I don't want to. I am sorry that you are dying. I wish you well. Goodbye." Ginny got up to leave, hesitated, and then planted a kiss on Dabney's shrunken cheek.

"Goodbye, Ginny." He closed his eyes slowly. "Thank you."

On her way through the kitchen, Ginny paused. "Mabel," she heard herself say, "if there is anything I can do for you, anything at all, please, will you let me know?" And she knew she meant it too, with all of her heart.

Settling back into her dorm room with Miriam turned out to be more of a challenge for Stuart than the interview with the Dean. It didn't help that her father had given Miriam all of her things.

"Look, if you want it, take it," Stuart said when Miriam took issue with her for attempting to put on a sweater that had belonged to her a scant 24 hours earlier. "He only gave you this stuff yesterday," Stuart said. "How attached can you be? Can I at least keep my underwear?" she added, thinking the entrenched Miriam would surely see the absurdity of her position.

"I've had to put up with feeling like I lived in your closet and that creep you were going with," Miriam whined.

"Miriam, honestly how much putting up with did you have to do? I wasn't here."

"I haven't had a roommate since practically the beginning of school."

"Less than three weeks," Stuart pointed out. "I wouldn't think it could have been all that bad to have a room to yourself."

The girl burst into tears, "Four, four weeks. That's the thing, college roommates are supposed to be good *friends,*" she wailed. "They do wonderful things together. Things they talk about for the rest of their lives."

Stuart turned her attention to folding the sweater as she felt her eyes roll. *Great, we have to be best friends forever!* she groaned to herself and fought the urge to say, *So you formed a lifelong bond with my clothes, Got it.*

Miriam wasn't finished. "Things they can teach their daughters," she mewled.

Oh man, Stuart thought. "This is just a guess, Miriam. I was clueless about how roommates conducted themselves. And I'm pretty sure I am not the only person that missed out on your roommate mandate. On this hall, I bet there are at least two other girls who didn't instantly form a lifelong bond just because they happened to share a room. Do you want to bet?" She looked at Miriam's tear-streaked face and smiled what she truly hoped was an encouraging smile, then flopped down on her bed to read her letter from Sallee.

Wednesday

Dear Stuart,

Ethel says I'm not supposed to talk about it, but I think it is ok if I write you. I'm about to bust wide open to talk to somebody about this. The day Gordy ran away, you knew that didn't you? Yesterday. When he came back, he didn't get in trouble so I can't give you any details, just that everything was all right even though he called Ethel a fat cow and told her to shut up. And he yelled all kinds of things at Mom.

You know she doesn't drink any more. I'm glad about that too because she promised God if I got well she wouldn't. That's a promise I don't want her to break on account of I don't want to get sick again. Gordy and Ethel say God wouldn't make me sick again no matter what Mom does, but I don't want to risk it.

Anyway last night Mom told us a story about when she was a kid and how Cy (you know that colored boy she had in her locket, remember I told you?) was her boyfriend and he wasn't colored because Black Sam was her Daddy's brother. She told us about her father and Cy and Black Sam getting killed in a car crash. She said that was why she didn't like Ethel's singing cuz Cy did it all the time and it made her sad thinking about it. I asked Ethel if she thought Black Sam was Granddaddy's brother that was when she told me I couldn't talk about it.

Hope you like school better than you did. Write back soon and tell me what you think.

Your Sister,

Sallee

Ginny went back to see Bertha the very next day. "Bertha, I know you aren't telling me what you know about my father.

I remember that you didn't like him. I want to know why." Ginny looked around for a place to sit. She was determined not to leave until she had the whole story.

"I want to know the truth. I need to. Please."

"Miz Ginny I doan feel right talkin' bad 'bout de dead. Whatever he did, it done died wit 'em." Bertha rocked hard and fast in her chair, looking tired and suddenly very old.

"Please, Bertha, it is important for me that I know the kind of man he was," Ginny pleaded.

Bertha's usual sweet demeanor changed ugly in an instant, so much so that Ginny was taken aback. The soft lines of her face transformed into harsh furrows and her mouth curled up into a cruel sneer. "I hated dat man wit' every once o' hate I could conjure, an' if I coulda I woulda conjured up mo'," she snarled as if she had unleashed a demon.

"He raped my baby sister an' den when she found out she was carryin' his child he sent her away. The wors' part was, he raped my mamma. Octavia was his *own*. His *daughter*. His own flesh an' blood."

Ginny nearly fainted. "Oh, my dear God," she whispered, not for one minute doubting Bertha's veracity. She knew what the woman was saying was true if for no other reason than the story was too wild to make up. "How could you work for someone like that?"

"I had a choice?" Bertha looked at Ginny with incredulity, as if she had suggested Bertha might have sprouted wings and flown away.

"Oh, Bertha, dear Lord in heaven, I am so sorry."

"Ain't none o' yo' doin'. It was the onliest work round. Yo' momma, Miz Bess, was a good woman. I don't know how she stood 'm or why, But dey ain't no understandin' love. I 'spect she loved him. She sho' put up wit' a lot. He used t' beat her blue when he drank. She wasn' takin' care of 'm like de story went. Gen'rally she was gettin' over what kinda beatin' he done t' her de time before. Sam was de enforcer. He made up dem stories. Dey was brothers wit' different mommas. Sam made sure ever'thang stayed covered up; look real nice from de outside. He wasn' such a bad man 'less you crossed 'm an' den yo' best be watchin' yo' back. He would be comin' fo' yo'. An' he was bad. I doan know what kind deal dem two struck wit' de devil, but I know dey struck some kinda one."

"Did Dad… uh, my father, did he do anything to you?" Ginny heard herself asking.

"He tried once. I bit down on him so hard he had t' let go. Drew blood." She peeled down her dress and exposed a shoulder to Ginny. "He did dis an' worse, but he never tried t' lay a hand on me again. I sweared 'afore God I'd killed 'm an' he knew I would, too."

Ginny shuddered as she fought back the rising bile.

"I made sure not one o' my girls knew a thang bout what was goin' on. Sam say I wouldn work no wheres if he ever heard tell dey was talkin'. I had to keep a sharp eye out when Ethel start workin' at the big house. I got t' be a right smart storyteller my ownself," She laughed for the first time since starting her story, cold comfort. "I doan think Cy had any idea. Wilson an' me both promised each ot'er we'd keep de chil'ren outta it. I doan know how, but if anybody could itta been Wilson. Wilson, God bless his soul, was a good man. He loved dat boy like he was his own."

"Did he know?" Ginny asked, "That he wasn't Cy's father."

"Course he did," she spat. "His daddy Sam made up de whole thang an' told Wilson dat was de way it was. Ain't no questionin' Black Sam. He say jump, yo' don't ask when or how, yo' jest get t' jumpin'."

On her way home, as the obscene truth of what Bertha had said started to make its way through the cracks in her defenses, she had to pull the car to the side of the road and vomit over and over again. She didn't need Sallee to work out that Cy was her brother, that her father was a monster and that her life was based on an unspeakable lie. "Oh, sweet Jesus," she whispered. She sat in the car drenched in a cold sweat, her stomach still heaving, watching the descending darkness and attempting to stop the freight train of images Bertha's story summoned.

Seven miles lay between the two houses Bertha's and Ginny's, yet it took a lifetime to get home. She laughed at that sad irony. She had been one woman going to Bertha's and was a decidedly different one coming back.

Pretending that she wasn't numb seemed the only option to propel her back to the house that other woman called home. She knew pretending all too well. As she went through the motions of a human being living her life, she was forced to reexamine every thought, every feeling, every belief. Her entire existence was a lie. Her mind screamed to pull into the liquor store as she passed, promising her the oblivion she so desperately wanted. She resisted, but just barely.

Finally home, she managed with an excruciating effort to get herself out of the car and into the house. Focusing on the tomblike solitude of her room kept her moving toward it. Ethel, dusting in the hall as Ginny approached, heard her footsteps and heaved the door open for her. With a weak smile of acknowledgment Ginny said, "Ethel, I think I might be coming down with something. I have a terrible headache." *It wasn't even a lie, well, the coming down with something was, but she did have a terrific headache.* "Would you mind staying until after supper? At least, head the children in the direction of homework." She was surprised that she had remembered the children, "If I get a little rest, I think I can corral them into bed, later."

"Yes'm. I'd be happy t' stay. Kin I get you anythang? How 'bout a little toast?"

"No I'm just going upstairs to lie down. Would you answer the phone? I don't want to talk to anyone, only Joe. Take a message. If Joe, calls wake me."

Ethel nodded and watched Ginny slowly climb the stairs. "Po' thing. Stuart an' her foolishness done took a toll on her. Now wouldn' dat be sompin' if she an' Mista' Joe got back together again." She ambled back into the kitchen, humming. And then as if she just couldn't help herself she warbled softly, "*O Lord my God, When I in awesome wonder, Consider hmmmm Thy Hands hmm hmm; I see the stars, I hear the rolling thunder, Thy power hmmmm the universe displayed.*" She had to work on not busting out in her full voice for the refrain. "*Then sings my soul, My Saviour God, to Thee, How great Thou art, How great Thou art. Then sings my soul, My Saviour God, to Thee, How great Thou art, How great Thou art! Hmmm hmm hmm.*"

The front door banged open. All three children scrambled into the house shouting and teasing each other. Ethel bustled out into the hall, shushing along the way. "Hush now, yo' Momma ain't feelin' so good. Y'all keep it down. She tryin' t' sleep. C'mon in t' de kitchen, I'll git'cha somethin' t' eat."

"I haven't heard you sing in a long time," Sallee remarked.

"Ain't had nothin' t' sing about," Ethel responded.

Sallee asked, "What changed?"

"I don't know, nothin', everythang."

"Like Cy? You're singing like Cy did."

Ethel cut Sallee a sharp, hard look, "Whad'da I tell you?"

Sallee raced to her own defense, "I'm just saying that..."

Ethel snarled, "Don't you be givin' me no *just sayin'*. I said I didn't wanna hear 'nother word 'bout dat from you. Didn' I?"

"Yeeees, Ethel," Sallee grudgingly acquiesced.

Upstairs Ginny lay down on her bed, terrified to think, upon hearing the children's entrance, that they might come up to see her. But then she knew as long as Ethel was there, they wouldn't need nor probably even want to. She couldn't quiet her mind, which dithered between whispering sometimes, shouting at others – nonsense -- nonsense she couldn't refute. It wasn't just the revelations about her father, Cy and all of those attendant feelings and repulsive images; Stuart also weighed heavily on her mind. That her daughter was a drug addict, any other time would have seemed completely preposterous. On top of this new awareness of the cesspool from which she had sprung, anything was possible. Though she was failing miserably, she did her best not blame herself for Stuart.

Who could she trust? The whole miserable pathetic house of cards that had been her life had tumbled and she was bereft, at a loss to know what to do about it. She probably ought to call her therapist, call Janet, yes -- but it was such an effort. It was such an effort and for what? Too bad Rebecca didn't have a phone, but then she more than likely wouldn't have called Rebecca either, so much effort.

Rebecca, what was her story? Why was she living in that rundown shack in that dreadful neighborhood? Why was she at AA? Who was she? Things certainly didn't add up about Rebecca as a whole, or even in parts.

Did she, Ginny add up? She wondered what her life looked like from the outside and shuddered. A ruin, that's what it looked like, a giant wreck. A failed marriage, a pathetic alcoholic, oldest daughter a dope addict and three younger children who cared more for the family maid than their own mother, not without reason either a real waste of a life.

Thank God, Joe was there with Stuart and he had found that doctor to help her – one that not only specialized in drug addiction, but that she liked. What a remarkable feat. But then Joe was a remarkable man.

That was one thing she knew for sure -- that they could all carry on without her. They might well be better off. Clearly, Joe was handling the situation with Stuart. The younger children were still besotted by their father and would love to live with him. Ethel might even be persuaded to help him out if she were out of the way. It was just all too much effort. She thought about getting up, going into the bathroom, but that too was too much. She lay there wishing she had the energy to do anything at all.

The *brrrring brrrring brri* of the phone yanked her back from the light drowse that had settled over her. She listened for Ethel's heavy tread. *Good, she got it*. Cursing Joe for not calling and the phone for waking her, she crawled off the bed and struggled with the covers, pulling them down, and carefully folded herself back up in them. For as much fighting back tears as she had done in her life, it was interesting that there were none now. Her emotions were stunning in their absence. As if she had cried every tear allotted her, wasted them on the petty little problems of a life that deserved none of them. Now here she was without a single tear left to shed, all so pathetically perfect.

Ethel answered the phone. Bertha started right in without even a greeting. "Ethel, did Miz Ginny make it home yet?"

"Yes'm," Ethel said, "she doan wanna be disturbed. Say she was comin' down wit' somethin'. Want me t' give'er a message?"

"No, doan 'spect she do wanna be disturbed. I think I done said too much. She look like a drowned cat when she left this here place."

"What you talkin' 'bout?"

"Honey, it a long story, one I ain't gots time to tell now. For de most parts, I told Miz Ginny dat her daddy rape my mother an' den he rape my sister, dat come from dat first rape. My sister's boy Cy was Miz Ginny's brother."

"Oh Lord Jesus save us," Ethel sighed sitting down heavily on the chair by the phone. "How she take all dat?"

"Dat's why I'm callin'. I doan think wha' I said done sunk in when she lef', but I shouldn' said wha' I did. Like dat box dat woman in de stories had, once dat lid was open I couldn' stop. Lord, what have I done?" the old lady moaned. "Ethel, I worry 'bout wha' she might do. Yo' know how prideful she is. I took it all away. Lef' her naked as a jaybird. Yo' go check on her, yo' hear, an' when yo' gets de time we kin talk 'bout what I said to Miz Ginny. I pray de Lord forgive me fo' wha' I did. Warn't right." She hung up.

Ethel sat by the phone with the dead receiver in her hand. "Lord a mercy." She shook her head heavily and tried to think.

Just then she caught a glimpse of Sallee and Helen heading toward the stairs. "Where you off t'?" she hissed. "Get on back in de kitchen an' do yo' book work. I'm s'posed t' make sure you done all yo' school work afore you do anythang else. Git on wit' you now. When you finish gwan out an' play 'til I call you."

The girls looked stunned, but decided by her tone that the best thing they could do for themselves was to comply. That old familiar feeling where asking questions only got you in trouble had started creeping back into their lives. They shrugged and returned to kitchen.

Helen whispered, "What's that all about?"

"Beats me," Sallee said, "She's cranky as she used to be back when she was drinking." Sallee stopped, "You don't think?" Helen's horrified look answered the question.

The Washington Post comic pages were spread over the table. Gordy, sipping sweet tea and eating peanut butter and jelly saltines, was engrossed in the latest episode of *Dick Tracy.* He looked up to find Helen and Sallee stealing a look in Ethel's purse. "What are you doing? Do you want to get killed?" he asked in a hushed shout.

Helen shhhhshed, "We're seeing if Ethel's been drinking."

Gordy got up and came over to the corner where the girls were huddled over the contents of Ethel's purse. "I don't know what's going' on here, but you better get that stuff back where it belongs before Ethel finds you. She hasn't had anything to drink in over three years." Helen ran from cabinet to cabinet, opening and shutting doors, checking all of Ethel's old hiding places. "You guys are out of your trees." Gordy couldn't believe the audacity of his sisters. "What would make you even think..."

"She is as cranky as an old bear. Like when she was drunk. She just yelled at us for nothing. Told us to go back in the kitchen. Do our homework, then go out and play," Sallee indignantly informed her brother. "Just like before!"

"That's some hard evidence there. No question she is drunk as a skunk. Do your homework and shut up." Gordy sneered as he whisked the newspaper off the table, replacing it with his schoolbooks. "You two!" He rolled his eyes while he opened his algebra book and dug around in his bookbag for graph paper.

Skip was what Joe wanted to do. He wanted to skip all the way to the Carlyle. He couldn't believe how much better he felt after spending time with Jacob Berke. The man was a genius in casting things so that you could see what was going on. Clarity, he called it. It was simple, actually, he thought as he reviewed the last few hours spent with Berke.

"You are right. Perception is the key," Joe had said. "Look what perception did for my old man." He laughed as he thought of his father, working diligently in his systematic way to place stop gap upon stop gap to protect Joe from what his father assumed was his son's slothful nature. "The man had no concept of me, his son. You can accuse me of a lot of things, but slothful would not be one of them."

"I could accuse you of being slothful," Berke pointed out as he sat across from Joe in his small office. "I could all day long."

"Right, I get it," Joe said, "Your accusation and perception of me doesn't make it so. Just your perception." Joe sat forward on the sofa, not wanting to miss a thing the man was saying. *Had he ever been so engaged?* he wondered.

"Yes." Berke picked up a small piece of what looked like jade from the table next to him and turned it slowly in his hands as he continued. "My perception only has a basis in your reality if you give it one. You are not slothful because you don't see yourself as so. It makes no difference how anyone else sees you. Perception."

"So, Pettit, Dad's lawyer, thought Pops made brilliant stock choices," Joe laughed. "Maybe he is right. His perception, but I guarantee you my old man bought those stocks because they were dirt-cheap. He never thought for a minute that they would amount to much. Theorems -- life was all about theorems for him. He probably even planned that Mother would have had to sell the stocks to get by after he died leaving no inheritance, and to insure that inevitability, he even built in a ten-year time factor giving the stocks plenty of time to flounder and fail."

Joe got up and moved over to a large lacquered oriental chest. "What is it?" He rubbed his hand over the old wood. "It's beautiful."

"It's a Chinese apothecary cabinet." Berke came over and opened a few of the thirty or so small drawers to show Joe how they were joined. "Beautiful workmanship."

"Did you just move this in here? I didn't see it the last time I was here."

"Been here since I have." He raised his hand his index finger pointing up, "Perception."

"Come on," Joe drawled.

Berke laughed. "If you don't perceive, it doesn't exist."

"Not sure I buy that," Joe replied.

"That's good, because it's not for sale." They both laughed. "You see, you don't have the market cornered on the truth. Your perception colors everything; take your perception of your father as cheap and unfeeling. This is how your mind has been programed to see him in all of his dealings with you." Berke took his seat. "It doesn't make a bit of difference that I saw him as a kind and loving man who cared deeply for his family and their well-being. He left you a legacy that you perceive as a series of ironic mistakes because that is how you have programed your mind to see him. Anyone else might see his legacy and the way he structured it as loving-kindness. Your mind is doing just what you have asked it to do: find cheap and unfeeling in all interactions with your father."

"Are you suggesting that if I were able to change the way my mind is programmed about my father things would be different?"

"We'll, things certainly would be less stressful, would they not?"

"So do I set a goal to see my father differently?" Joe asked.

"Try this. On a scale of ten to minus ten rate how it feels to think of your father as a unfeeling cheapskate."

"When I think of him at all it makes my blood boil."

"So what would that be on the scale?"

"Probably a minus nine," Joe said.

"So can you see your father as a Scrooge McDuck and you as Donald? He is counting his shekels and..."

Joe started to laugh, "What do you know about Scrooge McDuck?"

"How do you feel now when you think of your father?"

Joe stopped and thought about his father. Again he started to laugh. "That's amazing. Maybe a plus eight. The anger is gone. What did you do?"

"We just created a new memory for you. I'm still working on this concept," Berke said, obviously excited to share his new thoughts. "My idea is that our emotions about things are based on memories, if we change our memories, I am positing, we can change our emotions. Scrooge McDuck is a mnemonic device. When you think of your father you'll think of Scrooge. How do I know?" He supplied the question before Joe could ask, "You laughed and let the energy around your memory go."

"Son of a bitch," Joe laughed. "How'd you come up with this stuff? This technique wasn't taught in any medical school."

Berke laughed, "Since I was a very small child I could remember things easily. I don't know how I got the idea, but I naturally developed a habit of sticking what I wanted to remember to a funny or dramatic picture." He laughed heartily. "Like a carney at a carnival," he said, "I used to amaze family and friends with my uncanny ability to remember increasingly longer lists. Later I found that what I was using was mnemonics." He looked up at Joe earnestly, "People have been using mnemonic devices for centuries. It's not a new as you think. Recently," emphatically tapping his finger to his temple, "it dawned on me that past traumas were just memories." He shrugged. "Why couldn't we just change the memory and end the trauma?"

"It's brilliant. Does it last?"

"Yep, the trick is to make your images vivid. The more vivid, the more the new memory sticks. The scale is just to give yourself confirmation."

"I'm leaving town tomorrow." Joe said. "Despite the fact that my life might appear as if all is well, it's not. There are lots of complications at home, too many to go into now. I'm not sure Scrooge McDuck is going be able to fix it all."

"You don't want him to either. Different memory, different image," Berke cautioned.

"I would like to continue working with you. Assuming it won't conflict with your work with Stuart." The doctor smiled and shook his head. "Good, I suppose I could come and see you when I need help with this complicated life of mine?"

"You are certainly welcome to come see me. But it's not necessary. What I do can be done on the phone; as a matter of fact I have patients all over the world. I think it would be helpful if we set a time to talk weekly at the start. Does that suit?"

"Yes, good idea. So how did you come up with this mind stuff?"

Berke leaned back. "My passion as a young man was martial arts. I have studied many different types."

That explains the shape he's in, Joe thought.

"They all have at their core mastery of the mind. After I made the connection between power and the mind, I just followed where I was led, applied what I learned -- and here I am."

Joe closed the door on the phone booth, rummaged around in his wallet for the number of the pay phone on Stuart's hall, slipped the dime in the slot and waited. At the busy signal he hung up and called his office. "Reverse the charges, Hey, Judy, book me on the next flight home. It's around nine, I think. Leave a message at the hotel with the details. Everything going all right? Good. See ya later? Bye." Taking out all of his change, he dialed the number and waited for the operator. He put the dollar fifty in change into the phone and waited for Ginny to pick up.

"Hi, Ethel, is Ginny there? What? Oh." Joe was oddly disappointed. "Well, I'm on a pay phone, so I'll call back in a few minutes. I know she wanted to talk. Thanks."

Ethel crept up the stairs, trying hard to keep her fear in check. The stairs groaned under her weight. "Ain't nothin," she muttered, trying hard to be convinced. "These here stairs is goin' t' be de death o' me." When she got to Ginny's bedroom, she had to stand in front of the door stock still for a few moments to quiet her breathing enough to listen at the door. The floor boards protested with creaks every time she moved. She tapped lightly, whispering, "Miz Ginny, Miz Ginny? Kin I come in?" There was no sound in response. She tapped a little louder. Still nothing.

Screwing up her courage, she turned the knob and eased the door open far enough to stick her head in and look around toward the bed. The dead look in the eyes staring back at her jolted into action. She plowed into the darkened room. "Lord, Miz Ginny, wha' you done?" Scuttling over to the bed, she picked up Ginny's hand, sighing with relief at its warmth. "Miz Ginny, you all righ'?" There was no answer. "What in hell am I s'pposed t' do now?" Ethel asked out loud as she patted Ginny's hand. As she stood with Ginny's hand in hers for only seconds, though it seemed longer, the phone rang. Ethel startled, dropped the hand and picked up the receiver. "Hello," she shouted. "Oh, Thank de Lord, Mista' Joe, kin yo' git over now, Miz Ginny's in a bad way. I doan know what t' do. ...You ain't? Oh, Lord."

If she had risen from the dead, it wouldn't have jolted Ethel more, "I'll take that, Ethel," Ginny said evenly as she sat up and reached for the receiver in a dead calm. An unsettled Ethel backed out of the room, quite unable to stop her trembling.

"Lord, Lord, please don't desert us now." Ethel prayed.

"What did Ethel mean you are in a bad way? Has something happened?" Life just didn't seem fair. He had just swallowed his pride, gone to talk with Berke and was feeling good. *Bam! Here we go again. Does the crap ever end?*

"I'm all right, I had a pretty bad headache earlier." Even if she didn't feel it, she thought she was sounding pretty convincing. "How are things up there? Have you found a hospital for Stuart?" Her stomach hurt thinking about her eldest in a mental hospital, *a drug fiend*.

"She's back at school, and I am actually heading home." He laughed. "The story is pretty amazing, actually. It's thanks to a very interesting doctor. You should have heard what she said to the dean. I'll tell you all about it when I get there. Her speech was something. Our girl is quite the young lady."

"What? You said... she's what? ...Didn't you tell me she took an overdose of heroin two days ago? Wasn't she in a hospital? How on earth ... Joe, is this wise? You're coming home *now*? For God's sake, Joe. What about Stuart? Have you lost your mind?" Ginny flopped back against the pillow. "Joe," she sighed, "I don't understand...He must be a miracle worker." She ran her fingers though her hair. "It's not funny. It's terrifying. Yes, you will have to explain. When do you get in? No, not tonight. I'm exhausted. It has been a thoroughly unbelievable few days. You can come tomorrow for breakfast if you must. On second thought, come for lunch." Joe demurred. She groaned. "Okay, if you have to. I'll have to ask Ethel, though."

Ethel, still standing outside the door, fidgeted at the sound of her name, and the floor protested under her.

"Wait, I think I hear her.'" Ginny called, "Ethel? Are you out there?"

"Yes'm, Miz Ginny, I is." Embarrassed at being caught listening, Ethel started to justify her presence on the landing.

Ginny waved her explanation aside. "Joe wants to know if he could have fried apples and some of your sausage tomorrow for breakfast?"

Still on the other side of the door, Ethel brightened up. Yes'm, he sho' kin." *Thank you, Jesus.*

"She said yes. No, wait until 9 at least. Okay, 8:30. Don't you think about coming any earlier." She giggled, "Did you hear me? Joe? Damn you," she muttered as she hung up the phone. With a tiny glimmer of excitement, she climbed out of bed and pulled herself together.

Ginny came downstairs about a half hour after Ethel with newly applied lipstick and remarkably bright eyes. The children were outside. In the kitchen, Ethel had hastily cobbled together a last-minute meal and was just about to call them in. "Who was on the phone earlier?" Ginny asked.

"Momma," she said without thinking to lie and then kicked herself, anticipating Ginny's next question. Deciding on the truth, she answered. "She called cuz she say she done tol' you thangs she shouldn'a. She was worried 'bout you."

Ginny nodded, "Did she tell you what she told me?"

"A little. Miz Ginny, I..." Ethel began before Ginny cut her off holding up her hand and shaking her head emphatically

"I don't want to talk about it now. I might later, but not now. I would appreciate it if you wouldn't say anything to anybody about what your mother told you."

"Miz Ginny, I wouldn' think o' such a thang." Ethel huffed indignantly.

"I know it'll be Saturday, but can you be here a little earlier than usual tomorrow? Joe is coming for breakfast, and he insisted on being here by 8:30. I don't want to have him here for long, so the sooner he can have breakfast the sooner he can leave."

"Yes'm, I'll be puttin' breakfas' on the table at 8:30 sharp" Ethel smoothed her apron..

"Thanks, Ethel."

Chapter 12

As Joe pulled into the driveway at 8:15, Sallee and Helen ran out to greet him, dancing with excitement, yelling "Daddy, Daddy!" They pounced, seizing hands, arms, sleeves in their glee. From behind them, Gordy thought they looked like a pair of rubber balls bouncing back up the sidewalk to the house.

He had run out with the girls, but held back from the bouncing, not that he didn't feel like it, *just a little too old*. He had wondered if he was the only one who still held out hope that his parents would come to their senses and get back together. The greeting Dad was getting certainly belied his doubts. He was glad that his Dad hadn't married The Rose, that was for sure. What a bitch she was, he thought and then wondered why he thought that. Thinking back, he realized the only reason he thought ill of The Rose was because Stuart had said she was a bitch. He couldn't remember seeing her be anything but okay. That's funny, he thought, as he caught himself starting to skip up the walk after his father and the girls. Quickly he slowed to a walk, scanning the area to see if anybody had noticed. He was most definitely and defiantly too old to be seen skipping.

Even Ethel looked forward to Joe's arrival. She was placing his plate on the table just as he entered the house. All her former embarrassment and shame had vanished, she was delighted to realize. "Mornin' Mista' Joe," she said cordially. "Nice t' see you."

"Ethel," he exclaimed as he came over and gave her a hug. Numerous pairs of eyes bugged as he did so. "It's great to see you too. I can't wait to have some of that sausage. I can't tell you how much I have missed it. Well, hell, I've missed all of your cooking. Thank you so much for bringing the sausage today."

Ethel backed out of the room. No matter how pleased she was to see him, a hug was out of the question. *Lord, that man STILL doan know how t' behave!* she muttered to herself on the way to the kitchen. *Folk from de North …even aft' all dese years -- Ummh!*

Ginny arrived just in time to see Ethel's retreat, "What happened to Ethel?" she asked.

"Daddy hugged her," Sallee piped up. "You should have seen her," she giggled, "her eyes bugged out of her head like in the cartoons. You know when their eyes…" She held her hands in from of her eyes waving them around. Helen and Gordy laughed.

Joe asked as he pulled Ginny's chair out for her, "Was there something wrong with that? I was only letting her know I was glad to see her."

Laughing, Ginny said, "Hugging might be a little too familiar for Ethel. She is very proper, you know. Anything outside of her sense of propriety would not sit well with her. But you know that, Joe!"

"I didn't know hugging was off limits. She hugs the children all of the time," he protested in his defense as he dug into his breakfast with gusto.

"It's a long time since you were a child," Ginny reminded him with a little snort. "Besides, you aren't one of hers!"

Ethel arrived with more coffee and a pitcher of milk. Joe said, "Ethel, I'm sorry if hugging you was not the right thing to do. I was excited to see you. I certainly meant you no disrespect. I hope you'll forgive me." He laughed and rolled his eyes. "You'd think after all of these year I would have learned a little since the time I shook your hand at the dinner table. Do you remember?"

"Yes, sirrah, I surely do." She chucked, her jovial mood fully restored. "I nearly fainted dead away. You didn' bother me none. I jest didn' 'spect it, is all."

"So, can I have permission to hug you in the future?" Joe asked.

"Mista' Joe, you is a mess. Why doan we leave thangs as dey is?"

"Okay, no hugs for you then," he said smiling. They both laughed, while Ginny sat at the head of the table, rocking her head side to side.

"I think it's hopeless. These New Yorkers just don't know anything about gentility do they, Ethel?" she said.

"No'm, dey surely don't." Ethel gave an emphatic nod and returned to the kitchen, still muttering – or perhaps it was chuckling – to herself.

Ethel had just placed a second large platter of steaming sausages and apples on the dining room table when the doorbell rang. She bustled out into the hall to answer the door and groaned when she swung wide the big door and spied the agent from two days earlier with the same couple in tow. Barely greeting her, the man brushed, by leaving his client couple clearly embarrassed as they followed, averting their gaze. En masse they headed to the sitting room.

Ethel scurried into the dining room, "Miz Ginny, dey is someone here..." She stopped, not knowing how to continue, hoping that Ginny might be able to cut the intruders off before Joe was any the wiser. "Mista' Joe, kin I get you some mo' coffee?"

Ginny read the distress on Ethel's face and quickly got up to see what the problem was. She wasn't the only one who had seen that all was not well with Ethel. The giggling had died down as all ears attempted to listen for any scrap of information that might be in the wind. Ginny hurried out into the hall as the agent was leading his entourage toward her family. "I beg your pardon," she said as softly as she could manage and still sound commandingly indignant, "Sir, barging into my home without an appointment is completely out of the question. Would you be so kind as to leave this instant?"

"My office called yesterday afternoon and left a message. I regret that you'd clearly not been apprised of the situation, but that was not our doing, I assure you. My clients happen to have a few questions about this --" He gestured in a words-fail-me sweep of the arm, his arrogance trumping his attempt at civility.

"Your message was not delivered," Ginny snapped, her voice rising. "I have guests, and I would very much appreciate it if you would leave. I am going to take the house off the market. It won't be for sale."

The woman looked anxiously around at her husband as their agent began to bluster. "Madam, that is not the way things works in the real estate world. The house *is* on the market..." He turned to his clients and apologized "Don't worry, it will all be fine," he assured them as as they turned to leave. Ginny closed the door, leaning her forehead on it for a second as she attempted to pull herself together. *What else can go wrong?* she thought as she straightened her hair and took several deep breaths before reentering the dining room.

"Everything all right?" Joe asked.

"Yes," she sighed "just a misunderstanding about an appointment. "Not a problem at all." *Sallee, if you open your mouth, I am going to scream*, she thought as she willed her second daughter to resist doing what she was so prone to do. *Just keep out of it, please.*

Sallee was busy attempting to shove two pieces of toast piled with apples and sausage into her mouth as Ginny hazarded a look in her direction. She sighed inwardly with relief and was picking up her fork as Gordy announced, "Dad, you should have seen the farm we almost bought the other day."

"Farm?" Joe asked, "That's interesting," he said, looking at Ginny, whose eyes were riveted on her plate. "Tell me about it," he said with another wry glance in her direction.

All three children jumped in at once, while Ginny stared into her plate, wondering what she thought would happen.

He'd have had to know at some point, she reminded herself, *so what difference does it make now?* The difference, she noted, was that she hated having him know her business, just hated it. Especially under the circumstances -- Rose, the seller, the whole miserable business.

Attempting to change the subject, she said, "Tell me about Stuart and her doctor," then wanted to kick herself, as she recalled the children didn't know anything about their older sister's present situation. *What else could go wrong on a beautiful fall morning*, she wondered futilely.

Sallee having wrestled her breakfast into submission, looked up and asked, "Is there something wrong with Stuart? She said in her letter that she didn't like school. Uh oh..." *I wasn't supposed to say that,* she reminded herself a little too late.

"Nope, she is just great. I was up in New York with her this week. We spent a lot of time together. She loves her new school. Her roommate Miriam and she have lots of things in common, which keeps them both quite busy." He laughed as he thought of Stuart's description of the clothes wars. "I think she is very happy." Ginny looked at Joe with an over-exaggerated quizzical look, but to no avail as he continued blithely, "I want to hear more about this farm. It sounds very interesting. Where is it?"

"It's near Ethel's, about five minutes as the crow flies," Gordy stated matter-of-factly.

"Which road would that crow be flying from?" Joe laughed.

"It's north of town near the river," Ginny said grudgingly. "But it doesn't make any difference. It's not for sale anymore," she added, with a covert glare at Gordy. " It was just a thought."

"That's not ... What's the guy's name? Right, Taylor."

You should know, Mr. Can't-live-without-a-woman, she's one of your little friends, she thought, rolling her eyes.

"Is it new? With a pond and a barn? I know that place. I looked at it. I couldn't get him to come off his price. I thought he was asking too much, and then I heard later it was because he thought I had something to do with Rosemary leaving him. That's funny -- you, too? Even funnier?"

"Yes it is very funny, a riot," Ginny deadpanned. "Very funny, ha ha."

"I have a great idea," Gordy shouted, "why don't you both buy it and we can all live there together?" He looked from one parent to the other, wishing he had just blurted out anything else.

"Good idea son. Why don't we?" Joe looked straight at Ginny.

"Because he won't sell to us, remember?" she said as she folded her napkin, placed it neatly on the table, got up and left the room without another word.

Shortly afterward Joe tapped on her bedroom door, "Can I come in?" he asked softly.

"No, please go away. I don't want to talk with you," she replied evenly despite the urge she had to pummel him bloody.

"Ginny," he eased the door open a crack, "please, I am sorry. That was a shitty thing to do to you and the kids. I talked to them about what I said." Sticking his head in the crack, "I apologized for getting their hopes up like that and making you out to be the bad guy." He opened the door a bit more, "Please, can I come in?"

Oh, that makes it all better. You talked to them and said I'm sorry. Well then, I should be racing into your open arms just like in the movies. "No, please go away. What you did was reprehensible." *You selfish bastard!* "The children have been through enough because of us, especially me. Making it look like I am the reason we can't be one big happy family is just plain mean. Hateful." She started toward the door, thought better of it and turned her back to him. "Leave, please. It was a mistake to have you come for breakfast. Your being here is just too confusing for the children."

He pushed the door open all of the way and stepped into the room. "Why does it have to be confusing? Who says that parents can't get along, married or not?" He came right up to her and reached out to touch, then pulled back. "It seems to me what is confusing is pretending we don't like each other because we're divorced, so that we can justify our decision to get divorced."

"Obviously you don't listen to me. I asked you not to come in --" she turned, surprised at how close he was, and raised her arms in the air, palms open -- "and here you are. Why bother to ask?" Stepping back a few paces, she continued, "Then you tell me about --" gesturing expansively -- "*our* decision to divorce. If I remember correctly," pointing at him, "*you* were the one who wanted a divorce." She jabbed her finger at him with each "*you*": "*You* were the one that painted me as an unfit mother. *You* were the one who, after the judge didn't go along with your plans, brought one woman after another into their lives. Then *you* dismissed your lady friends without a single thought as to how it might affect the children." Dropping both hands to her sides with a steely look, she said, "I am going to ask again, and if you don't leave this time I'm prepared to call the police." She turned her back and stood looking out of the window with her lips pinched between her finger and thumb, offering cold comfort.

"Okay, you're right. I am sorry. Ginny, I love you." He swiveled on his heels and left.

Biting down hard on her lip, she watched him through the window as the children followed him to the car, turning away when he stopped, looked up at her and waved. A blue toile pillow lay on the floor. She picked it up and heaved it as hard as she could across the room, caring little what it might hit.

Sunday afternoon Stuart called. Sallee answered. She spent some time talking about her letter, or at least trying to talk about her letter. Feeling she had to speak in code made the conversation awkward, "Ya know, about you know who?" She wound her fingers through the big loops in the curly telephone cord as she spoke.

"Mom?" Stuart asked.

"No, you know, the guys I was talking about in the letter?" She sighed a lot hoping to get her point across.

"Gordy?" Stuart asked, "Sallee what are you talking about?"

Sallee stole a look around and seeing no one, ventured in an emphatic whisper, "Black Sam and Granddaddy! What do you think?"

"I don't know, honestly, don't have any idea. What difference does it make anyway?" Stuart said, adding, "So what? That was then."

Frustrated that she could elicit no interest, Sallee gave up, at least for the time being. "So you wanna talk with Mom?"

"Yes, actually I do. Would you get her?"

Sallee clunked the receiver down on the table and bellowed at the top of her lungs "M--O--M Phone! STUART!"

Ginny ran to pick up the extension in her room. "Oh darling, it is so good to hear from you. How are you? I wanted to call so…" Sallee heard before she hung up the downstairs receiver. "…so many times."

"Mom, I'm sorry it has taken me so long to call. I want you to know how much I love you and appreciate what you have taught me," Stuart exclaimed the minute she could get a word in edgewise.

When the dam of years of pent-up emotion finally broke, Ginny gulped and spluttered like a drowning victim between sobs, gasping for air. Wave upon wave of finally wept tears wracked her body until she finally put down the phone to manage the deluge. Unable to speak and frantic that Stuart might misinterpret her crying or just hang up out of boredom, Ginny battled to get her emotions in check. She picked up the phone and was just able to eke out, "I can't…" as a new jag of crying commenced.

"It's okay. I understand," Stuart edged in. "It's been a long, hard time for you, and I am sorry for the part I have played in it. I'll wait, you go ahead and cry." She paused. "Well, actually can you call me back? I don't have any more change and the phone is going to go dead any…"

Ginny rummaged frantically in her bedside table drawer for the number of the pay phone on Stuart's floor while blowing her nose with the other hand and tossing another tissue on the pile accumulating on the floor at her feet. Finally finding her address book, she riffled through the pages, ripping several of them in her haste to find Stuart's number. With shaking hands she dialed zero, and waited for the operator, "I want to make a long distance call." Her breath was coming in stuttering gasps; she gave the woman the number as she tried to calm herself. Finally Stuart answered. "Stuart?" Ginny gasped, "Is that you? I can't tell you how much I love hearing from you. You sound so well, so happy. I don't understand what happened this last week, but whatever it was, I am so grateful that you're okay – no, that you're fine!" Ginny stood up, then sat back down on the bed, unable to light in one place, still sniffing occasionally. "Thank you for calling – thank you for saying what you did – I can't believe it, I can't tell how much this means! I love you too -- so much – I'm so sorry for all the awful things I've done and said -- Ohhh." She sniffed a few times, wiped her nose and continued, "I have been so worried since your father called me the other night."

"I know -- I'm so sorry – really, I am. I'm not angry with you. I never was. It wasn't you." Ginny stood up, blew her nose, sat down and then stood again while Stuart continued.

"You were just the easy target, I know that now, and I promise it won't happen again. Well, I hope it won't," she quickly amended, with a rueful little laugh, "but I might fall back into a bad habit every once in a while, and if I do, I want you to promise to help me get back on track."

Stuart paused, then went on. "Another thing, Mom, Sallee told me about Cy, the stable boy, and your father dying in that accident, and all that. I never knew. I can't imagine how horrible that must have been for you."

Ginny broke in. "Stuart, why don't we let that be our little secret? You know Sallee likes to tell tales. I am sure she said far more than was..."

"No," Stuart stated unequivocally, "secrets are harmful. They keep things in the dark. Dr. J. says keeping secrets continues the trauma from one generation to the next. He said it was probably the worst thing that happened to any of us, keeping secrets."

"Oh," was all that Ginny felt safe saying. She felt like a little girl reprimanded for a wrongdoing, but she bit her tongue while fuming inwardly. *I can't stand that,"Dr. J.' foolishness, so unprofessional. Why in the world would someone go to the trouble of earning the title of doctor and then want to be called by an initial? How could secrets be bad? Especially if you save someone from getting their feelings hurt!* Happily, her daughter seemed oblivious to the effect her words had had, and Ginny manage to contain herself as Stuart promised to call soon and often before saying goodbye.

Just after the phone call, despite the feelings that the sense of being scolded had triggered, Ginny was elated that

Stuart sounded so happy, so seemingly well. But in no time, doubt crept in. It was just a little too good to be true, and in her experience, good didn't last nearly long enough. So she steeled herself for the other shoe to drop. *Nice while it lasts*, she thought, and on the tail of that thought, *Damn it, Sallee, I wish you would learn to keep your mouth shut. Oh, how could I have been so stupid as to tell the children my suspicions about my father? Particularly Sallee, who couldn't keep a secret if her life depended on it?* Another thought landed like a two-by-four. *Oh, God, she's going to tell Joe. Sweet Jesus, I've got to talk with that girl, and now!*

In her search for Sallee, she first checked the girls' room, then started toward the kitchen, until she remembered that it was Sunday and Ethel wouldn't be there. Out in the hall she called, "Sallee, Sallee?" There was no answer. The house was wrapped in a deep stillness and showed no sign of any of the children. As she hurried from front to back and circled back, checking outside at every window and door, she turned up nothing. A cold blast of a late October wind cut through her thin silk blouse, stinging her bare arms as she headed out of the front door. "I don't suppose it will do anybody any good if I catch my death of cold," she said out loud, and stopped. Turning back to retrieve a coat, she was suddenly bemused at the about-face in her mood from a two days earlier. As she struggled to put on her coat and close the door behind her, she noticed all three children loping across the leaf-strewn front lawn in her direction. Her arm by its own volition raised and waved gaily at them. Spontaneously, as if it were her lifelong practice, she gave a prayer of thanksgiving for them. Startled by the spontaneity of the deed and ashamed of the realization that this was the first time she had ever been aware that she was grateful for her children, she allowed her tears of gratitude and shame to flow freely.

Chapter 13

Monday morning, first thing, Ginny closed herself in her small study, sat down at her vintage rosewood desk and called her real estate agent. "I want to take the house off the market. I can, can't I?" she asked.

"Funny that you called!" said Sharon. "I was literally reaching for the phone, to call you. I have a full price cash contract for your house sitting here on my desk. They are willing to work with you on a closing date as far as six months out. You don't often see a full freight cash contract and flexibility on the closing, too."

Ginny groaned, "Oh no, now, what am I going to do? What happens if I don't accept the contract?" She twiddled a pencil on the desk as she gazed out of the window, seeing the scarlet sugar maple for what seemed like the first time. *That tree brings out the draperies beautifully, she thought. It must have been fall when I picked out that fabric. The coral is the same in the print. Well done, me!* She looked around. *I always did like the color of this room, such a lovely shade of blue, she thought as she half listened to Sharon.*

"It depends. You could be sued," Sharon said. "It will definitely cost you money, at least the commission. Look, why don't we see if we can get the Taylor property? You'll have cash with this sale. Your present mortgage is practically nothing. The kids loved the place."

"Oh," Ginny moaned, "you won't believe who else made an offer on that place." Ginny's pencil seesawed rapidly between her thumb and forefinger. "Bring over the contract. I'm going to live dangerously."

"Okay great. I'll be over in less than an hour. Who?"

"Joe," she groaned. "I'm not sure I even want it now … Just kidding!" she quickly added with a laugh, hearing the stunned pause on the other end. The pencil was now spinning on the desktop.

"Whew!" Sharon shot back, starting to laugh as well. Then, recouping her business demeanor, "They met every single stipulation. Let me talk to Taylor's agent. I'll call you back." She hung up, leaving Ginny to stare at the dead phone in her hand and wonder what she had just done.

But within the hour, Sharon was walking out of the door with Ginny's signature fresh on the contract to sell.

Back in her office five minutes after dropping off a copy of the signed contract, she was calling Ginny again. "You are going to kill me. The Trainer place has a cash contract on it, full price too. Wow, what a market! Let me get some properties together. Are you going to be around this afternoon? I'll call you after I do some digging. Bye."

A pencil lay on the desk in two pieces as Ginny left the room.

"Ethel I'm going to a meeting. Do you need me to get anything?" Ginny called into the kitchen on her way by.

Ethel came to the door wiping her hands on a dish towel, "No'm. Mista" Joe looked right smart d' other mornin'. Sure was good t' see 'im." She was hoping that Ginny had some time to talk and would be so inclined.

"I suppose," Ginny said. "Do you need anything? The meeting is just an hour, and I have no other plans. Do we have any bacon? I'd love to have one of your opened-faced tomato, cheese and bacon sandwiches for lunch."

"We do," Ethel nodded. She wouldn't have said so, and might not have been consciously aware of it, but Ethel knew in her soul that she could by sheer force of will create her desired outcome, so risking impertinence, she asked, "Would you be brangin' anybody home?" She hoped with all her heart that the answer would be, *Yes, Joe*.

"No, just me. See you in a little bit." Ethel turned slowly back to the kitchen and started humming to herself, then as Ginny pulled out of the driveway, singing full voice. *Hear the word of the Lord! Hmmmhmhmhmmm, hear the word of the Lord! Wouldn't that be jest somethin' if Miz Ginny and Mista' Joe got back together. Hmmmhmhmhmmm.*

She was vacuuming the living room when the doorbell rang. As she peeked around one of the sidelight curtains, she saw a man she didn't recognize standing at the door and two cars in the drive. She opened the door just a crack. "Yes," she said warily, "kin I help you?"

"Is this the Mackey residence?" the man asked.

"It is," Ethel allowed.

The man stuck out his hand to give Ethel something. She looked him up and down suspiciously. "Would you please give these to Miz Mackey," he said, "tell her compliments of Mista' Mackey." He turned on his heel and loped down the stairs. In no time he had climbed into the passenger seat of one of the cars and was gone, leaving a brand new metallic green wood-sided station wagon parked in the drive.

Ethel looked down at her hand where the man had put two leather-bound sets of car keys. "Lawsy," Ethel said softly "Mista' Joe is on de path. Thank ye, Jesus. My, my, dat is one mighty fine-lookin' car." She opened the front door wide and bustled out into the sunshine. Looking from the front porch didn't assuage her curiosity, so she walked down the path and circled the car, finally opening a door and peering inside. "Um umm, I love dat smell. Oh my, look at dese fine seats," she said, cautiously touching the deep tan leather upholstery. "Mista' Joe sure do know how t' go a-courtin' when dey's a strong-minded lady on t'other end."

Ethel hadn't been back in the house ten minutes before Ginny walked through the front door. "Hello," she called, "Ethel?"

Ethel turned off the vacuum and scurried out into the hall to greet her. "How do, Miz Ginny?"

"Whose car is that out there?" Ginny asked.

"A man come by an' he leave dese here." She fished around in her uniform pocket to pull out the two sets of keys. "He say, 'Give dese here to Miz Mackey. Tell her complimen' of Mista' Mackey.'" From Ethel's beaming face, you would have thought that she'd bestowed the gift.

"What?" Ginny practically shrieked. "Damn him to *hell.*" She marched past Ethel to the back hall, picked up the phone and started to dial.

Ethel stood looking down at the keys in her hand. "If dat doan beat all," she murmured, as she put the keys down on the mahogany hall table and headed back to the kitchen. "I never," she told herself emphatically. She was tempted to eavesdrop but thought better of it. The vacuum whirred back into service as Ginny informed Joe in no uncertain terms that she was not for sale. "And you will please have that – that *car* removed immediately," she concluded, just south of a full-on shriek.

"Calm down, Ginny, please," Joe pleaded urgently. "I'm not trying to buy you. Please. I wouldn't dare. Please just let me explain. While I was in New York, I found out I had come into a little money. I just wanted you and the children to have the advantage of some of my father's largesse. You're driving a six-year-old car. It's past time for a new one. This is the safest car on the highway. I don't expect anything at all from you. You don't even have to say thank you." He winced involuntarily at the sound of the phone being slammed down full force on the other end. "Ugh," he muttered. "When will I ever learn?"

Ginny came and went several times that day, leaving the new car exactly where it had been delivered.

Helen and Sallee got off the bus together, chatting about some goings-on at school and so engrossed that the car didn't register. Gordy was another matter. "Whoa," he yelled, as he banged into the house, "whose car is that out there. It's a beaut. Is it Stanley's?" he asked incredulously. The girls ran to the window and looked out at the car and the neat piles of leaves Stanley was raking into a tarp.

Ethel busied herself at the sink. "Y'all want somethin' t' eat? Wha' kinda foolishness you talkin' 'bout? Dat ain't Stanley's car an' he ain't here. You know dat. Ha ain't been workin' here fo' years now."

"Is too." Gordy insisted, "See for yourself. Whose car, then?" he repeated.

Floundering for a truth, she lighted on, "I doan know nothin' bout Stanley." Then with a shrug, "Some man jest lef' de car here dis mornin'."

"Man?" Gordy asked.

"Boy, would you get t' doin' yo' book work an' stop askin' so many questions. I tol' you I doan know nothin'."

Sallee and Helen gave each other, then Gordy, a knowing look while Sallee nodded to them to follow her. "I'm going upstairs to do my homework," she stated as casually as she could, considering what she thought she knew.

One after another they slipped away until Ethel was left standing alone in the kitchen, wondering how things could get so complicated so fast. "And where in de worl' did Stanley come from?" she said as she looked out the window.

"I told you she was drinking. Boy, what a grump," Sallee pronounced. "Whose car do you think it is, anyway?"

"Probably just some friends of Mom's?" Helen said.

"Yeah, but Ethel said some man..." Sallee insisted. "Where did Gordy go?"

Helen shrugged her shoulders, "I don't know. She could have a man that's a friend. Couldn't she?"

"I guess," Sallee acquiesced, looking out at the car. "There he is." She pointed to Gordy, who was prowling around the car looking in every window. She ran out of the room without a word to Helen.

The two of them each opened a door. "It's brand new," Gordy exclaimed, "Smells so good. I wonder how they do that?"

"Do what?" Sallee asked, already luxuriating in the passenger seat.

Gordy climbed into the driver's side and shut the door. It thunked solidly closed. "Make new cars smell so good. Man, look at the odometer. There are only five miles on this car. Wow, it is brand spanking new. I wonder who it belongs to? Do you think Mom bought a new car?"

"If she did, why would she be driving her old one?" Sallee asked. "That doesn't make any sense."

"Yeah," Gordy thought for a minute, "maybe she ordered it, and it just came, and she doesn't know it's here yet."

"Yeah, maybe so," she agreed as she waved to Stanley, who passed by, dragging a leaf-filled tarp. He nodded as he too checked out the new car.

Helen emerged from the house and was soon ensconced in the back seat, admiring the new car smell while investigating the tiny ashtrays in the door.

"I told you she was drinking," Sallee sneered. "You can always tell cuz she's snappish. Remember?"

"I don't know," Gordy said from behind the wheel. "Maybe. There is definitely something going on. That's for sure. I think it has something to do with this car." As he spoke, he fiddled with the gearshift. He moved the handle out of park to neutral. Parked on a slight incline, the car immediately started to roll. All three children screamed. Gordy tried to force the lever back into park, but it wouldn't go.

"Put on the brakes, put on the brakes!" Sallee shouted, finally resorting to screaming, "The brakes!"

With Helen's bloodcurdling shrieks in the background, Gordy panicked. His brain refused to cooperate as the car careened into a tree down the bank behind them. Three heads bounced off the seat backs and Helen's teeth chomped down on her tongue. Blood trickled out of her mouth and down her front. Ethel meanwhile was lumbering alongside the car, gasping for breath, and yanked open the back door, swiftly assessing Helen's condition before pulling her carefully out of the car. Speechless, she said with a single look all that the two in the front seat needed to hear. Without a word, they gingerly removed themselves from the car and scurried into the house. A silently bleeding Helen, clenched in a panting Ethel's grip, followed.

Still heaving to catch her breath, Ethel glared up the stairs at Sallee and Gordy. They had silently deduced that going to their rooms would be vastly superior to the tongue-lashing they were in for. Both hoped they'd reach safety before Ethel regained the use of her voice, or worse yet, their mother came home.

Without slacking her vise-like grip on Helen's wrist, Ethel, still gasping, half-dragged her to the kitchen sink and began scrubbing and patting her face and dress with cold water, ignoring whimpers of protest.

Upstairs, Sallee and Gordy moaned as they heard their mother's car coming up the drive. Ginny rushed into the kitchen, crying out, "What happened?" She stopped short when she spied Helen, still bloody, damp and wailing. "Oh, dear God! Honey, are you all right?" Ethel, still huffing for breath, stopped scrubbing for a moment and sought to reassure Ginny. "She all righ'. *She* all righ', but --"

Helen interrupted, wailing and a little garbled from the swelling in her mouth. "My tongue, my *tonnngue*, I bip my tongue in the wreck."

Ethel shook her head vigorously, "No wreck." She waved her hand in front of her face and gasped again, "No wreck."

"Are you sure you are all right, Ethel?" Ginny asked as she peeled Ethel's fingers from around Helen's wrist. "You stay here and catch your breath. I'll tend to Helen. Where are the other two?" she asked Helen as sternly as she could under the circumstances. "Something tells me they had something to do with this." Helen nodded emphatically in the affirmative. "Oh, what am I going to do with you kids?" Ginny groaned.

"Halloween! *Not* Halloween, oh puhleeeeze? I was going to be a convict," Gordy whined.

Ginny laughed at his choice of costume. *Fitting*, she thought

"This is my last year," he protested, ignoring her laugh. "You can't trick or treat after fifteen. Can't you punish me some other way, please please *please*? George and I had the whole night planned."

"Gordy, you should have thought about all of that before you wrecked the car." Ginny said.

"Mom, I didn't get into the car with the idea that I was going to wreck it. It was an accident. Is Sallee going to be able to go out for Halloween?"

"No, none of you are. None of you should have been in that car. It wasn't yours. You didn't know who it belonged to and now because of your trespass it's no longer..." She stopped. She didn't want to go into whose car it was and why she was planning on returning it.

"Whose car is it, anyway?" Gordy asked.

"Never you mind," Ginny snapped. "Do you have an alternative punishment that you would like me to consider?"

Shocked, Gordy said the first thing that came into his mind. "I could spend every day after school in my room for a month."

"I'll consider it. I forgot to call Dr. Anderson to cancel your appointment for tomorrow. I think it would be better if you and I went together and talked with him anyway. What do you think?" she asked, glad to change the subject.

"Okay. I don't think he does any good. But as punishment I could continue seeing him if you wanted," he offered, having just considered the magnitude of his first suggestion. "Just a couple more times," he added hastily.

"Somehow seeing a therapist as punishment seems counterproductive," she said.

"I guess," he said. "But if I have to stay in my room, then Helen and Sallee have to, too?"

"That is not for you to worry about, young man. I can't tell you how disappointed I am. You do understand that cars are dangerous?" He nodded." Not playthings?" He nodded again. "And very expensive?" Another nod.

"I have an idea. I could work off the cost of fixing the car," he said eagerly. "What do you think?"

"That's a good idea," she said. "I have to find out how much it is going to cost. I'm still going to think about the other options, though. Since you took the car out of gear and are the oldest, you are the most responsible, but none of you should have been in that car. Your father and I will have to talk about this. I'll let you know. Meanwhile get your homework done and until I come up with a plan, no TV." She got up to leave, but turned and gave him a hug instead. "I'm glad you weren't hurt."

Downstairs in the girls' room a similar conversation took place. Sallee offered to practice piano every day for an hour rather than miss Halloween. Helen said, "I don't see why I have to be punished. I bit my tongue, that should be enough."

"Young lady, had you not been in the car in the first place you wouldn't have bitten your tongue," Ginny pointed out.

"Yes'm," Helen conceded grudgingly, then switched to a whimper. "But I already practice piano for an hour every day." Sallee rolled her eyes but refrained from commenting. Helen sniffed, adding, "I guess I could practice *two* hours every day." Sallee couldn't help the groan that escaped her. "No, I'll just stay in my room for a month. I don't mind doing that," Helen decided.

"This isn't a smorgasbord. You don't get to pick the most appealing punishment. The purpose of punishment is to teach you to make better choices in the future," Ginny sighed.

Sallee said, "I liked it better when you just yelled at us or hit us. Then it was over, and we could just be mad at you. Didn't have to think so much."

Ginny flinched "Well, I didn't. I'm glad you weren't hurt. Get your homework done and no TV." She kissed them both.

———

"Joe, I hate calling you about this. I don't know what to do," Ginny said. "It's that blasted car of yours. The children were in it this afternoon. Gordy pulled the shift lever into neutral and it rolled down the hill and hit a tree. No one was hurt," she added quickly. "Well, Helen bit her tongue and Ethel practically had a heart attack, but other than that they are all fine." She sighed. "It's the damn car. I don't know what kind of damage was done. I haven't looked yet. I..."

Joe broke in, "I'm coming over. See in you in a few minutes." The phone went dead.

"Hells bells," Ginny swore as she hung up the phone. "That was not what I wanted to happen. Damn it, Joe." She sighed again.

Down in the kitchen Ethel was breathing normally when Ginny walked in. "Are you all right?" she asked and started to laugh. "You had me scared there for a bit."

"*You* was scared?" Ethel said. "I thought I was a goner. I just couldn' catch my breath. I was standin' lookin' out da winda at Stanley pickin' up leaves when I saw de car start t' roll. I knew righ' away wha' was goin' on. Doan 'member runnin' so fast ever befo' as I did. Like t' scare me t' death seein' dat car pickin' up speed wit' de chil'ren inside. Den de blood. I doan know how I didn' have a heart 'tack."

"You are fine now?" Ginny asked, then, "What do you mean Stanley was picking up leaves? You know as well as I do Stanley hasn't worked here in at least two years now."

"He was here dis day. See fo yo'self. Ain't a leaf in de yard 'cept what's left on de trees.".

Ginny went to the window and surveyed the yard. "Oh, damn."

Ethel looked at her quizzically but decided she best keep her mouth shut.

When Joe walked in the kitchen a few minutes later, Ethel had hard time not sashaying over and hugging him. "Well, if dat doan beat all," she said, then asked without thinking, "Is you stayin' fo' dinner?" She regretted it immediately when she saw the fire flash in Ginny's eyes. Not knowing how to extricate herself, she set to the task of fixing the meal.

"I looked at the car," he said, "And I think there is more damage to the tree." He laughed, "They couldn't have been going too fast." Ethel grunted. "Come out and look. If you give me the keys I could put back in the parking spot." Ginny shot a questioning look at Ethel.

"De hall table," she said, and quickly diverted her eyes back to the sink.

Ginny followed Joe out into the hall. "Since it's your car, I want to talk to you about an appropriate punishment, for the perpetrators." She couldn't help but laugh.

"It's your car. I already told you. Hey Gordy," Joe said.

"It's Mom's car? Cool. I'm sorry I broke your car, Mom," he said looking at Ginny, then turning to Joe, "...and Dad."

"It's not, Gordy. Never mind. Would you go watch TV." Ginny groaned.

"But you said..."

"Never mind what I said, go watch TV," Ginny insisted, "Now!"

As their parents went out to look over the damage, Sallee and Helen came into the kitchen. "Where's Gordy?" Sallee asked.

"In watching de TV," Ethel said. "Doan go nowhere, dinner'll be ready in two shakes o' de lamb's tail. Early's here so I's gonna put it on de table an' leave. Helen, would you set de table?"

Helen groaned, clomped over to the sideboard, and pulled out the utensils, slamming the drawer shut with her elbow.

"Okay, I'll go get Gordy. Is Mom having dinner? I don't guess this early," Sallee said, answering her own question. In the den she said, "You are goin' to get into some big trouble. She told us we couldn't watch it."

Gordy, enthralled with *Hogan's Heroes,* waved her away.

Put off by his lack of interest in her wisdom, Sallee marched over to the TV and turned it off. "Ethel says dinner is ready. Besides, you're going to get in trouble if you get caught. I'm doing you a favor."

"For your information, I was told to go watch TV," he said, flicking the program back on. "There's only a few more minutes. Tell Ethel I'll be right there."

Sallee stood rooted to the floor, watching the screen. "How come you get to watch and Helen and I don't? That's not fair! You were the one that wrecked the car."

Just then Helen appeared, "Damn it," she roared. Both siblings' heads spun in her direction, jaws agape. "I've had it! Not fair! You get to watch TV. You wrecked the car. I got hurt. I have to stay in my room. I'm watching the *Flintstones* tonight, and I don't care what anybody has to say about it." She stomped out of the room, snapping over her shoulder, "And by the way, dinner is on the table. Ethel says you better get in there."

Joe walked around to the back of the car to make sure nothing was hanging off, then got in and pulled it back into the parking space. Ginny watched from the walk, arms folded. When he got out of the car, she said, "Since you're here, I would like to talk about what kind of punishment you think is in order." She shivered, her thin sweater hardly a match for the falling temperature.

"Let's go for a ride," Joe said, still at the wheel. "Hardly a scratch on it. This baby is built like a Sherman tank." He laughed, "But look at the tree." She looked up to see hatch marks on the trunk where the bumper, now sporting a single small dent, had hit.

"I don't know. Ethel is just leaving. There's Early." She waved, realizing that he had been watching them the whole time they were outside.

"The kids can stay by themselves. We won't be gone long. If we stay here we won't have a moment's peace to talk," he said.

"Well, let me go tell them and get a coat," she said, turning back toward the house.

Joe insisted, "Come on, we'll just go."

She gave up and climbed into the passenger seat. "Oh, my, what a lovely interior," she said. "Look at these seats," She ran her hand over the soft tan leather, then reached for the door. "I need to get out. If I stay in here another minute, I won't be able to resist the temptation."

Joe quickly started the engine and slammed it into gear. "Too late, I got ya now," he laughed. "You deserve a beautiful car. I don't understand. What's the problem?"

"That's the thing, Joe, I don't. It's a long, complicated story, but, believe me, I don't," she insisted.

He picked up her hand, "Ginny, you have been too hard on yourself. You've had a tough time, and you don't give yourself enough credit." He ran his finger around the outside of her hand and along each finger. "I hate to see you continuing ... I mean ... I wanted to say this anyway: This doctor of Stuart's, Jacob Berke, is amazing. In less than the usual hour, he had me laughing at the problems I brought in. You should see what miracles he has wrought with Stuart. Honestly, it is a miracle. You ought to talk..."

She gently pulled her hand away, "What do you think we should do with the kids? Gordy offered to pay for the damages when I took Halloween off the table. He also said he'd see Dr. Anderson as a punishment. Sallee said she would practice piano for a month." Despite herself she had to laugh.

"It sounds like I was conducting a swap meet. I'll take one of those and give you three of these."

Joe laughed, "Gordy's offering to see Anderson speaks volumes about the man's effectiveness, talk about a setup for great results. Don't take him tomorrow -- just cancel the appointment. I don't see any point. He's already told me that Early did him more good in an afternoon than Anderson did in the past six months. I'm not even sure he didn't make things worse."

"He's going to charge if I cancel that late," Ginny protested.

"It's okay. Let him. I'll pay him. I don't think he is doing Gordy any good and I certainly don't see any need to send him just to avoid the bill," Joe replied. "What is it, sixty bucks? It's not a big deal."

"It is a big deal to me. Sixty dollars is a lot of money." She made a face when Joe laughed at that.

"There was a time when you didn't think so," he pointed out and then wished he hadn't.

"Things have changed. I am not quite as flush as I used to be, in case you don't remember. You are awfully free with your money these days, though," she said. "Speaking of which, do you know anything about why Stanley showed up out of the blue today? I can't afford to pay him."

"I, ah, um, called and asked if he would. I'll pay him. I didn't expect you to. I noticed the other day that the leaves hadn't been raked. I thought you might appreciate one thing off your plate with all that you have going on."

More defensive than she wanted to be, Ginny shot back, "What do you know about what I have going on?"

"The kids," he offered. "They've been difficult recently. What with Gordy running away and…" He decided to drop the topic of Stuart. "How about we don't punish them at all? Gordy is a good kid, they all are. They know that what they did was wrong." Joe was glad to change the subject. "I'm sure of it."

"I can't take the car back now," she grumbled. "I don't need or want it. I have a perfectly serviceable car."

"Is that why you want to punish them?" he asked, "Because you can't take the car back?"

Ginny sat up indignantly, "No, and I resent the implications of that." She reached for the door handle.

He grabbed her arm. "Don't go, please. Now that you can't take it back let's see how it feels to drive. You drive," he said while thinking, *Well done, guys!*

With a sigh she acquiesced. "I don't have my license."

"Ginny, that is just down right pathetic," he laughed. "If that's the best you've got, move over!" He jumped out of the car and ran around to the passenger's door, jumped in and kissed her on the cheek.

"Stop it! Don't do that," she implored, "please." She carefully put the car in gear and rolled gently down the drive. Five sets of eyes watched as they drove away.

"Let's go to the reservoir," Joe suggested, "You can drive there, and I'll drive it back." Without a word, she turned out of the driveway in the direction he suggested. "Aren't you going to talk?"

She didn't say anything for a long time as she delighted in the ease in which the big car handled. Finally she said, "I don't know what you are up to, but I want you to know I am not interested in getting back together with you. So if you got this car in hopes that I would swoon at your largesse, I'm telling you right now, it won't work."

Joe had to work hard not to react. "Ginny, I have far too much regard for you to ever think I could buy your affections." He pushed on, despite the risk. "I find it offensive, actually. As I told you, I've come into some money, and I want to spend some of it on you and the kids. It's important to me that you are well taken care of."

"You have to admit it is a rather about face," she said tartly. She turned off the highway on to a dirt road and marveled at how smooth the ride was. "It's amazing, you almost can't tell the difference between this road and the pavement, " she said, and he smiled.

"Do you like it?" he asked, hoping for a little break in the ice.

"It's hardly the point. Yes, it's a nice car." She stopped, put the car in park and climbed out. Just before she shut the door she added emphatically, "Do I want it? No," and walked around to the passenger door.

Joe slid over to the driver's seat. "Come on, Ginny. I'm sorry. I understand that you were hurt by the way I came after you during the divorce. I was worried. Your drinking..." *Drop that subject you, idiot,* he thought. "I was an ass. Can you forgive me? Don't you think it would be better for the children if we could find a way..." He fumbled for words, then plunged on, "...if we could get back together. Ginny, I love you. We went through a horrible time. Money was tight. Neither one of us was equipped to deal with all of the things we were dealing with."

"Oh, why was the money tight?" she snapped.

"I don't want to fight. I want to make love to you. That's what I want," he said, surprised by his candor. "Ginny, I love you."

Ginny's insides melted as a jolt of longing shot through her, completely surprising her and putting her defenses on high alert. "Can you take me home? I am uncomfortable with this," she said and wished she meant it. "I want to go home, and when we get there, I want you to take this car away. I absolutely do not want it."

———

"Have I been looking forward to this appointment!" Joe said to Jacob Berke that evening. "Maybe, I should schedule two appointments a week. Things happen so fast. It's a lot to keep straight."

"You can call me anytime you hit a wall," the doctor laughed, "You are doing a fine job. You also have the advantage of a daughter who has taken to this work like green to grass. It is second nature, once you blow the clouds of confusion away and gain clarity, you'll see."

"I'm going to start right off with my big win. It happened just this afternoon. I bought Ginny a new car. She made no bones about the fact that she didn't want it. She said she wasn't for sale." He took a breath, "There is a long story involved. Bottom line, I told Ginny I loved her."

"How did that feel?" Jacob asked.

"Good. That's not the huge win, though." Joe said, "When she accused me of trying to buy her affections, she threw the car, figuratively of course, in my face," he laughed, " but I didn't get mad. It took a little work. I saw the habit of getting angry, and I didn't give into it. That," he exclaimed, "felt fantastic."

"Well done. What did you do instead of getting angry?" Berke asked.

"I was honest with her. I told her what she said offended me, but I wasn't belligerent. I focused on what I wanted, which was to enjoy the time I was spending with Ginny," Joe said as he lay back on his bed and crossed his feet at the ankles. He laughed when he thought how Ethel would have a fit if she saw him doing this with his shoes on.

"You got it. Do you have anything you are resisting now?" Berke asked.

"Ethel and shoes on the bed," he laughed. Then he said, "Yes, I feel dishonest not telling Ginny about this inheritance. More than anything, I want to share it with her, but I don't want it to be about the money."

"Did you hear the *'don't want'* in there? Do you see that your double negative desire makes it all about the money? You're sending a message to your mind to look for the instances where it *is* all about the money. Your mind is very, very good at doing exactly what you program it to do. How could you phrase your desire to make it into a single positive goal?"

"I... want Ginny to ... love me and my money?" Joe ventured.

"Yes, good, and let's just clarify here a bit. The money is part of the whole package that is you. Separating you and the inheritance makes it about the money. Also, you have no control over Ginny, only yourself."

"Okay, how about this? My goal is to put my family back together in the clearest, most loving way possible, by sharing all of me. That is exactly what I want," Joe said, elated.

"Excellent! Is there anything else you'd like to talk about?"

"Nope, this mind training is amazing. I feel so much better, like I have power, real power for the first time. Thanks, Jacob, I appreciate what you have done for Stuart and me, for my whole family. I feel like a million dollars!" Joe laughed. "I even caught myself being grateful to my father today. That is big stuff."

Chapter 14

Ginny had to ask, "Was it as much fun as you thought it would be?" A resounding yes boomed back from all three children. She sighed, "I am so glad that it's over. So much ado about nothing."

In the back seat of the car, Gordy and Sallee exchanged bored expressions with a little eye roll. "Didn't you like trick-or-treating when you were a kid?" Sallee asked.

"We didn't." their mother said, glancing up in the rear-view mirror. "We didn't *go* trick-or-treating. We might have had a jack o' lantern, but none of the dressing up or begging for candy. The colored children did it, but we didn't. The focus was on today."

The children looked at her and then at each other like she was speaking a different language. "What do you mean? Halloween was a different day?" Gordy asked.

"Today is All Saints' Day. It was more important than Halloween when I was young," Ginny said, a little unsure of her facts now that she heard herself state them. Quickly changing the subject she said, "Honestly, I don't understand how you children can eat so much candy." She smiled, "All three of you look positively green. Did you eat all of it last night?"

"I didn't," Helen said primly. First one out of the door this morning, she'd claimed the favored spot, the front seat, for the ride to school. "I put mine away. I only had two Tootsie Rolls." Behind her back, Gordy squinched up his face, wobbling his head side to side and mimicked her words. Sallee suppressed a giggle.

Sallee jumped in to add, "I didn't eat all of mine, either." Gordy glared at her, then knitted his brows together as if to say, *you too*? "Gordy and I traded the stuff we didn't like." Sallee continued. She neglected to mention that she had made a sizable dent in her stash and probably would be down to the butterscotch hard candy by tonight. "I don't feel bad, though."

"It's a wonder your teeth haven't fallen out," Ginny commented. "I saw the amount of candy wrappers in your wastepaper basket this morning."

"Ha ha, old toothless," Gordy teased, poking at his sister as he wrapped his lips around his teeth, trying to look toothless. Sallee stuck out her tongue.

"I don't suppose there is much left of your treats, sir," Ginny said to Gordy.

"Well, there's some," Gordy hedged. "I didn't eat them all. I threw out all of the apples. I hate it when people give stuff like that, like raisins and fruit," he grumbled. "It's Halloween. Supposed to give *treats*."

"Maybe it's a trick," Sallee giggled, "They're trickin' ya. I didn't get a single apple," she crowed. "Must be doin' something right. I guess people didn't like having a convict show up at their door."

"Oh, like a witch was better?" Gordy scoffed.

"Guess so," Sallee retorted, "I didn't get any apples."

"Stop now. There is no reason for that kind of behavior." Ginny spoke over the bickering. "I want it stopped now. It's a bad habit and I don't want to hear it anymore, from either of you."

As they pulled up to the high school, Gordy stopped halfway out of the back seat. "Thanks, Mom," he said, shouldering his backpack. "Thanks for letting us go out last night. I didn't mean to hurt your car."

"I know you didn't," she said, hastily adding a reminder to everyone that despite the fact that the car was still parked in their drive, it was not going to stay. "It's your Dad's car. See you later. Try to stay awake."

After dropping the girls off at their school, she quickly did her errands so that she could be early for her meeting. She was looking forward to catching up with Rebecca. It seemed like weeks since she'd seen her. "If Rebecca isn't there, I'm going to go by her house and see if there is a problem," she said out loud to steel her resolve. Going to Rebecca's neighborhood was a terrifying prospect to her.

Ginny almost lost her nerve when she pulled up in front of Rebecca's ramshackle house. *Lord, it isn't much more than a shack,* Ginny thought as she picked her way across the rutted yard and on to the rickety porch. A loose board or shutter was intermittently banging, causing Ginny to flinch each time and heightening her sense of dread.. *For goodness' sakes, Ginny, get a hold of yourself,* she chided. As she knocked gingerly on the door, worried that she might knock it off its hinges, she found herself simultaneously hoping that Rebecca would and would not be home. "Rebecca," she called, "Are you here? It's me, Ginny Mackey. Rebecca?" She held her ear close to the door, listening. *There couldn't be more than two rooms in the house. Surely she can hear me if she is here.* She tried the knob. The door was unlocked. Slowly opening the door, calling all the while, she peeped inside.

"Rebecca?" The room, lit only by the meager light that managed to shine through two tiny windows shadowed by the porch, was drill sergeant neat and tidy, but cold. There was a small, unlit wood stove in the far corner next to a table that looked to be fitted out as a kitchen counter. Two clean jelly glasses were placed upside down on a dishtowel, and a frying pan was on the shelf underneath.

Ginny debated whether she should continue or leave. Her inclination was to run from the house. She combatted the impulse resolutely, reasoning with herself. *If Rebecca was in the other room, presumably her bedroom, she might not appreciate my barging in. But what if she's sick? What other friends … was she Rebecca's friend? There were the conversations after AA, it's true. Rebecca might not have anyone else to help, put it that way.* She crossed the room, still noticing the lack of furnishings. Tentatively approaching the door, she tapped lightly and then more solidly, "Rebecca," she called as she turned the knob and eased the door open. Applying her shoulder, she overcame the impediment of a bulge in the floor caused by a warped floorboard. The door scraped noisily over the floor, the black paint long since worn off. One neatly made mattress, one lamp and two baskets of clothes were all that Ginny could see.

She suppressed the urge to weep for Rebecca. *It's awful. Worse than I thought. How does she live like this?* She carefully closed the door. Standing in the front room, she looked around for a piece of paper and a pen or pencil. Finding neither, she went out to her car to write a note and tucked it in the door. As she turned to leave, it opened. Ginny jumped back, aghast. "Rebecca," she gasped. "You surprised me. I didn't see you," she stammered. "I was in…"

"I know," Rebecca said, barely audible. "I was in the ba….outside." She stood back from the door, holding it open in invitation. Ginny entered the room reflexively and again noticed the lack of heat in the room -- and then from Rebecca. Normally effusive, Rebecca was as cold as the dank room.

"Did I come at a bad time?" Ginny asked, then plunged on without waiting for an answer. "I hadn't seen you at meetings. I was worried that something might be wrong. Today, I decided that if you weren't there, I was going to come by and check on you." She reached out to hug her friend and was rebuffed. "Rebecca, are you all right?" Ginny realized that she was secretly hoping that Rebecca would send her away. Rebecca's strange, detached behavior did nothing to alleviate her growing sense of unease. An unbidden feeling of doom was settling in the room, cold as a tomb, and Ginny started to shiver, her eyes widening with alarm. "Come on, let's go outside into the sun. It's too cold in here." She wrapped her arms around herself and made for the door. "Rebecca, come on."

Hearing, "too cold in here" had done it, and a logjam of pent-up grief, rage, and guilt broke loose. What little control Rebecca had mustered to deal with Ginny's unexpected appearance evaporated as she dissolved into a torrent of tears. Ginny rushed to her, just catching her before she collapsed.

So recently close to abject despair herself, she knowingly held Rebecca tight, clear in herself that there were no words for this outburst. As the wave of grief subsided, Ginny led Rebecca, her breath catching in great gasps, outside to the car. Without asking, she opened the door and directed Rebecca to sit in the car's warmth, then retraced her steps back into the dreadful house. In no time, she reemerged with the two baskets of clothes, which as far as she could tell were the totality of Rebecca's earthly possessions.

She pulled the door closed with her toe and strode to the car, depositing them in the back seat. Rebecca attempted to whimper a protest, which proved to be too much for her, as Ginny started the car and sped away.

She banged open the front door. "Ethel," she called as she hustled toward the kitchen. "Will you make up the guest room? My friend Mrs --" she hesitated, vainly trying to remember Rebecca's last name, "-- Rebecca will be staying with us for a while. I would like her to have as much privacy as possible."

"Yes'm," said Ethel, bustling out of the kitchen. "I'll git righ' t' it."

Ginny started toward the door, then turned. "Run her a bath and make her some hot tea, too, please."

Rebecca had wept sporadically all the way to Ginny's, and Ginny had left her in the car to compose herself in privacy. As Ethel hastened to put Rebecca's accommodations in order, Ginny went back to the car to help her out. Rebecca sat in the front seat staring blankly ahead, and as Ginny gently touched her shoulder, she flinched. "Come on now," Ginny said encouragingly. "The first thing we are going to do is get you warmed up, a warm bath and some hot tea. You are cold as death." She instantly regretted her choice of words as she felt a shudder run through Rebecca's frail body. Once out of the shadow of the front seat, Ginny could see she had hollows deep as bruises around her eyes. She tried hard to maintain a casual demeanor, despite the fear that Rebecca's stupor had begun to engender. *Where was Charlie?* She wanted to ask but was terrified of the answer.

"Let's just get you in the house and warm. We can deal with the rest later," Ginny said more to reassure herself than Rebecca, who was moving ghost-like under Ginny's gentle guidance.

Between Ginny and Ethel, they were able to get Rebecca into the bath with a hot cup of tea perched on the tub's edge. "The poor dear," Ginny said as they crept down the hall together. "Ethel, I am so afraid something dreadful has happened to her daughter. She's a little younger than Sallee. She's retarded. I didn't see a sign of her at the house." She involuntarily shivered. "It's clear something awful as occurred, and I just don't know what to think. You stand by in case she needs you. You are so much better at this than I am. I'll go get her clothes out of the car."

Ethel nodded her assent, biting her lip as she turned back toward the bathroom door, and Ginny bustled off, glad to get away. *I don't want to ask, Lord knows I don't, so how on earth am I going to find out about Charlie?* The question worried her all the way to the car and back. By the time she arrived at the guest room door breathing hard, Ethel was chatting soothingly as she tucked Rebecca into bed like one of the children.

Ginny steeled herself to enter the room with the two baskets. She placed them on the big blanket chest at the foot of the canopy bed and smiled at Rebecca with what she hoped was calm encouragement. "Is there anything we do for you right now? Anyone I can call?"

Rebecca slowly shook her head, not lifting it from the pillow, and closed her eyes.

Back down in the kitchen Ginny immediately asked, "Did she say anything about Charlie – you know, her daughter, the little one who -- ?"

Ethel broke in. "No'um, not a word. Other'n t' thank me she did'n' say nothin'. But I feel it in ma bones, sump'n terrible done happen t' dat little girl. Her momma jes' too downhearted fer anythang else." She shook her head, muttering as she went to the sink. "Mhmm, mhmm, mhmm, sump'n' terrible."

"The house she lives in doesn't have indoor plumbing. Can you imagine?" Ginny exclaimed. "I just can't get over that house."

"Yes'm. Me an' Early didn' have indoor plumbin' 'til right recent like," Ethel said. "We got along fine," she added, as if it was an afterthought.

Ginny, a bit taken aback by this revelation, tried to extricate herself. "Well, yes, but you didn't grow up in a swanky apartment in New York City, either. I mean you all were used to it." She tried again. "I don't mean it was easy for you, either. Never mind, I don't know what I am talking about." She stopped. "Ethel, I hope I didn't offend you. I didn't think..."

"You did'n'," Ethel agreed, with a smile. "But I know wha' you mean. Me an' Early growed up widout thangs other folks takes for granted. Dat jes' the way it is. I 'spect it would be righ' hard t' git along widout if you wasn't used t' it. I'm here t' tell you, now dat I gots it, I sho doan wanna give it up." She laughed. "Kin I fix you some lunch?"

"I don't have much of an appetite. It sure makes you appreciate what you have when something like this happens," Ginny responded.

"Yes'm, it sho' do," Ethel replied, pleased to hear Ginny say so. "It sho' do."

When the children came home from school, Ginny met them at the door shushing them while explaining that she had a friend staying who needed to sleep. "Go on into the kitchen and get something to eat. I think Ethel has made some marmalade tarts." As they clamored off to the kitchen with Ginny shushing them from behind, she thought, *What was I thinking, asking Ethel to make marmalade tarts? They have had enough sugar to sink a barge.* Following them into the kitchen she said, "Don't eat too many. I forgot that yesterday was Halloween. And please be quiet. Rebecca has had a very difficult time and needs all of the sleep she can get."

As she turned to leave the room, Rebecca appeared behind her. Ginny jumped, with a little shriek, "Oh, you startled me." She scanned her friend, looking for improvement, "I didn't hear you come in. How are you doing? Did you get enough sleep?"

"Charlie's Mom!" Sallee shrieked, and ran around the table to embrace Rebecca. "Wow, what a surprise. I'm so glad to see you. Where's Charlie?" she asked, wrapping her arms around a surprised Rebecca. After a very long hug, Sallee turned back to the four astonished faces behind her. "This is Charlie's Mom, remember, I told you, Helen?"

Helen shook her head slowly, "No, you never told me."

"Oh right," she turned back to Rebecca, "I thought you were a dream, so I didn't tell anybody about that day I spent with you and Charlie. I think that was one of the most fun days I ever had." She hugged Rebecca again. "Where's Charlie?"

"She's in the hos...pital." Rebecca said choking on the word. "She has pneumonia. Ginny, could I use the phone."

"Oh no," Sallee gasped. "Is she going to be okay?"

Ginny scowled at Sallee, then turned to Rebecca, "Absolutely. Make... help yourself...make yourself at home. Whatever you need..." She spluttered trying to think of every scenario where she might offer help. "I'll take you there the minute you want."

"I don't know, Sallee. She's not okay now." Rebecca said and patted Sallee on the shoulder. She smiled wanly and looked around for a phone.

"Out in the hall to the right," Ginny directed as she rushed by Rebecca to show the way. As much as she wanted to know how Sallee and Rebecca knew each other, she was more intent on where the impending telephone conversation might lead. Standing stock still in the kitchen doorway holding her breath was all that Ginny could manage.

Not so Gordy, who immediately turned to Sallee. "How do you know her? What day and what was so special? Man, you act like she's your long lost friend. She doesn't look like Mom's kind of friends." He stopped to consider, then continued, "But then she doesn't have any friends anymore. Who is she anyway? Ethel, do you know?" But Ethel just shook her head with a steely look that brought him to a halt.

"Never mind," Sallee said, dismissing her brother with a wave of her hand. "I just hope she is going to be all right." Ethel came up behind Sallee and put her hands on the girl's shoulders.

"Doan you worry, now. The Lord'll look after her," she said reassuringly.

Turning to hug Ethel, Sallee said, "I hope so, Ethel. I don't think she was all too healthy before, though."

Ginny was so distraught over Rebecca's plight that she had to talk herself through the mechanics of driving. Desperate as she was to know more about Charlie's condition, she feared asking. She silently cursed Rebecca's laconic nature, although she understood it completely, having so recently been in much the same circumstances -- well-meaning friends hovering while Sallee might be near death. She tried on this emotion, compassion, new for her, as a spring dress. She found she was not averse to it -- though under the circumstances, she thought, she'd have taken the actual dress in a heartbeat, given the choice. "Do you want me to come in with you?" she asked as she allowed Rebecca to direct her to a parking spot close the door near the children's ward, an entrance Ginny knew all too well.

"No, Ginny, but thank you. Thank you for all you've done. I think they will let me stay tonight," Rebecca said, stringing together the most words Ginny had heard from her all day, "but if not, I'll be fine going home on my own."

"I absolutely won't hear of it," Ginny said firmly. "You call me, and I'll come get you. Whatever the hour, I insist. You can't take care of yourself and Charlie too," she heard herself pleading. "Please. Let us help." She held up her hand to head off protest. "You know I went through a similar situation with Sallee just a few months ago. If it hadn't been for Ethel's ministration, neither Sallee nor I would have survived as we have. Please!" She quickly searched her purse for a pen and paper and scribbled down her number. "Here, take it and just call me. I know it's none of my business, but you shouldn't try to spend the night. When she does wake up, it's so much better if you greet her like yourself instead of a shell of the mom she's always counted on. Honestly, I know. I've been there."

"You are right. It is none of your business," Rebecca said without heat and climbed out of the car. "Thank you – goodbye!" She shut the door and made for the hospital door.

Ginny sat as if slapped, trying to get hold of her feelings. Part of her shrieked in indignation at having her kindness thrown back in her face. A very much smaller part of her understood the pain Rebecca was going through, Rebecca's feelings of grief and guilt, and her fierce independence, her determination to handle all her problems on her own. Yes, she recognized it all. Hadn't she been doing the same thing? Hadn't she spurned all the offers of help extended to her, out of pride and shame? Wasn't she doing precisely that to Joe out of the shame she felt over her father's monstrous acts and the family legacy of secrets, of drowning it all in drink?

A rush of alien feelings welled up in her. The urge to push them back was tempting, but she resisted, closing her eyes, allowing them to come. *Could I have been so shallow that I have never felt blessed?* she wondered. Yes, always privileged, never blessed. She considered the light years of difference between the two. Such a sense of humility, so deep and foreign, fell on her that she could have fallen to her knees had she not been in the car. She heard a faint voice somewhere deep inside ask, *How can you judge?*

"What would I have wanted someone to do for me when Sallee was in the hospital?" she heard herself ask out loud, then felt foolish asking out loud, and even more so as she waited for an answer. Seconds later, she was sprinting across the street to a drugstore. At the counter, after catching her breath, she ordered chicken noodle soup to go. While the waitress waited pad in hand Ginny debated, *Do Jewish people eat meat?* Then she was asking the waitress, "Do you know if Jewish people eat meat?" With a blank stare the woman shrugged. *Right.* "Then, uh...yes, egg salad sandwich, also to go." Clutching her order, she raced back to the hospital and into the ward, taking all of the shortcuts she knew so well by now.

She slowed to a walk as she neared the nurse's station, and one of the nurses asked if she could help her. Ginny realized again that she couldn't remember Rebecca's last name. *Did I ever know it?* she wondered. "Charlie?" she finally asked. As she was about to explain that she didn't know Rebecca's name, the nurse said, "Room 356, second door on the right," pointing down the hall.

Reassured by her gift of food, Ginny walked into the room. Charlie, she immediately saw, was in an oxygen tent, eyes closed. Rebecca sat in a straight back chair as if she were doing penance. Her face hardened as she saw Ginny entering the room. "Please, she said, with a deep sigh, "I don't want to be ungrateful…but…"

"Then don't be," Ginny interrupted her as she set down the food on the table next to her. "You haven't eaten. You need food. Shut up and eat." Her words shocked them both, though Ginny gave no indication of it.

"I…don't…" Rebecca began an angry protest.

Ginny screwed up all of her courage and said in a commanding voice, "Rebecca, I don't give a damn whether you want it or not. Eat it." The words "dry drunk" came to her that instant out of nowhere. She'd never heard the term, at least not that she recalled, but it fit. "You are on a dry drunk. The only difference between what you are doing now and drowning your sorrows in booze is that you are not drinking. So shut up and eat. This little pity party is over." She sat down before her quaking knees collapsed under her.

Rebecca opened the bag of food. She slowly, carefully pried the top off of the cup of soup, dug into the bag for a spoon, and to Ginny's amazement, ate a spoonful. Unsure of exactly what to say, she opted for silence as she watched Rebecca eat another spoonful of soup.

At breakfast the next day, Ginny asked Ethel, "Does God talk to you?"

"I can't say as how He talks t' me direct. He doan say, Ethel, you is t' do dis or dat," she said, trying to hold her surprise in check. "Mo' like de Holy Spirit put ideas in ma head."

"That's it." Ginny brightened, "Do you think God would talk to me? I don't go to church."

Ethel effused, "Miz Ginny, God doan care if you goes t' church o' you doesn'. Dat's men's talk. You is one a his chil'ren. He love you no matter what. A course He gonna talk t' you." She wanted to dance a little jig for joy.

"Yesterday, I think he might have. I have never experienced anything like what happened, before. I had this clarity. I didn't know what I was doing and all of a sudden I did." She felt a little embarrassed sharing the experience, but if anybody would understand, it would be Ethel. She quickly changed the subject before Ethel felt the need to preach she said, "Rebecca should be down soon. I am not sure if she eats bacon, so maybe you could ask her what she wants rather than bringing ou... No, on second thought, when I buzz, go ahead and bring out what you've fixed for breakfast. There is no reason to make more work for you. She can deal with her issues with the food. We don't need to."

Ethel nodded her head as Ginny left the room, and she whispered to herself, *De Lord be praised! Miz Ginny is growin' up.*

Minutes later, Rebecca showed up looking more like herself. She smiled at Ginny as she pulled out a chair. "I feel so much better. Thank you for all you've done for me."

"You've have done more for me than you know," Ginny answered. "Thank you."

"Who's that playing the piano?" Rebecca asked, "It's lovely."

"It must be Helen. She is very good, I think," Ginny said.

Rebecca started to laugh, "I didn't know you were such an old hand at AA jargon. *Dry drunk*, I wouldn't have expected that from you."

"Neither did I," Ginny giggled, "It just came to me. I knew it well though, having suffered from it myself. I guess we're just a bunch of old dry drunks, you and me." They both laughed.

"The doctor said last night that he was very pleased with Charlie's progress," Rebecca went on. "She might even be able to come out of the oxygen tent soon. Did you have a hand in that too?"

"No, but Ethel might have," Ginny laughed.

Ethel appeared with a plate of eggs and bacon in one hand and a silver pot of steaming coffee in the other. "Coffee?" she asked.

"Oh, Ethel, thank you," Rebecca purred, "I would love some. I can't tell you how much I missed this." She waved her hands expansively, encompassing the whole of the room, then dug into her breakfast like a farmhand. "God, I'm hungry. This food is all so good." Ethel and Ginny shared a smile.

Ginny said, "Rebecca I've been thinking about this all night. I want you, before you dismiss what I am about to say, to think hard about it too. Okay?"

Rebecca nodded, "Promise."

"You would be doing me a huge favor if you would let me sell my old car to you."

"I can't afford..." Rebecca started until Ginny cut her off with a nod and a knowing look

"You promised! And besides, you don't have all of the facts yet, so you don't know. I know you have a fair amount of pride, it takes one to know one, so I'm not going to give it to you. I want to sell it for a dollar a month for a year." Ginny held up her hand to stop Rebecca's interruption and continued, "I have a darling old friend, Della Eades."

Sallee bounced in. "What did ya think? I sounded pretty good didn't I? Oh, hi, how's Charlie? You know I don't know what to call you?"

"Honey, I'm sorry, my name is Rebecca. You sounded great." She reached out to give Sallee a pat on the hand, "Charlie is doing better. It's sweet of you to ask."

As a reflex, Ginny was about to jump in saying, *Sallee you may call my guest "Mrs.* – until she remembered she still couldn't remember Rebecca's surname. She was disappointed that Rebecca hadn't given Sallee her full name, then thought, *Well, just take the direct approach,* and asked, "Rebecca, what is your surname? I think you told me once, but I can't remember."

"Levine, and Charlie's is Brampton. Her father's name was Brampton. It's complicated, having different last names. We make it work, though."

"What happen to her father?" Sallee asked. She ignored the scowl from her mother, "I'm so glad she's better, can I see her? I know how lonely it can be in the hospital when you're by yourself,"

"Sallee you don't ask questions like that," Ginny admonished.

"It's all right, Ginny. I don't mind," Rebecca said. "Charles died in a car crash before Charlie was born. You can't see her yet, but I'll let you know when you can. I know she would be thrilled to see you. She asked about you all of the time after that day."

"Why do you have a different name?"

Ginny gasped in horror, "Sallee!" then snapped, "None of your business. You don't ask questions like that!"

Rebecca looked first at Ginny and then Sallee's crestfallen face. She took both of Sallee's hands in hers and said quietly, "Sallee, your Mom wants you to learn to be sensitive to other people's feelings, and that kind of question might upset someone. It often happens that people withhold information because they have feelings they haven't sorted out yet. So it's best if you let them tell you what they want to in their own time." She gave Sallee's hands a gentle squeeze to see if her point was taken, as she looked her directly in the eyes. "Do you understand?" she asked with a smile.

Sallee nodded and said, "I'm sorry. I didn't mean to hurt your feelings or make you feel bad."

"You didn't, but you could hurt somebody's in the future if your Mom doesn't make you aware. That's all she was doing, and that's because she loves you so much." Rebecca smiled first at Sallee, then Ginny. Ginny tried to return the smile despite her embarrassment for coming down so harshly on Sallee. "To answer your question. He died in a car crash before we were married."

Ginny prayed Sallee wouldn't ask about the mixed-up order of things, given that thus far she'd been schooled that first comes love, then comes marriage, and only then the baby carriages. She hastily continued where she'd left off. "My friend is looking for a live-in companion. She's too old to live alone, no relatives except a bratty godchild. You would love her house. It's gorgeous, Georgian and chocked to the rafters with beautiful antiques. She is a dear, but I suspect a handful. I called her this morning. Told her about you and Charlie. She asked me to send you over as soon as it was convenient for you."

Tears streamed down Rebecca's cheeks. "Do you know, the reason I was in that dreadful little house was because my aunt, my mother's sister, had recently died. I was taking care of her. My cousins insisted that we move right after she died. I think they thought I was going to steal from them." She shrugged, "Who knows? People do funny things when they are grieving. Anyway, it was all I could find that I could afford. I had no plan to stay as long as we did. I'm sure that place was a chief reason for Charlie's decline." She stood up, her face still wet with tears, went to Ginny and hugged her. "What I am trying to say, but not doing a very good job of it, is thank you. It is exactly what I was looking for. You don't know how hard positions like that are to come by if you don't know people. Yes, I would love to buy your car even on your terms." She all but crowed. "To hell with pride!"

She looked at her watch, "Oh, dear, I've got to fly. Where are the keys to my new car?" She grabbed the last slice of bacon off her plate on her way out of the room.

"Front hall table," Ginny called after her.

Shortly after Rebecca left, Ginny got a call from her real estate agent. "Hello, Ginny, I have found the perfect place. I know you are going to adore it. Do you have any time to look today?"

"I don't, Sharon. I have so many things up in the air right now, I have no idea what I'm doing. Or even if I'm going to move."

"It's going to be expensive if you don't," Sharon cautioned. "I can tell you that. I talked to the buyer's agent. He says they are rabid to get in. I'll tell you one thing, that particular agent is not noted for letting a sale slip away without a bloodletting, so there is that."

"Okay, how much time do I have?" Ginny asked.

"Let me see." Sharon rustled through paper, "Six months from the date of signing. Not much. You have to be out by the end of May."

"Oh God," Ginny sighed, "I've got to think. I'll call you I just don't know when. It's complicated. Honestly, it's very complicated." She looked at her watch. "Sharon, I've got to go. I'll call you. I promise."

She rushed out of her study calling, "Ethel!" Ethel emerged from the girls' room, where she was making beds. "It's nearly 10. Joe is supposed to pick the children up, are they ready?"

"Yes'm, dey gone. Mist'a Joe say he was a little early. Hoped you didn' mind."

Ginny was shocked at how much Ethel's words disappointed her. *What was that all about? Was he sorry to have missed me?* "They didn't say goodbye," she murmured.

"I didn't see yo' car. I 'ssumed you was gone out. An' da's what I tol' 'em when dey ask where you was."

Ginny, just a bit desperate to know, was struggling with her pride. "Oh to hell with it," she said, "Did Joe want to see me?"

"He didn' say so, but I thought he looked a mite disappointed when I said you was gone. Is you needin' me t' do anythang else? I's got sump'n t' attend t', an' Early's plannin' on pickin' me up 'bout 10:30."

"No, you go ahead. Thank you, have a nice weekend, Ethel." Ginny gave her a warm smile and went to her own bedroom. For the first time in a very long time, an overnight without the children took on a long and lonely aspect. *What is going on with me?* she wondered.

In her room, she opened her dresser drawer, dug under her neatly folded silk scarves and pulled out the novel everyone was talking about: *The Group*. She removed it from the paper bag with a little thrill. *This weekend may be the perfect time to read this,* she thought as she perused the cover -- something she wouldn't have dreamed of doing in the bookstore. The sitting room was her preferred reading spot, but for this book her bedroom seemed so much more appropriate. After all Rebecca might come home. *How embarrassing!* she thought as she gave a little shudder, thinking of the titillating bits she had heard especially about chapter 2.

Late that night she put the book down, finished, and turned off the light. The rest of the night was spent sleepless, sorting out her tangled mess of a life. More than once she cursed herself for buying the book and Mary McCarthy for writing it. There wasn't a character that she didn't identify with in some way that didn't also scream for major changes to be made.

Despite not sleeping well, Ginny woke early Sunday morning. Seeing Rebecca's car parked in the drive added a little spice to what she had assumed would be a dull day. She was surprised, since she hadn't heard her come in last night. *Maybe I did sleep for a minute. If she came in late, she'll likely not be up until noon.* She looked at her watch and groaned -- *five hours!* She lay in bed with a mind abuzz, but hoping she might fall back to sleep. A luxurious morning languishing in bed was a habit she had always longed for but was unable to acquire, though not for lack of trying. Once she was awake, she was up. As she tossed, turned, fidgeted and fiddled, she struck a deal with herself. I'll get coffee and bring it back to bed instead of getting up. Going downstairs in a nightgown was unheard of. *What the hell. It's just me. Live a little,* she laughed.

As she opened her bedroom door, she ran headlong into a silver tray laden with her coffee service, two coffee cups, and sweet rolls. "Good morning," Rebecca chirruped. She was dressed in her plain cotton nightie. "I took the liberty," she nodded at the tray, "I hope you don't mind. I was looking for a creative way to thank you," she said, and I thought since the children were gone, you might enjoy a breakfast in bed. In fact, we both might!" She laughed a little nervously, seeing the look of total surprise on Ginny's face.

"I … I …never…yes let's do!" she finally got out, elated. She didn't even cover her silk negligee with a bed jacket as she crawled back on her unmade bed. Breakfast in bed was a decidedly new frontier. Rebecca placed the tray at the foot of the bed and crawled in on the other side. "How's Charlie?" Ginny asked.

"She is out of the oxygen tent, has real color and an appetite. She loves hospital food. Can you imagine?" Rebecca laughed as she made her way over to the tray on all fours, careful not to spill anything. "I hope coffee's okay. I didn't make tea. I thought you were a coffee drinker, but I can run make some tea if you'd rather."

"This is perfect," Ginny said. "What a wonderful idea! I have never done anything like this in my life. Such fun!" she bubbled. "And of all things, I read *The Group* last night." She picked up the book from her nightstand. "Have you read it?" Rebecca shook her head. "It sure does give me a new perspective on my life. One sorely needed I might add. And I love that you show up with breakfast in bed this morning. It's perfect. Time for a much-needed change." She lifted her coffee cup in a toast. "To change."

Rebecca filled her cup and raised it, "To change." And laughed long and hard. "That feels so good," she said as she plumped up a pillow behind her and lay back against the headboard. "I haven't laughed in so long. Everything has been so deadly serious."

"To laughter," Ginny raised her cup again. "Now you know why I was such a big drunk. I love toasts. To toasts! To AA! To – to wet and dry drunks the world over!" They cracked up. "Did you get home late?" she gasped, when they finally stopped laughing long enough.

"About nine. I saw your light was on. I didn't want to bother you, though." Rebecca said.

"Nine, I didn't hear you. I must have been reading chapter 2. Wow, that got my attention," Ginny snorted, setting down her cup in the interest of not spilling.

"I heard about it. Pretty racy stuff. I wouldn't have pegged you for a fan of erotica, though, Madame Mackey," Rebecca said, lifting an eyebrow. "Whooo-eee!" This set them off again.

When she was able to catch a breath and not gabble, Ginny gasped out, "Me neither, but here I am. I read it my room because I was embarrassed that someone might come in and see me reading this *smut,* as my mother would have called it. And I read the *whole thing* – in a *single sitting* – until I was practically *cross-eyed*!" Lauging until tears streamed down her face, she gasped and held her sides. "I'm not sure I have ever laughed like this. I think I had a very unhappy childhood," she said in mock seriousness then blurted out in a most unladylike guffaw, which made Rebecca snort coffee out of her nose, "I don't remember laughing as a child." She hooted. "Isn't that pathetic? Ohh, I gotta stop." She gasped for air amid sporadic snickering.

"I did too," Rebecca said, then she spoke in a deep, gruff voice, "My father was a rabbi, for him life was v e r y, v e r y serious." Setting down her cup, she laughed so hard that there was no sound, just her head thrown back and her mouth agape. Mustering some control, she chortled, "It was frowned upon to laugh at home. Like a jackass, I believed him." Peals of laughter ensued.

"How were you to know?" Ginny cackled.

"Speaking of jackasses," Rebecca giggled, "my father told me that Charlie's retardation was retribution from God." She stood up on the bed with her hands held over her head as if she were throwing down lightning bolts. In a very deep voice she pronounced, "Lying with a man outside of the sanctity of," and then shouted in deeper, stentorian voice, "matrimony." She shook her head and arms for effect and then collapsed on the bed in gales of laughter. The contents of the tray flew in all directions as the two women convulsed in hysterics.

"I'll raise you one except it's too new and raw, and I can't make it funny, yet," Ginny said, raising herself on one elbow and wiping her eyes, suddenly serious. "My son of a bitch father raped a black servant --" and before Rebecca could protest, Ginny raised her hand and continued, "If that wasn't enough, when their daughter was born and old enough -- how old do you suppose *old enough* would be?" she asked rhetorically, "he raped her too. And to make it absolutely off the charts appallingly ludicrous, the child of that unholy union was my very first love. Just imagine what your father would have to say about that." Neither spoke.

They lay there for some time, quiet in their own thoughts. Finally Rebecca said, "It's absurd, isn't it, that we were spawned from such bastards? No wonder we drank."

"No wonder," Ginny agreed.

"My God, what a horrible thing to find out about a parent, or anyone actually! You just found this out? How did that happen?" Rebecca asked.

"Yesterday," said Ginny, "you told Sallee that sometimes people don't want talk about things, because they haven't made up their minds how they feel about them. That is the story of my life. Since I was very young, I think I knew something was wrong. I just didn't know what. It was dangerous to go against my parents. I can't imagine why I say that." She stopped, sighed and ran both of her hands through her hair. "They weren't abusive. Strict, but not abusive. Maybe I just picked up the fear that permeated the household. The servants were, I have just come to know, terrified of retribution for missteps and were paid not to talk." She turned away and squeezed her eyelids together hard to staunch the tears.

With another big sigh, she continued. "Children sense so much more than you think. Well, than I thought, anyway. Hearing you speak to Sallee like you did yesterday made me feel so horrible."

"Ginny, I'm ..." Rebecca stammered.

"No, it's okay. I parent the way I was parented. I see that my parents were short and harsh with me, maybe even abusive, now in that light. It's like you said, no wonder we're drunks, look at the way we were raised. God, I hope I can make it better for my children. I feel so terrible when I think of all of the horrible things I've said and done."

Rebecca spoke up. "You can't blame yourself for what you didn't know. You just can't. It's crazy."

"How did you know? How did you know how to talk to a child? Did your parents treat you like you treated Sallee yesterday?" Ginny demanded.

"My mother was kind and patient, but that didn't mean I didn't do lots of things wrong. Her kindness was no guarantee I was going to be like her." Rebecca sniffed. "I was horrible to my mother. No respect, I bullied her, ran roughshod over her."

She continued, "I know this is going to sound alien to you. It wasn't until I saw my true love die, while I was pregnant -- then for Charlie to arrive out of wedlock, mentally retarded, and my father to reject me so that I could attempt to drown myself in alcohol. Turning those tragedies into blessings changed my life, so much so that I have you as a friend." She smiled at Ginny. "You saw how I was the other day, how prideful and haughty. We've all got a long way to go, Ginny. It's that we are attempting to change that makes the difference. We haven't given up."

"Well, what you said to Sallee and how you said it made me realize that I have to talk about this horrible thing. I can't just stuff it and expect it to go away. Now that the boil has come to a head, it is time to lance it, clean out the poison and let it heal." Ginny groaned. "But I am so embarrassed.

"For God's sake, get over that," Rebecca said. "Pride in disguise and we both know how ugly that is," she laughed. "Besides, *you* didn't do all of those dreadful things."

"Thank you for being such a good friend. I don't think I ever had a good friend. You are the first." When she leaned over to hug Rebecca her strap slipped off her shoulder exposing a breast. She looked down laughed and said, "If anybody comes in we're going be labeled lesbians for life," then threw back her head and laughed.

"Can't be any worse than being called drunks, I suppose," Rebecca giggled.

Ginny pulled up her strap, fluffed her pillow behind her and leaned back. "You know, Rebecca, I think I'm still in love with Joe."

Rebecca's clear, strong laugh rang out loud, "What do the kids say? DUH! I can't tell you how happy that makes me, to hear you finally admit it."

"Oh, God, was it that obvious?" Ginny groaned.

"As the nose on your face," Rebecca laughed.

"Ewww, how embarrassing. I know! More pride." Ginny laughed. "I kind of feel like I don't deserve him. I have been so high and mighty. Do I have to tell him about my father?"

"What do you think?"

Ginny shrugged. "I guess. I don't know." She paused, thinking. "Maybe."

Chapter 15

Saturday night, Joe and the kids sat or sprawled together on the big red leather sofa in his pine-paneled living room while Joe read them *White Fang*. "Man, I would love to have a wolf, like White Fang," Gordy announced, then looked over at Joe and asked, "could I?" Joe emphatically shook his no. "Didn't think so, but I'd train him just like Scott did. You know," he sat up and put his feet on the floor looking very earnest, "I bet ol' Lance would have gone for help if I had a broken leg."

"Maybe," Joe chuckled, "if he didn't pick up a scent first. Remember when he'd put his nose to the ground and then would take off. Lifting his head only to *baugh roo.* No amount of calling could get his attention." As he said this, he looked over and saw that Gordy's face had turned stormy, so Joe changed his tack, "He was a good dog. I bet you're right, Gord. He would have brought help for you. That old hound did love you." He patted his son on the shoulder. " And hey, 'bout time you got a haircut there, pal, don'tcha think? We could go together. You want me to pick you up after school sometime this week? I could use one, too," he added, combing his fingers through his hair.

"Sure, let's do it Tuesday. Is that okay with you?" Joe nodded yes. "Can I watch *Have Gun Will Travel?*" Gordy asked, on his way to turn on the television.

"Yeah. Helen, honey, you need to get upstairs and get ready for bed. You don't want to watch Paladin anyway, do you?"

"No, but I do want to draw some. OK?" Again he nodded. Helen, methodically gathered up her things, kissed him on the cheek, and left the room with her sketchpad.

"I'll be up in a few minutes." Looking down at Sallee, who was lying with her head in his lap, "What about you miss? What are you going to do?" he asked.

"Can I talk to you?" she asked. "In the other room?" she mouthed.

"Sure, let's go." He waited for her to sit up, then stood and held out a hand to her, and they walked out of the room together. "Is something wrong?" he asked as they sat down at the kitchen table.

Sallee pulled out a chair across the table from her father. Looking everywhere except at him, she put her elbow down on the table and propped her head on her hand. Sighing, she looked around the room as she thought about how she wanted to start. The red checked wallpaper with what looked like a picnic spread on it was hideous, she thought. Joe gave her a little verbal nudge. "It's pretty bad isn't it?" She nodded her agreement.

"How did you know that was what I was thinking?" she asked, unnerved.

"I didn't. I was watching your eyes and the expression on your face," he laughed. "You aren't exactly inscrutable."

"What's that mean?" she asked, "Is it bad?"

"Noooo," he laughed, "inscrutable means hard to read. You are pretty easy, actually. You wear your feelings on your face. And it looks to me like you have something bothering you. Yes?" He tilted his head in her direction.

"Yeah, I guess I'll just say it. When are you and Th- Rose going to get married? Cuz the other day when you came for breakfast, Gordy said, 'Why didn't you buy that farm, and we all live there.' You said it was a good idea. The thing is, I don't think that's a very nice thing to joke about, especially if you're going to be marrying somebody else. I think Mom got her feelings hurt."

Joe leaned over the table and put his hand on his daughter's arm, "Sweetie, I am so sorry. You are right. It wasn't a funny joke. And you're right about your Mom getting her feeling hurt, too." He patted her arm and then invited her to come sit in his lap. She thought about it and declined. "Still upset?" She nodded that there was more. "Rosemary and I aren't getting married," he said. "We're just good friends." To his utter surprise, she burst into tears.

"Stuart *said*," she wailed.

Joe left his chair and swiftly circled the table. He knelt by her chair and wrapped his arms around her. "Honey, I had no idea you were so fond of Rosemary."

"Oh, Dad," she groaned. "I can't stand her. It's because of her and me that Linda isn't around anymore. It's all my fault." She put her head down on the table and cried. She lifted it long enough to wail, "And now she's gone. She left me a note – when I was so sick – she didn't even wake me up to say goodbye!" She put her head down and brayed, "She's gone, and it's all – my -- *fault*!" Joe reached over her head, picked up a paper napkin, and tucked it under her hand on the table.

"When you finish crying, I hope you'll explain. I thought the reason Linda wasn't around was that she got a job closer to home, to be near her parents. I guess I was wrong," he said as he patted her gently on the back. The blubbering ebbed a bit. "Wait, are talking about the time you told Linda that Rosemary and I were getting married?" The blubbering flowed. "Honey, that was a mean trick Stuart played on me, and she used you to do it." The blubbering ceased entirely.

Sallee lifted her tear-streaked face, blew her nose and barked, "What?" Then, trying to hold back more tears, she said wearily, "Linda got mad when I told her you were getting married to…" *What the hell,* she thought, *I'm just going to say it…*"The Rose." Joe laughed at the name. "You weren't," she glared red-eyed at her father. He shook his head. "Ever?" she asked.

"Nope, not ever. Rosemary went through an awful divorce and needed a friend. That was all there was to it. We are just friends. She came with me to the hospital because she knew how upset I was about you, and she likes you. It probably wasn't the smartest thing I ever did to bring her along especially to the house, but what are you going to do."

"Yep, you got that right." She shook her head. "It wasn't very smart. So did Linda want to marry you? I liked her. I think I would have liked that."

"I think Linda wanted to get married, and she might have thought I was the one," he said with a little smile. "She wasn't mad at you. We talked before she left. She was disappointed, because she had sort of talked herself into thinking it would be fun to be part of the family. Except I was too old, had too many kids, and am still in love with their mother."

"You sure do have a funny way of showing it," she said rocking her head. "Dad, I worry about you sometimes. I bet you a hundred bucks," she stuck out her hand, "Mom has no idea that you still love her. Bet?"

"You got a hundred bucks? You better be putting your money on the table." He laughed as he shook her outstretched hand.

"I'll ask her tomorrow night," she said.

Joe gave a nervous little laugh. "Whoa, Sallee, hold on there. I'll take care of that. You don't need to get in the middle." He turned and looked at her with an askance glance. "You hear me? That's all I need!"

"I might be able to act as matchmaker," Sallee protested. "Rebecca told me that there are professional matchmakers in New York. I could practice on you guys." She was warming to the idea. "I think I'd be good at it."

"DO NOT get involved in it." Joe fought to keep his voice even, "If she doesn't know, I promise I'll pay up. Cross my heart."

"Okay, but you better." She smiled slyly then a cloud of concern passed over her face, "Are you talking about coming back home?"

When the children arrived home that evening, Ginny discovered she was again disappointed that she didn't see

Joe, who she'd expected would accompany them into the house. "Where's your father?" she asked. "I'm surprised that he didn't come in and say hello." The kids looked at each other and shrugged. "Did you have fun? What did you do?"

"We didn't do much. Helen informed her. "We mostly just played around his house. He had stuff he was doing with some guy that builds houses or something. They were looking at lots of big drawings."

"What about you, Sallee, did you have fun?" she asked, knowing Sallee's penchant for conveying information. *I'm acting like a schoolgirl,* she chided herself. *Mary McCarthy's character Lackey would die rather than moon around like this.*

"I don't know," Sallee answered. "I read the whole time I was there. Since, Linda hasn't been around it's not as much fun at Dad's." She covered her mouth with her hand. "Oh!" she exclaimed.

"It's okay," Ginny reassured her, "I know you cared about Linda, and I'm sorry she isn't around for you anymore." The unbidden thought, *I'm thrilled for me that she's out of the picture, though,* jumped into her mind on the heels of her last word.

"I didn't think you were here. Your car's gone," Gordy said as he flopped on the sofa.

"Rebecca has bought my old car," Ginny said. " I decided to keep the new one after all."

"Cool!" Gordy jumped up and looked out of the window. "Can we go for a ride? We haven't yet. Well, uh, not much of one, anyway," he laughed.

"Tomorrow when I take you to school," Ginny said. "It's late, and I bet you have homework to do. Am I right?"

Gordy sighed, "Okay, I'll go do it. Hey, Who is Rebecca anyway? And how come Sallee knows her so well?"

Ginny was about to say she was someone she'd met at AA but then remembered she couldn't. "She's someone I met recently. We started talking and liked each other. I don't know how she and Sallee know each other. I haven't seen much of her to ask since I found out." She turned to Sallee, "How do you know each other?"

Sallee squirmed a little as she tried to figure out a way to place the day without bringing up why she was in a position to have met Rebecca. "Remember that day I got sick? I was gone for a while, before. I was at Rebecca's house."

"How did you know her to be at her house?" Helen asked.

Sallee had to work out what to say in her head before she answered, "I was sort of sitting on a stump by the street in front of her house. You know she lives in a strange house. It's kinda fallen down."

Gordy asked, "Why were you sitting on a tree stump in front of her house." Sallee tried to glare at him to shut him up without Ginny seeing. "*Cuz*, is all. Just CUZ. Anyway, Charlie came out and started talking to me. She was fun. It was funny, when I first met her I couldn't tell if she was a girl or a boy. She's sort of strange looking, a little weird. But I like her," she added hastily.

"Was that the day I made you so mad at the drugstore?" Ginny asked. Sallee nodded and put her head down, waiting for the reprimand. "I'm sorry about that, Sallee. I think I deserved it. I wasn't nice to you or to Linda." She came over and gave Sallee a big hug and a kiss. "I hope you'll forgive me."

"Me too, Mom," Sallee whispered in her mother's ear before she kissed her back.

"I've got to do something about this situation," Joe grumbled out loud as he pulled away from Ginny's house. "The kids think I need to entertain them when they visit. It's my fault. I did at first. They are a little spoiled." *Or maybe I'm just being to hard on them, expecting too much*. They'd settled down all right on Saturday evening, but only after what seemed like an eighteen-round fight throughout the day – whining for treats, lobbying for a trip to the amusement park, insisting – the girls, at least – that they needed new clothes for some school event that he was quite sure Ginny had not mentioned. *And then there was that movie Gordy was so keen to see, what was it again? Something with Jayne Mansfield, yeah 'Promises Promises,' not a chance!* As his mind raced along, lighting on all of the disadvantages of raising children in two separate households, he tried to stop it. Thinking about the advantages to give his mind a more positive goal created more confusion. "Damn it, this controlling your thinking is not as easy as I thought, especially on my own. I need training wheels!"

Ok, he thought, *here's where we need "Dr. J," how does that thing go? Let's see, to give myself freedom when I get in a bind like this, "I'm free to think the kids are spoiled, and it's my fault. I'm not free to think they are spoiled and that I didn't do it." No, that's not it, how did it go?*

By the time he got home, he was cursing his inability to remember what seemed so simple just last week. "It's a good thing I have an appointment tomorrow. I need it," he said out loud. Meanwhile, he decided to confess his plight to Dr. Berke's star student. "Maybe Stuart can help." He pulled out his address book, checked for the number and dialed. "Can I speak to Stuart Mackey, please?" he asked relieved to have finally gotten through after five attempts were met with busy signals.

"Just a minute," was the bored reply.

Several minutes later Stuart answered, "Hello."

"How's my girl?" Joe boomed. "I am so glad to finally get you, I almost forget why I called."

"Hey Dad, it wasn't just to tell me you loved me?" she laughed. "I am great. I got two papers back with A's. I actually like my classes, and get this, Miriam has finally given up custody of my clothes. Now that the clothes war is over we're getting along really well. I even like her!"

"That's excellent news. I am so proud of you. And hey, you couldn't help me with Jacob's mind-bending, could you? I don't know how to do it." Joe complained.

"It's pretty simple, Dad. What's the problem?" Stuart asked.

"You know how when I first left your mother, I always had something fun to do on the weekends when I had the kids? Now they think it's my job to entertain them. If I don't have some activity for us to do, all I hear is complaints."

"Aww, poor Daddy. Are those mean little kids picking on you?" she teased.

"Are you going to help me or not? I don't need your smart aleck comments, Miss Prodigy." He laughed despite his irritation for having to ask. "Hey, I'm having a hard time with the tables turned like this."

"I don't understand. What do you mean?" Stuart asked.

"Fathers are supposed to be the ones with the answers. Calling their teenage kid up and asking for help is not part of the job description."

She laughed, "Aw, there is the rub. No wonder I was so mixed up!" she tittered. "It is one of the things I love the most about you. You are not hamstrung by the way things are supposed to be, not conventional like Mother is. You think for yourself. If I have an answer to a question you have, why wouldn't you call me?"

"Exactly my thought," he laughed, "so tell me how to bend my mind about the kids?"

"First of all you aren't bending your mind. You are giving yourself the space to see things differently. So have you done the freedom runs?"

"The what?" Joe sighed. "This stuff might be simple, but it sure ain't easy."

"Dad, such a whiner," she teased, "didn't Dr. J. talk to you about how important freedom is to the mind? One of the ways people make life hard for themselves is they don't give themselves the space to be. They try to wedge their thoughts into just one way of looking at them like it is the only way.

"The guy is a genius, Dad. I can't tell you how grateful I am to you for finding him for me."

Her enthusiasm verging on bubbling over, she continued with her explanation. "The way freedom runs work is, you say *I am free to be upset about the kids complaining because I am not entertaining them*. Then you say, *I am free not to be upset about the kids complaining.* You do that with all of the things you can think of around the problem of the kids being upset. Does that make sense? Like, I'm free to want to beat the holy crap of the kids for making me upset and I'm free not to want to beat them." She laughed.

"So I say, *I am free for the kids to complain and free for them not to complain,* like that?" he asked. "I'm free for them to be happy and I'm not free for them to be happy. I'm free to work when they are here and I'm not free to work when they are here."

"Not exactly. What you want to do is give yourself the freedom for both ends of the problem to be okay. Like this: I am free to be upset about the kids, I am free to be at peace about the kids. If you want to fix something you can say, I am free to fix it and I'm free not to fix it. I'm free to let it be and I'm free to not let it be. You have to be free for both ends. So don't say, I'm free to whatever and I'm **not** free to whatever. It's: I'm free to 'blank' and I'm free not to 'blank.' Get it?"

She was thrilled that her father called and asked her to help him with this. "I know it sounds weird, but I swear it works. You feel better when you allow yourself the freedom to have it all in any given situation. Like the papers I just got back. Before I handed them in, I did a freedom run on the outcome. I was free to get an A. I was free not to get an A. I was also free to flunk it and free not to. I'm not going to change the outcome of a given situation by doing freedom runs on them. I'm going to change just how I feel about the outcome. It's magic in how it changes your feelings, not how it changes the circumstances." She stopped, "You get that, right?" she asked and then added, "You know, the deal I struck with the Dean could have created a whole lot of unnecessary pressure which might have derailed my plans without this little trick Dr. J. taught me. I love freedom runs. You have to mean it, though. You do have to be free both ways."

"So I am free to want to get back together with your mother and I am free not to?" Joe asked.

"Oh, Dad, really? Are you sure?" She was silent for a minute, then said; "I guess the rubber has to meet the road sometime. I am free for you to get back with Mom and I am free for you to not get back with her. I do have a preference, though." She said. "I hope you know what you are getting yourself into. I don't want you to get hurt again."

"You, oh wise one, could be pleasantly surprised. Besides, if this stuff works as well as you say it does, I'm free to be hurt and I'm free not to be. Right? You know your mother's not been drinking since January. She's changed a lot. Wait until you come home for Thanksgiving, you'll see."

"I talked to her the other day. It actually did go well." Stuart admitted. "Maybe I changed, so I guess she can, too. I wish Dr. J. could get his hands on her. That would be something to see," she laughed. "I'm free for Dr. J. to help Mom and I'm free for her to be how she is," she said. "I have to work on that a little. I'm not that free for him not to help her. I would love it if she could be happy."

"I would love it if we could all be one big happy family. I'm free for that to happen," he said.

"Yeah, but are you free for it not to?" Stuart asked.

"I'll work on that," he said, "I love you. Thanks for setting me straight."

"Somebody's gotta do it," Stuart laughed. "Love you, too, Dad."

She hung up, sat for a minute thinking, then picked up the phone to call her mother. After Ginny accepted the charges, she poured out before Stuart had a chance to say a thing, "Stuart, darling, it's so wonderful to hear from you. I've been thinking about you a lot lately."

"Hi Mom, how are things going?"

"Things are wonderful." Ginny picked up immediately on the name change from Mother to Mom taking it as a signal that Stuart was relaxing into a more comfortable relationship with her. "I have had so much fun recently. This morning I laughed longer and harder than I think I ever have. My new friend Rebecca, who is staying with us for a bit, she brought breakfast up and we had breakfast in bed. I don't know why I hadn't done that before, except *we* didn't do those sorts of things." She laughed. "Can you imagine being run by people long dead? How ridiculous! Anyway, we talked about our childhoods and laughed like fools." Ginny hardly took a breath, she was so happy to be able to share her glee with her daughter. "About horrible, horrible things. It was so much fun. Laughing, by the way, was something *we* didn't do when I was growing up. How are you?" she finally asked. "I didn't mean to..."

"It's okay. Horrible things? It's great to hear you so happy." Stuart said, meaning it. "Tell me about Rebecca."

"Okay, but then you have to tell me all about you. The horrible things are just long dead stories, but some time I'll tell you. Deal?"

"Deal."

"Well, then," Ginny said, "let's talk about you. How's it going up there?"

"Great," said Stuart. "First of all, there were the clothing wars, did I tell you about that? And guess what, they're over, and I actually kind of like my roommate …"

Joe gave up trying to reach Ginny that night after about an hour of constant busy signals.

"Ginny, do you have plans tonight?" Joe felt like a fourteen-year-old, excited to finally speak with her after trying far into the preceding evening, and nervous at the prospect of asking for, well, a date. "I'd like to take you out to dinner. I thought we might go to the Gaslight. You like that place, don't you?"

Ginny struggled to keep her enthusiasm in check. "With the children?"

"No, just you." Joe bit his lip, *God, she can be so obtuse sometimes,* he thought. "I want to take you out on a date," he ventured, and feeling more vulnerable than he could ever remember, he added, "It's Veteran's Day, cause for celebration."

She managed to temper her desire to scream *Yes*. "I don't know. I'm not sure I can get a sitter."

"Ginny, you know damn well you don't need a sitter. I'm picking you up at 7:00." He hung up whistling. Until the thought *What if she used not being able to get a sitter as an excuse because she doesn't want to go* crept into his mind. He dismissed it. "It's tonight. I'm telling her all of it," he swore.

Ginny placed the receiver on the phone as if in a dream. She wanted to descend the stairs singing to little birds and mice like Cinderella in the movie. She opted for a more conventional descent, placing one foot carefully in front of the other, unsure if she could trust her feet not to take flight.

Rebecca looked up, "You look like you are in love," she commented, then laughed. "Who is the lucky guy?"

Ginny's lie surprised her, "I was just thinking about *The Group.* Such a good book -- you should read it. What have you in store today?"

"Didn't I tell you? Saturday, I met with Miss Eades -- Della," she corrected herself, "We got along so well, she wants me to move in and get settled so that when Charlie is ready to come home ... Wednesday," she gave a little hop of excitement, "we will have her room all set up for her." She came over to Ginny and wrapped her arms around her, "Thank you for the introduction. I think the situation is perfect for not only Charlie and me, but for Della, too. What a delight she is! She reminds me of my mother, a little."

"I'm so happy for you," Ginny said still wondering why she had lied about what she was thinking. "Can I help you? I don't have anything planned today particularly; that is until tonight."

"Fun, I hope?" Rebecca queried.

Ginny looked at her perplexed, "Huh?"

"Tonight, I hope whatever you have planned is fun," Rebecca explained.

"Oh, I suppose," she said, and let the subject drop. "Do you need any laundry done? I've got time, and I'm going to put some stuff in in just a few minutes." She waltzed back up the stairs, humming to herself.

Joe and Ginny sat across from each other with a too-small rickety table between them in the dimly lit restaurant. She looked around at the dark walls and drifts of cigarette smoke before saying, "I wonder if people would eat here if the lights were on. I always suspect dark restaurants of being dirty."

"Do you want to go somewhere else?" Joe asked. " I don't mind. I thought you liked this place."

"It's fine." She moved the ashtray. "You don't still smoke, do you?" When he indicated that he had quit, she called the waiter over and handed him the ashtray. "May I have an iced tea with lemon, please?"

"Bourbon and water and menus, please," Joe said. When the waiter left, he said, "I want to be sensitive to you. Would you prefer I that I not drink in front of you? I had planned to ask before I called the waiter, but..."

"I don't know. I don't think I can ask the world to stop drinking because I have," she said, looking as though she would like to.

He offered, "I can have tea, too."

"It doesn't make any difference," she said, although in truth she wished he had been sensitive enough not to have ordered a drink.

"Ginny, you are a pretty easy read. Something is eating at you. If it's something I have said or done, I can't fix it if I don't know what it is. I sure as hell don't want to keep doing something that annoys you." Joe leaned forward and reached for her hand. "I want…" She pulled her hand away, "…us to…"

The waiter plunked the bourbon down in front of Ginny then corrected his error, muttering, "Sorry, you were the iced tea?"

Ginny sighed, with a nod to the waiter. After he left, she said, "Sometimes it is so damned hard."

"Look, I can stop. I don't have to have a drink," Joe started.

Ginny interrupted, "If you didn't have to have one, why in the world did you order it? This isn't working. Take me home, please."

Joe pulled out a twenty and placed it on the table along with his napkin. With as much control as he could muster, he got up and pulled her chair out for her. Not saying a word, they walked to the car. Joe used every trick he had learned from Jacob Berke to keep himself in check. *My goal is to lovingly put my family back together,* he reminded himself. *That might take some time. I can't expect to rectify all of the wrongs in one evening.* In the car before starting the engine he said in an even voice, "I am sorry for all of the hurt I have caused you. It was never my intention. As much as I want to put my family back together, I can't be apologizing all of the time. I have forgiven you…"

"Me?" she snapped, then continued, slowing for effect, "How monumentally magnanimous of you! You have forgiven me for walking out on you—pregnant! Well done, aren't you just grand! You have forgiven me for accusing you of being an unfit mother. Wonderful! You have forgiven me for leaving you with a dead baby to deal with on your own." She pulled herself up to full height, "How dare you forgive me," she snarled. "Take me home, now!" She wrapped her arms up under her breasts, tucked in her chin and sniffed as she moved as close to the passenger door as she could. There, she sat in a brooding silence all the way home.

Joe started the engine, slipped the car into gear and drove slowly out of the parking lot. *What if I just ignore that outburst? What would happen if I just allowed her to be angry and didn't respond to it? I'd be a saint. Just get her home without losing your temper. That would be a big win. Just get her home.* As he pulled into the driveway at the house, he asked, "Did it ever occur to you that your actions might have brought some of this on? You might not have been a total victim. You might actually have some responsibility for what ended our marriage."

She slammed out of the car. Wordless, he walked her to the door, albeit behind her. Just as she reached for the door, it opened. Rebecca, startled, laughed, "Oh, excuse me. I didn't expect you so..." Ginny brushed past her and up the stairs without a word.

Joe watched her climb the stairs, then turned to Rebecca. "Hello, I'm Joe Mackey. You must be the Rebecca I have heard so much about from Sallee. I am glad to hear Charlie is getting better."

Rebecca looked up the stairs after Ginny, then back at Joe when he mentioned her daughter. "Yes, hello. That is very kind of you. Thank you. I hope nothing..." She looked back up the stairs, "Is there anything I can do?"

"Do you have a magic wand?" he sighed. "I am afraid she's not ready to give me a second chance. I had hoped... It was nice to finally meet you." He turned to leave.

Rebecca caught him by the elbow. "I know this is none of my business. And let me assure you I am a master of knowing how important that line is. Ginny risked it for me once, so I feel like I owe her." Rebecca plucked up her courage, because in spite of what she had just declared, this was new and shaky ground for her. "Are you still in love with her?"

"Hopelessly," Joe said, "but I'm afraid the feelings are not reciprocal and I am beginning to doubt they ever will be. I'm not even sure she ever loved me." He was shocked that he was saying this to a woman he had just laid eyes on. "I have never regretted anything I have ever done as much as this. I think I was half mad when I started divorce proceedings. When it took on a life of its own, like a fool, I just followed along." He looked up at Rebecca with a sad smile, "I'm sure it would be hard for you to believe, considering all that I am sure you have heard, but my family means everything to me."

"Let me talk to her. I don't know if you know this, but I met her through AA. I think I know what is going on. Without speaking out of school, I saw her this morning after your call. You did call this morning?" Joe nodded that he did. "She is a woman in love. Afraid, I suspect, of getting hurt, but there is no question in my mind that she is in love with you."

He smiled, feeling a little hope. "I don't know what you could do, though. Well, I just don't know. It went wrong when I ordered a drink. I offered...The thing is, she was well defended before that. You could almost say she was looking for me to fail."

"I bet she was," Rebecca mused. "It's a thing about us drunks. We don't trust ourselves or anybody else, except to hurt us. Let me talk to her."

"I can't stop you. I warn you, though, she is stubborn." He laughed ruefully. "And if she thinks you have overstepped your bounds, she can turn colder than a New York avenue in January."

"I had forgotten that you grew up in the city. Upper West. You?"

"I figured. Upper East." They both laughed. "Privileged," he laughed again, "No, maybe blessed is the more appropriate term."

"Aren't we just," she smiled.

Chapter 16

Rebecca wished that she had kept her mouth shut. Even if she did feel obligated, the idea of waltzing into to a person's life and telling them you know better than they how their life should go smacked of the kind of arrogance she hated about her father. Leaning against the front door that she had just shut after watching Joe walk away, she wondered how she was even going to start the conversation. She rehearsed. *Ginny, Joe and I talked. I know you love him...*and then another, *Ginny, remember when you said I was a dry drunk? Remember when you said it took one to know one? Well...*

"Damn, what have I gotten myself into?" she said out loud.

"Who was that outside? Is Mom home already?" Sallee asked, emerging from the den. "It sounded like Daddy."

"It was," Rebecca answered hoping that Sallee wouldn't ask any more questions, even as she knew very well that she would.

"Why didn't he come in?" Sallee wanted to know.

Rebecca went over to the child and put her arms around her. "Things didn't go quite how he had hoped. He was disappointed. I think he just wanted to clear his head."

"Where's Mom?"

"Your mom's upstairs." She nodded toward the steps.

"Things didn't go well with Mom? I hate her. She is always messing things up."

"Sallee, don't say things like that," Rebecca said. "This thing with your father is complicated. She didn't mess it up any more than he did. One person can't destroy a relationship."

"They can if that person doesn't try. She didn't try. She just felt sorry for herself and drank all the time is all." Sallee stamped her foot for emphasis. "She didn't…I wish she was more like you." Sallee hugged Rebecca.

"Sallee, your mother is a lovely person. It would be my honor to be like her. I understand that a lot of very painful things happened in the past, but please believe me, they are not all your mother's fault. Life is difficult. Sometimes it feels like drinking is all you can do. She doesn't anymore, though, and that is wonderful. Believe me, I know."

"Are you an alcoholic, too?" Sallee asked wide-eyed.

"Yes, I am. There is one thing I can tell you. Nobody wants to be an alcoholic. Once you have the habit, not drinking can be the hardest thing you ever do every single day." Rebecca put her arm on the girl's shoulder. "I don't expect you to believe it, but your mother is doing a fantastic job. Her life has been anything but easy, even now."

"I guess," Sallee said, all of a sudden sadder than she had been in a very long time. "I guess."

Rebecca steered Sallee back to the television and thought about sitting down with the kids before deciding she had better go talk to Ginny now or she might not do it at all. "I'm going upstairs to talk with your mom."

Gordy didn't even bother to take his eyes off the television, "You sure you want to do that? When she gets mad, she's not a lot of fun to talk with. She's a yeller."

"A what?" Rebecca exclaimed.

"A yeller, she yells a lot," he said flatly.

Rebecca laughed, "Gordy Mackey, you are a funny guy." She got up to leave.

"Ok, but you've been warned." He shot her a mischievous look. "Don't come running to me if you get your feelings hurt." She gave him an okay sign and they both laughed.

Rebecca approached Ginny's room quietly, trying to think of something to say before she knocked. Plucking up her courage, she gave the door a gentle tap.

"What?" Ginny snapped.

Taken aback and feeling more than a little timid, Rebecca answered just above a whisper, "Ginny it's me Rebecca. I wanted to talk. Can I come in?"

"No damn it, go away," she yelled back, "and leave me alone."

Rebecca stood outside the door for a minute trying to compose herself, surprised at the anger starting to well up. "Ginny Mackey, are we going to keep dancing this dance?" she shouted. "I lead, you follow. Then you lead." She couldn't believe how brazen she was as she turned the knob on Ginny's bedroom door. She stuck her head in the door and yelled like she was ten years old, "Dry drunk!" then stuck out her tongue and laughed.

Ginny was so shocked by her friend's actions that she burst out laughing. "You are an ass," she laughed. "Come in. I guess I deserved that."

"Yep, and if you keep it up a spanking too!" Rebecca pronounced with feigned solemnity.

Ginny sat up. "I sure made a complete and total ass of myself tonight. Damn, damn double damn. It's like I can't control myself. Everything he does makes me mad when I'm with him. When he's away, he's Prince Charming. Later, when I think about it I can't even imagine what I could have found that made me so angry." She stopped to blow her nose. "It's no use. We can't get back together. It won't work."

"You're right. Might as well forget it," Rebecca agreed. "Move on, find somebody else. There are a million fish in the sea."

"Hold on, what are you up to?" Ginny looked at her friend with suspicion. "Is this some kind of trick? You are not following your lines!"

Rebecca crossed the room, moved some clothes on the chair to make room and sat down. "Trick? Lines? What are you talking about?" she asked all innocence. "I am agreeing with you. It's not going to work. Joe is an insensitive clod. I just met him. You were right."

"Not funny, Rebecca. What do you think?" Ginny asked.

"You don't give a wit what I think and it's beside the point. It's what you think that's important. You said it wasn't going to work. I trust you. If you said so, it must be true."

"Okay, I get it. Maybe I was acting rather childish," Ginny allowed. "I want him. I just am so frightened that I am going to get hurt; that things will be hard. I'll start drinking again."

"All of those things can happen," Rebecca agreed. "Probably will, as a matter of fact."

"I'll start drinking?" Ginny retorted.

"You could. It's possible." Rebecca said. "Honestly, stranger things have happened."

"I just don't trust him, or you either right now. What are you up to?" Ginny sat up, "Damn it, Rebecca, stop playing games."

"I'm not playing games. I trust you. If it won't work, it won't work," Rebecca replied. .

"Well, I don't, damn it. I don't trust anything or anybody, most of all me!" Ginny shouted.

"That is a problem," Rebecca said. "Probably need some help with that."

"Ohh," Ginny sighed in exasperation. I think I'm going to call my therapist in the morning and see if I can see her before I talk myself out it." She half smiled, half grimaced, and shrugged helplessly.

"Don't worry," Rebecca said firmly, "I won't let you. You know," she added, "it's obvious you never had a good friend. You believe you're a bitch." She laughed out loud.

Her appointment with Janet, her therapist, wasn't until four o'clock on Wednesday. "What in the hell am I going to do for two whole days?" she groaned as she placed the phone back on the hook. It startled her when it rang before she had taken her hand away. With a big sigh, she picked up the receiver. "Hello,"

"Ginny, Hi, Sharon here. I hate to do this to you." Ginny rolled her head back and sighed again. "The buyers' agent called this morning asking when you were planning on vacating the property. I told him that you were still debating what you wanted to do. Things had changed and you weren't sure you wanted to sell. The guy went berserk. He started screaming at me. 'Going to call his lawyer, breach of contract, shouldn't have signed it if you didn't know what you were doing,' on and on."

Ginny sighed again, "I don't know what I'll do, but I'll figure something out. You had better start looking PDQ."

"Can we make an appointment to look and I'll line some things up? I know what you want."

Ginny had the phone cord wound around her finger for the fifth time and was busily unwinding but still laughed. "Glad you do, because I have no idea. I'm free all day tomorrow or Thursday. Let me know." She disengaged her finger and hung up.

She made a beeline to the kitchen. "Ethel," she started until she remembered that Rebecca might still be home. "Never mind," she said absently. "Do you know if Rebecca is still here?"

"Doan know, Miz Ginny. I ain't seen her dis mornin'."

"I'll go look for her," Ginny said, heading out of the kitchen. She stopped turned around and walked slowly back. "Ethel, if you wouldn't mind, would you say a little prayer that some place at least as wonderful as that farm near you comes on the market very soon?"

"God doan cotton much t' that much direction. He like t' work in His own way, but I'll ask fo' you. But you know, Miz Ginny, it wouldn' hurt none if you asked yo' own self."

"I have, Ethel, believe me, I have," Ginny said and went off in search of Rebecca.

Rebecca slipped her coat off. "I'm all ears."

"No, you were going out. It can wait," she said as her lip began to quiver. "Rebecca, I can't get out of the contract without having to pay a lot of money."

"What contract?" Rebecca asked.

"This house, I sold the house thinking I was going to buy the farm. We have to be out of here by the end of May. I swear, it is enough to drive a person to drink. Do you think one more thing can happen?"

"Count on it," Rebecca laughed. You'll be able to find a place before then. I'd love to go with you to look. It could be fun."

"It's all so hard. Joe and the house selling, Stuart, Gordy and then finding out about my father and Cy."

"Yep, it's a lot of stuff, but most of it has already worked itself out. I'm not sure I see the problem," Rebecca said, "You know you love Joe, right?" Ginny nodded. "You know he loves you?"

"I think." Ginny corrected.

"Well, I know he does because he told me he did. Stuart is happier than you can remember, according to you just the other day. Gordy seems to have settled down, and you just sold the house that you wanted to sell. Tell me what's wrong? Oh, and you have a new best friend." Rebecca leaned her shoulder against the doorjamb and folded her arms across her chest.

"When did you talk to Joe?" Ginny sniffed, finding herself miffed that Rebecca and Joe had talked behind her back.

"Hold on," Rebecca straightened and held a hand up for drama, not realizing that her audience teetered on the brink of rage. "Before you climb up on that high horse of yours and charge around the place all high and mighty lopping off heads and what not. I told you I met Joe last night when he walked you to the door. In the throes of a full-fledged temper tantrum, you might have missed it, since you were too busy stomping up the stairs, having left the man standing there with his heart in his hands. I couldn't just shut the door in his face. We said maybe fifteen words to each other. He said he was hopelessly in love with you and never regretted anything as much as he did divorcing you. Okay, maybe thirty words."

"You're awfully clever, and having far too much fun at my expense." Ginny lashed out indignantly.

"Ginny, it's a good thing I love you. It's pretty obvious that you have never had a real friend, because if you had, you'd know you don't treat people like this." Rebecca realized she had overplayed her hand.

Ginny ran up the stairs to her room and slammed her bedroom door. Rebecca shrugged, turned to put her coat back on and spied Ethel standing at the kitchen door. "Ever'thang all righ'?" she asked. "I b'lieve I heard a door slam."

"You did," Rebecca said, "I made Ginny mad, and she ran upstairs like she was a ten-year-old. Does she always act like that when things don't go her way?"

"Yes'm, she do." Ethel shook her head. "She always done ever since I knowed her."

"It's a damn good thing she ran into me, then," Rebecca said, laughing. "That kind of shit has gotta stop."

Taken aback as she was with Rebecca's language, Ethel could only agree.

Rebecca made a move to leave, "Hell, as my old Bubbie used to say, Living life is not like crossing a meadow." She took her coat off again and trotted upstairs after Ginny. Ethel stood at the bottom of the stairs drying her hands on her apron.

"Ginny," Rebecca called not waiting for an answer as pushed her way into the room, "Here's the thing. I can't stand by and let you do this to yourself. You are an exceptional woman with some remarkably bad habits." She stood in the doorway, hanging on to the edge of the door with both hands, swinging it gently. "Not your fault. Nobody taught you any better. I know you would be doing the same thing for me because you did, the other day in the hospital. Even though it didn't look like it at the time, I am infinitely grateful and frankly quite awed by your courage." She let go of the door and stood facing Ginny, "This isn't easy. Staring down the barrel of those blue eyes is intimidating."

Besides the I-wish-you-would-go-away-and-drop-dead stare, Ginny hadn't acknowledged Rebecca. Despite this fact, Rebecca forged on. "Just after Charles died, my mother insisted I talk with her good friend's husband. I think they met at synagogue, I think -- but that doesn't make any difference," she said dismissing it with a wave of her hand. "We met a few times before a drunk driver mowed his wife and two children down in front of him. It was terrible, as I am sure you can imagine."

She could see that Ginny was interested, so ventured farther into the room, pulled out Ginny's dressing table chair and sat down. "This man was amazing. Rather than retreat into his sorrow, something no one would blame him for even for a minute, he recast the horror into a mission to help people overcome trauma. I haven't seen him in years, but I have no doubt that he has accomplished it. What a role model. I started to go to AA because of his example." She didn't look at Ginny, afraid her next admission might make her even angrier, "Not because I have a real problem with alcohol, I don't drink, never have, except after Charles died. I go because it is a place where humbled people gather and take strength from one another."

Seeing no reaction, she continued. "I grew up in a very pious household, a household without a shred of humility or gratitude. Pride, privilege and arrogance were the gods my family bowed down to. That mindset put my mother in an early grave. It made my father into a monster who could banish his unborn grandchild because of the inconvenient timing of her birth and then find justification for his action when she is born an *imbecile,* as he so delicately put it. Putting that stuff behind me was the best thing I ever did, and you need to do it, too. It's poison. You are so much better than that," Rebecca implored. Ginny was sitting up crossed-legged on the bed now.

"I am almost sorry I embarrassed you downstairs. *Almost* because it's pretty clear no one has ever challenged you. They have out of misguided love protected you. That protection has spoiled you. When things don't go your way, you bolt to your room, to the bottle, to temper tantrums."

Ginny pulled herself up as tall as she could and said with an imperial air, "Are you suggesting you embarrassed me for my own good. Sounds like a lot of arrogant bunk to me. And you feel justified in your challenge why?" She shot Rebecca a venomous look. "You can leave."

"Ginny, don't shoot the messenger. Think about it. What have I got to gain by telling you this if my intentions aren't honorable? Why would I hurt you, you who have done so much for me? You took me in, stood toe to toe with my pride and stared it down. Don't I owe this to you? Why would I want to hurt you?"

"It's beyond me," Ginny said. "I can't imagine why you'd kick me in the teeth like this. Please leave and I mean, leave my house. Take your things and go, now."

"Have it your way," Rebecca sighed. "I'm sorry things have to end and in this way. I truly appreciate everything you have done for me." She smiled and approached Ginny to give her a hug. Ginny turned away.

On the way downstairs, Rebecca berated herself for pushing so much. *I had no idea that she was that entrenched. Maybe I was too flippant. Poor kids,"* she thought, then, *stop it, Levine, it will all work itself out. It's none of your business. Your job is to focus on taking care of yourself and Charlie*. When Rebecca saw Ethel standing at the bottom of the stairs, to her amazement she burst into tears.

"Didn' go so good?" Ethel asked as she wrapped Rebecca in her arms, "I didn' 'spect it woulda." She patted the woman on the back, "Doan you worry none, Miz Ginny'll come t' her senses in no time. Den ever'thang'll be righ' as rain."

"She told me to leave, to pack my things and go," Rebecca sniffed in Ethel's embrace. "I feel so awful, Ethel, I had no idea that she would be that upset or that stubborn."

"She doan hol' a grudge. She'll be down in a wink, askin' why you leavin'." Ethel assured her.

"That's not right, though. You know as well as I do. It's not good for the kids to have their mother act like a..." she searched for the word as she straightened, her dark eyes boring down on Ethel. "...a brat."

"Miz Rebecca," Ethel said, then corrected herself as she had been instructed, "Rebecca, you know good as me you can't teach an old dog..."

"New tricks," Ginny said standing at the top of the stairs. "Rebecca, I'm so sorry. I have been a perfect AA, what my sister-in-law would call an arrogant ass. Please forgive me."

Rebecca ran up the stairs and threw her arms around Ginny. They went back into Ginny's room, laughing. Ethel saw by the kitchen clock that they'd been talking for a good thirty minutes before Rebecca ran down the stairs, shouting over her shoulder, "Bye, have to fly, I have an appointment ten minutes ago!" as she dashed out the door.

By the time Ginny stopped feeling victimized long enough to take in Rebecca's hard words, they hit her like a bucket of ice water. The good hard look they demanded showed her how much of a bully she had become, maybe always had been. The similarity to her father made her shudder. She vowed to change no matter the cost. There was no question she did not want to live like that. Embarrassment and shame reared their ugly heads almost the instant she made her vow. "I know you," she growled out loud, "and you aren't going to win this time." She couldn't help checking to see if any one had heard her then added. "I'm not running away." With her new resolve, she picked up the phone. For the second time that day it rang in her hand.

"Hello," she said breaking out into a wide smile when she heard his voice, "Joe, I was just going to call you? Will you marry me?" She put her hand to her mouth. "Oh, my God, that wasn't what meant to say. I was going to ask you to lunch." She started to laugh.

"Yes," he joined in, "to both." They both laughed uproariously, setting each other off. "I'll be over in ten minutes – that's for lunch! I think the wedding might need a little more planning." They were still laughing as they hung up. Ginny sat down at her desk, shaking her head as she thought how amazing life was. A little over an hour ago, she was in the depths of despair, and the only thing that changed between then and now was the passage of time and her attitude.

Before Joe arrived, Ginny stuck her head in the kitchen, "Would you mind making lunch for Joe and me?"

Ethel flashed an ear-to-ear grin, "Yes'm, I would be happy t' do dat." Her humming had started before she opened the refrigerator door. Perusing the offerings, she pulled out her head and said, "How 'bout a BLT salad?"

"Perfect. He'll be here soon. Can you have it ready in, say," she looked at her watch, "forty-five minutes?"

"Yes'm," She didn't even wait, for Ginny to leave before warbling a strand of *What a Friend We Have in Jesus*. Ginny stood by the large front window, watching for Joe's car. When she saw it turn into the drive, she ran out to greet him. Soon after Ginny let the front door slam, Ethel stood in Ginny's vacated spot to catch a peek and saw the two locked in what appeared to be a very passionate embrace. She bustled back into the kitchen, warbling at the top of her ample lungs, "*Hmm hmm friend we have in Jesus, All our sins and griefs to bear! Hmmm hmmmm God in prayer!* Oh, YES, Lord," she exclaimed, pausing to affirm it, then started in again, "*What a friend we have in Jesus…*".

In no time, the table was set with a huge salad festooned with freshly cooked bacon-jest like Mista' Joe like it. Freshly made iced tea adorned with a thick slice of lemon sweated on the lace placemats. Ginny and Joe had made their way through all of the atrocities committed by Ginny's father and the inheritance left by Joe's, and four circuits of the garden. Ethel heard Ginny say, "Could we have the ceremony on our twentieth anniversary? Don't you think that would be just perfect?"

"Twentieth? Are you sure? We got married in 1943?" Joe asked.

"Yes, I am sure of it," Ginny assured him.

"That's two weeks away," Joe protested, feigned a groan. "But hey, on the other hand, I'd like that idea, since I already have that date committed to memory. No point challenging the old brain with another one." He laughed, then added, "But it would be a reason for two presents if we had two wedding anniversaries."

"You can just give me two presents on the one day," she giggled. "So we have set the date --November 22, 1963, yes? I think that's a Friday. That's sort of odd getting married on a Friday. Is that okay with you?"

"Yes, great, and if it's all right with you I want to give you a wedding present right now, okay?" Joe replied.

Ginny giggled, "You know I never turn down a present," then thought better of what she'd just said and corrected herself. "Well, almost never. But I did finally accept the car, so . . ."

Joe smiled, fiddled in his coat pocket for a bit then came up to her chair, and got down on one knee. Ginny started to giggle, wiping away tears. "Virginia Stuart Mackey, will you marry me, again and for the very last time?"

"Yes, Joe," she squeaked, so overcome with emotion that her voice failed her, then louder the second time, "Yes!" She kissed him hard and long.

Breaking off the kiss, Joe laughed. "I've got to come up for air so that I can give you this --" handing her a magnificent diamond solitaire -- "to make up for the lack of one before." She *ooohed* and *aaahed* as he slipped it on the ring finger of her left hand, admiring the perfect fit. "It looks like it belongs there." Ginny moved to continue the kiss. He stopped her, handing her a brown document envelope. "And this dear lady, love of my life, is for you, with all my love and devotion."

"What is it?" she asked taking the envelope as sparkles danced around the room like so many stars as the ring caught the afternoon sun streaming through the window. "Joe, this ring is gorgeous. Thank you."

"Open it," he said as he lifted his hand to shield his eyes from the reflected light of the diamond. "Sunglasses might have to be mandatory around that ring."

Grinning and giggling, Ginny worked at the metal clasp on the envelope with trembling fingers, finally managing to pry it open. She carefully pulled out some papers, looking at Joe and then down at the papers several times in the process. "I can't even imagine," she said as she glanced down at the papers in her hand. Before reading, she looked over at him, sticking out her lower lip and said, "I don't have a present for you. This all happened a little unexp…"

"Read, read," he interrupted her, barely able to contain his excitement. Still on his knee, with his cheeks aching from all his grinning, he watched Ginny's eyes scan the document.

She gasped, "Oh, my dear God," Her hands covered her face as she burst into a sob, "Oh, Joe, how on earth?" She leaned forward, wrapped him in her arms and smothered him with kisses. "Oh, Joe, I can't believe it. You are the most wonderful man in the world and I love you and I – Ohhh, I can't even think straight! Thank you, thank you, thank you!" She got up, reached out her hand and led him upstairs. Her bedroom door closed quietly behind them.

Ethel mustered every ounce of self-control not to start dancing on the spot. An hour or so later, Joe left. Ginny strolled into the kitchen. "Judging by your cat-that-swallowed-the-canary look and the tunes I have heard wafting out of the kitchen, I am quite certain you know what's going on. Yes?"

Ethel couldn't even attempt a pretense. "Yes'um. I'm so happy I could jes' bust wide open." She grinned.

"Please don't," Ginny laughed, "and please don't say anything to the children about it, either. Joe and I want to tell them all together. You know how word spreads in this family."

"My lips is sealed," Ethel promised. "I can tell Early, though? He'll be tickled pink."

Ginny, looking like a schoolgirl, nodded nodded laughing. "Ethel I want you to give me away. Would you do that?"

"You mean like I was yo' parent? Miz Ginny I doan think...Mista' Gordon or Mista' James dey be..."

"Ethel you are more family to me than any blood relation I have. Would you stand with me and Joe like a best man?" She laughed, "Best woman?"

"I doan think it woul' be quite righ', but it means de world t' me t' be axed. Kin I think on it an' let you know?"

Absolutely, it would mean so much." She bent over and hugged Ethel, "I'll be back later." She went to the phone in the back hall, canceled two appointments and left the house.

Sallee hustled breathlessly into the kitchen as soon as she got home from school. "Ethel, I am so glad to get you alone. I have the most wonderful news."

Ethel stopped her humming, flashed Sallee a broad smile, and chortled, "Dis must be de day for good news."

"Mom and Dad are going to get married," Sallee shouted, hopping on her toes. Ethel's face fell. Sallee asked, "What's the matter, don't you want them to?"

Ethel, too flustered to think, stood in the middle of the kitchen trying to come up with a plausible answer. Whatever she said would, in her mind, betray her promise. Finally, she settled for a remarkably inarticulate turn of the tables, "Who say?"

"Dad said so last night. He told me not to tell," Sallee announced as Gordy strode into the room and Ethel groaned.

"Den why is you?" Ethel demanded figuring that the situation called for a good offensive move.

Sallee slightly taken aback at Ethel's odd behavior said, "He didn't say I couldn't tell you, or Gordy or Helen, just Mom."

Ethel looked over at Gordy who shrugged with a wave in Sallee's direction and said, "She can't help herself. And I'll believe it when I see it."

Helen walked in, looking worried. "Wha's de matter wit' you, sugar?" Ethel asked.

"I don't know if I want them to get married," Helen stated in her usual unadorned manner. Ethel stole a look at Sallee, who looked back with a chagrined little shrug.

Ethel pulled out a chair and sat down with a mighty groan. "Lord, I doan know wha' I'm gonna do wit' y'all chil'ren," she said, and started to laugh.

That night Joe and Ginny's news left the parents nonplussed, as all three children reacted as if it were a rerun of *I Love Lucy.*

'Did Ethel tell you?" Ginny wanted to know as she sat in Joe's lap. "I wondered if she would be able to keep quiet. She looked like she was about to pop from excitement."

"No," Gordy answered, "Sallee did."

At which point Sallee piped up and said to Joe, "you didn't tell me I couldn't tell the others, just Mom."

Ginny looked at Joe. He smiled shrugging, "You had to have been there. I just told her I loved you – oh, never mind.

Besides, I didn't know you were going to beat me to the punch." He turned to the others. "You know your mother was the one that asked me. She called up and said, 'Joe would you marry me' just like that. What was I supposed to do? I couldn't say no, I would never hear the end of it." He shrugged helplessly and they all began to laugh, most of all Ginny.

"Okay," she said, "so maybe our upcoming wedding is already old news," she stole a bittersweet look at Joe. "I have some news that I am quite sure won't be." She waited as six eyes sparkled at her with excitement. "Oh, did I show you the beautiful engagement ring your father gave me?" she asked, milking the moment for all she could get out of it.

"That's your news, a ring?" Gordy couldn't hide his disappointment, "I thought it was going to be exciting."

Joe said, "Stay tuned, old boy. You might still be in store for a thrill."

"Drum roll, please," Ginny said. "Today your father gave me a wedding present -- the deed to the Taylor farm."

"The place with the swimming pool? Near Ethel and Early's?" Gordy asked crossing his fingers that the answer was yes.

"The very same," Ginny said, tears suddenly streaming down her face. Pandemonium ensued.

Sallee sat in the hall chair at the foot of the steps, swing her legs. She fidgeted with the arrangement of her new dress to make sure that she didn't wrinkle it. *This might be the prettiest dress I have ever seen,* she thought as she gazed down at the jacquard silk in a subtle teardrop pattern. She adored the empire waist, the adorable peter-pan collar and the simple but elegant line of the skirt – tailored, not frilly. Sallee didn't know much about clothes except she hated frou-frou and frills. Helen, on the other hand was wearing a dress in the same light gray fabric that made her look like an ice cream sundae with layers of frills and more frills. But she looked pretty. Ordinarily Sallee would have put her foot down. Wearing matching dresses was just too little-kid, but since the only thing that matched was the fabric, she could live with it. She felt quite sure that only the most discerning eye would even spot the similarities in the dresses. Her hair was pulled up and back in a half ponytail. She hopped up to check herself out in the large mirror. Yep, looking mighty fine. She carefully sat again, waiting for the rest of the family to ascend.

Gordy came down the stairs, so handsome in his new blue blazer and gray trousers that Sallee couldn't believe this was her brother. "Nice tie," she offered.

He grimaced. "Whatever I do for a living is definitely not going to require wearing a tie," he grumbled adjusting and readjusting it in the mirror.

"Did you tie it?" she asked.

"Yeah, but it took me half the morning," he laughed. "Where is everybody else?"

Sallee shrugged and pointed up the stairs. "You look handsome."

"Thanks." He couldn't help but beam. He thought so, too.

"You don't look half bad yourself. It's time to go, it's almost 1:30. It starts in an half an hour," he said, then shouted up the stairs, "Mom, Stuart, Helen come on."

Joe walked in, "Where is everybody?"

Gordy said as he headed to turn the TV on, "Upstairs."

"Don't turn it on, we've got to go," Joe said.

Ginny swept down the stairs looking glorious in a pale gray silk evening suit with a straight skirt and a scoop-necked jacket adorned with pearl buttons and bracelet-length sleeves. Around her neck sparkled a lovely diamond necklace. She wore white kid gloves and a copy of the pillbox hat that Jackie Kennedy had made so popular. Everyone in the hall gasped. "You look divine," Joe gushed, which induced a simultaneous eye roll from the two sibling onlookers. Stuart and Helen descended in their mother's wake, paling in comparison.

"Stuart, you take the kids and Ginny and I will ride together. Go straight to the church. We're short on time. Okay?"

"Yeah, Dad, how often does a kid get to see their parents getting hitched, we wouldn't miss this for the world." She laughed as her restored hair color shone in the hall light. "Mom, you look so beautiful." She went over and planted a kiss on her mother's cheek, " I am so happy. Come on, guys, let's beat them to the church." She raced out to the car with the others in pursuit.

Joe went over to Ginny and wrapped her in his arms. "I am in the happiest man alive."

"That makes two of us," she smiled.

"Man?" he knitted his eyebrows together, "Really?

She gave him a playful swat, "Get out of here, you." They both laughed all the way to the car.

Stuart stopped Gordy from turning on the radio. "Let's talk. It's been a long time since we were all together," she said as her three younger siblings exchanged surprised glances. "What have you guys been up to?"

"Gordy ran away," Helen offered up. "And he didn't even get in trouble." Gordy considered giving Helen a punch but decided against it.

"Running away seems like it was pretty popular these past few months," Stuart laughed. "Helen, I think you are the only one that didn't!"

"You ran away, too?" Sallee's eyes grew wide, while she sat back in her seat, pleased that someone else had noticed.

"Yeah, I got into a lot of trouble. But Dad found this great doctor who has helped me see so much stuff. I have to tell you later because here we are. I love you guys. I mean, I really love you guys," Stuart said as she pulled the car into the church parking lot. "Uh-oh." She was looking across the lot. "What's wrong here? Look at the parents. I hope they didn't get into a fight."

Worried the children hustled over to their parents to hear the sad news. "What are you going to do?" Gordy asked looking panicked. Stuart suggested that they give their parents some time to talk and moved off to speak to her uncles and aunt indicating with roll of her head that her siblings should join her. Sallee hung back watching while Helen and Gordy ambled across the parking lot kicking at stones.

As the family and friends poured out of the cars in the parking lot behind the church, all of their joy had been replaced with anxious, despairing looks. As each subsequent car pulled up, the uncertain occupants looked increasingly more despondent.

They gathered around in small clots waiting. Sallee stood off to the side, stricken that such a blight could mar her happiness. She was surprised at how few people were there. Hadn't her mother said that she had invited forty people, and she expected thirty? And it was past time now. The ceremony should have started. She gazed around. There was Jilly, She waved and got a wave in response accompanied by a weak smile. Uncle James with Aunt Lizbeth and Uncle Gordy. *Who was that tall, nice-looking man standing alone?* she wondered. *And where was Rebecca?*

As she watched, other questions demanded attention. *What are you supposed to do when a president gets killed, anyway? Is everything supposed to stop? Do you have school? Are post offices closed, and churches?*

Ethel and Early arrived. They too showed the sad despondency shared by the group. Sallee caught herself smiling as she spied Ethel's dark blue square-necked dress. On her head was a hat that reminded Sallee of the mushrooms in *Fantasia* with a touch of the dancing hippos, Sallee had to stifle a giggle. She was pretty sure it wasn't the look Ethel was after. She thought how strange it was that she had so seldom seen Ethel in anything but a uniform. When was the last time? *Oh*, she remembered, *at the beach when her baby brother Denny had died and then again at his funeral*.

Helen and Gordy made their way over to stand next to Ethel and Early. Helen reached for Ethel's hand. Early clapped Gordy on the back leaving his hand on the boy's shoulder. Stuart was busily chatting with the man Sallee didn't recognize. Why are we waiting? She wondered just as Rebecca came skidding in. She jumped out of the car, smiling from ear to ear. Sallee almost ran over to Charlie when she saw her climb out of the passenger's side but restrained because of the gravity of the recent events seemed to call for restraint.

Typical Sallee thought, she doesn't listen to the radio and doesn't know. Rebecca looked around the parking lot, waved at Sallee, and then shouted in amazement, "Jacob!?" and ran to the man talking to Stuart. She turned toward the car, "Charlie come quickly. I have someone I want you to meet.

"Jacob Berke, what," she stammered, "are you…How do you…What an absolute pleasure and a huge surprise seeing you here." She reached up and planted a big kiss on his cheek before hugging him. When she released him from the hug, she looked at Stuart. "I'm sorry I didn't mean to interrupt. You have to be Stuart. I would know you anywhere you are the image of your..," Stuart said "mother." At the same time that Rebecca said, "father." They all laughed. Charlie approached the group slowly looking nervous and uncomfortable. "I would like you to meet my daughter Charlie. I'm so glad we didn't miss the service I thought I was going to be late."

Turning back to Jacob she said. "My God, it is amazing seeing you. I was just talking to Ginny about you the other day. Singing your praises I was." Then to Stuart, "isn't he the best? I have been in love with this man since the moment I laid eyes on him." She slapped her hand over her mouth as if she had said too much.

Stealing a look at Jacob, she burned with embarrassment. "I assume you know each other," she laughed hoping to hide her embarrassment. Finally, noticing the somber air, she put her arms protectively around her daughter and pulled her close. "Has something happened?" she whispered. "Is something wrong?"

Before anyone could answer, the minister rushed out of the central doors of the church and down the steps, his robes flowing behind him. He went straight up to Ginny and Joe, bleeding solicitude. He worried his hands together as if addressing the bereaved rather than a bride and groom, "It is dreadful isn't it? I am so sorry, such a terrible event happening on this day of all days." His eyes rolled reverently upward. "I can certainly understand if you want to postpone the ceremony. It's terrible, just tragic –" Joe gently interrupted, asking the good Reverend to wait there for a minute. He took Ginny by the arm and moved away from the group. With heads close together they talked briefly, then came back to where the minister stood wringing his hands and looking distraught.

Joe cleared his throat and addressed the assembly. "Thank you all for coming out today to support Ginny, my family and me. I am sure the news of President Kennedy's death " —Rebecca gasped loudly, looking around with her hands to her mouth– "word of our president's death has come as a shock to all of us. We have suffered a devastating blow and the country is now in mourning. Nothing can change that. There is nothing we can do right now. Life, like the machine of government, goes on. We believe that it is possible to find joy even in sorrow. It's our job to find it."

He paused, looking around at their friends and family. He cleared his throat. "And so Ginny and I believe that it is vital for our family to go ahead with our wedding. We completely understand if any one feels the need to go home and be with your own family before or after the ceremony. We planned a small gathering at our new house afterward and we invite you to leave your bereavement outside the door -- don't worry, it will be there when you leave. And join us in celebrating the love that is who we are." With that, he took his bride by the arm, nodded to the minister to lead, and followed him into the church.

Afterwards, Early remarked to his wife as he held her elbow going down the church steps and back to the truck, "Dat was a righ' fine service. Dey all was lookin' grand. De flowers sho' looked pretty an' you looked proud as you could be standin' up d'ere by dey side. But you coulda knock me down when Mista' Joe stood dere sayin' what he say. I was sho' dey was gonna postpone de weddin'. Ethel," he smiled at her, "Wha' you think 'bout all dat?"

Bursting with pride and joy, Ethel announced from under her mushroom cap of a hat, "I think dey done growed up!"

About the Author

Mary Morony is an author who can write about tragedy from the inside and guides her readers through it to compassion, humor and recovery. She brings Southern charm, irreverence and wit to bear against subjects as vast as racism and as personal as alcoholism, always with a heart and soul that makes her work undeniably appealing.

Her *Apron Strings* trilogy, a series of novels that moves from the South to New York City and back between the 1950s and the early 21st century, draws on the life she knew growing up in Charlottesville, Virginia, at a time when Virginia was still very much a part of the Jim Crow South. Want to read more about Mary, the Mackey family, and Ethel go to

MaryMorony.com

Made in the USA
Lexington, KY
27 November 2016